SWALLOWED

Swallowed

A NOVEL

Réjean Ducharme

TRANSLATED FROM THE FRENCH BY
MADELEINE STRATFORD

INTRODUCTION BY DIMITRI NASRALLAH

ESPLANADE BOOKS

THE FICTION IMPRINT AT VÉHICULE PRESS

ESPLANADE BOOKS IS THE FICTION IMPRINT AT VÉHICULE PRESS

Published with the generous assistance of the Canada Council for the Arts, the Canada Book Fund of the Department of Canadian Heritage, and the Société de développement des entreprises culturelles du Québec (SODEC). We acknowledge the financial support of the Government of Canada through the National Translation Program for Book Publishing, an initiative of the *Roadmap for Canada's Official Languages 2013-2018: Education, Immigration, Communities*, for our translation activities.

Esplanade Books editor: Dimitri Nasrallah
Cover design: David Drummond
Typeset in Minion and Filosofia by Simon Garamond
Printed by Marquis Printing Inc.

LIBRARY AND ARCHIVES CANADA CATALOGUING IN PUBLICATION

Title: Swallowed : a novel / Réjean Ducharme ; translated from the French by Madeleine Stratford ; introduction by Dimitri Nasrallah.
Other titles: *Avalée des avalés*. English
Names: Ducharme, Réjean, author. | Stratford, Madeleine, translator. | Nasrallah, Dimitri, 1978- writer of introduction.
Description: Translation of: *L'Avalée des avalés*.
Identifiers: Canadiana (print) 20200306014 | Canadiana (ebook) 20200306189 | ISBN 9781550655537 (softcover) | ISBN 9781550655582 (EPUB)
Classification: LCC PS8507.U4 A6713 2020 | DDC C843/.54—dc23

Published by Véhicule Press, Montréal, Québec, Canada

Distribution in Canada by LitDistCo
www.litdistco.ca

Distribution in the US by Independent Publishers Group
www.ipgbook.com

Printed in Canada

~

CONTENTS

~

CONTENTS

The Case for Reading Quebec's Most Reclusive Author

By the mid-1960s, a young Québécois writer was staring at a small pile of rejection letters. His clutch of manuscripts had been turned down by all of the province's publishing houses. They deemed his writing immature, illegible, and too enamoured with breaking convention. So the twenty-four-year-old tried a Hail Mary: he sent a manuscript to Gallimard, the goliath of Parisian publishing responsible for the careers of many of French literature's great twentieth-century figures. The gamble paid off. Gallimard would publish Réjean Ducharme's *L'avalée des avalés* in 1966, as well as three more titles in quick succession.

The books, which display their author's fondness for wordplay and are startlingly Joycean in their range of allusion, astonished readers. During the tumultuous '60s—a time when every corner of Quebec seemed to beckon change but few people had any specific idea what shape it could take—Ducharme's novels defined the Québécois people as having a distinct voice in the world. But by then, the author was already plotting his disappearance from public view. Like J. D. Salinger, Ducharme had, in his early novels, elevated youthful ideals and held in contempt adulthood's corrosions. Equally Salingeresque, however, was his desire to shun the outside world. Only three known photos of the author are in circulation. The first, of Ducharme as a boy with a bow tie, is from a high-school yearbook. The second, of the writer as a young man, appears to be a passport photo. The third shows a grown man standing in a snowy driveway, his jacket open, two dogs watching over him.

By the time Ducharme died on August 21, 2017, nine days after his seventy-sixth birthday, he was a myth. His nine novels, four plays, two screenplays, and songwriting collaborations are part of Quebec's cultural psyche. Ducharme has earned "a place apart from the rest of Québécois letters, on account of his work, on account of the mystery that surrounded his life," wrote *La Presse* book critic Josée Lapointe, after Ducharme's death. For the rest of Canada, he is still very much a secret. His English Wikipedia page is exceedingly brief, all of six sentences. His French one is longer, yet nowhere near the length of his English Canadian counterparts, such as Margaret Atwood, Mordecai Richler, and Alice Munro. Yet as a winner of three Governor General's Literary Awards, a finalist for France's Prix Goncourt, and an officer of the Order of Canada since 2000, Ducharme is a French Canadian institution, widely taught in the province's college and university curriculums.

Ducharme's lifelong partner, the well-known film-and-television actress Claire Richard, died a year before him. The couple had lived in the southwest Montreal borough of Little Burgundy for their last twenty years together. She was his de facto spokesperson, accepting or rejecting accolades on his behalf. If he wrote anymore, Richard would often tell the media, she did not know when or where.

By the time of his death, he hadn't published a novel in nearly twenty years, not since *Gros mots* came out in 1999. Neighbours said Ducharme went for long walks in search of collectible trash he would then use in what he termed *trophoux*, "ready-made" sculptures, pieces where the artist assembles prefabricated items. He created these works under the name Roch Plante—building up a sizable oeuvre between 1980 and 2002 in that practice—which were collected in the book *Les Trophoux* in 2004. In 2017, a posthumous art book, *Le Lactume*, was published, containing 198 drawings the author created throughout the mid-60s, and this now serves as Ducharme's final publication.

It would be hard to overstate Ducharme's revolutionary effect on Quebec writing. According to Annabelle Moreau, editor-in-chief of the literary magazine *Lettres québécoises*, Ducharme "created a literature for the province centered around our use of the language, which by extension grew into our sense of culture and national identity."

Equally groundbreaking was Ducharme's acceptance into the French literary pantheon. "Not only did it establish him as one of the greatest stylists of our language at a time when Quebec suffered from an enormous inferiority complex in regards to France," notes novelist and translator Daniel Grenier, "but he did so by infiltrating their culture, by publishing his entire body of work in Paris, like a double agent of sorts."

Unlike in English or Spanish, the rules for writing and speaking in French are rigid and hierarchical, with Paris

9

assuming the indisputable center of the language for the wider Francophonie. Ducharme's exceptional skill at bending and stretching French prose, capturing Québécois parlance while earning the praise of the French language's highest gatekeepers, was seen in Quebec as a giant step forward for an entire people's voice. The burgeoning sepratist movement quickly claimed him as a sympathizer, but Ducharme wasn't keen on being co-opted by the politics that symbolically imbued his novels. "I don't want people to draw connections between me and my novel," he wrote to friend Gérald Godin in 1966, the year *L'avalée des avalés* exploded.

The run of work that he published at breathtaking pace in his mid to late twenties—*Le nez qui voque* (1967), *L'Océantume* (1968), and *La Fille de Christophe Colomb* (1969)—set the rules of play for a Ducharmian story. His debut was set against a backdrop of the Quiet Revolution, and themes of religion's stranglehold and rebellion abound, framed within deeply allusive portraits of family life. Ducharme's depiction of Montreal in its own street-level cadences, coupled with its wide-eyed imagination, ambition, and naïveté of youth, would win him legions of young Québécois readers who, previous to him, had no author to call their own.

His field of play would expand with each successive title. *Le nez qui voque* blurred the lines between family and Quebec's geography to create an aura of the province that is vibrantly alive but has a conflicted persona. In *La Fille de Christophe Colomb*, the explorer is an abusive father to his protagonist daughter. By 1973's *L'hiver de force*, protagonists Nicole and André Ferron are adults whose childlike inner lives primordially control their outlooks. "I read *L'hiver de force* in high school," says Moreau. "It profoundly affected me. Nicole and André's language, their immobility and imprisonment, really dissected the young woman I was at this time."

Published three years later, *Les enfantômes* is about siblings Vincent and Fériée, who are no longer even alive, but ghosts of children. It hinted that things were shifting creatively for Ducharme. His hand had begun to cool, and his legend was hardening into place. He wouldn't publish another novel for fourteen years. When he resumed, he released three novels that marked the end of his oeuvre: *Dévadé* (1990), *Va savoir* (1994), and *Gros Mots* (1999).

Perhaps his best-known works are a pair of screenplays he wrote for filmmaker Francis Mankiewicz: 1980's *Les bons débarras* and 1982's *Les beaux souvenirs*. The pair's initial collaboration is roundly considered one of the great films of Canadian cinema. It spotlights Manon, another child on the cusp of adolescence, as she tries to make sense of an unfair world. Set in the bucolic Laurentians region, the film captured Ducharme at his most accessible, his major themes shorn of symbolism and wordplay and made instead universal through the screen's imagery. On film, Ducharme's vision of Quebec was able to shine well beyond the Francophonie for the very first time.

One wonders why a writer as unique and as integral to Québécois literature as Ducharme hasn't been better served by translation. It's true, as has often been said, that his wordplay and culturally rooted symbolism—the very aspects that make him so resiliently Québécois—make him difficult to represent in another language. But he also hasn't benefitted from the kind of cross-cultural ambassadorship bestowed on a writer when a single translator or publishing house makes a mission of showcasing him.

After *L'avalée des avalés* made its initial splash in 1966, English-speaking interest in Ducharme surfaced first in the UK, not Canada. Barbara Bray, a literary academic, undertook a translation that was published by Hamish Hamilton in 1968 under the title *The Swallower Swallowed*. It was one of her first literary translations, and the book never made an impact with British critics and readers. It fell out of print long ago, and neither translator nor publisher ever pursued any of Ducharme's subsequent novels.

The first attempt to translate him into English in Canada came in 1980, when Robert Guy Scully undertook 1973's *L'hiver de force* as *Wild to Mild*, for a small press based on Montreal's south shore called Héritage Amérique. That same year, the author David Homel also translated an excerpt from *L'Océantume* as *Bittersea* for the literary journal *Exile*. Homel wouldn't return to Ducharme until 1986, when he translated the Governor General's Award-winning play *Ha ha!...* for the same publisher. In 2000, small press Guernica Editions published Will Browning's translation of Ducharme's fourth novel as *The Daughter of Christopher Colombus*. In 2003, Talonbooks published 1994's *Va savoir* as *Go Figure*—Browning's volley into late-period Ducharme. It would take another eight years for sophomore novel *Le nez qui voque* to appear as *Miss Take* with the same publisher. No other English translations emerged during his lifetime.

Timing is everything. Réjean Ducharme was fortunate enough to have written about Québécois life as authentically as he could and was lionized for emboldening the province's intelligentsia in the evaluation of its central existential crisis—is it subservient to the French language as dictated by Paris, is it Canadian as dictated by Ottawa, or is it something altogether more independent and self-determining? Unfortunately, no publisher came around at the right moment to make the case for what Ducharme's body of work can mean to Canadian literature. With his death, Ducharme deserves a re-evaluation. His books brim with adventurous precedents our writers and critics routinely seek outside our borders. It's high time English Canada saw that.

A version of this was first published in *The Walrus*, October 2017.

A POSTSCRIPT

I first discovered that *L'avalée des avalés* had been out-of-print in English when *The Walrus* magazine asked me to write the above appraisal in the weeks following Réjean Ducharme's death. The novel's absence struck me as a significant cultural omission. An important part of Québec's literary foundation was missing from Canadian letters. As an editor, I immediately sensed an opportunity, though I wasn't sure how realistic a pursuit it was.

On the one hand, times had changed since Barbara Bray's translation of the novel had first appeared in 1968. Canada now had a publishing industry that was half a century strong. The oft-tumultuous relationship between

English and French Canada had calmed and matured over the past two decades. Generations of legislation in Québec pertaining to the French-language had also groomed a wealth of homegrown translators who were better equipped to tackle Ducharme's slippery prose, complex wordplay and multi-layered allusions.

But there were other obstacles. Gallimard is half a world away and used to selling English-language rights on a global scale, while Véhicule Press is a boutique regional independent in a country that is itself a subset of their North American territory. Surely a half-century-old book from their back catalogue was a low priority for an organization preoccupied with international book fairs and a raft of contemporary titles to sell. They could consider our market too small for them. Would we attempt a Hail Mary like Ducharme and approach the venerable institution responsible for publishing many of the twentieth century's great authors?

An exchange began with their rights department. They were initially receptive to the idea, but had little background on the linguistic particulars of our region and no prior knowledge of our modest publishing house. Would we not want to publish the existing Barbara Bray translation? they asked. Our ambition was to have the novel retranslated by someone who had a natural understanding of Québécois idiom, and who could communicate the particularities of the original French in a way they had never before been served. Without a track record in international publication deals to bolster our cause, we were concerned our publishing circles were too far apart; Gallimard probably had more pressing activities underway.

As luck would have it, in March 2018 I was invited to attend the Paris Book Fair to promote my novel *Niko*, which had just been published in France. With a trans-Atlantic visit in hand, we restarted the conversation with Gallimard, to see if I could meet with their rights director in person and articulate the unique case for bringing Ducharme back to Canada. I am grateful to Camille Cloarec, at the time the Book and Debates Officer at Consulate General of France in Toronto, for taking up our cause and communicating our desires to Gallimard from a much more reputed vantage point than our own. Margot Miriel at the Parisian house, was instrumental in our discussions. A few days later, I found myself in Paris, standing outside the unassuming door of the legendary publishing house, with less than two hours' sleep after an overnight flight.

Once we were able to sit down in the same room, we were fortunate enough to hit it off and an agreement emerged quickly. It turned out that Anne-Solange Noble, the head of English rights at Gallimard, was born and raised in Montreal. She understood the underlying cultural value of what we were proposing, and saw it as part of the ongoing unique relationship between the French and English languages in Canada. We rhapsodized about the city, its street life, as well as people she remembered from Montreal's Anglo literary community of the seventies. A new English translation, she agreed, could be useful to Gallimard in brokering rights requests in other markets.

Two years have passed since that fortuitous meeting. In that time, translator Madeleine Stratford has produced this new translation of *L'avalée des avalés*. *Swallowed* differs from Barbara Bray's *The Swallower Swallowed* not only in its translator's proximity to the regional roots of the original French, but also in its rendering to a looser and more figurative, more acrobatic English. Stratford's translation of Ducharme is, to my ear, playful and lyrical and utterly timeless.

After more than half a century of languishing out of print, the book that transformed Québécois culture during the Quiet Revolution is finally available for Canadian readers to discover.

Dimitri Nasrallah

April 2020

Swallowed

1

Everything swallows me. When my eyes are shut, my own stomach swallows me, chokes me from within. When my eyes are open, what I see swallows me, smothers me from within the stomach of what I see. Everything swallows me up: the river is too great, the sky too high, flowers are too fragile, butterflies too fearful, my mother's face is too pretty. My mother's face is pretty for nothing. If her face were ugly, it would be ugly for nothing. A face, be it pretty or ugly, is good for nothing. You look at someone's face, a butterfly, a flower, and you feel disturbed somehow, or even annoyed. When you let that happen, you get upset. There should be no faces, no butterflies, no flowers. Whether my eyes are open or shut, I'm always enclosed—the space around me suddenly runs out of air, my heart tightens, and I'm overcome with fear.

In the summer, the trees wear clothes. In the winter, the trees are bare naked. They say the dead are pushing up daisies. The gardener found two old barrels in his attic. Do you know what he did with them? He sawed them in two to make four pails. He put one on the beach, and three in the field. When it rains, the water gets trapped in the pails. When they're thirsty, the birds fly down and drink from the pails.

I'm alone and afraid. When I'm hungry, I push daisies down my throat and the hunger goes away. When I'm thirsty, I dunk my face into one of the pails and suck up the water. My hair unfurls into the water. I suck up the water and it's over; the thirst is gone, as though I'd never been thirsty in the first place. You wish you were thirsty enough to drink the river dry. But after one glass, your thirst is already gone. In the winter, when I'm cold, I go inside and put on my big blue sweater. I go back outside, resume playing in the snow, and I'm not cold anymore. In the summer, when I'm hot, I take off my dress. My dress doesn't stick to my skin anymore and I feel great, and I start running. We run in the sand. We run and run. Then we don't feel like running anymore. We've run ourselves bored. We stop, sit down, and start burying our legs in the sand. Then we lie down in the sand and bury our whole bodies. Then we get tired of playing in the sand. We don't know what to do next. We look around, as though we were searching for something. We look and look. But we find nothing worthwhile. If you pay attention when you look around like that, you realize that what you're looking at is hurting you, that you're alone and afraid. You stand powerless against your loneliness and fear. Nothing helps. There are daisies for hunger, rainwater for thirst. But nothing for loneliness or fear. The more you try to soothe them, the more they struggle, the more they scream, the more they sear. The stratosphere sinks, continents collapse, and you're left to live in that void, alone.

I'm alone. I just need to shut my eyes to know it. When you want to know where you are, you shut your eyes.

When you shut your eyes, you end up where you are: in the dark, in the void. My mother, my father, my brother Christian, and Constance Chlorus are there. But they're not where *I* am when my eyes are shut. Where I am with my eyes shut, there's no one but me. There's no need to care for anyone else—everyone's elsewhere. When I speak or play with others, I can feel that they're outside, that they can't get in where I am, and that I can't get in where they are. I know all too well that loneliness and fear will take hold of me once more as soon as my silence drowns out all of their voices. You shouldn't worry about what happens on the land's or the water's surface. It changes nothing to what happens in the dark void where you are. Nothing happens in that dark void. Waiting is all there is in there—always. Waiting for you to do something to make it end, to get out. Others—that's far away. Others flee, like butterflies. A butterfly is far away, as far as the stratosphere, even when you hold it in your hand. You shouldn't worry about butterflies. You suffer for nothing. In here, there's only me.

My father is Jewish, and my mother, Catholic. Our family is not doing too well; it's no smooth sailing for us, no piece of cake. When they got married, my parents agreed on some sort of divided custody of their future children. They even signed an agreement before a notary and witnesses. I know: I eavesdrop on them when they fight. According to their arrangement, their first offspring would go Catholic, their second, Jewish, their third, Catholic, their fourth, Jewish, and so on until their thirty-first. First-born Christian belongs to Mrs. Einberg, and Mrs. Einberg brings him to church. Born second and last, I belong to Mr. Einberg, and Mr. Einberg brings me to shul. They have us. They're sure that they have us. They have us and they keep us. Mrs. Einberg has Christian and she keeps him. Mr. Einberg has me and he keeps me. It took me some time to get it. It doesn't seem so hard to grasp, but when I was younger, I thought it made no sense at all that my parents might not love each other or us like I loved them.

Mr. Einberg gives Mrs. Einberg the evil eye when he watches his property play with hers. He sits on pins and needles when Christian and I play together. He thinks Mrs. Einberg is using Christian to get to me, lure me, steal me away. Mrs. Einberg says that I'm hers just as much as Christian is, that a mother needs her every child, that a boy needs his little sister, that a girl needs her older brother. I pretend to play the game Mr. Einberg claims Mrs. Einberg is playing. It makes Mr. Einberg's blood boil. He lashes out at Mrs. Einberg. They fight nonstop. I spy on them. I watch them yell at each other. I watch them loathe each other, hate each other, their eyes and their hearts filled with utmost ugliness. The more they yell, the more they hate. The more they hate, the more they hurt. Fifteen minutes into the fight, their hate is so great that I can see them writhe like worms on fire, I can feel their teeth grinding, their temples throbbing. I like it. Sometimes it pleases me so much that I can't help laughing. Go on hating, you fools! Hurt each other so I can see you suffer! Writhe in pain, so I can roar with laughter!

They sent Christian away from me. What an honour! They stuffed him in an envelope and sent him off to scout camp. Go be a good boy, Christian, far from your toxic little sister! When school is out, one of us invariably must leave. If I'm not sent on tour with the choir, Christian is sent to scout camp. This doesn't sit well with Mrs. Einberg. Why can't you just leave those children alone, you maniac? Mr. Einberg, master of departures, won't hear any of it, won't let go. If you don't send your brat off to camp to do some good, I'll send my sprat off to practice her scales! Travel shrivels the mind! she yells. Travel broadens the mind! he yells back.

I'm just a girl. Einberg has me, but he's not happy about it. He's envious of the other. He would much rather have Christian. Girls are no good—they're good for nothing. I couldn't care less. Let *them* deal with it! I wait for Christian to come back. He never does anything bad. He never says anything harsh. All he says and does is soft, soft and sad like a flower, like water, like all peaceful things that leave you in peace. Christian is soft like a thing. There are things, animals and men. What a load of cow crap! Right?

2

When Einberg brings me to shul, he holds me by the hand most tenderly. He holds me so tight that you would think he wants to rip out my arm. He shoves me around. He pushes me and pulls me as though I were the neighbour's dog that just plowed through his flowerbeds. It gets on my nerves. I tell him to get a grip. He tells me to watch my tone when I speak to my father. Watch your tone! We end up fighting. I kick him. He slaps me.

"Stay still! Pray! Listen to what the Rabbi's saying!"

Rabbi Schneider opens his big red book with the gilded edges, and starts reading.

"The evildoers will burn like straw."

In my head, I see Christian burn like dry grass. Pray Yahweh! The more you pray, the better your seat, much closer to the ring. If you pray ferociously, you may get a front-row seat to watch the evildoers burn. It makes me ashamed. It makes me eager to be an evildoer myself. If Einberg didn't drag me to shul, I would never set foot in there. Synagogues smell like blood and ash—that smell works them into a frenzy. Some are eager for their fathers to die so they can stop going to school. I'm eager for my father to die so I can be as evil as I want. You fools! To think that they mistake me for one of them! Rabbi Schneider speaks about those who don't fear the one true God. He tells us what the God of Armies said: He shall strike those who don't fear Him, and He shall leave them neither root nor branch. Rabbi Schneider is dead wrong if he thinks he's scaring me. The only chills I get from His "God of Armies" are chills of anger. The more he talks, the more I hate him. They have a God like them, in their own image and likeness, a God who can't help hating, a God who hurts so much from so much hating that he grinds his teeth. When Rabbi Schneider talks like that, I think about my elm tree. My elm stands in the middle of our great island, alone like a plane in the sky. It must be evil. I've never seen a single leaf on its branches. It sheds in strips—the bark peels off like paper. Under the bark, the trunk is smooth and soft, so soft. When the wind blows, its long dry limbs crack—you would think they're full of human bones. Let their God of Armies come and tear off my roots and branches! I look forward to it. Let him ruin me! Let him go all out! He can have my roots and branches. When he's finally torn every last one off, there won't be a shadow of doubt left. I can be sure that he's not taking me for one of his chosen ones, for one of his slaughter worshippers, thirsty for blood and ash. And I can rest easy. Rabbi Schneider is handsome. He seems sweet. He conducts the choir. He says I'm his best soloist. This choir's name is as long as your arm: The Children's Choir of God's Children Exiled in Canada. Last year, we spent the summer on tour in South America. Cha cha cha. After his gory speeches, Rabbi Schneider comes to speak and smile to me. I'm almost sure that he doesn't believe a word he says when he preaches. His looks clash with his words when he preaches. That big red book of his, the one with the gilded edges, must be working him into a frenzy.

3

The elm is my ship. When I run out of things to do, I set sail. I've fastened a yellow flag to its crest. My anchor is an old rusty can hanging down from a string. Cast off all continents! Hoist all horizons! Here we go! I set course for steeper, more volcanic coastlands than are to be found in this country. I straddle the highest branch to check if there are reefs peaking out of the mist. My foot suddenly slips and I lose my balance. I topple over. During the fall, my face hits a rock—I black out and sink to the bottom of a dark and dull ocean. I'm drowning. The elm floats adrift, keel over deck. I end up in a hospital bed. When I regain consciousness, I feel something missing inside my mouth. No wonder. My four front teeth are gone. I can't help pushing my tongue through the gap. Mrs. Einberg is sitting by my bed. She eagerly reassures me. Your teeth will grow back! With little girls like you, everything grows back, recovers and heals. I'm nine years old. Christian is eleven. Einberg and Mrs. Einberg are as old as my anchor. They've hit rock bottom, they're over the hill.

Einberg is rich and important. As we reach the stairs of the synagogue, people start swarming toward us, gathering around us. They all know I fell from a tree, went to the hospital, and broke my teeth. After their ritual grovelling to Einberg, they fall back onto me, awfully proud to have something to say, to show the extent of their compassion for a child's misfortunes. Open wide! Let us see those poor teeth of yours! They all want to see my teeth. They make me open my mouth and peek inside with overly sad eyes. What a shame! Poor girl! How she must have suffered! I have to tell them everything that happened to me in all the boring details. I leave things out. I tell them I fell from a tree, lost consciousness, was brought in to the hospital, and spat out my four teeth without even realizing it.

Constance Chlorus is nowhere to be seen. I can see her brothers, but I'd rather not speak to them. They don't like me. I'm not sure why. They glare at me, evil-eyed.

"Hello there, little Apache."

After greeting me with those words, Rabbi Schneider reaches below my arms to lift me up and sit me down on his lap. He's our choir conductor. We sing. He moves his arms around. He says he's setting the beat. If you ask me, he's just beating the air. He's sort of handsome. My eyes are drawn to him. His big cow eyes are bright and black, vibrant, as soft as the wind. He plays with my nose, my ears, my braids. It bothers me, annoys me to the point of feeling hatred. When he sits me on his lap and starts touching me, I lose it, get angry, see red. I forget that he's handsome and laughs all the time. He turns into this inhospitable giant shamelessly capitalizing on his superior strength. He's just another one of those crazed maniacs who would squish a small bird in their fat hand while stroking its beak with their fat fingers, convinced that the birdie likes it, that it will even feel gratitude and love. I don't want to be played with as though I were a thing, a mere wristwatch. Only dogs, cats and other such prostitutes let you finger them. Not a single goose would stand it. What does Rabbi Schneider take me for? I'm not his cocker spaniel. I'm not a man's best friend. I am someone: my own person. How would he feel if I walked into his home and started fingering his tables, his chairs, his figurines? Leave my tables, my chairs and my figurines alone!

"Are we wearing this finely embroidered corsage for the first time?"

If you have nothing fertile to say, you should always keep your mouth shut. He parts my lips to see my teeth. His fingers are inside my mouth. I want to bite them. Go ahead, Rabbi! Keep acting like this is your own mouth! Make yourself at home!

"It looks like we'll have to do without our brilliant prima donna for a while. Next time, you should seek my advice before engaging in another hoplomachy."

"I don't need anybody's advice. And I'm glad I can't sing anymore."

"Did *you* eat the lion? You're no typical gladiator. Usually, it's the gladiator who gets eaten with a knife and fork."

Rabbi Schneider fancies himself funny. He laughs. His belly and thighs are bouncing, making me bounce. Now, that's a good one. Looking stern, with his hands in his pockets and vacant eyes, Einberg waits for him to be through with me.

"How's your lovely mother?"

"Why don't you ask my lovely mother? How should I know?"

I suddenly pity Rabbi Schneider. He likes me. He goes out of his way for me to like him back. Is it his fault if he's so ham-handed? I should have never talked back to him. But regrets are always useless because they always come after the fact. And how about him? Does *he* pity *me*? Does *he* respect *me*? Crappy cow crap!

I find my only true joy in solitude. Solitude is my palace. Inside, I have my own chair, table, and bed, wind and sunshine. When I sit down anywhere else, I'm resting in exile, on misleading land. I'm proud of my palace. I'm keen to keep it warm, soft and glorious, like I could entertain butterflies or birds. If I had any more pride, I would kill and exterminate all those who endanger my solitude's welfare, who breathe roaring hate in the chimney, who pull sadness over the windows. I would murder Einberg and his wife. I would murder Christian and Constance Chlorus. I'm alone. Sometimes, I'm away from my palace. Some take advantage of my absence to sneak in. I banish them as soon as I come home. When someone sets foot inside my palace, it means I was careless. That makes me ashamed. It's so hard to throw Constance Chlorus out, to show Christian the door. But my palace is too fragile for me to entertain friends. When friends walk into my palace, my walls start shaking, and darkness and fear sweep through the windows of light and silence, which they break with every step they take. When I'm not alone, I feel sick, at risk. I must conquer my own fear. In order to conquer your fear, you must see it, hear it, feel it. In order to see your fear, you must be left alone with it. When I lose sight of my fear, it feels like I'm losing consciousness. Maybe this happens because I was weaned two days after birth. They're the ones who cut me off. I prefer to think that I weaned myself, and that, suddenly swelling with pride, I bit my mother's breasts with rusty metal teeth until gangrene set in. I imagine all kinds of things, believing them true, making them impact me as though they were real. Only what I believe true, what I dare to believe true, is real. Einberg wouldn't let Mrs. Einberg feed me. It sickened him that I was just a girl. When Einberg is away on a trip, I go to church with Christian and Mrs. Einberg. But I mustn't say a word. The church is smeared all over with ash and blood, just like the synagogue. Having faith means that you quiver like a vampire when you hear about blood and cemeteries. You filthy ghouls! I make sure Einberg knows that I went to church. It sickens him.

4

My face is laced with pimples. I'm as ugly as an ashtray filled with old cigar and cigarette butts. The warmer the weather, the more painful my pimples. My face is yellow and red, as though I were suffering from both jaundice and measles. My skin hardens, thickens, burns. It sheds in strips like the trunk of a birch tree.

We set foot in the synagogue, where we spend half our time. We're steady shul mice. I'd rather we be drunk as skunks. Einberg holds me by the hand. He sends my hand flying and shoves me onto a bench. Rabbi Schneider starts reading from his big red book, the one with the gilded edges.

"All the proud and evildoers shall burn like straw. The fire is coming that will set them ablaze, says Yahweh of Armies, and leave them neither root nor branch."

"Crappy cow crap!"

I sift through the bleak herd, peeking between their shoulders and over their hats. One face after another, I keep seeing the same anonymous, repulsive replica. I see no sign of Constance Chlorus.

"But to this man I will look: he who is humble and broken in heart and spirit, and who trembles at my word."

"Broken in heart and spirit... Crappy cow crap...! Like in love songs!"

Rabbi Schneider comes to see us. He meant to shake my hand and pinch my cheek, but given the state of my cheeks, he settles for a handshake. When he comes to see us like that, I wish I'd never learned to speak. I wish I could stay silent for the rest of my life. I want to leave and forever be gone. Someone who addresses me is someone who wants something from me, who's got something to give in exchange for something they believe more worthy: that someone is up to something. I see them coming a mile off. They have something to sell. Thanks, but no thanks! Try me later! And when you do, I'll be ready for you. I'll have plenty of snakes up my sleeve to throw at your heads. When I need something, I take it, like a giant. I never ask for permission. I never give thanks. And I never smile before or after the taking.

We leave the synagogue. Outside, the wind is so strong that streetlights and shadows are shaking. It's hot out. Einberg takes me by the hand. Our car is waiting for us at the other end of the sidewalk. We walk behind a convoy of creepy men in black suits and black hats. Einberg can't walk fast; he was wounded in a war. Flying shrapnel or sharp nails. Oh. Oh. He has a limp. I want to prance around. He holds my hand and squeezes it tight. Prancing is out of the question.

"Crappy cow crap!"

"I forbid you to swear. You will *not* use those words."

"Crappy cow crap! Crappy cow crap! Crappy cow crap!"

"Keep that up and I'll slap you good and proper."

"Your wife says 'crappy crap' and so much more."

"I forbid you to call her that."

"Crappy cow crap!"

"You say that one more time and I'll lock you up in your room for the rest of the day. Without lunch or dinner."

"Crappy cow crap! If you think that scares me!"

I'm not afraid of him. In fact, he never carries out his threats to lock me up for the rest of the day. When he takes the trouble to slap me good and proper, he feels that he's fulfilled his fatherly duties for quite a while.

"Why do you always hold my hand?"

I try to break free. The more I pull away, the tighter his grip. Adults are so strong! Constance Chlorus takes me by the hand. It's not the same.

"Why do you never answer any of my questions? Why don't you leave me alone if I mean nothing to you? Why are you so mean?"

Einberg says nothing. He looks at the houses.

"You know, Einberg… the proud and evildoers…"

"The fire is coming that will set them ablaze, said Yahweh."

"He will leave them neither root nor branch, like the elm."

When I grow up, I'll be proud and do evil. My roots will be as thick as the pillars of the synagogue. My leaves will be as wide as sails. I'll walk with my head up high. I'll see no one. When the coming fire comes, it will scorch my skin, but my bones will withstand the flames and I will stand tall.

"I'll hide my head in the sand when the coming fire comes. I'll feel too ashamed. I don't want to stand on the stage when all the evildoers are slaughtered."

I won't walk alongside Yahweh. I'll walk against his flames, against his armies. I prefer to be on the wrong side of things, if I must choose a side. The thought of my pimples comes back to haunt me. Suddenly, I start enjoying the way they burn my skin. I let the pain in. I stir it up. I savour it. I revel in it. It arises from the same fire that will burn the proud and evildoers.

"Einberg, you know… the others, the humble ones, those who tremble…"

"Yes! Yes!"

"If they tremble, isn't it because they're scared? Isn't it because they're not proud or brave enough? This year, a boy in our class let the girls beat him up. They stole his marbles and he ran crying to Dame Ruby."

Einberg has stopped listening. From the very first word of my story's very first sentence, he'd already heard enough. His ears are sealed. Most of the time, he just ignores me. You idiot! When Mrs. Einberg is not fighting him for my custody, he finds me utterly uninteresting. He has to make an actual effort to punish me.

I'm walking around the marsh, from one poplar to the next, my face buried in poplar leaves. The marsh is heaven's floor. Poplars are dancers attending the ball. I have water and arrowheads up to my knees. I fell flat on my face a few minutes ago, and my new dress is drenched. Einberg buys my dresses himself. Poplars have legs, just like humans. Like women, they wear skirts; theirs are made of foliage.

They roll them up to dance in the water. Trees grow in soil. When you look up through their branches, the sky is filled with leaves, and it looks like trees grow in sky. The wind lashes and whips, making the leaves whizz. It's as if a storm were slapping the pavement. As though it were raining coins. I'm sitting still, up on a hill. Looking. Waiting. Until the ringing leaves and the sultry wind are done with me. Waiting until I'm fully done dissolving into the wind, into the leaves. Leaves have two sides: one is dull, the other is shiny. A frog leaps onto my feet and stays there, frozen. The frog is cold and clean. My feet are hot and dirty. It slowly lowers an eyelid, as though it were falling asleep. Splash! It jumps back into the water. Frogs have bulging eyes and no eyelashes. Like leopards, they have ocellated skin. The frogs you see in the grass are green. Those you see in the fields are brown. Women who wear red shoes carry a red handbag. Those who carry a black handbag wear black shoes. Christian still isn't back. I'm in waiting mode.

5

When I was little, I was kinder. I loved my mother with all my pain. I always felt like running into her arms and hugging her hips and sinking my head into her belly. I wanted to be grafted onto her and be part of her softness, of her beauty. Then pride came along with reason, making me hate the bitter hole that eats away at your soul so that you can love. Now, what I need is to make a clean break with

Mrs. Einberg and make that woman perfectly worthless. I hate needing someone. The best way to need no one is to wipe everyone out of your life. I know what I must do: ward off all the powers the world is hoarding against me and respond to all attacks on my solitude with attacks of my own. I must grow up, expand upwards, outranking all else until I tower over the highest mountains. I must erect a scaffold, build a ladder, a ladder tall enough to touch the great blue sky. When I come down, my hair will be saturated with sky, like your hair is saturated with water when you come out of the river. My mother is a bird. Birds don't like us. As soon as they spot us, they fly away. When you catch one of them, it struggles. Even if you tell the bird how much you love it, it wants to fly away, refusing to stay with you. Dogs and cats like being petted. Birds don't like it. Once I tried to hug a hen. I found it pretty. It squealed to death, slapping me in the face with its wings. It even scratched my arms until they bled. My mother is like a bird. When I would take her in my arms, she would grow stiff and struggle. Stay still! Go out and play! You're hurting me! That's enough! It was as though I were a nuisance to her, as though she had something more pressing to do. She loves me, but in the queerest way. I used to feel like there wasn't enough room in her life for me to exist. I wanted to sleep with her. I would sneak into her room in the middle of the night. I would climb upon her bed, a large bed with dumper wheels instead of legs. I would curl up against her. She would wake up, smile at me, lift me up on her shoulders, and take me back to my room. Be a good girl! When she was sitting in the flowers, I would go sit on her lap and hug her neck. Go on and play like a good little girl! Leave Mommy alone! Mommy's tired! When she was taking a walk, I would tag along, hanging on to her dress. She would let me follow her, without minding me. Then she would turn around and tell me she'd played long enough with me. It's over now. I'm done loving her. I wasn't going to spend my life being pushed away like some foul-smelling thing. I'll take care of myself. I'll never try to hold her gaunt falcon gaze anymore. I won't seek her gaze. All her doors and windows are sealed shut: she's an abandoned house. In the end, no one has a mother. In the end, I am my own daughter. Now, when she smiles at me, I turn away. When she tries to hold my chin in her hand, I wave it away. When she takes her gun and says, "Let's go to the mainland!" I tell her to leave me alone. When she speaks to me, I don't answer. Let's climb on rooftops! Leave me alone! She often climbs on the roof of the abbey. She likes to walk on roofs and straddle their ridges. Rooftops are steep, and shingles loosen under her feet. She's often drunk. She drinks at night. She drinks slowly, sitting in the dark on the couch of the small living room. Resting her bare feet on the tapestry wing chair, she strokes her cat with the tips of her toes. You can hear it purr. You can hear alcohol flow into the tall round glass. Then nothing. *And I still ponder on that ship gone down, my twenty years in a starry sea now lost* (Nelligan).

6

This here is an island. It's a large field surrounded with cattails, arrowheads and small flashy poplars. It's a tall anchored drakkar, awash near the shore of a great river. It's a lofty ship whose steel and coal-loaded flanks are almost sunken, whose only mast is a dead elm. We live in a drystone abbey, big enough to get lost. Its four red tile gables are sharper than axe blades, steeper than cliffs. Our abbey is so tall that, if you sit on top of the roof, you can see the city spread like an enormous grey web beyond the forests, you can see the river flow into the ocean. But the bridge is even higher. The abbey looks like it has four gables, but there are in fact only two, crossing each other in such a way that, from a bird's-eye view, the building looks like a crucifix. Mothy Mouser explained why, but I didn't understand a word. Anyway, Jesus Christ died on a cross. A small tower stands at the bottom of each valley: four watch turrets. The nuns used to climb up there to shoot the Indians. The railway bridge spans across the roof. I always fear it will collapse and crush the abbey to pieces. The bridge blocks out the sun. It's always dark in the abbey. The bridge is so wide that the abbey, hugged by its enormous black iron pillars, looks like a fawn sleeping between elephant legs. "Miss Berenice!" That's the gardener calling me. The old quarry winch, taller than the Ferris wheel at the fair, still works. The nuns built it to mine coal and iron. They used the coal to melt the iron. They poured the molten iron into cannon moulds, and used the cannons to shoot the Indians. At dinnertime, I run and hide in one of the winch buckets, waiting for the gardener to come and find me. "Miss Berenice! Miss Berenice!" He knows that I'm hiding in the quarry winch, but he doesn't know in which bucket. He's too old to climb. To find me, he needs to activate the winch. I look up at the sky and when the wheel starts turning, the clouds start running.

We have dinner in the lower part of the refectory, at the old beam table where five hundred nuns sat to eat two hundred years ago. The table is so long that Mothy Mouser and Einberg, at each head, seem to be sitting at the far ends of a road. Christian and I sit midway, opposite each other. Mothy Mouser fills the roaming bishop's seat, a tall and wide stall. The back is carved more intricately than a bas-relief. Where the armrests should be, two inlaid lions stick out their tongues. Mothy Mouser dislikes daylight. When sunshine pierces through a gap in the drapes and lands on the floor, her face becomes tense and gloomy. Despite the need to hate her, my mother fascinates me, like a bird. I admire her. As I watch her be and act, I tend to emulate her, feeling like this is how I should be and act. Everything of hers is beautiful to me: her eyes, her hands, her mouth, her clothes, the way she pours tea. I watch her eat as you would watch a pelican eat. I watch her sitting there as you would watch a swallow fly. I fear her like you would fear a witch. When I catch myself lifting my head, stroking my lips or staring like my mother, I get angry with myself. That hold, that spell must be broken. That's the enemy I must kill.

My mother is always daydreaming. When I catch her passing through my life with her nose up in the air, a look of surprise in her eyes, it's as though she were somewhere else, wandering in another century, drifting through a fairy tale to the sound of a horn between tight rows of bowmen clad in silk brocade coats. She walks past me, eludes me, slips away from sight as water slips through my fingers. In my mind, there's no doubt: she's a danger, a terrible threat. She's a sun that would burn my soul if I didn't shirk away or try to fight it. She stands on the threshold of my life, and her presence is huge, heavy, almost stifling. She whips my life around like the sea whips the husk of a ship. If I open the door, even just an inch, she penetrates me, floods me, sinks me, and I end up drowning. She unwittingly casts spells. She bewitched Christian. Without the slightest effort, she imposed herself on him like hands on clay. For him, only she exists: she's his one obsession, his only strength. I find that despicable. Each time he sees her, he looks at her as though she were a vision. He could eat her up. When she's sad, he's desperate, thinking he must have done something wrong. When he cries, it's because he saw her cry. It drives me mad to see them together. It sickens me. It reminds me that I used to be like Christian. I try to make him understand that he must fight back. He won't hear of it. He's hopeless. She hypnotized him like a snake charmer. Were I enchanted like before, I would be so sad and suffer so much! My mother is like a bird. But I don't want her to be like that. I want her to be like a dead cat, like the corpse of a drowned Siamese cat. I demand that she be something ugly, as repulsive as can be. My mother is as repulsive as can be. My mother is ugly and repulsive like a dead cat, a mothy mouser. It matters little that she looks nothing like a mothy mouser. You need to see people and things in a different light to avoid being swallowed. To avoid hurting, you need to see only what can free you from what you're seeing. The only truth is what I must believe to be true, what serves me well when I believe it true, what I need to hold on to so as not to suffer. Mrs. Einberg is *not* my mother. She's a dead, mothy mouser. Mothy Mouser! Mothy Mouser! Mothy Mouser!

We masticate quietly, in silence, like cows. The thick velvet drapes have been drawn over the hollow windows. Only the pallid yellow diamond chandeliers shed some light, hanging by sheer magic, it seems, from the shadowy depths of the metatomes. Grey foliage scrolls run down the black central pillars. Only a few rays shine on the varnished floor. The abbey has four wings. Our rooms are in the one facing the widest part of the river. Mothy Mouser sleeps in the attic, just above the water, on llama skins carelessly thrown over black and grey tiles. Moonlight turns iridescent as it gleams through a stained-glass wall that Mothy Mouser assembled by haphazardly welding together shards from the chapel's mosaic. The chapel, which now has a ceiling, was turned into a living room. But we still think of it as "the chapel." Mothy Mouser is in love with trains. What she likes most about them is the racket they make at night. Many speed over the bridge every night, just above our heads, as though they were running right over the roof. They shake the walls and rattle our beds. When they whistle from afar, Mothy Mouser wakes up, gets out of bed and runs to open the bull's eye window. Standing on the tips of her toes, she listens to them come, pass, and go. A causeway connects the island to the mainland. Mothy Mouser loathes that isthmus. She talks about killing, crucifying it. When the causeway is flooded in the spring, she rows around the island in her canoe everyday, many times a day. In the spring, the river rises and swells. Sometimes, the water floods the whole island, overflowing the land, leaving but the elm, a few poplar crowns, and the quarry winch protruding through the white and sleek mirror-like surface. The abbey belongs to Mothy Mouser. I don't like living here. I just live here in the meantime, dormant. Christian is away. His place at the dinner table, opposite mine, is empty, as empty as his place in my mind should be. September already… Christian should be coming back soon. We'll spend a couple of weeks together. And then… Einberg claims that a boy his age should go to boarding school… Everybody is fighting to keep him away from me. Christian is like a trophy. The strongest will prevail. Christian, Einberg, Mothy Mouser: they have it all wrong. I'm the strongest. I will prevail, have him to myself. I'll steal him away, like I'll steal Constance Chlorus away from her dreadful family. Having someone on your mind is like having a sword. I want to penetrate Christian's mind like a sword, and break his own sword over my knees. And snap Constance Chlorus' sword. And smash the God of Armies' sword. As for my own heart, I'll rip it out and throw it in the river.

7

Christian will be back in the morning! Off to bed! Falling asleep is too hard… This night will never end! Before I surrender to sleep, my boat circles the globe a hundred times and my bird flies a thousand times to the end of the world and back. I wake up. Too early! I shut my eyes. I wake up again. It's still night out. I wake up once more. Daytime. At last! I'm beside myself. I jump out of bed, out of my room. I laugh, scream, scamper through the hallways. I swirl and twirl like a swarm of white moths around a lantern. I run to Christian's room and rip the door open. I dive into his bed as though it were a river. I relentlessly bounce like a ball on his sleeping field. Christian! Christian! I break into war cries and gestures like an Apache charging into battle. Blankets, bed sheets and curtains fly around the room like ghosts in a haunted house. It's snowing feathers all around, non-stop, like in a blizzard. I tickle his soles, and his toes curl up. I tickle his armpits, and his arms snap shut like traps around my hands. Christian, who's just come home, all rheumy-eyed and puffy-faced, is groaning, growling and barking threats, but he remains flaccid, refusing to lose his temper. I go all out. I throw myself at him, mess up his hair, shake him up by the nose, by the ears. I shower him with insults. His body eventually stiffens, tightens, tenses up—he's about to erupt. The sharp turn in his demeanor triggers an actual earthquake. I catch him by the foot and yank as he desperately clings to the bedposts. I exert a powerful pull. He lets go, and bang! He rolls over the ground. There it is! He's angry. He gets up and comes after me. If he catches me, he'll wring my neck. I slip right past him, quick and swift like a stream. He runs faster than I do. I'm caught in a corner. I'm a desperate little lamb. I seize a flying bedsheet and throw it to his face. He gets caught as in a net, and I manage to flee. He's at my heels once more. He'll fall down upon my shoulders. His jar of beads sits proudly on the dresser. I grab it as I run past and gracefully scatter handfuls of beads under his feet as though I were sowing seeds. He stomps in pain and anger. He sways and swings until he loses his balance. He finally keels over. I laugh to the point of stumbling, drunk with my own laughter, which slowly drains me, wears me out. My legs buckle. I can barely stand. I fall to the ground, struck down by laughter. He grabs me, crushes me, punches me. I let him. I'm too intoxicated to react. His blows gradually sober me up. I manage to flee. He catches me right away. We both fall down in our embrace. Take that, you toad! Take that, you skunk! We grapple, like little bear cubs, like fighting cocks. Since he's taller and stronger, I feel no shame in resorting to the cheapest shots. We roll all over the ground, slamming and bouncing against the walls. Dressers get stripped, chairs collide, and the bed is spinning. Call it quits! No! He holds me down on the floor, his knee locked on my throat. Call it quits! No! Never! I lift up my head and bite him viciously, piercing the muscle to the bone with the teeth I have left. I clutch at his pyjamas. The buttons of his shirt blast away like firecrackers. But he's twice as tall and twice as strong as I am and he'll eventually overpower me. All my sweat and tricks only delay the inevitable: my unconditional surrender. I'm gasping for air. My throat is on fire. He's twisting my arm. I can't take it anymore. I give up. I wave all flags. I call it quits. I beg him. He demands that I pick up his beads. Never! Never! Burn me at the stake! Drop an atomic bomb! You can pick up your own damned glass eyes! I would have died in the dark closet where he dragged me and locked me up if the gardener hadn't heard me screaming and come to my rescue.

We sit down to dinner. The gardener is serving us soup. We act like nothing happened. Nothing must reveal we had a fight. It's a secret. We've really put one over Einberg. We stare at our soup so that our eyes won't meet. Just thinking about him will set me laughing. Christian covers his mouth with one hand.

"Look under your bowl!" he says in a flat voice.

Suspicious, I lift my bowl still full of soup. A note. I quickly palm it and unfold it on my lap. Something falls to the ground. On all fours under the mammoth table, I fumble for it in the dark. I get ahold of a shoestring donned with something shiny like a cat's-eye. It's an ivory sun bristling with opal and sapphire rays. Opal and sapphire! It's so pretty! So shiny! I let out a cry of joy and spring back up, glowing with bliss. Without thinking, out of sheer enthusiasm, I show Einberg the necklace. Look, Einberg, how pretty, how bright it is! Christian gave it to me! I read the note, sniffling with emotion and love. "I hope this morning's beating has taught you a good lesson. This is a real talisman. With real precious stones. A Zulu scout gave it to me. Your brother Christian." I tie the shoestring to my neck. And in a sharp voice, I swear to Christian, before Yahweh, that I shall never take it off. Mothy Mouser is smiling at the back of the room. At the other end of the table, Einberg is clenching his fists, grinding his teeth. I see Christian shake in his boots. Einberg shoots him a poisonous look—a death stare.

"What is that thing?" he barks. "Answer me! What is it?"

"It's a talisman," answers Christian in a high-pitched voice, his ears red with shame. "It's a Zulu sun. An object of worship."

"Take that off at once, Berenice Einberg! Give it back to him *now*! And ask forgiveness to Yahweh for that ridiculous oath. As for you, Christian, leave my daughter alone!"

He makes me fume. I've had enough of that crackpot's hogwash! I'm fed up with their Thirty Years War.

"Don't you think for a second that I'm scared of you, Mauritius Einberg! I said I'd keep the talisman, and I will. If you take it from me, you'll regret it. I'll kill you!"

Mothy Mouser makes a stand, coming to my rescue. She would never miss such a perfect opportunity to lash out at Einberg.

"All this huffing and puffing is completely absurd, Mauritius Einberg! You're a sick man! Mad with hate! You always have to overrule everybody, don't you? Destroy everything? The slightest sign of happiness horrifies you, drives you mad! You feel intimidated each time the children are having fun. Their love for each other makes you retch and fester. Poor you! I really feel your pain!"

"I reserve the right to raise my daughter however I please! If you want to turn your son into a half-wit, be my guest! But you stay away from my daughter!"

"I reserve the right to protect my children from the sick hatred you harbour!"

Wham! Take that! Catch that load! Bam! In your face! That'll teach you, you cow! Pow! Right on the schnoz! That'll teach you, you louse!

8

Mothy Mouser refers to love as a walled village, a haven no evil can reach, an oasis of bliss, a luxurious enclave sheltered by a living roof of flying finches and tanagers. When she speaks of love, her words find peaks and troughs to bounce off within me. But no matter how safe a haven may be, isn't it always a cage, a prison, a gloomy, gluey tunnel? I find life's calamitous immensity more appealing than any of its cozy cluttered cocoons. A bay is of no interest to me. I want the whole continent—all continents. I want to sail through continents and deserts. I want to conquer chasms and pinnacles, jump from hell to heaven. I want it all to swallow me, if only for the sake of crawling back out. I want to be attacked by anyone or anything bearing arms.

I stand against love. I rebel against love like they rebel against loneliness. To love is to feel interest and affection for someone or something. To love is to experience. To love is to surrender. I don't want to experience life: I want to provoke it. I refuse to surrender. I want to strike. I refuse to suffer.

When I grow up, there will be no heart in my chest—just an empty, dried-out wineskin. Christian will leave me cold, completely indifferent. Our only bonds will be the ones forged by my own hand. Nothing will drive me toward him: I'll walk up to him with my own feet. I like to imagine that we're two stones I've decided to graft together with my own blood. Two stones will engage in a dialogue. I'll be crowned with success. I'm an alchemist driven insane by mercury vapours. Mine will be a loveless, painless love, as though I were a piece of quartz. I'll live without a beating heart—without a heart.

Love stories bore me. In my mind, when your life is a beautiful love story, you live a mediocre life, a failure, a waste of a life. It's always the same story. A girl and a boy. Coming from opposite ends of nowhere, they fall into each other's arms. They don't know each other. They come face to face, they look at each other, and they feel their hearts kindle, bleed, swell. They love each other. I love yours. You love mine. They're in love and, suddenly, thousands of bells are chiming, conjured up from Earth's darkest depths. He's enraptured, yet it's none of his doing. She's in heaven, yet it's none of her doing. Something they were not seeking happened to them. They surrender to some kind of pressure, some kind of pull. How weak! How shameful! They fell into a trap where they now find themselves at ease. They were played and they blindly rejoice, as though they were brain-dead. They're two victims of one conspiracy, deceived by some scheme. My name is Berenice Einberg, and I won't let myself be fooled. You must never let yourself love. It's like letting yourself go.

I'm learning to scorn what I spontaneously like. I'm training myself to seek what I spontaneously shy away from. Things and people that bear no beauty cause no pain. It may be ridiculous, but less so than naively following the voice of your emotions—emotions that came out of nowhere. Born out of nothingness, they opened their eyes, found emotions in their souls, thinking, "These emotions are mine." What matters is to want, to have a soul of your own making, to have what you want in your soul. They wonder where they come from. When you come from yourself, you know where you come from. We must turn our backs to the fate that steers us and build our own. In order to do that, we must constantly overrule unknown forces, outside impulses. We must create ourselves once more, giving birth to ourselves anew. We're born like statues. When we come into this world, we're statues; something made us and we just have to live as we were made. That's easy to do. I'm a statue striving to take on a new shape, to sculpt herself into something else. When you create yourself, you know who you are. Hubris demands that you be who you want to be. What matters is satisfying your hubris, never losing face before yourself, projecting splendour in the mirror, maintaining honour and dignity at the expense of the out-side forces plaguing your newborn soul. What matters is knowing you're responsible for your every action, rebelling against the life some deep-set instinct was imposing on you. You must be flogged so as not to fall asleep, like the dark giant guarding evil spirits. If need be, I'll rip off my own eyelids to keep my eyes peeled. I'll choose the ground beneath each of my steps. With what little hubris I have, I'll reinvent myself.

There's no need to live very long to draw proper con-clusions about happiness. I sneer at both joy and sadness in equal and full swing. I know joy is immanent and that, no matter what I do, I'll always have to fight off its blows, as regular as a clock's tick-tock. What I mean is that you can't help it if you're happy one day and sad the next. One day you're merry. The next you're crabby. There's nothing to do about it either way. When you're wise, you try your best not to care and go on living your life. That constant switch from joy to sadness is an uncontrollable, outside phenomenon, like rain or sunshine, like night and day. We shrug and we keep going. Crack that whip!

Christian! Constance Chlorus... Who are they? I'm the general and they're fortresses for me to seize. I make them mine. I steal them from whomever owns them. I yank them away from themselves, take them into captivity. I use my powers on them. I'm inclined to love them, but I don't. Because I don't want to. I must triumph over their will and over what leads me to love them. They're my battles. My only battle. Mothy Mouser is my battle. Einberg is my battle. Everything is my battle. Bang! Fire that cannon at the Indian's nose! Wham! Fling that shoe at the Indian's ear! Whatever wits may be guiding me tonight, whatever force may be stirring me now, Christian and Constance Chlorus are still haunting me—I seek them, I wait for them, I should own them. I should stop suffering because of them. I should only know their faces. I should see them only as the fool and the queen on a chessboard. But I would get bored. You shouldn't suffer. But you must risk to suffer a lot. But I love winning too much not to pursue every single battle and risk losing everything. Go to bed. Crappy cow crap!

9

This week, being Christian's friend is easy, undemanding, exhilarating even. It's so easy that it's almost not worth it. Later, though, it will be hard, exhausting, almost impossible. I have plans. We'll leave each other cold. Like rocks. We'll need to forge a new friendship as we go along. We'll only be friends out of pride, for the beauty of building, of creating something, of running the show. I want Christian, in time, to despise and loathe me. Only then will he be my friend in spite of us both. Only then will our souls' efforts to remain friends leave us sweating buckets and make our eyes bleed, make us burn. Life doesn't take place on earth, but inside my head. Life is inside my head, and my head inside life. I'm all enclosing and enclosed. The girl the swallowed have swallowed.

Christian has a way to love that melts my heart. He loves little things, things that have no strength, no shape, no weight, no beauty. He leans close to them, and I can suddenly see them, before my very eyes, radiate the best of humankind. He delves into them, discovering them. He only needs to point at them or take them in his hand, and his love suddenly makes them marvellous. He could even make a boa constrictor fall for the leg of a chair. When I'm alone by the marsh and see spiders running on water, I feel nothing. When Christian is with me, the spiders fill my view like a fleet of ships—they light up so that I can see them, open my gaze to let them in. The rushes he picks up become houses. He opens the ends, and something quickly crawls out: an insect, a small creature, some tiny human being or a rhinoceros no bigger than a pinhead.

We head toward the marsh, taking off our shoes the minute we reach the water's edge. He rolls up the legs of his trousers and I tie a knot in my skirt. We hold hands as we walk in the cold, perilous clay. I carry his hunting bag over my shoulder. Let me carry your hunting bag! It's filled with nets and jars equipped with clever traps. He suddenly stands still, squeezes my hand, and points at something.

"Look!" he whispers. "A Livia! Take a good look at her. See how transparent her wings are. You can see her body below them; she looks like she has no wings at all. Look at her belly! See how it's really black but looks green when it glitters. Her wings are so perfectly square, like they were drawn with a triangle. Look at her head! It couldn't be more square! And you'd think it's adorned with a silver drop. You'd think she's wearing a helmet. See how still she is, pretending we're not here."

At first glance I thought it was just a big fly. Then I believed it was the work of a goldsmith, and that he had pinned it to that petal as you would slip a diamond ring on your finger. But the Livia is something else entirely. I learn that it's an adventurer, a killer. Christian tells me the bloodiest Livia stories he knows. He takes a swatter from his hunting bag. My chest tightens. Swift as lightning, Christian strikes. And the Livia, that, just a moment ago, was sitting on a petal, looking like an arrow about to be shot, now looks like a mere larva, squirming weakly in the viscous water.

"You crazy fool! You broke it! It's all broken now."

I open the jar and he drops it in. We resume our exploratory journey. The Livia comes back to life. Its little legs tense up like violin strings. Its wings tighten like drum skin. It has regained its glow, now standing erect, alert and cautious. I watch it dart every which way, throw itself in vain against the glass walls of its prison.

We hold our breath. We dunk beneath the dark and mysterious surface the hemp cloth we use as a net. Holding it tight from all four corners, we slowly, smoothly, relentlessly scrape the rugged bed, carrying it deeper and deeper, to ever more hidden spots. We must be very careful not to disturb or move anything: the greatest wonders are the most fearful ones. Christian gives me the signal. Slowly and smoothly, shrouded in the most stifling silence, we claim our catch. This is the moment when we experience bliss, purer every time. We watch the water drain with wide-open eyes and gaping mouths. As our faces inch closer and closer to the little cloth hollowed by the weight of the liquid, we're more anxious than if we were sifting auriferous sand. The water flows between our legs until it runs scarce, coming to a drip. All that's left is a thick soup made of silt and algae. The muddy water starts moving. It comes alive, comes to a boil. I imagine that something—goodness knows what—will soon emerge from the tremors of this unbearable gravidity: squirming earrings, tiny finned fairies, vibrant daisies or dahlia blooms. Things swarm, wriggle into recognizable shapes. Backbones shine through. Tails spring up. I can already see a brood of black tadpoles squiggling about. I expect to see more—bigger ones: fair and tepid like sparrow eggs, white-necked, limp like cheeks, with bumblebee legs at the end of a beautiful sharp tail already wearing away. Next to the smaller ones, they look like giants: marvellous, monstrous even. They fill your fist when you tighten your grip to feel them fight for their lives. Every time the water disappears, some kind of miracle happens. A leech as long as a shoelace leaps up, breaking into a full body shimmy. A real ornamental fish, a small see-through fish, shining green or shining blue, surfaces through the bulk of little black tadpoles and still shellfish.

It's nightfall when we head back home. I walk far behind Christian, kissing poplar nymphs along the way.

10

Twilight has fallen and it's rather cold out. I look up at the sky, trying to understand the dismal excitement, the dizzying fever it elicits within me, this anxious intoxication consuming my whole body. High over the horizon, a bank of jet-black clouds, as massive as a wharf, frame the blazing top of a wall that once contained the violent flares of the fall sunset. We're besieged. The sky is about to be seized.

The wind is blowing in the right direction. It will soon rain. This may be our last chance. We must burn the grass *tonight*. We go see the gardener. We've been hassling him about this since the beginning of the month. Look, Gardener, it's going to rain, and the grass will be wet! Look, Gardener, the wind is blowing the right way; it'll drive the flames toward the river! Defeated, utterly out of strength and arguments to fight back, the gardener gives in. He stands up, puts on his cap, and heads to the abbey to ask Einberg for permission to burn the grass.

Wielding firebrands, we set fire to the waterfront skirting the width of the island. We kindle the waist-high, rampant, bone-dry grass—broom, whin, cat's tail and witch grass. We witness at once the extermination, slaughter, deflagration, disaster. As soon as the grass is ablaze, a single blow of the wind makes the flames roar, rise above our heads, spread on all sides—it's as though we were caught in a flight of tufts. Before long, the flames strike, surge, scream from shore to shore, their plumes billowing below the clouds like tight herds of great white horses. Entangled in black fumes, rekindled by a mist of sparks, the flames furl and unfurl like a tidal wave. Titanic, terrifying, untamed, they sweep and spread like a tsunami, wolfing, razing, wiping everything. All they leave behind is a fine black lace of ash that turns to dust under our feet. The night sky casts a red glow. The moor crackles throughout. Christian and I are not done. We're firebenders. That, believe me, is no small feat! We must manage the scope of the burning wave, making sure it doesn't miss a single twig or straw. We must help it past rocky ridges, revive it when it hits a puddle, stir and feed it where the grass is scarce, bring it back to life when it dies out. We must continuously meld its countless masses together. We must look after every detail. Feckless and heedless, distracted, the gardener leaves everything to chance. I put my hands on my face. It's burning hot. I put my hands on Christian's face. Our eyes are crying, our lips are laughing. Neither of us can stop coughing. From the shadows, cradling her cat, Mothy Mouser watches us. Around the elm and the quarry winch, we have to corner the Hydra, hem it in, fend it off, fight with it. We swing our shovels relentlessly at every raised head. The wind dies out. The rain slowly starts to fall in small icy lumps. Intoxicating at first, the pungent fumes now make us a little nauseous. Our arms are shaking. We head home. The last gleaming glitters are fading, fainting as they reach the water's edge. All that's left glowing in the night are a few scattered pockets of ember. I follow Christian, exhausted, wobbly, holding my belly as I laugh in flurries, clinging with one hand to the hem of his shirt.

11

Four sparrows spring from crumb to crumb before the door of the gardener's lodge. A freezing blast of wind forces them under the cornice. Last year, at the first signs of winter, I put my tongue on the gate's corbel and it stayed stuck to the surface, so hard that all the skin came off when I pulled away. I take off my warm mittens. I plant myself right before the gates with my clammy hands, reaching to touch the cold iron corbel tinseled with white fluff. I'm scared. But the iron corbel is too inviting. I retreat and recoil many times, but eventually proceed. I shut my eyes and seize it with both hands, letting out a little squeal. Ow! This is worse than holding a fistful of embers. The metal is boiling cold. I can feel my skin melt as my palms adhere to it. My heart grows faint. My mouth opens. Do not yell. Swallow those sinful screams, Berenice Einberg! I try to pry my hands off the gates. My skin tears from my flesh. Suffer but do *not* scream! Think about Father Brébeuf, who stayed still when those Indians slipped a white-hot iron collar around his neck. Amazed by the courage of the frail white man, the tough warriors fought over his heart. Do not lose your mind, Berenice Einberg! Suffering only offends your flesh. Screaming like a banshee offends your entire soul. The Indians knew that Father Brébeuf was suffering, but that was not enough for them. They wanted him to wail, to writhe, to lose his wits. They wanted to crush his pride. Do not lose yourself, Berenice Einberg. Keep squeezing your soul tight. You'll always find enough strength in your heart to resist screaming like a banshee. Since last year's adventure, I learned that, in such cases, there's only one way to walk free without getting flayed alive. You have to suffer and wait for the metal to warm up. My hands are on fire. Surely they'll warm something up before long. My pain is greater than Father Brébeuf's. Yet I still haven't screamed. I got my revenge. I conquered the corbel. I smile to myself, gloating. Last year… Like last year, alas, the grand duchess of Mingrelia is here for the winter holidays. She arrived yesterday from Dnipropetrovsk, in all her glory.

It hasn't snowed yet. It was very cold last night. When I came out of the abbey, early this morning, a thick frost dusted the land and the metal-bearing sand, coating the naked poplars and the motionless rush, cloaking the elm, the quarry winch and the gardener's lodge.

At first, we tentatively tiptoe onto the thin jet-black tiles that paved the channel a few hours ago, in the secrecy of night. Since it seems to hold our weight without creaking or cracking, we shakily steal away from the shore. Leaning on each other, we carefully slide our feet across the surface. Old inlanders believe the channel is unfathomable on this side of the causeway. If the abyss has a bottom, it's far below. One day, a long time ago, engineers came to measure its depth. They brought a plumb line so long that its weight threatened their boat. The whole line had unwound but the plummet still sank. Last year, as we were probing the ice much like today, something thundered below our feet. As the fear paralyzed us, a large crack ripped the ice between our feet, sped forth, branched out and disappeared into the reeds throughout the shore, imprinting the shape of a tall white tree on the black surface. The ice is not cracking. It shows no sign of weakness. We move forward with greater confidence. Our steps grow bigger and heavier; soon we run to the beat of a mad race, a crazy country-dance, laughing wild. We still have our doubts. We still lack a more tangible proof. We let ourselves fall onto the dark mirror, testing it one last time, pounding it with all the strength of our cleats. The ice flakes but it doesn't break. Victory! The ice is good! We run back to the abbey and tell Mothy Mouser, who raises an eyebrow and consults with the gardener.

"The ice is good," he confirms.

I clap my hands, jumping up and down.

"Don't make so much noise!" whispers Mothy Mouser. "Mingrelia's still asleep."

We put on our skates, sitting on the mat before the revolving door so as not to damage the floor haphazardly. Mothy Mouser helps Christian tie his laces. She must exert extreme pressure on the intersections while Christian threads them through the next eyelets. She presses with the tip of her long, beautiful finger, adorned with a pink, precious, ogival stone. Christian blushes like a young bride. And I've never even seen a young bride. Your skates must be tied really tight for you to feel steady. I had to urge Mothy Mouser to let me lace my own skates. I'll do it alone, as I please. So be it! Mothy Mouser wraps a woolen scarf around my forehead and neck. She strokes my face with her beautiful, long hand—her soft, delicate, flower-scented hand. She wrapped me like a mummy. I can't breathe.

"Christian!" she calls out as he opens the door. "Take good care of your little sister!"

He takes me by the hand. One day, *I* will take good care, *I* will take by the hand. Diamond dust flies and stars shatter under Christian's feet. There he goes! The flurry takes him, carries him away. Now he slides like a sailboat. Now he sways and waltzes away. I don't know what's wrong with my feet, but I've never been able to skate. I'm dying to catch up with Christian and take part in the game, let him carry me away as though we were rolling down a hill, be introduced to the enchantment that gives him so much grace and joy. How hard can it be after all? I watch him closely. You let yourself glide on one skate, then on the other, and there you go! Let's try once more! I slide one foot forward. The ice is so slick, so slippery, that I lose control, skid, and crash down. I get back up. I give it another go, slip and slide again, falling flat on my face. I give up and start walking, but I grow impatient and reckless and I start to run. My skates turn sideways and my legs suddenly spread apart. I lose balance. I bash my head and break my tailbone. Again. I call Christian for help. He takes me by the shoulders and

I manage to skate over a dozen feet without falling. He says I'm skating like a champion and ditches me, skating away. I won't lose hope. That comes with time. Pretending that Christian is still supporting me, I try again. I give it my all. No one ever tested their bums at such speeds, with such zeal. The short timespan I was willing to spare to possess my art to the fullest has elapsed to no avail. I have no desire or strength left in me to stand back up. I wallow in despair. Now on my back, then on my belly, I punch and kick, damning my impotence, my plight, and so on. Again, I call Christian for help. Intoxicated with sheer ice and open air, he delights in dazzling me with his talent, taunting me, adding insult to injury. He swirls around me as swiftly as a shooting star, now with one leg up in the air, then backwards. He jumps over me. He brakes just under my nose, rasping the surface, showering me with frozen flakes. To make things worse, the grand duchess of Mingrelia comes to join us. Skating is no joke to her. She's wearing a tutu and breeches. Pulling entrechats, she speeds ahead, twirling and swirling forth, looking like a true ballerina, a butterfly that flutters from flower to flower. All the more reason to seethe with rage. I pound against the ice with my head and teeth. I swallow my pride and, on all fours, start chasing Mingrelia. Our precious Christian won't teach me how to skate. Will *you*?

12

We go skating. I'm making progress, coming along in leaps and bounds. Now, when Christian and Mingrelia grab me by the arms to perform those breathsucking pirouettes with me in tow, I manage to stay on my feet. I deserve even more credit since nothing makes them laugh harder than seeing me spread-eagled on the ice, since laughing with each other is, for them, like kissing each other. I need to predict when they'll make sharp turns, stops, pretend missteps, or furtive attempts to trip me. If I am to believe them, I've been making amazing progress, leap-frogging, rocketing forward. They share the same look, the same clever smirk, claiming that I've been blessed with an unparalleled gift for figure skating. They even compare me to Barbara Ann Scott.

Christian and Mingrelia share a secret. I can smell it. When they smile, you could swear their teeth were hiding treasure. When they look at each other, an unworldly sun, not the sun you can see, makes their eyes shine bright. They're skating in an invisible realm. My skates glide along with theirs, but I alone am skating in the real world. Long live solitude! Crappy cow crap! I can tell that I'm a third wheel—unwanted, annoying. I couldn't care less. No need to play shy. I take malicious pleasure in intruding on them, cramping their love, breaking their spell, troubling their little bliss. To get rid of me, they skate off on a tour of the island. Their dizzying flight brings them beyond where I can see, and I've run out of ways to throw wrenches in the gears of their secret. I guess I could always crawl after them.

But I would never crawl fast enough. Slow and stealthy wins the war.

The grand duchess is leaving us. *Vaya con Dios, ma chère Fräulein*! I shall be delighted not to suffer your presence anymore. She's a wolf in sheep's clothing. What irks me even more is that she seems to favour me when she gets one of her affected bouts. She must be thinking, "That one doesn't look too bright. She's got an empty head. Let's fill it!" With me, she's so confident in her superiority, so sure to convince me with her regal bearing and her petty pizzazz that she manages to shake my strongest beliefs.

I'm ugly. My hair is straight and scruffy enough to break a bulldozer comb. Mingrelia is as pretty as the day is long. Her soft, shiny, black hair falls in long, heavy ringlets that curl and twirl around her fine neck, no larger than a wrist. My words are as rough and clumsy as my limbs. She has the grace of a butterfly and the manners of a queen. I've only ever left the island to go to school. She's sampled the finest restaurants in the biggest cities of all five continents. She's attended the theatre in Hamburg, and the opera in Oslo. I have no notion of chemistry, geometry, Greek, Hebrew, music, ballet, horse riding, or sex. These sciences, languages, and arts have no secrets for Mingrelia, who has learned, guessed, or broken them all. I beg in vain for Christian's smile and attention, endlessly sacrificing my pride for his friendship. Mingrelia has subjected my brother to her face. She's pulling his strings with her eyes, her cheeks, her lips, like a puppet master. Also, what's even worse, she's evil, heartless. Instead of feeling sorry for me and flying to my rescue, Mingrelia deliberately takes advantage of my innate, natural, and acquired shortcomings to scorn me and sneer at me, belittling me as much as she can, mocking my humblest efforts. However, I'm not overly worried about all that. When I grow up, my glory will have successfully dissolved Mingrelia's shadow in the bountiful glow of her mighty effulgence.

They send Mingrelia my way year after year. She supposedly comes to share the Christmas sadness of a misguided Jew like me. The town has been embellished, decked with multi-coloured rosaries of light. Mothy Mouser had a tamarack erected in the chapel. She wreathed it with garlands, overloading the lushly fragrant branches with tinsel and shiny balls, as well as tinted figurines. But that's none of my business. I should be happy, for all of it alienates me, and alienation is salvation. It's the complete opposite. I'm filled with sadness. It's New Year's Eve. Mothy Mouser laughs as she welcomes a giddy party of family and friends. They won't stop hugging and kissing. They perform Polish dances, sweating the night away. At midnight, they sit down to a candlelight dinner. Usually, the gardener pulls up the walkway bridge as soon as we cross it. Tonight, it will stay down all night. Mingrelia and I are allowed to make but one appearance merely pro forma, in our pyjamas and slippers. Christian is showered with gifts. As expected, Einberg turned down all of Mothy Mouser's gifts to us. She only gives me Christmas presents to force his hand, to make him boil, to mock and spite him.

I go to Mingrelia's room and ask her if she would let me in her bed. I'm hoping to melt her heart with my woeful misfortunes. She turns a deaf ear. Her misfortunes are far more woeful than mine. Where can she possibly stuff all those boys? She smells supremely good. I interrupt her to tell her.

"You smell so good, Mingrelia."

"That's easy. You would too if you bathed more often."

"Do I smell like hell?"

Mingrelia's nose comes near my neck to check.

"No, you don't smell. And don't tell Christian what I told you about Serge."

Her eyes are shut. I look at her. I imagine that Christian kisses her, then that I kiss her. She belongs to a superior realm—the same one where butterflies, trees, stars, and all things beautiful belong. She's like Mothy Mouser. Her sheer existence makes her glorious. I must make constant efforts to find myself worthy. She just needs to be herself for me to find her fabulous. Who cares if she has no soul? Does a butterfly? I would trade my soul for any flower's petals, any parrot's feathers. I'm sad and I hate it. Sadness makes me hate myself. Sadness weakens the soul. Sadness is a cesspool. When you want to be fabulous, you can't let your soul rot in a cesspool. Pull yourself together! Gaiety makes the soul shine as bright as the sun. Be gay Berenice, gay!

Even though Christian betrayed me out of base complacency, I'll remain loyal to him! Even though he's never thought twice before mocking me to please his mundane, hollow Mingrelia, I remain gay and loyal to him! Even though he's clearly proven that he's just as heartless and soulless as that half-wit, I still love him! Even though he's willfully chosen to stay blind to her blatant schemes, I still love him! Even though in his shameful soul, the slightest sign of attention from that piece of trash is more important than my most bitter disappointment, I still love him! Smile, merry maiden, smile! I'm distraught.

13

Mothy Mouser tells me that my old nanny has died. Here's the story I made my old nanny tell me a thousand times.

That year, spring came at lightning-speed, without warning. Besides having to withstand the attacks of seasonal fevers, the nuns had to cope with the brutal passing of an abbess they worshipped and then look on helplessly as her domain was desecrated by a young stranger with a sharp tongue and a stony stare who was rumoured to owe her high office not to her piety or charity but to her noble birth. When tragedy struck, however, daily life had apparently returned to normal, following what seemed to be a new order to which everyone had grown accustomed.

That night, the new abbess, who had been more haughty and moody than ever for a week, had not attended any of the services, and nothing appeared to justify such serious omissions. The nuns didn't worry. They took offence. Inflamed by the bitter influence of their older sisters, they rejoiced in having found fault in the arrogant abbess. No one dared to dig any deeper. The new commandment was that Mother St. Denial's sleep was not to be disturbed under any circumstance.

Sister Sacristan loves to run. She whooshes through the whole abbey at full tilt, dark gloomy hall after dark gloomy hall, making the walls crackle with the sharp rattle of her ratchet as she rallies the troops for Low Mass. Without realizing it, she runs past Mother St. Denial's cell. She slows down. She stops. She looks back and stares at the door, waiting, hoping that the abbess will finally give some sign of life. Nothing. The door just stretches out in silence, shrouded in ever-greater mystery. Sister Sacristan wavers. Then she makes up her mind. Poor Mother St. Denial may be gravely ill. She doubles back and, standing right in front of her superior's door, starts to rattle her ratchet frantically. She stops to catch her breath. She cocks an ear. Nothing. She switches hands and starts over. She keeps knocking on the door, harder each time. No response. She calls out in vain, again and again, "Mother St. Denial! Mother St. Denial!" wondering what to make of it all.

Suddenly she thinks she has heard something move in the rock-hard silence behind the door. Something coming from within the wall, like the distant rumble of a great storm. She presses her ear to the lattice. As the noise becomes clearer, it grows ever less familiar, ever more frightening: cries—thousands of them—faint, short, strangely steady. They sound like peeps from an overpopulated aviary. Sister Sacristan tries the lock. To her great surprise, the latch moves freely in the catch. She knocks one more time, calls one last time. All she has to do now is turn the handle. The door swings wide open, as though struck by a violent blow.

At that moment, seething shrieks go off like shockwaves as thousands and thousands of rats, big ones, explode out of the room; thousands and thousands of big black rats with diamond eyes. Flocks, legions of rats fighting and trampling up to the lintel blast out of the walls of that mysterious cell, streaming out, spilling over, stumbling down, spewing and spurting out of the room like a tidal wave. Within seconds, all four wings of the mazy abbey are swarming, teeming with rats—they have spread over the whole island.

A pungent smell pervaded the new abbess' consumed cell—the potent smell of burnt hair. The fire had damaged, destroyed, or downright devoured everything in the room, from the marble Jesus to the small iron bed. The floor was littered with ashes. Strangely enough, most were at the foot of the bed, forming a wide eminence. Considering how uncanny the whole scene was, nobody paid much heed to the uncanny mound. But when a sudden draft scattered the top ashes, screams pierced the halls. Eyes widened as they saw the red velvet coat—untouched, immaculate. Flipping the rich fabric, the exorcist uncovered two charred skeletons, huddled with their backs against one another. The next day, the nuns resigned themselves to leaving the rat-infested island. A hundred years went by before anyone dared to drop anchor anywhere nearby.

"That new abbess... Was she pretty or was she ugly?" I would ask my old nanny.

My old nanny would shrug, unsure.

"She was young... she must have been pretty."

Then, I would conjure up the new abbess. I would feel her live within me. It seemed to me that if she had been ugly like me, nothing would have happened. If she had not been pretty, everything would have happened for nothing.

14

Winter is over. Spring has begun. Green strands are piercing the straw bed where the snow used to rest. Soft hair is growing everywhere under my feet. I'm walking on earth, on air, behind Christian. With our notebook, pen and inkwell, we draw up a thorough list of our fauna. Like Christopher Columbus, we explore the island one square foot at a time. Forty-two crickets. Twenty-three ants. Three dung beetles. One cat. Everything is accounted for, even Mauriac, Mothy Mouser's beloved cat. Christian records it all in the most beautiful handwriting. We can barely move forward without stepping over a rat's tail. Christian wrote there were two thousand of them, rounding it out. Diamonds are the Republic of South Africa's greatest resource. Rats are ours. We spot two water snakes coiling behind the cord of wood against the back of the gardener's lodge. A sad, scraggy fox is wandering through the rushes, looking in vain for a trail the melt washed out. Six groundhogs are keeping watch outside the coalmine. They will stay above ground as long as they're sure to be the only living souls out there, and vanish as soon as they see something move. They look around, twisting and untwisting their necks at incredible speed, spending their whole lives watching their surroundings to make sure that no one else is there. Christian hits a rock with his stick. Two weasels bolt out. We count two squirrels with tails bigger than their bodies. When they run, their tails float behind them like ostrich feathers on the helms of charging spearmen, like ostrich feathers on torpedo tails. The two squirrels chase each other into the tunnel, their claws clanking on the metal like hail. A plane dropped a big grooved cylinder one night, and that tunnel stayed right where it fell, lying askew across the sand at the back of the island. Christian says that we may not even know all the animals we don't have. However, we feel extremely embarrassed that some we do know, such as dogs and horses, are nowhere to be found. Tomorrow we shall have our dog. We'll befriend the first stray dog we cross on our way back from school. When we walk home tomorrow, we'll carry a bag and we'll fill it with everything we can find: crickets, grasshoppers, cockroaches, snails, rhinoceros, or elephants. The more animals on our island, the richer we'll be. We wrote a letter to Mothy Mouser. We'll slip it under her plate before Einberg arrives. It's a request listing with utmost precision all the missing animals. "Dear Mother, a goat, a cow, a pig, a horse, a boa, a panda, a kiwi… Signed: Christian & Berenice." Christian thinks it will make her laugh.

Rats all come out at the same time, as profusely as dandelions. For a month, they thrive; the whole island is swarming with rats. Each spring, Einberg swears to wipe out their species. However, he has never been able to launch the orgiastic hunt of his dreams, always running up against the peasants' terror. He had to resort to a ruse, luring more of those obsessed mink and muskrat poachers to the island to set their evil traps. Mothy Mouser feels the deepest reverence for animal life, and circumstances— not the least of which being her Thirty Years War with Einberg—brought her to play a leading role in our rat preservation campaign. Like me, but for other reasons, she ended up growing attached to those dreadful rodents. She became obstinately passionate about them. When anyone speaks ill of them, her heart and eyes ignite. Personally, I had nothing against rats or the plague, rabies, diphtheria, malaria, or any of the terrible diseases they carry. While I waited for events to help me understand what I thought or felt, I blindly trusted Christian's thoughts and feelings on the matter. Besides being the rats' general, Christian is their mother, their brother, their doctor. They bit him a few times, but he was so good to them that over time, they learned to value his presence and friendship. When he sees a rat that is limping or huffing and puffing, he brings it over to the clinic he set up in the abbey's cellars so he can treat it. He warms up some milk, disinfects its wounds, mends its broken bones. Since the start of the season, in great secrecy, we've been conspiring with Mothy Mouser to go on a crusade against Einberg and his poachers' cruel operations. We've been chasing traps. Wearing boots, armed with sticks, we spend beautiful days sweeping through the wheatgrass and rushes. All the traps we dig up are ruthlessly disarmed, destroyed, and thrown into the waters of the bottomless channel. Under the railway bridge, at the foot of a pier, we witnessed a tragedy that blew me away; it was so grim and so glorious that the memory of it still unsettles my soul. Splashing mud all over the rushes, a trapped muskrat is struggling to free itself, whistling as though it were weeping. The iron jaw has seized its leg, relentlessly tightening its grip. Knowing it might never break free, the great rat doesn't waver or wait for a miracle. Young and spry, it decides to cut the Gordian knot with its sharp and strong teeth. It starts eating its own leg! It's biting and gnawing at it, making every possible effort to dull the pain. Blood flows. Bones crack. It's vivisecting itself, imbued with an almost wicked willpower. It's hacking at its leg, furiously biting off the flesh, wringing out the lacerated limb, now crushed to a pulp, while its whole body writhes. It's like mad, out of its mind, erupting—like lightning, like thunder.

"Do you see…" says Christian as he slips a hood over the possessed muskrat's head so he can operate without running the risk of losing a finger.

Yes, I saw. And now, I can tell from his teary eyes that he also saw it. We're disinfecting the leg and securing it into place with twigs. We're so in love with the small wounded creature that we only have eyes and ears for it.

"Leave it!" someone suddenly shouts behind us.

Christian barely has time to turn his head before the young poacher's fist lands on his face, striking him down. I barely have time to realize what's going on. Christian quickly scrambles to his feet and takes off. He flees without looking back, leaving me alone to shield the poor muskrat— that was almost killed by its own freedom—from the big brawny poacher. A rat has a bellyful of courage. A Christian doesn't have enough to fill a pinky toe. It's fine to be friends with a coward—it's better than catching the scarlet fever, swallowing rat poison, or sucking on mothballs.

15

We're caught in a storm. It's raining so hard that the drops burst like tiny bombs when they land on the sand or the river. We run to the tunnel for cover. When I'm alone, I like to let myself be whipped and soaked by the heavy rain. When I'm with Christian, I'd rather hide with him in this cramped cocoon and convince myself that we're facing a common threat. Today, we talk about our future, our careers—for the first time. I tell him that I won't stay here rolling and cutting stones until tedium kills me. I'm not of those who build cathedrals. I'm of those who can't wait to spread their wings across the whole sky, like the stratosphere. When I grow up, I'll travel far and wide, across the world, felling all the lions in tedium's den. I'll own a big cannon and banish boredom to the day I die. Christian says that he sees what I mean. I doubt that he's being earnest. How could he possibly see what's hidden so deeply within me that it hurts? I can't see the wolves howling inside my cage.

"Are you in a hurry to leave?"

"No, Christian. That's not it. My soul holds me tight like a spear. It's about to throw me real, real high and real, real far. My hands just allow me to hold on tight until I'm strong enough to be launched across the sky. And I truly madly deeply can't wait!"

In confidence, he tells me that he also can't wait to throw something and be strong enough to do it. He too wants to throw a spear, but it's no human spear. It's made of wood. This confession startles me so much that I don't understand what he means. He has to repeat it all. He wants to be a javelin thrower. He dreams of setting an all-time record, playing for Canada in the Olympic Games.

"What now? Javelin thrower! You can't be serious... You're crazy! Come on!"

Unimpressed by my outburst, Christian shrugs. You must be mad to have such ideas.

"You don't want me to be a javelin thrower? What would you have me be?"

"My brother, my friend..."

"And what's a brother, what's a friend to do? If I spend my life being your brother and your friend, I won't have done much with myself."

The wild grey rain is thinning out, dying down. We walk back to the abbey surrounded by rolling thunder. Christian brings me to his room. We sit down on his bed.

"So where's your javelin?"

"Hush! Mother can't know. Don't forget: it's a secret!"

"Why don't you want Mother to know?"

"I'll tell her when it's a sure thing, when I'm sure to make her proud."

"A javelin thrower can't make his mother proud."

"Our mother is one of a kind. I'm sure she'll get it."

"Mother is pretty, isn't she?"

He tells me about the Zulu scout. He says that he's his best friend, that they write to each other. Apparently, the Zulu scout could effortlessly throw the javelin across the whole abbey. He's quite the man! He was selected to compete in the Brisbane Olympic Games two years from now. By then, he won't even be sixteen. Christian climbs onto a stool and takes a large notebook out of his closet. He blushes, stutters, and clears his throat as he opens it and hands it to me. It's a scrapbook where he glued paper clippings and photos depicting the triumphs of javelin throwers. Christian speaks out the American names of those unsung heroes—most of them black, their features almost simian—with great fondness and pride, as though they were the Latin names of various rat species. Cesar Lincoln Cash. Shakespeare Washington Blake. To please him, I make him repeat them so that I can learn them by heart.

"If this is what you want, Christian, I want it too. I'll help you train."

"But please don't tell Mother, bless her heart! She thinks I want to be a biologist. I'll try to throw the javelin. If I fail, she'll never know and I'll go on studying biology like nothing happened. She's so proud of me. When she talks about me, it's like she's talking about herself. 'Christian is so intelligent! He's so serious for his age! And he has such lofty ideals!' She'd be crushed if I told her I may be training to be a failed javelin thrower. But if I succeed, she'll understand… I'm sure she will. She'll share my joy, and we'll share laughs."

"Never mind her! Poor Christian! Don't you see that Mother and Father hate each other enough to kill each other, so much so that they can't see straight, that they can't see us, and that they're using us to hit and hurt each other?"

"Father will never understand. I don't mind. He'll say to Mother, 'Look what you've done with my son! A javelin thrower! A primeval torpedo launcher! An athlete!'"

Yesterday's brother was a rat saviour. Today's brother is a javelin thrower. I wonder what all those brothers are doing here. I'm alone as I let my soul crumble under the very belfries I erected to guard it. How can I honestly say that I love Christian? In order to go on loving him, I must love another. I must trade one Christian for another as Christian keeps turning into a new version of himself. One minute he's worthy. The next he's spineless. One minute he's in love with Mingrelia. The next he hugs a sick rat under his sweater to keep it warm. From one minute to the next, he's a javelin thrower. How stupid is that? I like to think that I love Christian, but I don't love *him*. I love the *idea* of him, something within my soul I call Christian—the Christian I dreamed and embodied the way I wanted to dream and embody him. I know Christian would be different if I saw him through the eyes of another consciousness. I'm realizing that I just need to change the way I feel about my inner Christian for outer Christian—the one I only know by sight—to change and adapt accordingly. Therefore, Christian doesn't exist. Which means I have created him. Why, let's go on creating him, then! I remember dubbing him a knight, and then following him around, as I would have followed Gautier Sans-Avoir in his crusade against the Niam-Niams. I remember seeing him fall gloriously before the walls of Nicea. I remember wrapping my clothes around his remains and burying them in a desert of snow, freezing to death as I lay on his grave! I also remember how I often wished Christian to be ugly, spineless, devoid of any charm, like a stone, so that my love for him would become even stronger. Christian lives alone in Christianland, and he sees me differently than I see myself. I'm choking from within my bones, holed up, filled with self-loathing. I see

Christian through every foul and ugly inch of myself. I picture him as a cluster of stars shining at the bottom of a sewer. All revolting things brewing within me are like all things sealed inside a blood-heated coffin. Go on and open that coffin after ten years—my age! Crappy cow crap! No trace of Christian. The same way that Christian, to quench our respective thirst, finds a mom where I find a Mothy Mouser, there are many Christians, as many as there are people around to create a new Christian. And that leaves me feeling alone. If there's no Mothy Mouser, no Christian, then there's no one but me in the sun. And if I'm indeed walking alone in the sun, then the sun belongs to me—I'm its maker and owner.

Summer again. Once more. Constance Chlorus is leaving me yet again. I barely saw her this year. She's going on tour with the choir. I love her. Tonight, Constance Chlorus, you're the only face I love. The otter has an otter's face. Constance Chlorus has the face of a Constance Chlorus. Like otters, humans have but one face. When I look at an otter, a rat, Christian, Constance Chlorus, Mothy Mouser, I can only take in their faces. If I'm not off with Constance Chlorus and the rest of the choir, it's in honour of my cousins. From Poland, Russia, and the United States, my many cousins run over to greet me. Welcome them with open arms! That was one of Mothy Mouser's ideas, another one of her blows to Einberg's long snout. I have no clue what most of my cousins look like, but I fiercely hate each and every one of them. Does that mean anything at all? I need to hate. Therefore I hate. Period. It only strengthens my lifelong belief that Berenice Einberg, ugly as she may be, has control over all of creation. Didn't I only have to crave for my cousins to be hateful for them to become so? May blackness be green! Believe it or not, darkness, for me, has a green, blue, pink, red, or white hue. What is a green U next to a green night? What is an I-beam? Crappy cow crap!

16

I counted them, just out of curiosity, just to see how good I am at math. I have more cousins than I have fingers. In total, there seem to be fifteen no less. Impressive! And who knows what the future still holds? The American delegation is yet to come—it will strike a balance between the Guelphs and the Ghibellines. For now, the Catholics outrageously outnumber the Jews, enjoying a pornographic numerical advantage. Performing, as always, the most thankless task, Einberg takes me aside, enjoining me to beware of my blond cousins' attentions. He tells me that the Poles have a bone to pick with me because I'm Jewish. They're not evil per se, but history, propaganda and envy, he says, has led them, like all Goyim, to wish harm on my race and on my person. Berenice, my child, watch your back and keep your distance. If they try to shame you for being Jewish, fight back. All right, Father, I'll turn a deaf ear and a blind eye. I'll tell those uncut bullies to buzz off! Mothy Mouser gives me her own little sermon, saying that my heart belongs to all, and that I should divide it in equal pieces to offer to each and everyone of them. She talks about my heart as though it were a cake whetting all my cousins' appetites. I have strange cousins: they like pus and vinegar cakes. She tells me that some of them don't speak a word of English, and that I should take the opportunity to learn their language. Knowing many languages enhances your personality. All right, Mother, I'll learn Russian, French, and Polish. And when I grow up, I'll master so many and have such a stunning personality that when they happen to run into me, they'll mistake me for Venus de Milo. I'll have legs! Eyes! A waist!

Mothy Mouser is making quite a fuss around our cousins' invasion. She's spared no expense preparing for it since the beginning of the year, constantly switching between hostility and diplomacy, swinging a hammer, scaling a ladder, running her mouth, or running her pen. With the sole help of the gardener, she renovated the West wing of the abbey in the dead of winter, often withstanding sub-arctic temperatures. She refurbished enough rooms to be able to give them a proper homelike welcome. She would have stopped at nothing to rub Einberg's nose in her endless benevolence, making him suffer every single inch of her loving, compassionate heart. My name is not Christian. Her well-meaning charade doesn't fool *me*.

We spend two weeks fixing, caulking, and rigging the old cutter we fished out of the ship graveyard. Well-assisted by the gardener—a retired fisherman, odd, yet handy—Mothy Mouser runs the show masterfully. Like galley slaves, our cousins work splittingly hard, feed on hay, and sleep like pigs. Astounded by the great number of great things they had to do, they joyfully and vigorously got down to work, giving it their all. Boys and girls, young and old, white and black, red and green, the Guelphs and the Ghibellines are all sweaty-faced, sharing laughs, pushing ahead like clouds, without seeking to clash. I thought it best to stand out. I drag my heels. I deliberately drop beams onto their feet. Tonight, as planned, we launch the cutter. It sways a little, but it floats. We stay silent as we wait to see if it will sink. Later that night, anchored in the harbour, our boat raises its mast into the dark, spreading out its evanescent blue sails in the glowing flames burning on the shore. Ready to go, it trembles with excitement, stretching its belly to convince us to board. We're lying exhausted around the bonfire. We landed there as though we'd been hit by a hail of bullets. We keep quiet, marvelled to tears. My cheeks swell up to take in the fire, and let it burn me. My nostrils flare to take in the smoke that smells like bark, like branches, like the bush. I'm almost asleep. Suddenly, a Russian girl starts to sing, her voice light as air. It must be Mingrelia. Who cares?

I let myself be won over, but without much conviction. I tried to hate them, but I've run out of hate. We set sail in the thick, milky-white morning light. Some are sporting petasos, and others, morions. Each of us is armed to the teeth. No two shields are alike, but we all carry one. Those who don't have a wooden rapier have a wooden scimitar or a wooden yataghan. Mingrelia graciously allowed herself to honour those ridiculous uniformity requirements. Christian sanded his sabre so that she wouldn't get gashed if it grazed her skin. My axe's shaft is worse than a porcupine, but Christian couldn't care less. They're waiting for Mothy Mouser, Captain of our fleet. Some are fencing, others hitting the hull with their blades. They got up early;

some didn't even take the time to rub the morning gunk out of their eyes. I keep away from them, gun-shy, almost apathetic. I'm neither unhappy enough to hate, nor happy enough to love. But I'll sail along, if only to enjoy my solitude all the more among the large travelling party. At last, Mothy Mouser appears, obviously tired, but smiling broadly. She's wearing a Gallish helmet with two horns—the type that looks like a wing nut. As it happens, she comes armed: a long, engraved, copper wheel-locked pistol—the most beautiful piece of the collection Einberg is so jealous of—is hanging from her waist, carelessly tucked under a large jewellery belt. Poor Einberg has only ever taken that masterpiece off the chimney hood to polish it.

This is all just a game, but everything unfolds in accordance with the finest naval traditions. Mothy Mouser assigns us duties, pointing her pistol at the people she selects.

"You will be my Lieutenant…! You will steer the ship! I'm naming you topman… and you, linesman! You two will be sailors… I entrust you with the sails! And you three… off to the jibs!"

We hoist our crimson and golden flag displaying a headless silver skeleton. We're sailing on high seas. Here, the river is so wide that the shores draw but a thin shadow along the blue skyline in the distance. The wind sweeps us off. Our cutter speeds down the river as though it were falling down a cliff, furiously flapping its wings, as though it meant to take flight. The topman takes out his telescope. A rather strange vessel is heading toward us, slowly emerging from the far horizon. It gets bigger by the minute. It seems to be inflating as it comes closer. We try to identify it.

"Chap ahoy!"

"It's a tanker, a black tanker."

"What flag does it fly?"

"The worst: Netherlands'!"

"Rudder, right! Straighten the sails! Hold on tight!"

It's been decided: we'll board it and sink it! We charge ahead, feeling quite bold. We're sailing close-hauled, so much so that each side wave almost makes our cutter capsize. Alas! We're no match. We must call back our troops, take down our ladders, and retreat after taking four point-blank broadside hits from 97 cannons, each more than a foot in diameter. Mothy Mouser is beaming. She's tall, blond and beautiful, like Baldovinetti's "Virgin." As though she were made of gold, our cousins have turned her into a Goddess and thrown themselves at her feet to worship her. They swarm around her, buzzing like bees. They tilt their heads into the light, so that they can see her face better, and so that she can see theirs. She strokes their hair with her long, beautiful fingers. She hugs them tight, two by two, lovingly. There are enough hugs for everyone. You just need to wait your turn. No free passes! Queue up quietly! No pushing! As I sit on the boom with my back to the sails, I let daylight devour me, I let wind sheets whip me. I couldn't care less. Standing over the shrouds, Christian watches her, biting his lip, staring at her with sad, dreadful eyes. Someone is looking jealous. Someone doesn't seem to enjoy seeing his mother prostitute herself. Much ado about nothing, Christian! Mothy Mouser has no use for such cheap romance. All that matters to her is proving what she must to those who need it. All that matters to her is winning her war against Einberg. Absolutely nothing else matters—not the very least. She has no use for me, or Christian, or any of those snots. It must melt her heart to see herself be so motherly to other people's brats. She must be thinking quite highly of herself; she must love herself dearly.

17

The Ellice River flows from the Barren Grounds into the Queen Maud Gulf, south, way south, of Prince Patrick Island. Unfurl your red sands before my feet as far as the eyes can see, Kyzylkum Desert! Weep, sweet halcyons, weep!

Christian is slipping away from me. He's over the top in love. He loves the grand duchess so much so that he can't get his head out of the clouds. He's so swollen with love that he floats above earth and water, like Yahweh. They're crossing the channel in their rowboat. They've supposedly gone hunting geometer moths in the mainland bushes. I decide to swim after them across the channel, following their fright. Crawling on all fours in thick, damp, bug-ridden peat moss, I follow their fright. Sneaking on all fours under thorn cradles that dig into my dress, sink into my skin, and suck my blood, I follow their fright. Feeling offended and humiliated, I follow their fright. They stop. They're in a small clearing graced with a huge, hollow, black, century-old tree stump. With one hand in his pocket, his pants bulging with something like a box of sweets, Christian dawdles, letting Mingrelia grow restless as he laughs up his sleeve.

"Do you have them or not? You're such a baby! Come on! Gimme!"

Mingrelia comes to blows. She manages to stick her hand into Christian's pocket to fish out the hidden treasure. She opens a small case: it's full of cigarette butts. She sticks the longest one between her lips, waiting for Christian to light it up. He lights hers before lighting his own. They both start sneezing. With each drag of smoke, they cough and spit and choke and turn red. I've had enough! I throw dead twigs at them. They panic. I laugh—at the top of my lungs. Christian grabs me by the neck. Mingrelia pulls my hair and calls me an ugly bitch.

"Go away! Go!" hisses Christian.

He pushes me off and lets Mingrelia spit on me.

Christian has stopped looking at me. He doesn't know me anymore. He remembers nothing. He passes me by without noticing me, looking straight ahead, pouting like a free judge of the Vehmic courts. When I go wake him up in the morning and surprise him, like before, he gets white with rage and drives me out of his room—he could kick my ass out. At the beginning of spring, he and I, in the utmost secrecy, put together a biological lab in a crypt, a kind of clinic where we could heal rats and study some specimens of the moorland fauna. Since Mingrelia arrived, I'm banned from the crypt. Now, he spends his days locked up in there with *her* instead of me.

I come back from the mainland with my head down and my heart crushed to a pulp. I go hide in a cold, dark corner of the shed where the gardener splits and stacks his logs. I settle on the floor and comfortably lean back. I rest my head—so heavy, so weary; my head is overwhelmed with everything that keeps invading it through my eyes, ears, mouth, and nose. Then I start to cry. I quietly cry my heart out, whining softly. Whimpers drive to tears like music drives to dance. Unwind, let your heart swell, let out a faint whimper, and tears will stream down your cheeks.

"What's wrong, sweetie?"

Mothy Mouser stealthily snuck to my side. Her face appears so suddenly over mine that I gasp. She's playing sad, distressed, dropping her arms. It's only fitting to look sad next to those who weep. It's not hard to look sad: just avoid laughing. I start crying anew, now out of rage. She's fooling herself if she thinks her inflated hieratic poses will soften my heart.

"Leave me alone, you Mothy Mouser! Don't touch me, or I'll bite!"

"Why so grim...? There, there, little bat... Let Mommy comfort you."

The more she talks and touches me, the more I feel broken, lost, betrayed. She smiles—a sad, most beautiful smile. She lifts me onto her lap, cradling me, kissing me. I feel all tense and tight. If she keeps drooling on me like that, I'll kill her. I wrestle her as though I were possessed. I kick and punch her as hard as I can. I scratch her arms and face. I even bite her. I warned her. She should just keep her hands to herself. There will be blood! She finally lets go of me. I push her out of my hideaway with both arms, with all my strength. Go away, you witch! Leave the good guys to cry in peace! I can see her face: she's weeping—for real. Her calm composure is fully crippled, severely damaged.

She runs away as fast as she can, her face buried in her hands. Her exit leaves me as cold as her entrance. I hate her! Mothy Mouser! Mousy Mammoth! Mousermoth! Mousermoth! My brain, blinded by hate, digs up an old scheme, one I have long wished to execute, one I've been itching to carry out—one that will soothe me, pull a few blades out of my heart. I empty the content of an iodine vial into Mauriac's—Mousermoth's beloved cat—tin bowl, and mix it with milk.

"Here, kitty kitty cat! Here, sweet pussycat!"

The cat is rather suspicious of me, but it's just another glutton with a sweet tooth, and it's already gotten a whiff of the nectar. It meows, bowing its head. Do I promise not to hurt it? It timidly approaches the bowl. It starts rolling its tongue—in and out, and in and out. It licks it clean. It now wobbles away, careening like mad. Boom! The cat is down. It stiffens, quakes, pukes, kicks, and croaks. What an easy victory! Crappy cow crap!

18

Today is Cherry-Rush Day. All of us migrate to the mainland. The gardener, carrying the wicker baskets, is the last one to leave. In the kitchen before leaving, we swiftly assembled as many banana sandwiches as we'll be able to wolf down, fighting over the butter dish and throwing knives at each other. We won't be back before dinnertime.

"Brace yourselves, children! We're going cherry-picking! Here are twenty big wicker baskets to fill, one for each of you. We're going to make wine. The more cherries you pick, the more wine we'll have when you all come back in a few years, old enough to get drunk."

Skirting the oat field, shrouding the barbed wire fences, the cherry trees stand in a single file as far as the eye can see. Their frail branches buckle, chock-full of fruit, packed with red sapphires. No host was ever this hospitable, no king has ever burnt this much incense, sported this many shiny jewels, set such sumptuous tables, or offered such a munificent welcome. It seems like we would just need to reach out our baskets for them to fill up and spill over. When you snap off a cluster, you can feel your hand start to float, you can feel it expecting and then see it expand beyond the horizon and be covered with lakes, forests and castles. The cherry pickers who love each other too much harvest in pairs. But most of them disperse as far as they can to find a great big cherry tree for themselves alone. Where did Christian and Mingrelia go? As through the bones of a skeleton, you can see everything through the old ramshackle boards of the abandoned shed. I sit down in the shadows on the footings of the ruined barn, where I can get a malicious eyeful. They're playing in the rotten hay. What they're drinking from Mingrelia's wineskin is not water. No, this nectar they stole at great cost: it's Mousermoth's cognac. They light up a cigarette butt and take drags in turn, blowing smoke into each other's eyes. Mingrelia tries to stare back at Christian as solemnly as he's staring at her. She's having a hard time: the temptation to laugh is biting her lip. She shuts her eyes. She starts stroking his face. They stroke each other in turn. It looks like they do this often.

You shut your eyes and I stroke your face. I stop stroking yours, I shut my eyes, and you stroke mine. Mingrelia has it best. Christian strokes her face for much longer than she strokes his. She barely brushes around his eyes and over his lips with her finger before she drops her own eyelids. Mingrelia grows bored of having her face stroked. Her face shies away from Christian's hand. She rolls in the hay and laughs, and keeps repeating how drunk, how crazy, how great she feels. Suddenly, she screams her head off. She's gotten hurt. She bursts into tears. A fork was hiding in the hay, prongs pointing upwards. The long teeth pierced her bodice all the way through her skin. She sees blood staining her dress and quickly pulls it over her head. Uncomfortable, Christian turns the other way. She's wearing a bra, like a real woman. She takes it off. She tries to remove the blood with spit, to suck it out of the fabric. The stains are stubborn. She looks upset and truly disappointed. The holes in her chest are not bleeding that much. She looks at Christian. She calls him over. He answers yes without daring to turn around. She calls him over again, more gently. She wants him to look at her.

"You can look, if you want. It's not a big deal! You're my lover. And I'm not *that* naked… Come on! I'm not a Gorgon. You won't turn into a stone statue. It's not a big deal! A Russian boy would look. I don't get you Canadians at all! Look at me, Christian! Blood, rich blood, beautiful drops of blood…"

I'm fed up with their puppy love. I'm sick and tired of it. Something's been brewing inside me for too long. It's high time to let my lid pop off. Leaving my basket behind,

I take off at full speed. As I mow down daisies in great strides, I carefully choose my words. The idea of revenge overly troubles me, makes me want to laugh. They were mean to me. They had it coming! I shall not be defeated! I'm not one of those weaklings who cry in their beers!

"Come, Mother, quick! It's sweet Christian and sweet Mingrelia! They're naked in the shed, over there! Naked!"

"Oh dear! Oh God! That can't be. You must be mistaken…"

I grab Mousermoth by the hand and pull. We must hurry. If Mingrelia can get dressed as fast as she can get naked, time is of the essence. I arrive first at the shed. Mingrelia, still naked, stands in one of the sunbeams cutting across the dark, readjusting the buttercup wreath sitting on her brow below the dome of her hair. She's so pretty, even without her clothes on, that my revenge suddenly feels silly. I turn around to see what's happening to my revenge. Mousermoth is petrified. With her mouth half-open, one hand still in the air and one leg in front of the other, she looks like a wind-up doll with a broken spring. Once again, she's lost her beautiful composure, fully bent out of shape. Slowly, in the dark, her face takes on a white glow, growing radiantly pale. Her big blue eyes turn black, like when she's fighting with Einberg. I can tell she's about to explode. I get out of her way.

"Crappy cow crap!" she suddenly screams, shaking her head emphatically.

Wrath, in one blow, has swallowed her whole. She's out of control. She charges and pummels them both, one after the other, showering them with bucketfuls of insults.

87

"You dirty little slut! I trusted you like my own sister! I thought you were a lady! You fraud! You hypocrite! Christian! Christian, you've stabbed me right in the back! I thought you were virtuous and true! You make me sick! You make my skin crawl! I'd rather see you dead! Who taught you such depravity? I feel so alone, my child, so deeply alone! I could've done without your filth!"

She slaps them more and more violently, as though she meant to hurt them as much as they've hurt her. Christian is crying, begging, babbling. Mingrelia is acting like a world-class felon or fugitive who got caught. She clenches her teeth and suffers the blows. She was ready for what would happen if she got busted. She'll be more careful next time. Exhausted, blinded by her tears, Mousermoth collapses, sinking onto the harrow below her bum, then drops her face into her hands, pressing her temples. She apologizes. She humbly beseeches the guilty pair to forgive her violence. For her part, she's already forgotten all about their momentary indiscretion. She doesn't know what happened to her. She must be at the end of her rope. Being left with twenty children overnight, that takes its toll on a lady, she explains. She stands up, sniffling, and helps Mingrelia hook up her bra and button up her dress. She even helps her blow her nose. She wipes away her tears just as you would your own. She calls her "little baboon." Mingrelia refuses all forgiveness, stubbornly sulking with her arms crossed to hide the bloodstains. Mousermoth takes them both by the neck, leads them out of the shed, and invites them to come and join herself and the others to play more amusing, age-appropriate games.

"As soon as we're back on the island with all of our cherries, we can start preparing the must. The clock is ticking! We're undermanned! Fifteen days at sea!... And so much to do before we can set sail! Or have you naughty boys and girls already forgotten that we're leaving tomorrow at the crack of dawn, in a few hours, by the time it takes for the sun to set and rise?"

They don't seem to remember much. Mousermoth's voice is loud and clear, peaceful and constant as streaks of forgotten tears dry out on her cheeks. She often cries. Mousermoth's tears are Christian's greatest torment. Mousermoth's tears leave me cold. Christian says that she cries often because she carries too heavy a burden. I say she cries that often because she enjoys it, because it suits her, because she likes to see and hear herself cry, because she thinks her tears are so pretty, because she *wants* to cry. Someone who doesn't want to cry won't cry.

Tomorrow, we're supposedly leaving for a two-week cruise on the Great Lakes. I know how tirelessly fertile Mousermoth's imagination can be. I'm afraid that this epic journey will turn into a stupid picnic across the river. But since Einberg is also going on a trip, who knows what might happen.

19

Under a collapsed burial mound where a chalk-white mast stands and a black flame squirms, Isolde's bones are turning to dust and disappearing into flower-growing soil. In the ballroom of the palace, roly-poly baronesses are dancing with ruddy-rosy baronesses. Suddenly, as tall as a tree, a crystal chandelier falls from the wainscot and crashes on all those baronesses dancing with other baronesses, slipping, splitting and scattering at full speed over the jet-black tiles, showering the steel baseboards with a thousand bouncing stones, making them chime. I see a ship sail across more than a hundred acres of ocean. I'm sitting on deck with my legs hanging overboard, like on the edge of a narrow spit of land. This is a high-speed wharf, a tempered glass wharf, a massive wharf made of translucent rainbow beads. What carries me off like this on a senseless drift is a thick stained-glass cliff. Sitting between heaven and earth, between night and day, in one of the buckets of the quarry winch, I dream up impossible things. The world is an oyster and I am the pearl, and while darkness creeps upon us, I dream up things that will never be. There's a weeping willow across the channel, just before the stone bench where Mousermoth is sitting with her head down. I carefully watch the weeping willow weep and soak its soft wooden locks in the stream. I look at the willow: I throw myself at the willow. When a pearl of the world throws herself at a willow, the willow becomes a pearl of the world. The willow looks at me: it throws itself at me, it swallows me, and the pearl of the world becomes a willow. The sea is a big teacup. A storm at sea is a storm in a teacup. Not a single torch is burning as our cousins hide in the bushes, waiting for the night to turn pitch-black.

It's Mousermoth's birthday. This is why she went to sit on the stone bench with her shoes dipped in the water and her head tilted sideways. She's not yet thirty and she has nothing left to do. Just stay there and wait. She can't leave the abbey: she's married. When you're married, you must stay with your husband and with your children and wait until the rest of yourself disappears into thin air. She can't move anymore: she's an easy prey for death. With her head bent, her neck exposed in the dissipating shade, she looks like she's surrendering to a slayer's sword. There, there, little bat, yourself! As the night grows darker, the river becomes cleaner and calmer. A white pool rises and retreats around her feet, moving back and forth like a hand. Her hand moves back and forth on the grey back of Mauriac II, the cat standing in for the cat she loved. At night, all cats are grey. And the back of a grey cat is grey. Earlier I could see the willow weep. Now I can't see it anymore: the night is black as pitch. Things change. Everything changes.

Lights are blossoming deep in the bushes, as in whiffs. Suddenly, our cousins charge toward Mousermoth as though they were shooting out of the ground with their freshly kindled torches, screaming their heads off. They now surround her, singing *Happy Birthday* in Polish. They hold each other by the hands or the sleeves to start a round dance. They swirl. Their torches draw a red circle, a swirling red circle. They split up and pretend to be horses. Slapping their flanks, they stop running and start galloping; they stop singing and start laughing and throwing firecrackers at each other. Then the round dance turns into a fantasia, a mad whirlwind of rockets.

Our cousins conspired all week. They made Anna Fiodorovna, their baby, learn Théodore de Banville's poem "*La Mère.*" They stop moving and grow still. Anna Fiodorovna's booming voice breaks their silence twice like two last sparklers, "*Niet! Niet!*"

Tiny Anna Fiodorovna seems buried under the huge wild rose bush she's been loaded with. She takes two steps sideways, steadies herself and steps back. Pushed by some and pinched by others, wanting to get this over with as fast as she can, she doggedly wobbles ahead. Unable to see where she's heading, she almost runs into the stone bench. The screams stop her dead in her tracks. She lets out a loud sigh and proceeds to blurt out in one go, half-sobbing, in cockeyed French, "Déothore de Panville's boem '*Ma Lère.*'" Mousermoth reaches over to receive the lavish bouquet. Somewhat desperate, Anna Fiodorovna drops the wild roses on the sand and throws herself into her open arms. Mousermoth laughs and kisses her. Everybody laughs and claps. The beating Mingrelia got in the abandoned shed righted nothing but her head. Now, she shamelessly scorns; she rebels overtly. She runs the show while, with his cheeks flushed, Christian dances to her tune as best he can lest he should lose her. She shows up for dinner smoking a cigarette, holding a wineskin filled with cognac. If Mousermoth stares at her for too long, she forces Christian to take a drag of her cigarette and a slug of her cognac. She tells anyone who'll listen that Christian is like her slave; that she can make him steal all the smokes and booze she wants. She says that she likes him, but nothing more, that her true love is Serge, that Christian is just one of her cruise or layover flings.

"The more he loves me," she says, "the more he'll smarten up. He's a real baby. He still runs crying to mommy every chance he gets. When he kisses me, he thinks of her and speaks of her. Don't laugh: I'm telling the truth. He says she'd be sad if she saw us kissing."

Mingrelia has sworn to destroy Mousermoth, to annihilate her, to wipe her from Christian's heart and from our cousins' hearts. She's got her hands full. Everything Mingrelia has made him do during the day, Christian undoes at night. He goes straight to Mousermoth and cries by her bed, kneeling, confessing, and making amends. Christian is riddled with needs. He's weak and wimpy. A born parasite. Like thistle, he clings to everything that touches him. Like a plant, he focuses his every effort on taking root; his arms can't defend him or attack. Like a plant, you can pull him out of one spot and plant him elsewhere. He tries to take root, by himself or by force, wherever he lands. He can't go or take root where he would thrive. Christian will just blossom and wither in the garden of whomever prevails. I'm not jealous... I'm waiting for my strength to be full-grown, until I'm strong enough to pull him away from all other gardeners.

20

Since Einberg went away on his trip, the order he usually enforces at the dinner table has turned topsy-turvy, disorganized. The Good and the Bad (Guelphs and Ghibellines) now eat shoulder to shoulder, love and hate presiding over the selection of immediate neighbours.

Because now, emboldened by Mingrelia's example, everyone loves and hates as much as they please. Anna Fiodorovna reserves the seat on her right for tall and handsome Nicolas. And I already cry mercy for any girl who dares to steal him away from her or for any boy who dares to sit in his place. Anna Fiodorovna may not have large claws or long teeth, but cutlery knows no age; forks and knives are as big in her tiny hands as in those of the colossus of Croton. And who's deserted the wandering bishop's monumental seat to come and sit beside me wherever I've chosen to sit? Mousermoth. She looks me right in the eyes and asks me why I've been hating her so much lately. I know what she's after. She wants me to love her like before. She's barking up the wrong tree. She'd better sit back on the monumental seat of the wandering bishop, the slandering bishop, the sanderling bishop, the bird bishop. It's over, my dear, between good intentions and me. Over and done! Enough waiting at faces' gates! Christian's attitude over dinner couldn't be more ambiguous, more challenging. Half his face must laugh along with Mingrelia as she mimics Mousermoth's distressed priestly poses, while the other half must laugh along with Mousermoth who winks at him mercifully. Both halves of his laugh are bound to be hollow. I've never seen my pretty older brother look so ugly. Some own palm or apple trees, others own dogs or monkeys trained to eat with a fork and a knife. I'll have more than that; I'll have a human of my own: my brother Christian. It's not hard to speak with a human, to kiss a human, to marry a human, or to bring a human into the world. What's hard and most interesting is to own a human. It would be best to own a human as beautiful, as wild, as evil as Mingrelia. But it would be a waste of time to try and get hold of such a specimen: it would never let itself be caught. So I shall make do with humans like Christian and Constance Chlorus. They're relatively low quality specimens, but they're still better than monkeys, dogs, palm and apple trees, diamonds, or works of art. Humans make the best lapdogs. No other creature can handle a fork and a knife more brilliantly.

Mingrelia stands up on the bench. Christian struggles to make her sit back down. His efforts are for nothing: she will not take her seat—she will speak out. She calls for order and, turning to Mousermoth, she takes the floor.

"Auntie, I have great news to share with you and a small favour to ask. Christian is a javelin thrower. For real. He didn't tell you because he thought you'd be upset. I believe, instead, that you'll be very pleased to learn that he's so good at throwing the javelin that he got noticed and selected to play for his school in a great big athletics tournament. Auntie, the event happens to be tonight. Please allow Christian to compete and please take us all to the tournament."

"No, Mother!" Christian cries out while everybody is cheering him. "I don't want to go! I don't want to! I'm not ready. I haven't touched a single javelin all summer."

The secret I've been keeping like a cabbalistic sign is now going around the table, becoming everybody's business.

In the jeep, we're packed tighter than sardines in a can, than eggs in a basket. Tonight, now that the air and the insects are quiet, we're just a pile of humans on hot wheels hedgehopping between two bushy waves. Only the jeep's tires touch the ground; the jeep's body and ours are flying between heaven and earth. Through narrow twists and turns closely lined with houses, we drive into the heart of the city. I feel cold, crushed. Inflamed by Mingrelia, they're screaming and laughing. Christian is bleakly holding his javelin, like he's being led to the slaughterhouse. He's not ready! He'll be a laughing stock. We walk into the stadium. It's a large field surrounded with tall iron masts fitted with a hive of spotlights shining into the night. The bleachers are full, brimming. Christian is panicking. The other javelin throwers look feisty, vicious. They're hopping around. Hopping like that makes them look like dancing, dangerous kangaroos. Away from the others, standing completely still, his arms gone limp, Christian looks like an automaton whose snack got stuck in the automat. He drops his javelin. He picks up his javelin. Our cousins are chanting his name and tapping their feet. He can't even hear them. He is lost. He has already lost. At the timekeeper's signal, he lines up with the others along the white mark. He's wearing number 14. Holding the starter gun up in the air, the official shoots. Aiming for the sky, five hundred javelins soar up like thunder from the ground. Christian's javelin breaks away from the bulk, falling far behind. Our cousins tense up and strain forward as though they were pushing the javelin. It's a lost cause. While others fly ever higher, ever faster, Christian's javelin lands on the grass, quietly. We drive home, silently.

"Why didn't you tell me you were a javelin thrower?" asks Mousermoth.

"I neglected to do it!" Christian yells back in shame, crying hard over his defeat, breaking his javelin over his knees.

"I've never considered the business of sport undignified. Quite the opposite! I myself was a fierce fan of many sports before the war. I even took part in Dublin's show-jumping races."

"You were an Amazon!" declares a fierce fan of Mousermoth. "Please do tell!"

"Is it true that Amazons burn off their right breast?" asks a perfect fool.

"It is," says Mingrelia, laughing her heart out. "Do you know why? So they can throw the javelin with greater force!"

Mingrelia is quite proud of that one! Well done! She led us from one misstep to another as though she were making us dance the polka. Christian was beaten to a pulp and Mousermoth, humiliated, outplayed at her own mom game. Everyone is disappointed to have thoroughly believed in the victory of a javelin thrower who turned out to be the worst javelin thrower in the world. Mingrelia led us on a merry-go-round and round until things turned ugly. Bravo! How nice of you! That will teach me! Christian is sad like a cormorant whose beak broke pecking at the Koran. I like to see him sad. The sadder his life becomes, the more he'll need someone to pity him. And come time for pity, there'll be no one left but me.

21

Our cousins left—all of them in one go, one gunshot. That gets a phew out of her ladyship. I walk up and down the halls of the west wing. I find pleasure in it. They've regained their resonance—they can hush or echo. It's as though, during the night, all humans and animals had deserted the world. It's as though, during the night, all humans and beasts had boarded Noah's ark. I'm walking on the shore. I find pleasure in it. The shore is just as it was before: cousin-free. The wind blows hard, so hard that it yanks sparks out of the clouds: raindrops. The river spawns its autumn swell, taut and grey, tired from having borne so many ships.

Our cousins left in the strangest way, almost without realizing it. Mousermoth kept the day and time of their departure a secret until the very last minute. You could feel that something was about to happen. It was three in the morning and everybody was still up. We were playing Greek theatre in the chapel. Holding our playbooks, we mouthed off the centuries-old lines of a comedy whose author I forget—something like Aristophanes or Terence. What started as a table-read after dinner quickly degenerated. The attics were raided, and old trunks and old dressers plundered. Masks, buskins, spears, trabeae, peplos, purples—all that was needed was found, and we got up on stage. The later it got, the looser our screws. Tired to the point of feeling numb, drunk with sleep, we laughed at anything and found ourselves brilliant, sustaining long-winded to-what-length-Catiline arguments without taking a single look in our booklets.

"Children," said Mousermoth suddenly, taking her mask off. "I think a little fresh air will do us all good. Leave your masks, buskins, and spears behind. Let's go on a little jeep ride."

The crisp night air knocked everybody out. When Mousermoth woke us up, we were in Dorval, on a runway, below the belly of an airbus. Departure struck our cousins hard. Mousermoth handed each of them their tickets. Those who could realize what was happening couldn't believe it: their eyes widened, their jaws dropped. Most of them could barely keep their eyes open. They were shaking and stumbling, still in their retiarii, hetairai and Heautontimorumenos costumes, as they walked up the stairs leading onto the plane, holding on to one another so as not to tumble down.

Einberg comes back at noon. He slams the door, chewing on the trabucos matching his soul's stormiest spirits, and he shouts, spits and curses. When he sees the chapel's floor littered with masks, buskins, and spears, he goes after Mousermoth and charges her. This house is a dump! A true pigsty! But she too happens to be in a nasty mood.

"What is it, Mauritius Einberg? Your mistress didn't enjoy the kind of Egypt you fashioned for her? Did she recklessly fly off your gold and diamond handles?"

Pointing at my intrusive presence, Einberg feverishly motions for her to pipe down.

"Don't you fret, Mauritius Einberg. You've raised your daughter well. She hears nothing her mother says, nothing at all. Why, she barely even sees her."

Hell is about to break loose! Fuses will blow. I love it when hate flares. They disappear into the apsis, also known as the den. The door slams shut, almost bringing the wall down. I'm quite familiar with this door. Of all the abbey's doors, this one is bestowed with the largest and most welcoming keyhole.

"Well, I do! There! I have a mistress. But you're not jealous, are you? Good friends should never make each other jealous! Good friends! That's what we are, right? What we'll always be… right?"

"Go on! Please do… I sense you still have a whole lot to tell…"

Mousermoth sits down on her couch, spreading her legs out on her wing chair. When you expect to get stuffed, you might as well get cozy. Einberg pulls the zipper of his briefcase as though he meant to rip it off. He takes out a large framed photograph and throws it on Mousermoth's lap.

"You're jealous on empty, my good friend. She has nothing on you to justify such jealousy. As you can see, she's not even pretty, her fashion sense is off, and she doesn't even look clever. She can't carry her head, but what does it matter to a man who has no use for a head? She has a vagina between her legs, carries it high and well, and a vagina, my friend, a woman's vagina such as the one you must be pained and shamed to have, is all a man needs when he takes a mistress. She copulates, and it doesn't make her stomach turn. She looks at herself naked, and it doesn't make her sick. I heard she washes her vagina as often as she cleans her ears. Apparently, it's completely natural for her to sit on her butt when she's sitting. What's worse: she told me that she treats her vagina the same way she treats her stomach. When one or the other is hungry, she feeds it. When you meet a friend, you hold out your hand. Well she also holds out her vagina. She's a curious specimen of a race scarcely anyone wants to belong to anymore: the human race. What's more, she finds me delightful. She thinks I wear tasteful ties. She loves me."

"Your mistress can find you as fetching as she pleases. That doesn't impress me much. I personally find you more disgusting as time goes by. Every single day, you manage to find a way to add to my disgust. How can you forget that you're not alone, that Berenice and Christian are here, that they didn't do anything to you, that they're so young, so beautiful? You're not alone in your filth: Berenice and Christian are right there with you. They're in over their heads with you in that filth. It's about time you get a grip. Think of it: they're asleep, they've seen nothing yet! Think of it: they'll open their eyes and realize they're lying in filth, in *your* filth! Dear God! What a way to wake up! Spare them! You old freak!"

"You weren't so dismissive when I found you in Warsaw, in the gutters. Your brothers, gentle colonels, were collaborators. Your brothers, gentle Poles, had just raped you... I gave you chocolate. You were so hungry that you ate it out of my hand."

"Yes, my brothers were collaborators! I should have followed their lead! Between the four of us, we'd have killed more Jews! There wouldn't be as many now. You may not have been among those who lived."

"I offered you a cigarette. You were so starved that you ate it."

"I was mad, Mauritius Einberg! Despair drove me to madness. I was thirteen. I was hiding in the gutters to survive. I had to leave my beloved brothers. And those monsters recognized me and they assaulted me. They thought I'd come to spy on them. When you found me, I'd gone mad. You saw it. And you used it to your advantage! When you married me the next month, I was still mad; and you knew it! You took advantage of a young, thirteen-year-old girl, who'd also gone mad! If I were you, I wouldn't stir those repulsive ashes."

There they go again, conjuring up their past.

I'm having a nightmare. Everything here is white, glaring white. The pillars are white. There's a chair, a white chair, glaring white. And everything is mine, everything belongs to me. There are girls standing before white windows, half-naked girls, like Mingrelia in the abandoned shed. My heart explodes: they too are mine! I clap my hands. The girls turn their heads. They all have the same face: Mingrelia's face. They're all so pretty! All my humans are so pretty! Everything here belongs to me. Everything here is mine. It's so wonderful in here! So white! You would think that we're inside the sun, inside snow.

22

Einberg is sending me off to California. There, I shall catch up with the choir. There, I shall meet Constance Chlorus. Travel broadens young minds but never minds old minds. Since he's come home from his trip, Einberg has gone back to his old tricks: he's never been more true to form. I don't want to go to California. I plan to spend the last days of summer actively taking care of Christian. Mingrelia's sudden departure left him aghast: all I have to do is finish him off and take him. Dead humans belong to their killer. I don't want to leave at all. I take Einberg aside to talk.

"I know you're just sending me off to California to protect me from your wife's evil influence. There's no need. She has no influence over me anymore. I hate her: she'll tell you herself. Everything she says goes in one of my ears and out the other. No joke. I swear. She can try all she wants. She'll never fool me."

Einberg wouldn't hear of it; he didn't even try to believe me.

I'm here with Constance Chlorus. On the bus, we sit on the same seat. In hotels, we sleep in the same room. She helps me forget that my exile made me miss my chance with Christian. He was wounded, wallowing in his own blood. I would have just needed to give him the kiss of death. Anything wounded can be easily fooled. Once, in a ditch, I found a crow, a great big crow with wings as long as my arms. It was in agony. I took it into my arms. It didn't resist. What a wonderful feeling to hold such a large bird! I wrote, so as not to lose it all, "Dearest Christian, I miss our friendship a great deal. Our friendship makes me miss the grasshoppers and the rats of the island. I forgive you this summer's misconducts. I have wiped them from my memory. I know that deep down, you suffered much more than I have, and that you wish you could forget about it as quickly as I have. I hope that when you have restored order within your heart, I can reclaim my place. If you still recall, I am small; I do not take much space. It was Einberg who drove us apart, who sent me here, far from you, and kept you there, far from me. You tell him how I hate him, how I despise him. You tell him that he is wasting his time, his bombs, his woes. His hatred and his blows will not prevail over the bonds between us. I kiss your beautiful Zulu sun; I take religious care of it. I also send you kisses, with all my heart, so that you will soon feel better. Berenice, your sister, who loves you now and forever."

I have a new inclination for reading. I delve into all the books I can get my hands on and pull myself out as soon as the curtain falls. A book is a world, a whole world, a world with its own beginning and end. Each page of a book is a town. Each line is a street. Each world is a home. My eyes scan the street, opening each door, entering each home. In the house called "camel," there's a camel. In the coop called "goose," a goose awaits me. Behind the many windows of the mansions called "indissolubility" and "incorruptibility," I catch a glimpse of Robespierre's incorruptibility and indissoluble marriage. I'm crazy about travel literature. I spent the night with *The Travels of Marco Polo*. I had the most wonderful adventures in there, but I can't remember which. I don't seek to recall what occurs in a book. This morning, when I stepped out of my book, I felt deliciously drunk and free, moved by a great impatience, by a magnificent desire. All I ask is that a book should fill me with energy and courage, tell me there are more lives around than I could possibly take, and remind me of the urgent need to act. If almost all of last night's words brushed past my eyes like waves past the flanks of a ship, the few words I recall carved an indelible mark on my mind. For instance, I vividly remember when the Emperor of China gave Marco Polo *his order for their having free and safe conduct through every part of his dominions.*

A war just broke out between Israel and the Arabs. Rabbi Schneider sobs when he talks about it. Yahweh is sounding bugles, beating drums in all our hearts! His land and His people are under threat. Yahweh is enraged; He's waking the world. Around the globe, he's calling out, "Judith! David!"

"You and I, my children, are Judith and David. I shall go. You shall go. Many of you are already there."

Many uncles, cousins, brothers and fathers of the choir members are indeed already on their way to Israel. I can't say that I don't care. When I listen carefully, I too, it seems, hear a voice calling me, "Judith! David!"

23

Christian's handwriting runs wild, at breakneck speed. Here it straightens up and stands tall. There it slants and cants, almost falling on its back. Stems swing like pendulums, from the far right to the far left. Many syllables, several words, complete sentences have been crossed out, cruelly obliterated. The margin is plaited with small thoroughly blacked-out polygons. Christian's letter looks like a storm. You can tell that he slaved away at it, that he had to wring his brain out to the last drop to fill out that page. He's never written to me before. I sent him countless letters over the past three years. He never answered a single one. When I returned from exile and scolded him for it, he answered that he'd received nothing, that Einberg surely intercepted the mail. I stretch out the letter by the corners first, then by the sides. I hold the letter on my palm, like a plate. I drop the letter on the floor. Then I pick it up. I pin the letter to the wall with pretend coffin nails. What a victory! I shall look for a very long time at that first letter from Christian, my fearsome friend, before I have used up all its joy, before I have sucked it bland. I shall pat it for a very long time before I have exhausted its fabric, before I have exposed its every face. It's divided into four paragraphs and, like in a symphony, each one has its own tempo indication. Finally, he forgot to sign, which is hardly surprising.

"*Andante.* I received your letter at two o'clock. It is now two thirty. I hasten to reassure you. I know how I failed you this summer, how much I hurt you by behaving the way I did. But you forgave me, and for you as for me, that bumpy ride is over. All that madness is a thing of the past. Now that things are back in order, I see that Mother Brückner, Father Einberg and you still occupy every single inch of my life, taking even more space than there really is. *Allegro non troppo.* Mauriac II, after twenty vain assaults, finally climbed on top of the pedestal shaped like a conductor's stand. There, kicking his paws, swinging his head and charging at it shoulder first, he managed to knock down the gouramis' aquarium—which, as you know, is shaped like Puget's famous bust of Louis XIV. As he hit the bowl, Mauriac II swallowed the gourami couple in one gulp. Basking in the glory of his acrobatic chase, licking his chops, he brushed Mother's leg so she would pet him. The heated, threatening tirade Mother, sobbing hysterically, unleashed on the assassin while he continued to rub against her with his tail up, turned out to be such a hilarious prosopopeia, such an untimely jest, that our guests couldn't help but laugh. *Furioso*. Your attitude toward Mother is beyond comprehension. It worries and pains me as much as Mother herself. When I told her I had received a letter from you, she asked me if you mentioned her. Your attitude toward Father is no better. If he keeps you isolated, it is because he fears for you. If he fears for you, it is because he loves you. If he loves you, his intentions are pure and you have no right to judge. He is grooming you to take possession of a marvellous heritage. Father only sends you on narrow roads so he can lead you more safely to a castle whose foundations are the very roots of Earth. Soon, shortly, if you obediently let him guide you, you will discover its gold and silver halls. Believe me when I tell you how much I envy you for holding the beacon that Noah and Lamech received from Methuselah and Enoch, who received it from Mahalalel and Jared, who received it from Caïnan and Enos, who had been entrusted with it by Seth and Adam. *Maestoso*. Our mother and father love each other more than you think. Their ephemeral quarrels only aim at affirming the might and majesty of their friendship. I am your friend just as before, forever and always."

24

Christian is off to boarding school. Last year, he only came back to the abbey once a month. This year, he'll come home every week. I'll have him every Saturday and every Sunday. A child needs to have some semblance of family life, said Mousermoth to Einberg, who would have preferred the young satyr to spend the whole year locked away. As for me, I must walk all the way to the village to get an education. Last year, I would spend mornings at Dame Ruby's and afternoons at Rabbi Schneider's. Rebecca Ruby, a waspish, skinny old hag who pledged all her strength to Knowledge so it would avenge her on Beauty, meanly taught me to read and write, forcing me to learn Nelligan's poems by heart when she thought I wasn't listening to her hard enough. Thelonius Schneider, as fat as a pig, constantly laughing, softly taught me math, biology and calisthenics. This year, things are changing, and not for the better, as you might be tempted to think. They're changing for the worst, jumping out of the frying pan into the fires of hell. Determined to take an active part in the festival of great intellectual thrills that Einberg and he call their holy war, Rabbi Schneider announces his official resignation as schoolmaster. Ruby is called in to fill the vacancy, and she accepts… the cruel cow. What she made me suffer all morning, I'll now have to suffer all day. The war I had to fight all morning I'll now have to fight all day. Along with October comes the time to sharpen your pencils and put on your boxing gloves. This year, Dame Ruby will get in my hair twice as much as last year, so I have to make my boxing gloves twice as big as last year. Some summon up their patience. Others, like me, put on their boxing gloves. Patience is no good, not even the kind you can summon up. Patience is just the skin of stagnation. Insurance companies say that speeding kills. Speeding kills you at some point. Stagnation kills you straight away. I pray for Dame Ruby to escape fatal damage. She and her dewlap-covered throat, where the handful of pills she gulps down all melt! She and her rotten apple face, and her head shaped like a head that passed through the hands of a bunch of headshrinkers! In her big green parlour, there will be Anna, Paula, Louisa, Albert, Bill, Sam. Gloria and Jack won't be there. Good riddance! Respectfully seated on her beautiful *Japan sofas* (Nelligan), there will be a few I still didn't have the horror to meet, a few who, just like the ones I already have the horror to know, will have a gift for exasperating me, instinctively knowing how to drive me to hate until blood is shed. Also present, since nature has it that balance must rule, will be Constance Chlorus, the palest, most colourless of all the prettiest human beings, the sweetest, most exquisite, divine, authentic gazelle. I almost forgot Eliezer, dull Eliezer, flaming Rebecca's lame husband; the man she sends to wipe the blackboard and to sharpen our pencils, the one she relies on to turn the score pages on time when she sits down at the piano, the blond, chestnut, reddish, black piano. In the Bible, Eliezer is Rebecca's valet. At Dame Ruby's, things happen like in the Bible. You just need to shut your eyes to feel like you're sailing to Mount Ararat on Noah's speedboat. The rain is falling hard, to the point of drowning Dame Ruby's voice. Smack in the face.

You're not listening, Berenice Einberg! Well, well, well! I'll have you memorize the "Song of Wine"! That will teach you! I've never seen one word flow out of Eliezer's mouth. He quietly wipes the blackboard. He quietly sharpens our pencils. When Dame Ruby calls, he appears, quietly dragging his sorry slippers across the floor in small swift strokes. He quietly lets his back hunch a little more each day. He quietly lets arthritis, lumbago, and so on consume his life under his very nose. All he dares to do is tighten his face as hard as he can in order to look mean. But he scares no one. Everybody knows Dame Ruby will put him in his place should he be so foolish as to play Frankenstein. I don't pity Eliezer; I despise him. When I look at him, I see all that I hate in Dame Ruby. All I see is her strength, a strength I would admire if old age didn't make her so ugly, so pathetic, so useless. I'm scared of old people. They're witches and warlocks. They know the past and the future. They see into death. They lay curses on me. They show me images, real enough to take my breath away from what I'm becoming. They spoil all my nasty surprises. I often get this nightmare where I'm pinned to the wall at the far end of a long corridor, alone with a blind old woman. She's walking toward me, laughing. She's about to die. The closer she comes, the faster my heart beats. I can see the skin wither on her hands and her face. She's a few steps away. She's rotten: she reeks. Under her blouse, I can see the swarming sickening viscera, a sludge reminding me of the rat's insides that Mauriac II was eating one day. The old woman corners me, squishes me. My heart is failing me. I can't breathe. I wake up in a cold sweat.

25

I'm talking with Christian, at night. I'm kneeling on the season's first cold floor with my hands folded on his bed.

"I've had enough. Let's run away."

"Where to?" he asks, yawning.

"Wherever."

"Whatever!"

"I've had enough. Nothing ever happens around here. Let's leave. Let's unleash the greatest dramas. Let's leave! I can't even feel my heart beating anymore."

"What's the matter?"

"Nothing. Nothing. Can't you see: nothing! My matter is squishing my shape right and left. I thought I'd fallen into a world. I've fallen into a sarcophagus spreading its wings to look like a flat surface, a large area where you can run and make yourself at ease. Its ten pairs of leaden wings spread out above me without casting a single shadow, close in on me like arms, squeezing me like a single fist… I'm suffocating. I'm choking. Let's leave! I'm decomposing. I'm liquefying. Life is deserting me, flowing through me as through a sieve. I'm hardening. I'm fossilizing. I'm petrified. Let's run away! Let's hurry! Before it's too late, let's claw our way out of the amplectant prefoliation woven by inaction, whose fibre is contracting, shrinking, slashing through our flesh. Let's burst through the stratosphere, now smaller than a dome. Let's shatter it to pieces and flee as fast as the wind. Enough wait-and-see! Let's see some eagerness, some craving. Let's leave! The faster we run, the more desire, need, and impatience we'll gain."

"Who cares? We're happy here, like this. Aren't you happy here like this?"

Far into the night, I still can't sleep. I press my pillow against my ears so as not to hear the blows, the beats, the drums. I'm alone, still, and I'm afraid to die. Drums, frosty drums, permeate the dark, triggered by the minister of Death, invincible master of the mountains of graves, a scrawny black cuirassier riding, erect, a herd of yellow mares, one foot on the back of each. At first a repetitive hum, a recurrent ruffling of my eardrum, pulsing dots almost invisible on the horizon of silence, the muffled sound of its unbridled race slowly grows louder, opening up, invading all, swelling disproportionately in strength and quantity. The hooves concentrate their roulades into sharp, quick, powerful blows. They echo inside my ears as though they were pounding on the walls of my room, as though a wild, winded heart had taken hold of the whole abbey, as though the sky were hitting the ground with cymbals. Chilled to the bone, contorted with fear, I'm waiting for the skeletal horseman to seize me, drag me out of my bed and take me away, back into nothingness, releasing me. He comes in at once and falls, crashes down upon me, destroying me. I scream. I hear myself screaming, as from the bottom of an abyss. My screams make me come to myself.

I'm screaming so loudly that I'm scared I may have gone mad. I get up and walk. I shake it off. Something must be done. I put on my best Sunday gown, my beautiful Damask laced-up gown, my white, sculpture-like gown, the one that falls all the way to the floor and buries my hands: my coronation dress. I'm talking out loud so that I won't be scared of what I'm doing. I spew nonsense. My gown! My brown! My clown! My crown! My down! My frown! My town! I put on warm socks. I wrap a shawl around my head. Then, shoes in hand, I run over to Christian's room to wake him up. I won't stop talking to him. He won't hear any of it. He doesn't get what I'm saying. I persist and proceed to explain further.

"Why should we whine on a stage? We can pile up mountains onto mountains, climbing them up to play hands deep in the stars. We can grasp, take it all. Everything belongs to us: we just need to believe it. Why should we stand by, day after night? We just need to go to the scene and claim possession. Why wait? We just need to leave. All the kings of this world—usurpers, the lot of them—have dethroned us! We just need a sword. We just need to wipe out the pirates from all rivers and seas. When will we oust all priests, choirboys and choirgirls from our temples and basilicas? All these pretty women are yours, Christian. Until when will you put up with them being passed around as though you didn't exist? Let's leave. We'll fly and kill like a couple of livias. Torch that vermin whose burrows we call houses. Disembowel gold mines, precious stone mines, ring and clock mines, pumpkin and lemon mines, daisy and violet mines, snow mines, nail and plank mines, cod and eel mines, elephant and panther mines. Rule once again. Leave. Reclaim it all. Recall our cannons. Rouse our citadels. Resurrect our fleets and armies."

Gasping for air, Christian switches off the lamp and turns his back on me. I take one of his hands in mine—a cold, limp, toothless hand. I'm so moved by the hopelessness of my own words that I start crying.

"That hand! That hand! When will you give it back its sceptre?"

I stroke Christian's head, that beautiful coward's head.

"All the crown's pieces that those puppets, those so-called kings, are wearing, we shall smelt them on this brow."

Christian says nothing. He has no voice. Even if he wanted to, he couldn't answer. After a long silence, I get back to business.

"We're the strongest, no doubt. But we need to go and prove it to them. It absolutely must be done. How else would you have them believe us? Leaving. We must leave and defend our domains, the ones we inherited from our fathers who inherited them from their fathers."

That last sentence I didn't finish out loud. I whispered half of it. I realized that Christian was fast asleep, like a log. I climb on the bed. I shake the sleeper in vain. I crawl under the duvet. I press my body against the sleeper's back. I'm alone in life and I cry. I don't want to sleep and become one more of those sleepers. But I eventually fall asleep in my white Damask gown, cradling my shiny leather shoes.

26

To throw myself upon a sword. To run into an ambush.
To hit the deck. Hit the rail. Hit the road. To leave. To have
never set foot on this earth. Days go by, predictable, most
impudently naked, all their secrets now exposed, all inside
in and outside out, right side well up and well known,
effortlessly digestible. Routine reduced everything to two
motions and two movements executed at an ever-increasing
pace. Repetition pounds the beat, routine orchestrates, and
boredom conducts the piece. I can now go through it with
my eyes shut, my ears plugged with emery paper, and my
hands and feet bound. I can let myself drift along, leisurely,
without even making the effort to realize that something
is propelling me forward. Your life doesn't need you to
be lived. Days need no one to be counted or to count one
day, over time, in the eyes of everyone. There's no need for
you to fret, Berenice. At the end of the day, come rain or
shine, after being painlessly handled by automated seesaws
and mechanised carousels until you've gone round the
mulberry bush, until you've walked, eaten and slept, and
learned something about grammar, history and geography,
you'll end up older, better educated, and knee-deep in
filth. The great machine of time, after some fidgeting and
teetering, felt its gearings and joints finally getting filed and
oiled, collaborating. Bit by bit, its cams, cogs, and shafts
combined—to the micron—and the machine started to
produce massively and deliver surely, efficiently, rapidly,
drawing from one hope, thanks to the exact key patterns
and precise meanders of its time functions, the phenomena
to be continued in the next episode that it must generate

and force the soul to watch every time a new day comes. The tree I used to love now bores me. It keeps repeating its once scary stories stupidly, relentlessly, without changing a single word, faster and faster. I've seen the very same yellow streak be drawn so many times, in the very same place and at the very same time that it's ceased to offend my gaze, that it merely bores me, almost puts me to sleep. I felt the very same artery throb within me so many times that it ossified and I stopped feeling the pain. If they had amputated both my legs two years ago, I would have gotten used to having no legs by now; I would have my share of small joys and small sorrows, as though nothing happened and I still had my legs. Legs are good for nothing. Life has no need for human legs to be lived, to ride its half-blue, half-black train half the day and half the night. That's pure cow crap. Cow crap was meant for cows. But since there's nothing else, humankind must settle for it, thus risking to end up on all fours before long. I call for chaos. But no one comes. I call and call. Nothing comes. The few chickens that heard me take my words for threats and disperse in fear. I call for humans to wage war against what they created. Chaos! War! Confusion! Fight! Total mayhem! Takeover! I call and call. Nothing. Must I be the one who shoots the first bullet, who sets off the powder keg, and who'll be hanged to death for doing it? Must it fall upon me, who's calling precisely because I feel like I'm not living enough…?

Tally-ho! Tally-ho! The huntsmen lead the charge in unison. Sitting in their steel horses, they're coming for me.

"We're going to get you!" they scream. "We're going to get you!"

They're coming after me as if I were a killer, and I didn't kill. But they're no fools. They don't want to take me down for nothing. They know that I hate them, that I hate what they've done, that I hate what they did with the life they gave me before they gave it to me. I'm to murder what flame is to fire. And they know it. A fire mustn't be left alone to burn. I must flee like a thief, yet all I took was my own life. But I'm not fleeing for nothing. I know you can't take your own life, that when you do, you take life itself, that people who take their own lives and flee also flee with everyone else's lives. Hate hasn't yet crystallized into crime. I've done nothing yet. Yet I feel like they're persecuting me, and not for nothing.

My name is Neurasthenic. The doctor says that of all children my age he knows, I'm the only one called Neurasthenic. Neurasthenic thirty-year-olds aren't uncommon. But there are no eleven-year-old Neurasthenics. Neurasthenic is a name that suits adults best. I'm not sick. I'm dead. I've become a mere reflection of my soul. I'm floating, as light as a memory. I'm drifting in the ether of outer space, supremely and indefinitely indifferent. I've stopped eating. My body rebels against everything the living call nourishment, food, meal. I vomit—on the spot—whatever they force me to eat. Do I not wish to live, or have I stopped to think? I'm losing weight by the minute. My skin sticks to the bars of my cage. Like any good corpse, to whet the worms' appetites, I let the shape of my bones show. They're keeping me on bed rest. Mousermoth claims that I'm suffering from love. When I'm sleeping, she sneaks into my room to watch over me. When I wake up, I chase her away.

117

Einberg diagnosed me with a kick-in-the-ass deficiency. He starts a violent discussion with the doctor, who himself diagnosed me with a thyroid deficiency. Christian promises me that we'll leave as soon as I'm well again, that we'll go anywhere. Anywhere is where you can find anything, namely everything. Constance Chlorus brought me an armful of gladiolas.

27

I look into the night through my red eyelashes, my long and straight doll-like lashes. I see someone in the dark; I see them—her and her cat. She's in my room. Protecting me. I'm sick, weak. I can't keep watch. She keeps watch for me. She stays with me to help me ward off Death in case she dares to show up and strike. Alone in this room, in my state, she would have it easy. She would just need to come and take me. She's in my room. She's in my life. But there's no ground to be sentimental. At times she's in my life, at times she's in Christian's, and at times she's in Einberg's. I'm just another face, and the room of her lonely almightiness, like that of countless others, is full of faces. She's much too busy. She has much too much to do. I don't want to be one face among a thousand. In those thousand-face rooms, I prefer to be no face at all. It's much too dangerous. You could be forgotten, lost, victim to all kinds of errors. In the single soul that holds a thousand faces, the one called Berenice could be confused with the one called Antoinette. I only feel perfectly safe inside a soul that holds only me, like my own for instance. If Mousermoth had wished it so, we would be friends by now. We would be together day-and-night, hours on end. We would be on an unending journey. She would be the sole denizen of my life and I the sole denizen of hers. She would be proud to have me, being so fond of the ugly. I would be proud to have her, being so fond of the pretty. To be a soul's only face, you have to oust all other faces. Yet in the soul of an adult like Mousermoth, so many faces have piled up—faces of the dead and faces of the living, faces of things and of animals and of humans—that you can't even hear yourself speak. Go away, Mousermoth. With a soul such as yours, you're good for nothing, absolutely useless, harmful even: you're just wasting my time.

Mousermoth takes a sip of cognac. Mousermoth strokes her cat the wrong way and it's giving off sparks. Something in her fascinates me, attracts me—something like a void. I'm in so much pain that the dark is burning my eyes. I need her, need to be sheltered, need her to hold and stroke me like she's holding and stroking Mauriac II. It's as though she were the only house in a sea of snow. She *is* my mother after all! Should I let myself go, I would feel all soft, all gooey inside. Should I let myself go, I would fall into her arms and love her, and feel warm, and cry almost with delight. This is all just instinct, cowardice, despair, heresy. To love must not be: to let yourself be passively pushed into someone's arms. Love must not grow inside your soul like a nail at the end of your finger. Do not let yourself go. Hate instead.

28

Why bother to deny, cry out, defy or destroy? I'm trying to find myself, like the doctor said. Why bother? The more I dig into myself, the more I crumble. I'm looking for the nub of me, but I'll never find it. I know there isn't one. I aspired to recreate chaos within me, to go back to square one. I'm afraid that when you get back to square one, you have nowhere left to go. I'm trying to find myself, like the doctor says. That doesn't mean much. I'm alive. I don't know what being alive entails. I've got life. I've got no clue what I should make of it. I don't know what to do. I've groped everywhere around me, leaving no stone unturned. I've found nothing. I've found myself in a land where I'm bored to death. Take your own life, turn every stone, or let yourself go. When you're keen to be the law of your life, there's no taking it, no turning stones, no letting go. I wanted to let myself die, for no reason, as a form of distraction. In order to make myself a soul, I destroyed my heart, burnt every shred of spontaneity. I've barely hacked at the clock than it's already stopped, I'm already sick and I bitterly regret it already, already wishing I could mend, restore, repair it all, finding all the nuts and bolts. I'll recover. Obviously. But I can never rewind the clock. Whether you hack at the clock ten or a thousand times, you can never rewind it with a single blow of your axe. That petrifies me with fear. When we're born, we run perfectly well. If you let yourself go all your life, you'll run perfectly well until you reach the end. The engine powering me escapes my intelligence and my will. And that bothers me. Wielding an axe, I open up my engine. I get an eyeful, investigate, understand. The spark blows up the gas. The strength of the explosion pushes the piston, which activates the crankshaft, which cranks the main shaft until the differential transmits its motion to the wheel: it's Columbus' egg. But it dawns on me: that engine doesn't obey me. If I talk to it, it doesn't listen. It does whatever it wants. If it doesn't obey *me*, whom else? I won't let such forces run my life. Blow by blow, I break it all: the spark, the gas, the piston, the crankshaft, the main shaft, and the differential. That wheel will turn the way *I* want! I put my shoulder to the wheel and push. We might not go very far, Berenice, but we'll go as we please, and without outside help. I get tired, I get sick. They call for the doctor. The doctor says that he can make the engine run again, but that it will never run like an engine running on its own again. I've lost all faith. The gears and springs of my feelings are ruined. I have faith in no one. I have faith in nothing. All I have left is my wheel and my will.

Enough with this slaughter! The foreign forces controlling me are not just despicably almighty; they also have their soft spots. They don't just grab you by the throat. They also, sometimes, grab you by the neck. Let them. Release. Let go. Who knows where they're leading you? Don't you wish for surprises and discoveries? Nothing is more devoid of surprises, nothing more boring than the countries you yourself created. Let *them* create you, let *them* surprise you, lead you into the unknown. Those who try to find themselves find nothing. Those who look for themselves are looking for someone other than themselves in and of itself. If they go all the way, they find protozoa.

And beyond protozoa is matter. And beyond matter is void. Humans developed from protozoa. You can't seriously want to go back to square one without going back to being lifeless. But before you do, you must go back to being a monkey, a saurian, a trilobite, a protozoan. At the sight of me lying still in this bed, doing nothing but letting my heart beat and my lungs hold air, you could think I've reached the last stage of species evolution in reverse, that I'm close to the nub of it all, close to infamous sources: death, torpor, vacuum, void.

My doctor is as much an expert in psychiatry as in endocrinology. With his pharmaceutical screwdriver, he plays with my head, with my radiator. He cleans the spark plugs of my thyroid gland. He tells me that my radiator pump has stopped sucking, that he must take it apart. He doesn't give a damn about me. I don't give a damn about him. We make each other laugh. Since he's been patching me up, life doesn't feel more interesting, but it feels less impossible. We talk about combustion engines. *To be or not to be.* Once again, without faith, for no reason, just because life is such a heavyweight, I've chosen to come back to life. I have my expectations.

29

Einberg threw the doctor out, and here I am, back to protozoan square one. I have a sweaty forehead and shivers running down my spine. My back is cold like cold sugar and my face is hot like hot sugar. My temples are throbbing like barley sugar. The doctor wanted to charge inflated fees. He told Einberg that a doctor who, on top of being a doctor, is also a psychiatrist and an endocrinologist, is duty-bound to charge inflated fees. But Einberg is not the type of man who'll let himself be inflated by fees. He told the doctor to go to hell with his inflated fees. Wait around or die? I'm firmly resolved to let myself die. Anyone who wants to give me back a thirst for life will have to be a damn good liar. They'll have to be dead eloquent. I've stopped talking. I've promised myself I would never speak again. I don't even speak to Christian. Since the doctor's defenestration last month, I haven't uttered a single word. Eating no evil, speaking no evil, hearing no evil, seeing no evil. Getting used to being dead. Countless headaches and sleepless nights. Tough it out. Tough as nails. Tough to kill. Rabbi Schneider is leaving. Once more unto the breach, dear friends, once more. He came to bid me farewell. I let him talk to himself. He slaps his belly and says it will make him lose some weight. I let him slap his belly. You can slap your belly all you want, you fat Lope de Vega. Fifty more men will hop on the same plane shortly. All of them came into my room. Eager young men with hooked noses and concentration camp numbers tattooed onto their wrists—they look like great warriors, like the Ten Thousand. They're all willing to shed their blood. Ticks, leeches and vampires beware! Among the fifty, I recognized Abel, the only brother Constance Chlorus has left. The three others died last week. The tank they were in got blown up. When you don't want to commit suicide, you ride on horses, not in tanks. I'm glad they died. They hated me. I can't wait for Abel to get killed. He's just the same.

They're boarding the plane shortly. Einberg is sponsoring their expedition. They'll land in Tel Aviv around midnight, if they don't sink into the Dead Sea on the way over. Those who, like Constance Chlorus' three hateful brothers, die on the battlefields, let their dentures sit unused. Notice to all denture seekers! Time to get on board! Time to go get shot! Enough fake teeth rationing!

Mousermoth worries as much for the Arabs as Einberg does for Israel. She welcomes as many fez-wearing ambassadors in the parlour as Einberg welcomes hook-nosed consuls in his study.

"Everyone supports Israel on this continent. I've had enough. It's too unfair! The poor Arabs will come to hate us. There are enough hate walls in this world without that war—that filthy war, which, like all wars, is just some kind of business between bigheads and bigwigs—building more walls."

Upon which Mousermoth has launched a relief effort meant to help Arab families affected by the war. A hundred fez-wearing petitioners went around with baskets collecting cans, cigarettes, dollars and kicks in the teeth. The relief effort might just as well be meant to help suffering families on both sides. According to Mousermoth, though, there are already enough relief efforts meant to help Jewish victims. The newspapers are really roughing her up, accusing her of homicidal ignorance and criminal blindness. They claim that there's only one rule of law, that when two parties fight, all the good people are on one side, and all the bad, on the other. They claim that if she knew anything about history or politics, she would defend a truer cause.

Mousermoth replies that most of the Arab children and elderly affected by the war can't read or write, so they don't know any more than she does about history or politics. She replies that, even if there were, all in all, only half a rule of law, she would take all the rights it entailed. Someone, then, makes sure to remind her, off-colour, that her brothers, the Brückner Colonels, collaborated with the Nazis at the start of the last war. She proudly replies that she has no more memory than a poor Arab baby, no more memories or resentment than an Arab baby. She replies that surely, if she had any memories, they would only inspire her contempt and resentment. Einberg and Mousermoth are speaking so loudly that I can hear them as well as if I were sitting next to them in the parlour.

"This war is just as holy to the poor fools on the one side as to the poor fools on the other. All the silver tongues sang them the same tune: 'The rule of law is on *our* side!' But all those silver tongues are careful not to tell the poor fools that it's the law of the jungle, that the only ones ruling are those who have the most killers and the most killing machines."

"What's this got to do with your brothers this time? Who are they now? The poor fools or the silver tongues? Because it's always about your brothers in that little head of yours, right? You may have been only thirteen when I married you, and you may have been a real nutcase, but let me tell you this: you were single-minded. You only ever opened your mouth to advocate for those dearly beloved brothers and urge your little husband to use his influence to save them from the gallows. When it came down to making him write to a judge or a minister, there was no hesitation: clothes came right off, tiny arms opened wide. When you decided to sleep in a separate bedroom, it had to do with your brothers. Again. I just had them released from jail, so there was nothing you could get me to do for them anymore. You no longer saw any reason to put up with me sleeping in your bed. The Arabs are a bit like your brothers, aren't they? They share a striking resemblance… Like those beloved Colonels, they're fanatical, bloodthirsty Anti-Semites… We must protect them! We must rush to their rescue!"

"What I did for my brothers has nothing to do with blood. I would have done it for a perfect stranger. In fact, you know perfectly well that for the past ten years, my brothers have been perfect strangers to me. There's an abyss between us, a vast abyss, a thousand-year abyss, as large an abyss as between me and Reccared I, Visigoth King of Hispania."

"Reccared I! Reccared I! What a load of nonsense! The abyss between you and Reccared I is nothing next to the one between him and myself. I heard that savage converted to Catholicism. But *I*, Mauritius Einberg, will never convert to Catholicism."

"If you ever convert to Catholicism, Mauritius Einberg, I'll kill myself. I'll be so angry at God for giving you grace that I'll kill myself!"

What a load of nonsense!

30

I have a skeleton. Through my flesh, growing thinner each day, I can touch it, feel it, get to know it. I can poke my fingers through the large sockets it has instead of eyes. It has tibias instead of legs. It has zygomata instead of cheeks. My hands are just gloves casing its bony hands. My hair is just a wig stuck onto its bony skull. My eyes are just two little coloured lightbulbs stuck in eyeless sockets. I'm just a skeleton's garb. I'm getting skinny, twiggy as a toothpick. The skeleton that has me will catch its death. Tough luck. It should have picked a dumber acorn. I make a point of refusing to eat. It wouldn't be fair for me to eat since the sight of food is enough to make me sick to my stomach. If I were a flower, eating would make me bloom. When you're human, eating just brings out disgust, dread, and dung. The thought of all the bile, the fear, the filth that can be avoided just by pushing away each bowl of soup, each potato and a half, each slice of beef, almost restores my will to live. My fever rises and rises. I let it rise. I let myself braise, like ham. Oftentimes, after the sharpest pangs, the sorest pains, my fever becomes intoxicating, giving me the sweetest pleasure. I shut my eyes, stay still, and feel like I'm falling, endlessly falling, like when you look at a high steeple from the foot of the church. I'm sterile, empty. I'm light, lighter than a bird. I'm now just a pair of swallow wings, swimming in thin air.

Devoutly, defiantly, Mousermoth spends her nights by my bed. I can hear the cat purr, and it's like I'm hearing love streaming from a basin. What's here, sitting beside me with a bottle of cognac between her legs, isn't Mousermoth: it's a bottle filled with love. And that bottle sometimes stands up and leans over me, extending its neck all the way to my lips. I'm dying of thirst. I shall not drink. My tongue is rough like sandpaper. I shall never drink from your spring.

A scream rips me out of a nightmare. I open my eyes on her beautiful face. My eyes penetrate the fresh, clear blue of her eyes. I feel her want, crave. That face, velvety soft, standing two inches from my squid ugly soul, is starving skin. That breath, as sweet as a flower's fragrance, sending shivers down the rock of my soul, is wishful wind. Gently, her nose says "Take me." Gently, her eyebrows say "Take us." Gently, the gondolas and gondoliers on her nightgown say "Help yourself." I close up, blindly. I fold my arms, shut my mouth. I keep telling myself to beware, blindly. Keep your pretty knives and your pretty forks, you pretty drawer! I want nothing, you pirate trunk of the South Seas! I choose my own misery over your bounty, you garden! All you have is what you are, you aquarium filled with iridescent fish! And what you are is yours and yours only! For a long time, she keeps leaning over me, reaching out, expecting, waiting for me. Waiting for me to take her in, her hand, soft like bird wings, strokes my scorching, prickly forehead. Waiting for me to take her in, her long locks, soft like bird wings, fan out over her cheeks, folding like sashes over her face. Suddenly, she leans back. Suddenly, her eyes slip away from mine.

"Are you thirsty?" she asks.

"Yes you *are*," she asserts. "Let me run and get you some water."

She comes back with her water. I don't want her water. She doesn't insist. She changes my sweat-soaked sheets.

I watch her. I don't often allow myself to watch her like that. But tonight, I'm too weak to fight back. She strokes me some more. I let her beauty play with my mind. But I only allow myself to watch her when she's not looking. Her hand roughly runs a comb through my hair. As though rotten from the roots, my hair, it seems, breaks with the slightest touch. Several strands stay stuck to her fingers.

"You're shedding, little lemur," she says, laughing.

Mousermoth must laugh up her sleeve. In this self-inflicted state, I've become for her a weapon more powerful than an intercontinental nuclear missile. During her Thirty Years Trial with Einberg, I've become the ironclad proof, the shatterproof piece of evidence. Nothing could be easier than telling Einberg, her eyes filled with crocodile tears, "Look at what you've done with my daughter!" Christian says that, since I got sick, she's constantly picking fights with Einberg, screaming at him and sobbing to his face. She accuses him of poisoning my life. She accuses him of being less tight-fisted when it comes to buying guns in Israel than when it comes to pay for Berenice's doctor. She charges him at full speed. And she takes full advantage of the situation. I may not be sick much longer.

"She's frustrated! You've defrauded her of her most innocent needs! You offended and humiliated her, treated her like an animal!"

Take him, Cicero! Do not let him get you, Verres! The last time I spoke to her, in a fit of rage, I told her that she would never be more than a panther, an egoistic, lonely creature, a deaf, blind creature stuck with herself as her only love, reason and pride.

"And you," she answered, smiling and stroking me, "will never be more than a little lemur, an ugly, grimacing, sneering, angry little beast."

Recalling the little bat episode, she now calls me little lemur. Little bat. Little lemur. Lillehammer.

31

The wind blows in gusts. The rain lashes down. Thunder rolls. Lightning strikes. Mousermoth is standing in the deep embrasure of my window, with one hand on the espagnolette. She's wearing snowy white pyjamas that look too big for her.

Mousermoth is sitting sideways on the big Chippendale, with her back against the cold, hard backrest whose bulging twin pillars rise up to make a portal. Her hyaline, selenic blue stare embraces the storm. Her eyes are aquatic. They shine like twin water holes on the surface of her face. Eyes, open eyes, fascinate me. I adhere to open eyes with an open-eyed soul, be they human or animal. I look at her eyes. I look at those eyes, blinded by their inward gaze. Because trees don't have eyes, they can't speak or walk. Eyes only allow you to choose whom to hate, whom to love. Eyes are what allow you to cry when you cry. Eyes are the reason why two human beings may not agree or see eye to eye. Eyes allowed man to crawl out of the infinite depths of the dark. Thanks to his eyes, man reached the surface by himself, thought he saw other men, and imagined that other men may be challenging his lonely almightiness. When his eyes opened, the truth, or rather the lie, came out, and man was filled with deception, and his deep mountain of darkness, his warm God hole, started teeming with the worst hallucinations. Eyes made him imagine that he wasn't the only one anymore to cry or suffer from loneliness and fear. Eyes make the mother bird realize the baby bird died. Man grew eyes *before* man grew legs. Upon seeing what he saw when he started seeing, man was scared stiff and quickly grew legs (why the hell didn't he grow wings?) so he could run away, seeking another mountain of safe and still darkness, seeking another God hole. Eyes made man realize man could die. When man saw man die, he screamed at the top of his lungs: that's how he acquired speech. He screamed so loud that ears sprang out of his head. Tired of running, man sat down (origin of the chair). While resting, he tried to understand what had just happened (origin of misunderstanding). When a man would meet another fleeing man, he only had two choices: to avoid or to attack the daunting alter ego who appeared to wrestle away the quiet enjoyment of his bosom of darkness. Avoiding came to be called cowardice. Attacking came to be called love when one submitted to the other, and hate when either one refused to submit. Eyes claim a high price for the plays they allow man to see, for giving man the illusion that he's not alone. Men who buy glasses to see better are fools. The more clearly you can see an illusion, the more real it looks. If men lost sight, we would soon see them stop, hush, settle on the spot, grow roots and leaves, bear fruit. While their roots would grow, their mountains would close their fake door to the sun's fake light, and we would see the puppets they're holding tight slowly turn into a sceptre and a crown.

While I'm having all these thoughts, Mousermoth, whom I've been staring at, stays still. Her blond locks are as fine as cobwebs. They fall down perpendicularly around her head, almost in chunks. On her neck, they arch, almost into a corbel. When she tilts her head, they lean forward, part, and unfurl like waves on a shore. Only hair, eyes, nails, and teeth aren't covered with skin. Mousermoth's blond locks switch on and off in the lightning bolts. Suddenly, she moves. She takes a sip of cognac. Her lips are moistened with cognac, her Kabylia lips, smooth like the rim of a glass, thin like the edge of a pail. I imagine that, with a slate hammer, I'm driving nails into her broad and smooth brow. I imagine that, thus nailed, she now hangs from a wall, between the ceiling and the floor, like a Velasquez painting. She has a finger planted into her cheek. Her teeth are showing through her half-open lips, *like a flock of sheep coming up from the washing*. With her head down, she's looking down at her loving cup, as though she were watching a play at its very bottom. She can spend hours looking down at her loving cup, completely still, without moving a finger or batting an eyelid. Mauriac is lying across her naked feet, taking a nap.

You watch over the sick. Mousermoth watches over me. She's not too watchful. Her head is often in the clouds. She abruptly turns it toward me. She sees me watching her, letting her beauty play with my mind. She seems surprised. She thought I was asleep. She recovers from her surprise, smiles at me, puts her hand on my forehead.

"Hi there, little lemur!"

She smiles, visibly embarrassed. She should be. I swore to ignore her presence. For a month, I pretended not to see her. And here I am, staring right into her eyes. Here I am, not looking away.

"What do I see here! What should I make of it? Can you now see me or are you just pretending that you can? Are you actually bothering to notice my presence? Or is that just another ruse to make me waste my breath? I see a twinkle in your eyes. Is that ember glowing from the back of your cold head? Let's blow on it, quick!"

Since my most hateful faces can't defeat her happy face, I turn my back. She stands up, leans over me, takes my elbows in her hands. And, softly, warmly, in shallow breaths, she blows in my ear. Just like that, it's over! I'm done for. I lose control. Just like that, within me, floodgates fail, dikes and dams burst. I know that woman is a fake; I tell myself, I keep telling myself. But it's no use. Utterly bedazzled, I forget it all, lose it all. I tumble down every one of my peaks and crash. I lose balance, I free-fall. Everything slips through my fingers. Suddenly, as though triggered by an active volcano, I turn around, stand up and run, rush into her arms, holding on to her neck. She hugs me firmly, without saying a word. Long minutes go by. The silence is so deep, so thick, so rich that I can't breathe, like at the bottom of a lake. I'm warm, deliciously warm, so warm that I feel like I'm melting, evaporating.

"Don't move. Don't speak. I love you. Stay. Stay here. Stay like that."

I keep repeating the same words, a hundred times over.

I need to speak. My throat is holding back so many words that I'm choking. In one move, in a single gesture, she tears me from my bed and lifts me up to the ceiling. She's showing me off like a trophy. She's laughing. She brings me down, leading me into the most ridiculous, disorienting dance. We twirl on the floor like a thousand tops, in fits and starts. We swirl so swiftly that our feet are all over the floor, all over the country. The room's four thousand walls rotate as fast as the wheels of Phaethon's carriage. Furniture and pillars overlap and blend into each other, becoming vaporous, turning into whirling horizons, dissolving into a maelstrom, a mist. She's laughing. So hard! At last we stop, drained of all strength. Stumbling and staggering, she lets herself fall down, spread-eagled. I collapse beside her. We huff and puff, lying flat on our backs, holding our stomachs. She turns serious, stiffens up, starts to cry.

"Whoever you may be, sweetie, I love you. Don't you forget it! Whoever you may become, sweetie, you'll always be my child, you can always claim your right to me. Wherever your search for happiness may lead you, I'll be there at every turn, waiting at the end of each blind alley with my arms wide open. Never forget that I love you. Please."

She gets back up. She reaches her hands to help me up. I find what she just said utterly ridiculous. But what wouldn't you forgive such a beautiful thing?

"Go to sleep now…"

I want her to lie beside me. I don't know how to tell her.

"You must be tired…" I say hypocritically. "You've spent all of your nights watching over me for more than a month now… Come lie beside me for a bit. Look: I made lots of room."

At first, she refuses. I insist. Plead. At last, she condescends. Seeing her cry makes me want to cry. My heart is heavy. My nose itches. My eyes fill with tears. Lying there, right beside me, in my own bed, she looks like she's letting herself belong to me, like she's letting me have her. Lying where my dolls used to be, she looks like she's my doll, like she's all mine. From here, I can't see her well enough, can't enjoy her being here to the fullest. I get up and go kneel close to her belly. The view is better from here. I see her like I wanted to, have her like I wanted to. Watching her lie under me in my own bed, in the ship of my fears and nightmares, I forcefully feel like I'm taking her, keeping her, holding her inside my soul. I'm a country. And she's in the country of me like the island is in the water. I want to touch her. I want to grab her, seize her with my hands. I want to run my hands all over her body, from head to toe.

"Give me your hand."

"Why?" she asks mockingly, upon which my own seriousness makes me blush.

"To look at it."

"It's too dark in here. You won't see much. Should I switch on the light?"

"No! No light! No switching!"

I listen to my own words as though they were someone else's. She extends one hand, showing me the back, the tanned part, the part that makes up a fist, the part you see when you close your hand.

"You have no feelings. Those who have feelings show their palm first, the part you discover when you open your hand, the softest, least bony, most intimate part. You're showing me the slapping side."

"I have bad manners."

I take her hand, that beautiful cluster of fingers crowned with a pink diamond. I tighten my fist around one of her fingers, soft, thin like tall grass. I move up and crouch next to her face. With my finger holding a pretend piece of chalk, I trace the bridge between her closed eyes, the bay line of her brow, the basket-handle arch of her jaw, the crest of her nose.

"You're pretty, you know. There's nothing prettier than you. You're prettier than a tree."

She cracks a little smile and her nose lets out a disgruntled sigh. I lie on her breast and ask her to put her hands over my eyes. She lowers two cold palms on my burning lids.

"Press harder. You'll see: it's funny."

She presses a bit harder. Then I move my lids and ask her what it reminds her of.

"What should it remind me of?"

"When you hold a caterpillar tight in your fist, it struggles and it tickles like that."

"That's awful!" she cries out, a shiver shaking her breast.

I slide my face down onto her belly. It's soft, soft like snow, warm snow. I press on her belly with my face really hard, hard enough to break my nose.

She folds her hands behind my neck.

"You're not alone anymore, sweetie. Go to sleep now. Sleep. Sleep."

"If you say so. Why sleep? So that the dull of life can come back sooner?"

"The dull of life...?" She laughs.

We fall silent. Love has fertilized me. Love runs through my veins. And, until dawn, every time my heart beats, I feel like I could die.

32

I love her! I love her! Make her come back! Please! Night has fallen. I'm waiting for her! What is she waiting for? Here she comes! I'm kind of scared. Now the door opens, and Mauriac II walks in with its tail up. I clench my fists and want to scream. My belly is filled with a thousand screams, longer and louder than eels. I love her so much! I've gone mad. All night long, I will let myself go mad, as mad as I can. But this second night will be the last. Mad women must be bound.

I leave the doors and windows wide open. I don't have enough eyes to look at her, not enough ears to hear it all, not enough voice left to tell her everything. I'm festering, pores fully dilated. If need be, this will last until dawn, or drag on into the afternoon. I have all night. I will take as much time as I need to wear the glamour out, break the charm. I talk to her, touch her, as quickly as I can, as madly as I can. I'm relentless. No loitering! She pours a little cognac into her loving cup. She stares into it, deep into it.

"What's so beautiful in there? Let me look!"

Motioning me to keep my voice down, she throws me the angry look of an angler who wants you to stop throwing pebbles in the water. She's holding the loving cup really tight. If she makes the slightest move, troubling the air, what the loving cup contains will escape, fly away like a hummingbird that hears something stir in the branches. She motions me to come closer and take a gentle look inside.

"Look, sweetie, a sunken city."

At first, I see nothing sunken but the diamond-carved crystal at the bottom of the cup. Then I grasp that you have to strive to see a city inside a glass.

"Is it a Mycenaean city? Is it Atlantis?"

"See the red, green, blue and yellow shimmers? That's a big city at night, a city that stayed exactly as it was a moment ago, before sinking to the bottom of the sea. Its red, green, blue and yellow signs still shine."

"I see it now. I see! Don't tell me. Allow me. It's a harbour city. I can see a tall lighthouse. I can see the waterfront lights ruffling the water."

I just need to strain my eyes a bit to see all I can think up. I'm amazed. I'm there. I can see a tall lighthouse. I can see bright wharfs and dark warehouses. The night is wearing away, fleeing as fast as a night train. The night is over. My love goes back into its shell. When I wake up, the romance will have become sweetness, a sweet secret. It can only live on between me and myself, unseen, in underground pockets of light and darkness.

Crappy cow crap! I'm cured now, perfectly cured, cured to the bone. I'm healthy again, healthy as a rock, clenching my jaw so hard I could break my own teeth. I'm so healthy I could kill the world with a single punch. I go back to Dame

Ruby's. If I had a saw, I would saw her legs off. If I had a funnel, I would hit her on the nose with it. If I had an atomic bomb, I would make her eat it. If I had scissors, I would cut her ears off. I'm healthier than ever! All is for the best in the best of all worlds! Samba samba! I love life! I walk in long and steady strides, like all those idiots convinced that nothing's going around in circles, deluded with the idea that the faster you walk the sooner you'll get somewhere. I walk light-hearted, like all those idiots who can't see they're only getting up to fall right back into the same miasma, the same mistakes, only laughing to fall right back into the same monotony, the same tepid tedium, only keeping their mouths shut to repeat the same trifles, the same nonsense, bland enough to suck your own blood dry. I walk holding my head up high so as not to see that everything is going around in circles, going to hell. Humans aren't going around in circles. I'm not going around in circles. If you pay close attention, you'll see that we're standing still, in a stranglehold, and that what's going around in circles is a grinding wheel as big as Earth, gnawing at your flesh a bit with every turn, blunting your soul a bit with every turn, killing you a bit with every turn. I walk in long and steady strides, light-hearted, with my head up high. And don't think for one second that zigzagging is enough for the gyratory motion to stop! My romance with the blue-eyed white panther is over, done. It lived as long as all sweetness: the time it takes to clear the confusion. It's her fault! She's a fool. She's rock-thick-headed. She has it all wrong. I loved her like a boy loves a girl. When I was alone with her, I couldn't look at her without feeling like I was doing something bad. She has it all wrong. I kissed her with my darkest passion, convinced she was kissing me back with her highest fever. That fool just saw whimsy, mischief, kid stuff. That fool never caught on. Dumb Mousermoth wiped the floor with dumb Berenice. If she had felt the strength, the seriousness I summoned to do all we did together, she would feel ashamed. She would have touched nothing. Everything would have stayed in that room. Everything would have stayed hidden deep within her soul. She never suspected the truth for a single second. She never doubted her truth for a single second. She tells everyone about it. She brags about it. And when she tells people, there's no shred of shame in her eyes. She destroyed everything. She opened that room to the four winds. All its fragrances dispersed. She hung all over the city walls the pictures we painted together in that room. She tells the whole world how the two of us jitterbugged those two nights away.

Since I recovered, she's been showing me off. I'm her show bear. That's all she remembers of me and my passion for her. I'm her proof. I am proof that she was right. I'm the flag showing her victory over Einberg. I'm the one Einberg had killed, the one she resurrected with her motherly love. Einberg said I needed a few good slaps, and she said I needed motherly love. She was quite right. She gave me motherly love and I'm healed. Thanks to Mousermoth's motherly love, I'm alive again, alive and kicking, cold hard cured. See how alive she is since I gave her a taste of motherly love! The day before yesterday, she showed me off to the Glengarrys. She told them how Einberg had killed me and how she resurrected me.

"Right?" she asked me.

"Right," I said.

Yesterday, we were at the Jovitches'. She told them the story of the caterpillar caught in a fist and of the sunken night city at the bottom of the sea. They were quite entertained.

"Right?" she asked, turning to me, all smiles.

"Right," I said, bursting with bile.

"She held me so tight in her little arms that I couldn't breathe."

"Right," I said, bursting with bile.

Tomorrow, we're going back to the Glengarrys' for an encore. I let Mousermoth do her little show. I play her little game. I let her believe anything she wants. I let her believe that she actually performed a miracle, that I was actually dead, and that she actually resurrected me. She's the fairy who healed me with the touch of her wand. I was desperate and ill. I'm now so happy and healthy I could pop. When I've had enough playing the part, I'll send her to hell.

I scold Christian. He promised to bring me to the end of the world as soon as I would be cured. He's done nothing yet.

33

Christian shows up, as white as a sheet. This is the day, he declares, true to his word. This is the day. A man of honour is true to his word. He said that he would bring me to the end of the world. He now brings me to the end of the world. Here we go.

We'll leave under the cover of night, at the darkest hour. We'll swim away from here. There's a dinghy, but we won't use it. What would we look like if we fled in a dinghy? We might as well flee on a bus or a charter plane, or a motorbike! We'll go big.

"Let's pretend we're breaking out of a war camp."

"Sounds good," he says.

He asks me to set a time. Set the time, to the minute.

"Any time? Any minute?"

"I'll see. Try me. There's two of us. If I don't like it, we'll talk it over."

"In thirteen hours and thirteen minutes."

Overly dramatic, Christian slowly winds up his watch, excessively slow. We walk up to my room. Overly dramatic, I slowly wind up my cuckoo clock, excessively slow. I synchronize my clock with his watch. We spread out a map of the area over the bed. We kneel down with our elbows on the mattress, and he teaches me how to read the map. The railway that runs over the bridge that spans over the island is designated by a funny black line with stripes—funny because it looks like a never-ending centipede, a skinny megapede, a gigapede that hasn't eaten for two millennia! There. The railway overarching the abbey branches out into three tracks when it reaches the city. We're interested in the one that skirts the waterfront. With the tip of his pencil, Christian follows the corresponding multi-legged line. The water is blue. The ground is yellow. Where the harbour is, the ground breaks down into tiny rectangles: those are the docks.

Affectedly, in a deep voice, Christian signals a dock by the name of Victoria.

"This will be our stop."

"And after that? What will we do? Board a ship out of the blue? Oh! Christian! Oh!"

Christian stays dead silent, mighty mysterious. Then, like a magician pulls a jack of clubs from his sleeve, he pulls a thick wad of printed sheets from his pocket. It's a newspaper page that he carefully unfolds and smooths out. He starts reading, dead solemn:

"*The* Elga Dan, *a Danish liner moored at Victoria Dock, will be sailing tomorrow at daybreak. The ship's departure marks the end of one of the busiest seasons of our country's greatest harbour. Canada Ports Corporation announces that the harbour will open two weeks earlier than usual in the coming season. The river will have to be widened and deepened.* And so on… The destination of the *Elga Dan* hasn't been disclosed yet. Are you happy?"

"Unknown destination! Oh! Christian! Oh! I could kiss you!"

"I want to get away from here too. I've had enough. I'm fed up. I want to die."

"You want to die? You? For real? What's wrong?"

"Maybe I'll let you know. Maybe not. Anyway… it's appalling. And I'm sure you must have figured it all out. You're such a snoop."

"Unknown destination! Let's go to bed, Christian! Let's go to sleep so that time can go by more quickly. It's cold outside. We'll have to dress warm."

I can see myself there already. We're crawling on the iron deck, under the portholes of the officers' cabins. We're creeping in the shadows, like rats, holding our breaths. I don't know how we've managed to sneak aboard. The deckhand on watch must have been asleep or watching a lunar eclipse, or gone down to the hold to get some matches. We nose about, fearing the worst. Threats are looming all around. Every shadow is the enemy. Every noise is dangerous. We're huddled behind the rescue boat we've chosen as our hideout. But rescue boats are wrapped in tarps, and those tarps are secured by cables tied so tightly that they're impossible to lift. We anxiously struggle to loosen the cables keeping us out of our rescue boat. There! The knots give way. We dive head first into our rescue boat. We're starving and freezing to death in our hideout. We hug each other so as not to cry in despair. Hanging from its davits, our hideout rocks and rolls. But not all is lost. Beyond the silence, beyond the dark, officers are barking orders, sailors are swearing, dolphins are playing leapfrog, albatrosses are sliding up and down the wind, the sun is shining, the sea is bubbling at the bow: the *Elga Dan* is sailing forth. Soon, we'll reach the end of the world. It's a twenty-coloured pentapolis with twenty doors, whose laugh is greater than air, whose dance is wider than a bird's flight, a pentapolis clustered around an apse.

"Wait for me on the dock. I'll be there in thirteen hours and thirteen minutes."

I'm waiting for Christian, and this task is time-consuming, all-absorbing. The last minutes of my old life are ticking by. I anxiously listen to the last minutes of a bleak life fleeing out of me, a mean and miserable life, a life as flat as an atlas. A new, clean life is floating my way on the dirty water, all white against the night, all warm against the cold. My new days and my new seasons aren't the kind that can be counted like sheep or that drop like flies. My new days and my new seasons spread out into the void like a mural on a wall. My fifty thousand new seasons aren't fifty thousand little sun corpses sinking to my feet one after another; they're one sun, one breath, one land, one sea, one single road. It's a moonless night. The wind is cold and so biting that it blows through my clothes and flesh, right into my splanchnic cavities, it seems. I'm wearing trousers, a sweater, trainers and a beret. Christian pops out of nowhere, startling me. We bring nothing with us. When hunger hits, we'll eat dirt or bite the dust. Our teeth chatter. It makes me laugh. Christian doesn't seem to be in a laughing mood. On the dock, we push pebbles into the water between the cracks with the tips of our feet. The dinghy's mooring is squeaking—that boat is too shabby for our great escape. The more I look at Christian, the more he looks sad to me. I nudge him gently to lift his spirits. No use. Suddenly, I'm seized by the greatest fear: it will all go down the drain! I join hands, drop to my knees and fervently invoke the chthonic powers. I take Christian's wrist and roll up his sleeve. Thirteen hours and thirty minutes have gone by! It's time.

"It's time, Christian. I beg you, Christian, let's take off our clothes and dive in!"

"You can't be serious, Berenice. We'll catch our death."

"That's not true. Some people go swimming in the middle of winter. They even dig a hole in the ice if they have to. Beavers spend the winter underwater."

I kick off my trainers and send my beret flying with a

shake of the head. In a flash, I rip my sweater off. Abruptly, brutally, Christian grabs me by the shoulders and tightens his grip.

"Listen, Berenice. Behave. Let's not leave for real. There's no end of the world. You're smarter than that. Come on! It was just a game. We played the great escape. The game's over now. I don't get you anymore. I thought we both knew we were just having fun. It's late. Let's go home. You were sick to death a few days ago and now you're shivering with cold. Let's go home. Let's go to bed."

He's avoiding my gaze. He's such a cruel disappointment! He inspires such bitter hatred in me!

"You've got nothing! Nothing! Nothing! Christian Einberg. You disgust me! You're just a… a… Aw, you're not a man! I'm just a girl, and I'm braver than you!"

I pummel him. I'm so angry that I'm grinding my teeth. My resentment is so vicious that I'm spitting fire.

"Loser! Lame duck! Limp soul! You're just a sack full of loose flesh and stale blood! You say you want to die… I don't believe you. To have a death wish, you must first feel alive. And there's not enough life left in you to activate the eyelids of a worm! Look at me! Have mercy! Let's at least pretend to leave, Christian. Let's at least pretend, please! I'm begging you! Make an effort. Love me enough not to let me down, just tonight, just this time."

"All right, Berenice. But promise me you won't catch pneumonia."

"The mere illusion of leaving will boost my health enough to dream for the next thousand years."

Slowly, as though he were walking to the gallows,

Christian takes off his clothes and folds them. Like me, he rolls them into his sweater and wears the bundle like a hat, with the sleeves tied under his chin, so that they can stay dry as we swim across the river. Without waiting for him, I sink half-naked in the delightfully freezing water.

We take the road to the village and stop at the grade intersection. Then we take the railway, the railwaves, the railhole. We're walking where only trains have run before. It's as though we were walking where birds fly, where fish swim, where stars spin. We walk for long, delightfully mad hours on the railway, on the birdway, the fishway, and the starway. Sometimes, we each walk on our own rail with our arms outstretched, like funambulists. We often lose our balance. We try to reach out and take each other's hand, but our arms aren't long enough. Sometimes we walk between the rails, matching our steps to the sleepers' beats. The sleepers are too widely spaced-apart for us to walk effortlessly, but not enough to run with ease. We often miss our steps, and our feet often get caught in the ballasts. We swing our legs from one sleeper to the next as we would hop from one stone to the next to cross a river. But we must watch out too much, hold back too much. We quickly tire out. So we switch over to the embankment. And, with our heads up in the air, for miles on end, we run at full speed on the squeaking, sliding, sinking ballast. Suddenly, shortly after a switch, we stumble upon a tall iron mesh fence. Our ascent and descent prove to be perilous, painful, and indeed bloody. The diamonds are so small that we must hang on to the fence by the tips of our feet. Climbing by the sheer force of our fingers and toes, we reach the top to face a whole boom of spears. We lose our strength, control, balance. Straddling the fence, we tear our legs, our arms, our clothes. That knife-rest refusing to let us set foot on the other side, we decide to jump. As we hit the ground, we break every bone in our bodies. We've landed in an oil refining plant. The further we go, the more it stinks. In the distance, towers emerge, all kinds of high ovens and scaffolds emerge, filling the horizon. A giant pink flame is floating at the very top, at the end of a chimney. The tracks are gradually packed with tank cars. We hit them with our sticks. Their gong voices sound out. As though sitting on knolls, huge black vats are flanking us, stamped with big words written in white. Pipes of all sizes run all over the place. The one skirting our feet is as thick as four boas. Some zig-zag between heaven and earth, others burst out of the ground or out of the dark. We faithfully follow our railroad. Suddenly, behind the last tank car, the tracks curl up into formidable fangs, coming to an end. It's over.

"You chose the wrong track on purpose, Christian Einberg!"

"Come on!" he cries out, licking his ragged palm. "If I hadn't listened to you, we wouldn't be in such a mess."

Sneaking behind the gatekeeper's house, we manage, without being noticed, to reach a nice wide street, as bright as day. Stretching his arms out every which way, Christian tries to find his way around. He's not getting anywhere. I laugh at him. The sky is moonless, starless. The only suns around are the bulbous street lamps. We take a cross-street that leads us onto a four-lane boulevard. We make a right turn, then a left, then another right. We end up at the end of a cul-de-sac. We're lost, truly lost, truly, madly, deeply lost. I laugh hysterically. What could I possibly fear? All this is just make-believe after all. All this is so far from the end of the world. All this is pure madness too. The black car following us really slowly has a gyrating red light on the roof. The police. Let's run, Christian! Quick! Or at least pretend to.

"Where are you off to?"

"You should take your hat off when speaking to a lady!"

The policemen tell us that they mean no harm. They want to know where we live.

"Gentlemen, we live at Mr. and Mrs. Man, Planet Earth, Solar System, Universe. Now take your hats off, you boors!"

It's wonderfully warm inside the car, wonderfully pleasant, mild like an August night. I'm worn-out, washed-out, knackered, beat. There's something like a coat between me and the car's warmth. I'm wearing a thick coat of cold, of night, of tracks, of oil. My hands are all stiff, scraped by sky and soil, feeling out of place. I remind myself of a fish fresh out of the sea, struggling in the sand. I lean and snuggle against Christian, asking him to put his arm around me. I shut my eyes. Christian's shoulder is a beam at the bottom of a hold. Giant waves are breaking against the caravel's hull. We're sailing to an unknown destination.

"You made me very happy tonight, brother. It was wonderful."

Sniffling from emotion, filled with the nostalgia of what could have been, I pledge my undying allegiance to Christian. Outside, everything is now white with silence, heavy with silence. It's dawn or daybreak. At the abbey, the hustler greets us, ready to pounce, and the harlot greets us with caiman tears and warm cow's milk.

Something is wrong with Christian. He was dead serious when he told me he wanted to die. I'll make him spit it out. I'll worm it out of him. When there's nothing productive to do, you can always play with worms.

34

I watch Mousermoth pacing on the dead grass. With her arms hanging loose and her thumbs hooked into her pant pockets, she wanders in that slow, graceful, listless motion I've always envied, craved, tasting all that sweetness down my throat. She reminds me of one of those chubby cats that are too lazy to round their backs and bare their teeth, one of those fat creatures that stay limp when you pick them up and, with utmost indifference, will let anyone and everyone hug them or pet them, as though they were always drunk or sleepy. Her camel pants, too wide, flutter in the wind. For whatever reason, she's rolled the legs up to her knees. She's wearing her tennis shoes. She'll take them off before she comes in, leaving them on the mat before the revolving door. I'll see them when I pass by, smeared with spring sludge, summer grass and black char from the fall fires. The gardener is burning waste in a barrel. She walks toward him and speaks to him. She and the gardener look down the barrel like children down a well, watching the fire burn. The gardener leaves with his head down. She goes on looking down the barrel, watching the fire burn. This year, we won't burn the dead grass. No one cares about such things anymore.

"Winter already!" states Mousermoth, walking barefoot into the chapel.

I look at her wind-woven hair, at her wind-wet eyes. She's so beautiful! I look at her feet. She has dirty feet. I tell myself how beautiful it is to have dirty feet.

"How time flies! How quickly past turns into present! When I was a child like you, time would never go by fast enough!"

When I grow up, I won't spend my time leisurely wandering on dead grass. I'll be gone to a place of no return, to a place you reach via other places where no one ever stops. Riding Pegasus, I will launch an attack on Olympus, like the Titans, like Ajax of Oileus, like Bellerophon. I will die at full strength, from the very outburst of my own violence. I will fight against Death when the day is full, fully awake, and in full glory. I will march over to her and strike the first blows. I know the outcome of the battle. I know I will fight in vain. I know my soldiers and my horses will be charging from the edge of a cliff. But I will fight anyway. If you must lose, let it at least be a beautiful loss. If my soldiers and my horses must fall into the abyss right after taking their first steps, let them at least be the fastest horses and the bravest soldiers.

I don't have to do much to make Christian talk. He freely spills his poor scentless secrets, his tasteless secrets. A soul lies inside each body. Christian opens his mouth and shows me his poor pathetic soul, as sad as a boiled potato, as boring as soup. Some, like Leander, swim across the Hellespont, while others swim across the Channel. Christian, sitting comfortably in his chair, is drowning in a religious crisis. This is a religious crisis of titanic proportions that compares to Phalaris' infamous torments: it's *his* religious crisis. I tried to feel, to share his agony, his terrible agony. I felt nothing, shared nothing. His terrible agony lies inside his soul, and his soul lies inside his body. I could only feel his agony by entering his soul, and I could only enter his soul through his mouth, his body's biggest door. My fist doesn't even fit into his mouth. How could my whole body possibly fit? This summer, Christian committed mortal sins with Mingrelia. He kissed her on the mouth, for instance. I listen to him talk. I listen with all my strength. I don't know what prevents me most from hearing him. Is it jealousy, spite, hatred? Or is it just tedium? I let out deep sighs of impotence.

"When you commit a mortal sin, you lose the grace of God, and to get it back, you must go to confession. Without the grace of God, you're not allowed near the communion table. If you go near the communion table anyway, you're guilty of sacrilege. And a sacrilege is the biggest offence against God, so great that if you confess to it, you may not be absolved, and you might even be excommunicated. Do you get it, Berenice? If I died just now, I'd go straight to hell. You get it, right? I've often run to the confessional to admit the sins I committed with Mingrelia. Fear seized me every single time. And I made one false confession after another. You know, when it's a big sin, you must describe it in every detail, you must leave nothing out... I couldn't do it! I can't! My jaw seals itself shut. My tongue swells. And then I go on taking the Holy Communion with Mother every Sunday so that I won't disappoint her, disgrace her in front of everyone. I'm sacrilegious, Berenice! Don't you see? I'm damned! Damned! No one can save me now! I might as well kill myself! If I confess my sacrileges to the priest, I'll be excommunicated, get it? Excommunicated!"

I love Christian. I must take him seriously, I must be moved. Despite the absurdity of the situation, despite my own cynicism, I make every effort to take him seriously, to be moved.

35

With me around, cats are goners. I'm the only human awake on the whole island. The gardener is asleep. The others are away. I snatch Mauriac II and tie it by the leg to one of the beams of the quarry winch. I grab a heavy bludgeon and hit it until it falls stone dead. I dig a hole in the middle of the gardener's shed where I drop and bury the corpse, nefariously making sure that the tail still shows. You can see the tail quite well, as stiff as the stem of an onion, like a periscope piercing the sea surface, like the cross of Christ protruding from the Calvary. As soon as she's back from her errands, Mousermoth starts looking for her beloved cat. I offer my help and lead her cunningly toward the shed. She falls to her knees, breaking into tears and sobs. The gardener's recent behaviour has been particularly queer and hostile. Suspicions immediately fall on him, who never planted a single cabbage yet receives a handsome pay. Livid with anger, Mousermoth goes to his lodge and knocks on the door. No answer. She pushes the door open. We storm in. On the table fenced with empty green beer bottles, the gardener is lying dead, with his throat slit. Weak at the knees, we step into his blood. He killed himself. One murdered cat and one suicide gardener make two dead. The police show up, take photos and give me caramels. Violent deaths attract boneless beings. Every single boneless being of the mainland, including Constance Chlorus, hurries to the island. Dull eyes getting an eyeful.

The sand on the shore is concrete hard. Constance and I sit down on the sand.

"It's cold!" Constance Chlorus cries out, rubbing her bum to warm it up.

It's dead cold, Constance Chlorus, stone cold, cold as a log. Cold cold cold. What do you want me to say? I have nothing to say, so I say nothing. Let her speak if she has something to say. Tell me something extraordinary, Constance Chlorus. I'm all ears. She has nothing to say. Instead of talking, she picks her nose and bites her lip. There are tons of words. But there's nothing to say. There are tons of things. But there's nothing to do. I brought her here so that I could be alone with her. I'm alone with her now: a lot of good that does me. I feel lonelier than ever. There are hundreds of trees. What can I do with them? I would gladly chop them into tiny pieces, but I don't have the tools it takes. I could always count them.

"Let's count the poplars, Constance Chlorus. Don't count them out loud. We'll compare totals."

I count eleven poplars. It's too boring. I stop counting and, with all my eyes, all my ears, and all my soul, I try to find something else—something fun, something radiant. The world is wide. So wide! The world is so empty! So full of nothing! The universe is infinite. The universe is like numbers. You can count to a thousand million and keep going. You can count your whole life without reaching where numbers end. I scan the universe, listing its contents at first sight, and it's as lame, as meaningless, as when I try to count to a million before I go to sleep. Number three means nothing to me. Number thirteen means absolutely nothing to me. Number three hundred and forty-two means absolutely nothing to me. There's nothing in number five, nothing in the trees, nothing in the wind, nothing in the clouds. Constance Chlorus is carefully counting poplars with her dirty little finger. I try to stop her and make her understand how silly it is to count poplars. She won't hear any of it. She starts counting at the top of her lungs so that my voice won't make her lose count. She's incorruptible. It's no use. She keeps counting poplars, and will go on counting them until she bleeds to death if need be.

"Two hundred and thirty-nine! What about you? What's your total?"

"I stopped at eleven… I was bored to death."

"You're mean. You made me count all those trees for nothing."

"There are billions and billions of numbers... I've got an idea! I don't know how to tell you… There are billions of numbers, much too many to know them all, to remember them all, to carry them all in our hearts, to love them like you would love your tree, your home, your brother. If you say, 'I love numbers', you don't love much. If you say, 'I love human beings', you can't feel yourself love. But if you say, 'I love Christian', you see someone in your head, you feel your heart carrying someone's weight, you remember the things you did together. Here's what I suggest: let's pick a number, any number. It will be our number, and we'll love it with all our heart. Out of all those billions of numbers, this one alone will have a face. I'll let you pick."

"Two hundred and thirty-nine: the number of poplars... Okay?"

"Okay. Berenice's and Constance Chlorus' number is two hundred and thirty nine. May the geese and all the other birds spread the word! Sun, take note! Moon, take note!"

Constance Chlorus is thrilled with it all. She stands up. With her hands cupped around her mouth, she repeats our number at the top of her lungs until her voice breaks. We each arm ourselves with a sturdy dead branch and, for fun, we start tracing the biggest two hundred and thirty-nine ever in the rock-hard sand.

One cat chases the next. So-called Three succeeds late Mauriac II. Three came to us by mail from Abyssinia, like a letter. With its slender build and its fierce look, Three looks more like a panther than a cat. As hard as shells, as large as barn doors, standing on end, its triangular ears are unlike anything I've ever seen in the animal world. Looking good, Three! It'll be a fun fight! Wherever a cat comes from, be it Abyssinia or elsewhere, its days are numbered when I'm around.

36

Today is Friday. Mousermoth and Three are waiting for me in the snow-covered jeep. I slam the door in Dame Ruby's face, run, and hop in, forgetting Constance Chlorus; we head for the train station to wait for Christian. When I see his hunched back and shifty eyes, I understand that Christian hasn't yet managed to confess his sins of lust.

"You're still unwell, darling, aren't you?"

Once again, Mousermoth inquires in vain about the true nature of his distress.

"Stick out your tongue!" she orders him callously.

Looking pitiful, he stretches out his tongue a bit.

"That's nothing!" decides Mousermoth, inspecting the tip.

She lifts his right eyelid, then his left.

"Tongue is fine, eyes are fine, forehead is fine; it's hard to tell… Got it: it's a heartbreak. Could you have fallen in love with someone other than me?"

Christian's ears turn red. Playing the femme fatale, Mousermoth takes a step forward with her hands on her hips, puffing up her breasts and shaking her mane.

"What does she have that I don't have?" she asks, throwing him a sad look from her pretty blue eyes.

With all that funny business, she eventually succeeds in cheering him up to her liking. And, while she showers him with kisses, now reassured, Three is spreading terror among incoming and outgoing passengers. Terror is not too strong a word, trust me! Some are climbing up the Threes. The faintest of heart may spend Three months in the hospital. In a nutshell, it's worse than the Peach Three War. We head down to the cellars. We carve our way through the dark, into the abandoned crypt. We sit down face to face in our rat clinic—also abandoned. Like every Saturday for the past month and a half, we go through the dress rehearsal of "The Confession of Sins Christian committed with Mingrelia."

"Father, I accuse myself of kissing my cousin five times on the mouth. Repeat after me. Close your eyes and repeat. When your eyes are shut, you're alone. If you close your eyes at the confessional, there'll be no one else but you. Repeat: Father, I accuse myself…"

Obedient as ever, Christian squeezes his eyes shut and repeats.

"Father, I accuse myself of kissing Mingre… my cousin five times on the mouth."

"Father, I accuse myself of seeing my cousin almost naked once."

"Father, I accuse myself of seeing my cousin… I'll never be able to do it! It's no use!"

"You're alone in the world, Christian. You're the only person on Earth. Who are you so afraid of? Father, I accuse myself of having impure thoughts about my cousin thirteen times. Come, Christian. It's only me. Don't be scared. There's no one here but you."

"Father, I accuse myself of having impure thoughts about my cousin thirteen times. You're right, Berenice. I *am* alone. I can't count on anyone but myself. If I don't confess to those profanities, nobody will do it for me, nobody will go to hell for me. Father, I accuse myself of taking communion seven times in mortal sin… He'll never absolve me. I'll never be able to do it! It's no use."

"I'm sure he'll absolve you. Didn't you tell me that Christ redeemed all the sins of the world when he died on the cross?"

"That doesn't mean *everyone* is granted absolution."

"Christian Einberg, you told me yourself that God only refused to forgive those who wouldn't repent. That's not your case. You repent so much that you'll end up mad. You're just complicating things at will."

"You don't know everything. The sins I've been keeping from you are far more disgusting than those I confessed."

"Tell me everything, Christian! If you're still so sad, it's precisely because you haven't told me everything. Pour your heart out. Unload it all on your little sister. Your heart will feel so light once it's empty. Your burden is too great to bear. Unload it all on your little sister. Let go of it all. Leave your burden in her useless arms."

I sit down on the floor at his feet. I hug his legs, pressing my head against them. One minute, my heart suddenly feels full of cynicism. The next, my heart suddenly feels full of compassion, of kindness, of mercy.

"Then again, Mingrelia was so pretty. If I were you, I'd be proud of it, brag about it. I'd go running to the priest. And instead of telling him: Father, I accuse myself... I'd say, Father, I congratulate myself... You think you're filthy. If you ask me, I think you're lucky. Not all boys get to kiss such a pretty girl on the mouth. I'm so ugly. I don't care. I don't need to be pretty. I'm your sister... Shhhh! Listen... Listen... I hear steps... Someone's coming..."

Christian hears the steps. He blushes, grows nervous, tries to pry his legs away from my head. I fight back, tightening my squeeze and pushing my head harder into his legs. The more he struggles to set himself free, the more I struggle to hold him captive. We break into a ridiculous fistfight.

"That's why you're hiding!" shouts Einberg, outraged, brutal, hateful, arrogant, convinced he caught us off guard.

Today is Sunday. Christian is going to mass. I take him aside to urge him one last time to be wise, to be brave.

"Shut your eyes. Squeeze them tight shut. Tighter. There's no one else but you. Imagine that you are in the rat clinic, that I'm the only one listening. She was so pretty."

Under Einberg's furious stare, I walk along with Christian and Mousermoth to the other side of the bridge. Christian is shaking like a leaf, as though he were about to be scalped. Before I leave him, to give him confidence, I madly, desperately seize his hand with both of my hands and give it a kiss.

"Berenice!" Mousermoth cries out, looking exasperated. "I've had enough of your little schemes. Children, there's nothing I hate more than shifty, devious hypocrites."

"What's going on between you and your brother?" Einberg asks me, grabbing me by the arm. "Go on! Speak! What's going on between the two of you lately?"

"Nothing…" I answer, making the face I make when I'm lying.

"I smell a Brückner rat! Confess! They're trying to make you convert! They're conspiring!"

"Religion has nothing to do with it! I'm fed up with all your religions!"

There you have it! Christian has crossed the Rubicon! He has come back from church transformed, radiating freedom and joy. How happy that makes me! I throw myself into his arms.

"I'm so happy! At last! At long last!"

I give him a long, passionate hug, so that Mousermoth and Einberg can't help but wonder and take offence, and feel targeted. Like in the rat clinic this afternoon, Christian anxiously seeks a way out. But I can hold my ground.

37

Three, Mousermoth and I see Christian off at the train station. Everything is snowed in: the sky, the jeep, my arms, my ears. I then fall back into my room, into my bed, into silence. In all that void, only my heart is moving. In all that stillness, my heart feels like a fish stuck in air, a bird stuck in water. I unwittingly, incessantly think of Christian. His image keeps striking my soul like a hammer strikes a nail, inescapable, gruesome, repulsive. The same thing happens every time. As soon as I'm back in my room, alone, he starts to fill my heart and head, making them swell until it hurts. The longer it takes to fall asleep, the more the thought of him grows strong, sharp, insistent, the more it hurts. It's silly. I'm well aware that I wouldn't care about him at all if he were still here. When he's here, instead of brimming over with him, my heart and head are fully devoid of him. It's dead silly. There's no peace of mind, no sleep. I get up, turn the light back on, and sit down at my desk to write him a passionate letter, a long, crazy letter, a string of screams ending with a death wish. The next morning, I feel silly for writing that letter drenched in blood and tears; I destroy it, filled with hatred. But tonight, my despair is greater than ever. And I will mail that letter soaked with blood and tears—out of cynicism, out of self-hatred, in full surrender to the Master of Mockery.

"Christian! Christian! Come and get me! I am burning up! Come and get me! I am erupting! I give myself up to you with every fibre of my being! I give you my heart and soul! Come and take me! Come and save me! My love! My precious love! My darling! My sweet darling! You cannot possibly not want me! I am so pretty! I am so rich! I am full of fuel, vinegar and acid! Come and get me! You will make millions out of me! My friend! My dear friend! I shall shoot and strangle anyone who stands in our way, I shall pump potassium cyanide into their boiled potatoes! To love is to choose someone and let that someone take you. Come and take me! I love you! I need you! Carve your way through the dark and show your face! Come! Come! Come! Do you not recognize me? Do you not know who I am? I am the madwoman trapped within me! I am your friend, your love, your angel, your sweet, your mother, your brother, your sister Berenice. How is the weather over there? It is awful over here. Over here, it is discrustickinasting!"

I'm not stupid. When I entrusted Einberg with the task of mailing my letter, I very well knew that he wouldn't resist the desire to open it, and that after reading it, he wouldn't resist the desire to make a scene. Mrs. Glengarry is coming to dinner. I walk over to the table laughing up my sleeve. I sneak a peek at Einberg: he's laughing up his sleeve. Everything is right on track, Tanyatuva! After he's done eating his boiled potatoes, Einberg raises his arms, calling for silence and attention. All smiles, Mrs. Glengarry, peacemaker extraordinaire, friends with both the Guelph and the Ghibelline, puts an immediate stop to a fascinating dissertation on roses, determined to hang on to the Guelph's every word. Taking his sweet time, dragging it out, the Guelph now pats his thick flabby lips dry with his dainty batiste napkin. We're all ears. He then wipes his little lamb chin. He pulls out my letter from his jacket's inner pocket. He unfolds it. He proceeds to read it, in a tense, monotonous voice.

"Christian... Christian..."

He's reading slowly, interspacing words with long floating pauses, and sentences, with endless pauses, staring diabolically at Mousermoth. He only lifts his eyes from the page to shoot her evil, hateful glares. He's only sprinkling his performance with such long pauses to spare enough time to eyeball her like she deserves, voraciously, as violently as if he were punching her. He's completely unaware of Mrs. Glengarry and me: we're of no concern to him at all.

"Over here... it is... discrus... ticki... nasting..."

As Mrs. Glengarry walks around the table to give Mousermoth a warm neck hug, Einberg starts staring at me.

"You're the one who wrote all that filth, correct?"

"Yes! I did! And this is not my first rodeo! You missed my best lines!"

"What does that mean?"

He gets up from his seat and leans toward me, ready to pounce, just in case.

"Whatever you want, you monster! I love Christian! And if it bothers you, I'm glad! That makes me love him, adore him, worship him a hundred times more!"

Curious to see how I'm doing, I look over at Mousermoth and Mrs. Glengarry. It's as if they were standing on the tips of their eyes. Mrs. Glengarry seems perfectly lost. Mousermoth tries to understand me, support me, but she's overwhelmed.

"Christian is your love, isn't he... your precious... your sweet..."

"He's much more, much worse than that. He's like a husband to me..."

Einberg is comforted by my arrogance, by my ability to support and flesh out his theory. He straightens up and sits back down, relaxing. He wants to laugh, but he holds back.

"And what is love, exactly?" he asks me in a saucy voice.

"Don't you know, you old geezer? It's what you have with your mistress."

I didn't mince my words. Pleased with myself, I throw a wide look at each of their faces. Mrs. Glengarry is compassionately rubbing Mousermoth on the back. Mousermoth herself is leaning on the table with her head buried into her folded arms, shaken with sobs. As for Einberg, he's tapping victoriously on the edge of the table.

"Well!" he says. "Very well! We'll advise. We will indeed. Something is clearly wrong with this household. Changes, big changes will be made."

Mousermoth leaves the dining room, bent over in half, supported by Mrs. Glengarry. Dishevelled, her dress half undone, Mousermoth is lying face down, crying in her hide nest. Downstairs, Mrs. Glengarry, with her perfectly curled, perfectly fried hair, is lecturing Einberg, scolding him. What a mess! What a mess! I collapse on my bed and slip under the covers with my clothes still on. Lying flat on my stomach, like Mousermoth, I'm under the very distant illusion that I am her. I try to cry like her. I fail. A thousand hours later, I get up and switch the light back on. Where can I find peace or sleep? I open the door, the window. I open my dresser's drawers. I open books. I find nothing anywhere. As I open the closet, my eyes fall on my skates. My skates inspire me. Let's go skating, on and on, until I fall dead or asleep on the ice! I put my skates on, lacing them up. Winded by the task, I let myself fall back on my bed. I shut my eyes. I feel sleep seeping into me like water. I wrap the covers tight around my body and doze off.

38

Einberg calls me into his study and makes me shut the door. He tells me to sit down. I remain standing. I answer that I only sit down when I feel safe. He leans forward, resting his elbows on the chrome surface of his oak desk. And, skimming the lines with the tip of his gold stiletto, the one with the gypsum handle, he starts reading aloud from his first edition Bible. If he carries on like that, he'll go through the whole Book of Ruth. I'm shifting my weight from one foot to the other. In a proud motion, I square my shoulders. In a desperate motion, I let them sink. I cross and uncross my arms. I rub and rub my eyes. He reads slowly. His reading, it seems, must last as long as infinite bliss should last.

And Obed begat Jesse, and Jesse begat David.

"You're leaving for New York on the 24th. This isn't a holiday. No. You'll be there to stay. You're to leave this home, this hell. You're switching families for a long time, for a number of years, maybe for life. Desperate times call for desperate measures."

He pauses to yawn. He must be bored or tired.

"There will be major changes when you're gone. Your mother is a misfit, a lunatic, an overgrown child. Our marriage was bound to fail… One day you'll understand. I'm entrusting you to a family of saints. Try to make yourself worthy of their hospitality. With them, you'll come to your senses, you'll learn how to live a good life, how to think good thoughts, how to behave well, eat well and sleep well. We might see each other again… In a year or two. Forget the life you were given to live here, and fast. Forget this island and this creepy abbey, forget your brother, your mother… And if it's not too late already, you may very well get to lead a healthy, happy life. That'll be all, my child."

Let's quickly switch topics. Anyone who listens to Dame Ruby spout all that stern, scholarly nonsense for days, weeks, or months on end will want to commit suicide. To survive, Constance Chlorus and I came up with a code, games, a black market of shenanigans, a clandestine trade of kind words. We enjoy surreptitious dialogues the most. A surreptitious dialogue is a perilous exchange of scandalous lines scribbled on scraps of paper.

Here's my slip: "Away from you, dear Dame Ruby, my sterling beauty, I float adrift, and I might as well say it, fall apart. Since we started meeting but every five minutes, each day feels like a century. You are still glowing with youth. I have one foot in the grave. When you grow one century older every day, cruel love of mine, you cannot grow old very long. What has become of the Homeric times when we met every five seconds?"

Her slip: "Shut up, Eliezer, and wipe that blackboard! Rub it! Harder! Don't be shy! You won't wear it down! It can outlive seven times seventy old wrecks like you! And stop dragging your feet like that! It distracts the students!"

Mine: "Pretty Dame Ruby! What has become of your grace, your mirth and your ample girth? What of the day you were so heavy that, stepping on it by mistake, you blew up the scale meant to weigh the trucks that carry the iron meant to fill my late father's fob pockets with gold?"

Hers: "Now you accuse me of marrying you for your father's money! You are wide off the mark, old fool! Your ramblings are turning to mush, old duteous dog! I only married you because I needed a hand to wipe that blackboard!"

Mine: "Baby, oh baby, please remember! You opened your eyes so wide when I wrapped my arms around your neck that your glasses, the beautiful focus spectacles you used to wear at the time, exploded like a football whose pressure rises in the summer heat, under the repeated touch of the players' hands."

Hers: "No footballs in the classroom! Quick! Hand me that vulgar thing! And you can kiss it goodbye! I will burn it!

The nerve! I could have swallowed my dentures whole, my rotten verdigris-ridden false teeth! Don't you dare do that again, you worn blackboard wiper, you wannabe athlete, you weightlifter who can't lift his own weight! When words must be wiped off the blackboard, make them gone! When there are none, make yourself gone! Go stand behind the door and don't say a word until I call you back! Blackboard wipers are meant to wipe blackboards, not drop footballs in full view of children who haven't eaten for two days!"

Mine: "You are making a mountain of a molehill, my beautiful wilted beanpole. Those children do nothing but eat. Take little Constance Chlorus. She looks like an ogress next to you. Of course, it should be noted that apart from your big toes, nothing in your body is really really big or very very obese."

Hers: "Watch out, Berenice! She saw us!"

39

Have I lost the inward curve of Mousermoth's back? Does that mean I'll never see her wondrously hollow back again? Today, on the eve of my great departure, I feel strong, able to laugh. My room is full of suitcases—I tower over it. I'm the queen of small, medium and large pieces of luggage. My proud luggage tribe obeys my will, my thrill. I've played a dirty trick on everyone: I am thrilled, I am strong. Let's go, sweet suitcases! When are we actually leaving? Where is that famous departure so we can shower it with laughs? I'm raving mad. I stand up on my bed and start stomping, my mouth foaming with laughter. I jump up and down, throw punches, salute à la Hitler, bow before roars of cheers, shake hands with Blalabaleva, Sargatatalituva, Skararotukiva, Sinoiroisardan, Allagatatolaliev, and other merry men. I am Berenice the Great, the victoriose, unbridable baredevil! I am Berenice across the St. Lawrence River, throughout the Milky Way. I am Berenice all the way, down to the four little black feathers lost among my pillow's billion little white feathers. Come and get it, you filthy humans, you withering goners! The little speech Einberg gave me two days ago left me depressed, deeply disappointed, despite me knowing he could never love me, despite him proving it over and over. Yet I still thought that I made him feel *something*, that because he was my father, he had to be overcome with some kind of animal warmth, some kind of blood affinity. I was dead wrong, which is why his speech was so terrifying yesterday. I could barely hear him. His voice seemed to be coming from the depths of an abyss, from the other end of a desert. My ears floated in a void. My ears were in one place, and his voice was elsewhere. My father's voice was not in my father's house, but in the house of perfect strangers. Yet how could I blame Einberg for being unfeeling? How could I blame him for being so effortlessly unfeeling, when I wish I could effortlessly disregard him myself? I love everyone. I'm an easy girl. Life is no cakewalk for us easy girls.

It's high time that I rifle through the barrel of my soul and regroup. No more dithering. Nothing matters here but me. I'm inevitably, hopelessly alone. If I can't stay true to this truth, I'll be a consenting sap, the biggest sissy ever born. I'm alone. That's no war cry or death rattle. None of that, please. Let it be like a finger count. This hand has one, two, three, four, five fingers. How many are we here? We are one… How many soldiers are in this camp? One. I'm alone. It's a simple calculation, a simple headcount. Nothing else.

Come here, Christian! Come here! Hurry! So I can turn you into a god! Hurry! So I can grovel to your feet, so I can let myself fall into your arms and be freed from that burden! Hurry, you small sickly swallow! So I can pick you up and make you eat from my hand, and warm you up, and shield you from harm. Easy, there. Don't fight it. There! Covered with blood from fighting my last battle over you, I'm now your mistress by warmth and weakness. Hurry! So we can sit alone with each other, under this elm, while the others fight each other under the burning sun! Hurry! Before I must, for your sake, go back to battle! Hurry! Before you deny it! Hurry! Before you realize what a wreck I'm turning you into, and foolishly, stupidly take offence!

I won't be alone in my exile. I'll be with Constance Chlorus. I have Mousermoth to thank for that charming sweetener. After two days of hard-fought struggle, she snatched her from the jealous hands, alive and dead, of her large family, and managed to convince her sworn enemy to make the necessary arrangements himself for her to be given a proper welcome in New York. What a gem you are, Mousermoth. I guess I should thank you now, show gratitude, feel a bond, show my love. That last shot across the bow was for nothing, Mousermoth. You missed me: you always have and always will. You're fighting in vain. Shoo! You'll never have me! All your devotion, your favours, your hugs, your pretty eyes are just tricks, hooks, fences, and chasms. I am not Christian. For me, a trap is a trap, be it pretty or not, good or evil, just or unfair; a trap has teeth, a web has tangles. Those who want me want to hurt me. You'll never have my scalp. I am of those who'll bow before a slave and look a queen straight in the eye.

I may have just seen Christian for the very last time. Einberg specified that any letter we would write each other despite his ban would be intercepted and destroyed. We skated until dark. Ignoring his cries of protest, I walk into his room and lie down beside him. Before, he would say nothing when I came to sleep by his side. He now finds me queer, fears me even. His observations make me laugh up my sleeve.

"You love me too much, Berenice. And you're not natural…"

"I'm supernatural," I respond, stroking his forehead with one fingertip, shutting his eyes like the eyes of a corpse, so that he'll stay silent and go to sleep.

"You're not natural. You look like you're forcing yourself to love me, like you think you have to. You even look like you have something bad up your sleeve."

"When we see each other again, I'll be a woman, and you'll be a man. It'll be a great surprise! Write to me. I'm sure Mother will find a way for you to get my letters and for me to get yours. You don't trust me, do you?"

"You think this is funny? Is this a joke to you?"

"Close your eyes, sweet brother. Go to sleep. Don't fight it. Let my hand help you to sleep."

"I really don't get you anymore. I really don't."

"I'm evil."

I'm pregnant upon leaving the bed of my childhood. My belly is about to burst. Crimes have nested in my loins—they're now growing, thriving. It shall not be pretty when I give birth! And they shall tremble when I stroll down the sidewalk with my swarm of crimes. And if they do not, they shall vomit or spit in my face.

40

Crowned with phylacteries, we pray every morning and every night. Now that's saintliness. It's no joke. We get to New York City like whales in an aquarium: cramped. We get to Zio's like tuna stuck in a tin of sardines in oil. There's no room in the ninth cage of the ten-cage prismatic columbarium where he's put up his brood. Those who live in igloos, Miss Berenice, do you know what they're called? They're called Inuit, Ma'am. And those who live in tenements, Miss Berenice, do you know what they're called? They're never called, Ma'am, they're not worth it. They're people, Miss Berenice, human beings! You tell tall tales, Miss Berenice, tall tales indeed! My cousins wear multi-coloured skull caps, like bishops. And they only take them off to sleep. At the end of their shaven temples, they grow out ridiculous, caudal ringlets. Zio didn't put his family up at the top of this columbarium because he's poor. No. He's quite rich. He's put them up there out of saintliness. When you're a saint, you must look poor. Those who, based on hearsay, question the saintliness of Zio and his brood, should just come and see for themselves. Zio's long moth-eaten beard and his sons' pigtailed temples are categorical, they leave no room for doubt. In my mind, saints or not, they're monkeys. Mammoths! Rabbits! Pigs! I'm vulgar. Ever since I've been living saintly, I've grown vulgar—out of austerity, not avidity.

Zio, Zia, and our two male, and two female cousins welcome us most warmly. They shake our hands to pieces. They're delighted to make our acquaintance.

"Pleased to meet you. Hope you like it here. Come on in. Let me show you to your room."

They're dead friendly. Dead happy. They're dead happy because they're dead saintly. They're dead saintly because they're dead welcoming. You should set foot into this house as though you were stepping into a crocodile pit or a hippo swamp. Right from the threshold, you can see their hearts open huge maws full of sharp swords, prey-trapping pitchers set to swallow you whole. When I walked into this house, I closed up like an oyster in danger. They're much too nice. And I've never trusted human touch. A touch is a breach, an opportunity for deception, disappointment, bitterness. Before my cousins, I display a slight hostility tinged with deliberate indifference. I have cousins for nothing. My cousins are good-for-nothing. I want nothing to do with them, nothing from them. Dear cousins, just pretend you don't exist!

I'm learning Hebrew. It's compulsory. Most exciting. When I know Hebrew, Zio will reward me. He will grant me the honour of adding me—like his wife, his sons, his daughters, and Constance Chlorus—to the list of those who have the privilege to read aloud from the Bible before dinner.

The room we were assigned is a famous room. Historically reserved for philanthropic purposes, it's filled with the ghosts of the lamest, saddest children ever. The last two who stayed in this room—two sisters, daughters of drunkards—met an unfortunate end. They were found dead one morning with their mouths half eaten, their lips gnawed, torn to shreds, bleeding from nose to chin. In a fit of despair, they silently broke the lower pane of the guillotine window and quietly chewed away the glass, shard by shard. Zio doesn't approve of me reading Homer and Virgil, that Turk and that Italian. But his irritation only whets the shady appetites he and his holey saints have awoken within me.

Still, now, tonight, as I rest my legs against the cold little legs of Constance Chlorus, I feel calm, pretty, holier than thou, almost happy. I object! I have no right to feel almost happy. It's ludicrous! Illogical! What? Me… happy? After all they've done to me? I discard those ludicrous, illogical feelings. I recall hate and despair at the top of my lungs. In the heart of an ugly girl like me, born for nothing else but pain, there's only room for hate and despair. Quick! I must start to cry and grind my teeth again! They took my brother! They took my mother! They took my island! They banished me! They locked me up with holey saints!

"We couldn't care less about that," answers my voice. "We're almost happy tonight, resting our legs against the cold little legs of Constance Chlorus."

That can't be true! What else have they done to me? Oh Satan! Help me remember!… I'll take back what they took from me! I'm regaining my strength... I feel wings growing at my body's expense, spreading out, swelling randomly in the gusty wind until they tear me away from the ground. I'm making myself free. I grow claws as well. They're already coming out of my fingertips, their ivory tearing apart the ugly, filthy molting that is my skin. They're already twisting my fingers, tensing my palms. Soon I'll be able to look straight at the sun without being dazzled, like an eagle. What a queer dream I'm having... I'm in a huge hypostyle temple. I'm at the end of a long cloister with cross vaults so high as to make my head spin. Mousermoth is holding a black and yellow snake hissing with rage. She ties the snake around my hips and it turns into a belt of icy stones. Suddenly, as though I were to be knighted, I'm down on my knees and she touches my shoulders with the flat of a heavy rapier. Like the stone-belt, the sword is ice cold. I turn around. The lower windowpane is broken and the wind is blowing snow right under the covers. Mousermoth again. Nursing me. Her milk is wonderfully warm. Her breast becomes a crystal ball clutched in the hooked fingers of a witch. Once inside the ball, I dive into a thick forest where I see an ugly creature running; although it has no head or arms, it laughs loud enough to burst my eardrums as it strokes my forehead with its fingertips.

41

Light has taken shape, released from the ocean of air that gave it the ethereal quality of shadows. The sun has iron spokes. The moon has wooden spokes, like a carriage wheel. I'm calm. I'll never scream again. I understand it all. I know. When you know where and who you are, you can pounce like a cat on a bead rolling on the floor, pretending it's a dragon. Once you understand yourself, you can run all over the great armillary sphere, pretending that, like a caged squirrel, you're playing and being played. You must first understand if you want to own yourself. The only hands that can catch life are inside your head, inside your brain.

I'm not in charge of myself and couldn't be. Like everything that's been made, like that chair or that heater, I'm fully unaccountable. A bullet that hits an animal right through the heart isn't guilty. It was shot and couldn't avoid its target. I was pushed and can't avoid my path. Smarter than a hail of bullets, I might want to fight the push and hit other targets, but my flesh and blood are packed with one track, and I can't change its course any more than a sealed bottle can change contents. In other words: I was made to be Berenice like the heater was made to be a heater. I might resist Berenice and try to become otherwise, but, like a heater will never turn into a boa, I'll never turn into Constance Chlorus. When you were made indifferent, mean, and hard, you can't be sensitive, kind, and soft. How can things hurt you if they're meaningless? You can resist being mean, but you'll still be mean. A stone can strive for softness, but it will stay hard. A wine lover can't avoid loving wine. A wine hater can't avoid hating wine. You're done. Period. You're a heater. You can't do anything about it. Humans are the only heaters who can kick up a fuss, bend out of shape. A human is a heater that may not be content with its own shape and want to assume others. But a sardine swimming up a fuss in the sea still won't make waves. To be someone is to have a destiny. Having a destiny is like having only one destination. When you only have Budapest, you have one alternative: either you go to Budapest or you don't. You can't go to Belgrade. I'm not guilty of anything I do: I've never wanted to be or had time to want to.

You're not born upon your birth. You're born a few years later, when you realize you're alive. I was born around five, if I remember right. Five years old is too old to be born, because at that age, you already have a past, and your soul has taken shape. The second a butterfly is born, it tries out its wings. The very first thing it does is dive into the sky, punch-drunk. Butterflies are pretty. When I was born, I thought I had a choice, and chose to be a butterfly with yellow-orange stained-glass wings. Then, supremely confident, without giving it a second thought, I jumped off the roof of my dungeon. Unfortunately, I was no butterfly. I was a buffalo. Or a rhino, truth be told. For half a decade, I was something other than a butterfly. What was bound to happen did: I crashed on a parvis, and the parvis split in half, and I ended up in the hospital. When you're a rhino, it's no use trying to fly. What did I ever do to be fitted with a rhino shield? What did I do so wrong to deserve such a thing? I asked myself so many questions! So many theories ran through my mind! I told myself so many stories! It's all over now. I now understand.

When I was born, I was five years old, I was someone: I was swimming in the deepest depths of my destiny, in the strongest current of my cravings, grudges, fellow humans, and filth. I screamed in horror, in vain. I swam against the stream like a maniac, in vain. I was mad. I tired out; that's all.

Here's what I am: a cloud of arrows that think, that know they're flying and can see their targets. Therefore I can think. I'm thinking! Thinking! And what am I thinking? What a great question! I think it's time to think about playing, about having fun. I just have one face that I didn't make, but I can choose to pull thirty different faces. Which one will I choose? What a great question! I choose laughter. Laughter! Laughter is the symbol of light. When light suddenly fills the dark the child was so afraid of, she bursts into laughter. I want to rip out some nails with pliers, saw some ears with a razorblade, kill humans and hang a garland of corpses from the picture rails all over my walls. I want to burn villages and bombard cities. I want to shake the sea surface, crush continents against one another, fly across the universe on the back of a star like you slide across a torrent on the back of a rock. I'll do all that, just so I can laugh! Laugh! Laugh to death!

Let's switch topics. Let's move away from theory and turn to tactics. I send long letters to Christian, c/o Mousermoth. What's most important is not that Christian should receive the letters, since they're not real. What's most important is that Mousermoth or Einberg read them and get scandalized, dispirited, stunned, disgusted. I received nothing from Christian. Mousermoth's three words are all I've received from my lost loved ones over the past three months. I can still see the blue envelope that contained those three words, trembling in my hand. The stamp, the beautiful big stamp from Czechoslovakia, is all askew, stuck upside down in the lower left corner. I try in vain to decipher the postmark. I don't open the blue envelope just yet. I play greedy. I lay it down on the *bonheur du jour*, throw myself backwards on my bed and, folding my hands behind my head, I look at it lying on the *bonheur du jour*, waiting, getting restless. "My dear, I will return to America in a couple of months. Then, I will come and knock on the thick wall that was erected between us. Do not be mean to me. Do not be needlessly hard on yourself. You will not turn a deaf ear. You will come running. Between the both of us, we will soon bore a hole in that wall, big enough for us to hold hands again. I need you even though you may not need me. Mom." My dear…! In a fit of rage, I tear the letter into a thousand confetti. I regret it immediately, feeling warm and fuzzy to tears. And, in a fit of pity as strong as my previous fit of rage, I shower the envelope with kisses, determined to keep until the day I die the big, beautiful, multicoloured stamp picturing a miner cutting coal. Two days later, the stamp and Mousermoth mean nothing to me, and I drop the carefully preserved stamp through the cracks of a sewer grate. Besides, Mousermoth didn't put any return address. Mousermoth, Christian and Constance Chlorus suddenly make me hurt so much. Then they suddenly leave me so cold. They make me feel great pain, or absolutely nothing. I hurt either way. When they make me feel nothing, I hurt because I was wrong, because I said and thought things that have stopped being true, because I did things that are now meaningless, because I hurt for nothing. They leave me cold most of the time. When I hurt because of them, I scream, I squeal, I throw whining tantrums. I scream like someone who's just lost both arms. And what does it look like when the new armless fool, in the deepest pit of despair, once she's cursed and trashed every possible thing, once she's screamed all possible screams, suddenly sees her arms grow back, growing once more indifferent to said arms? It's quite funny. Dead funny. Time to laugh! How can Constance Chlorus stay so constant, so true to herself, so consistent in everything she does, says, and feels? How can Zio be so steadily saintly? How can so many cousins be of one single kind? They're all doing it on purpose! Constance Chlorus, as pale as fall pastures, as pale as sand, as ashes, as anything sterile. She's to leave me at the end of the month and come back to me in September. I madly love Constance Chlorus, yet she leaves me supremely cold. One minute I'm ecstatic about her great beauty, her great sensitivity, her great depth of thought, the next I couldn't care less about any of it. Naïve, selfless, she sacrificed herself for my sake: she gives me anything she can find, within herself or elsewhere, that could possibly please me. Clever, alert, she's never out of resources or surprises: one flattery chases away the next, one nonsense rolls off another. Only Constance Chlorus can claim she was born in 1687, a year when, according to her, there was no 4th of May. She stares at me intently, eagerly, her eyes suffering from some kind of nystagmus, as though she feared I could hit her.

"What I'm saying is silly, eh?"

"It's not silly, Constance Chlorus, because it's true. There was no 4th of May that year. What's so silly about that? If there wasn't any, that's the way it was. You were born in 1687, the year there was no 4th of May. I believe you, I promise. Don't you think I believe you?"

Constance Chlorus shakes her head in denial. She's glad: she tricked me. She made me talk. She watches me fire up, get sucked into the game.

"You're just trying to make fun of me."

"I'm not! I'm free to believe whatever I want, and I believe you. I believe with all my strength that there was no 4th of May and that you were born in 1687!"

"I believe you, Berenice. Isn't it wonderful to be able to believe all kinds of crazy things? Let's pretend to believe all kinds of crazy things, okay?"

"Let's believe that stars have eyes! That humans have three arms!"

She keenly replies to everything I say, and we pretend to believe in all kinds of crazy things until we're out of breath.

"Let me tell you really silly things... okay?"

"Nothing's silly!" I say bombastically, believing her clever language lures to be sincere, against my better judgement.

She takes place. Blushes. She concentrates as though she were about to recite something she learned by heart. She clears her throat. Begins.

"We're friends. You take me along and I take you along. We take a walk in my forest. I teach you the names of all my grasshoppers, of all my crickets. Grasshoppers have boys' names. Crickets have girls' names. Jean-Pierre feels you with his long limp antennas: he's grumpy and doesn't like strangers. 'Who's that?' 'My friend Berenice. You can trust her.' 'That friend of yours doesn't seem too nice. She hardly smiles.' 'Berenice hasn't had it easy. With her, you must smile first. Come on, Jean-Pierre, smile at her.' Marguerite arrives: she's an old gossip. She raises her long stiff spiky leg. 'Pleased to meet you, Miss. You're a friend of Constance Chlorus, I suppose? Berenice! You must be Berenice… She can't stop talking about you. Wait! Don't go! I'll get Yolanda, Eunice and Paulette.' Wasn't that story downright silly? I've said enough. Your turn! Come on! It must be downright silly. If it's not downright silly, it means you'll leave me one day."

Constance Chlorus knows as much as Christian. I'll have to introduce them at some point. She knows the Latin names of each of a beetle's twelve parts. She's a botany buff. A zoology whiz, if you will. Termites have kings and queens, and soldiers. Termite kings have wings, but termite queens don't. Termite queens are so fat they can barely move. Their white bellies are as big as a finger and their heads, as small as a fly's. Constance Chlorus told me all that.

Constance Chlorus scampers after me. When I walk faster, she scampers faster. When I cross the road, she crosses the road. She doesn't ask questions. She follows me quietly. She quietly scampers along, wherever I go. She'll only mention herself to ask if she's bothering me.

"I love you because you're sad, always sad, as sad as a sad picture."

42

Bitterly, I revisit every Saturday Christian and I have ever spent on the island. On Saturdays, we'd run from dawn into night. On Saturdays, we were so busy, in such a hurry that we'd lose our appetites. On Saturdays, we'd become raging truants. We'd tumble down those narrow nooks of books and desks, landing on allodiums of clamour and light. We'd skip all day like goats, from one discovery to the next. Always hungry for more.

Here, we have Shabbat on Saturdays. And all the biblical decrees for the day Moshe said should be devoted to boredom are strictly obeyed. Everything becomes *verboten*, especially anything that isn't hunger, thirst, silence or complete stillness. On Saturdays, Zio abstains from any type of food, be it solid, liquid or gaseous. He welds his lips and sews his nose shut so he won't swallow air. But, Yahweh be praised! He doesn't impose such extravagant fasting on the whole household. A few good turnip roots are usually left soaking in the kitchen sink. If you're not scared to let the others starve to death, you can get up extra early and grab a couple to stave off stomach cramps until evening. Tolerant to death, Zio doesn't just tolerate that we sink our teeth in turnip—he also tolerates that we sink our teeth in water. However, he won't suffer any offence committed against the laws he enacted to banish all non celestial light. On Saturdays, lighting a cigarette in the ninth cage of the columbarium is punishable by electric chair. You can't touch the refrigerator because the electric bulb inside will automatically turn on should you inadvertently open the door. When night falls and the street lamps and neon signs are about to turn on, all the blinds of all the windows have been pulled down in the ninth cage of the columbarium. Pulling up the blinds, even by mistake, is punishable by electric chair. Often, unable to resist the pleasure to take risks, I pull one up. I've survived quite a few electric chairs. I'm lucky: the light shining in Constance Chlorus' eyes is considered celestial.

When, after twelve hours spent in so-called meditation, the hour of salvation finally comes, it's welcome all right. When, tied to a chair and muzzled since sunrise, dying to laugh and run wild, vainly craving wilderness and wind, we're finally allowed to retire to our room, it's about time. We can't believe our legs as we sneak up to our room. Fearing that there's been a misunderstanding, that the great boredom isn't over yet and that they'll call us back, we sit down on the floor with our backs against the door, waiting for our doubts to subside. Five minutes have gone by without drama, so we let out big sighs of relief. We hug and pat ourselves on the back like hockey players who just scored a goal. Then, with infinite caution, taking off our shoes so as not to be heard, we step into a forbidden realm. Parting the heavy drapes with panache, I take in the town's nightly view as though there had never been anything behind those curtains, letting my eyes wallow in heaps of stars, in this heaven on earth. Meanwhile, playing hide-and-seek as always, Constance Chlorus has slipped under the bed. I call her, in vain, to amuse her. To amuse her, I pretend that I'm looking for her, unable to find her. I look everywhere, except under the bed. I look under the pillows, behind the calendar, inside the can sawed in half that we use as an ashtray. Suddenly, one of the studs of the piece of furniture I'm crawling under resonates loudly as I hit my head. Constance Chlorus can't contain herself anymore—she bursts out laughing. Her laugh, fitful and quick, is infectious. Her laugh, a marmot whistle, takes my laugh by the hand, dragging it on a mad race. Let's dive into the thick of the story. Fearing that it might escape, Constance Chlorus folded all of her ten fingers around the tiny candlestick we plucked from one of the branches of the seven-branch candelabra. It is fire, light, evil. I strike the match. The sulphur head cracks, bursts, ignites. Our hearts are beating on empty. Our eyes blink and itch. With our mouths open from all that soul struggling to commune with what we're seeing, we watch the fire engraft its inflorescence to the white wood, enfolding it, blackening it. We watch the flaming petal split in two, leap, and land like a bird on the tip of the tiny candlestick's black wick. Constance Chlorus blows on the match, and we can hear the fire crack like a whip, roar like a motorbike. As I look into Constance Chlorus' big black eyes, I suddenly see my face and the candle reflected on both surfaces. Like spherical mirrors, Constance Chlorus' eyes are distorting my face, shrinking my own eyes, already too small, magnifying my nose, already too big. Constance Chlorus' eyes are like tunnels. The opening is different from the middle and the end. Looking into Constance Chlorus' eyes is killing me. It's so... fascinating. No, it doesn't fascinate me. It swallows, chokes, smothers me. I tell Constance Chlorus that I want to beat her up and kill her. We've been stealing all week. We sit down on the floor in the middle of our room and proudly display, between our embracing legs, the inventory of our robberies: meat, fruit, vegetables and sweets. We stole from butchers, greengrocers, candy makers and bakers. We stole from everyone. Our tummies rumble. We eagerly devour it all, swallowing without chewing. With our oesophagi blocked, our cheeks swollen like balloons, and our hands brimming with food, we both cast mean looks at each other, coveting the Hungarian sausage, the damsons, or the nougat—objects of burning desires. At first, I had a hard time convincing Constance Chlorus to participate in these sabbatical orgies, despite her obvious aboulia. She didn't seem to object for specific reasons. When I offered her suggestions, she would only say she wasn't ready and ask me to wait a little longer. All of a sudden, as if some invisible object had just hit her in the head, she stops laughing and stuffing herself, and looks incredibly sad.

"I know you're making me do bad things, you know."

She spoke slowly, in a voice so soft, almost bitter from so much softness. Her words make me angry. She realizes it, hastily lays her head in penance wherever she can on my body, and to finish me off, claims that with me, she doesn't mind doing bad things. She fluffs the pillows, wraps me up in the covers like one would wrap a mummy in bandages. She kisses me on the forehead. Then, sitting down by my bed with her back real straight against the chair, she reads me her favourite poems as though she were reading to a queen. She's madly in love with Nelligan, with Émile, the poet who went mad upon reaching adulthood, the poet who would lock himself in churches at night to scream his verses at the Virgin Mary. The poems she reads to me as though I were a queen are the same that Dame Ruby would make me learn by heart when she got heated with me, but they couldn't be more different. I listen to them as though I were sinking my teeth into Constance Chlorus' big black eyes. When I would read "Wald-in Dreams" and "Sentimental Winter" aloud, they smelled sour like my breath and they made me sick. In her mouth, they taste like maple water and barley sugar: my eyelashes get wet, and I get goosebumps.

"Far windows limpid eyes whose looks I drain unsoiled by any gaze of commoner, with Norway ice the fields like metal are, may Winter chill warm up our hearts again, like troops mourning the wrecks of Theban war, let us, my pet, treat our rancours tenderly and, scorning life with its songs of sophistry, let good Death lead us down to Hades' door, you'll visit us like an icy spectre, we shall not be old, but weary of life's faults, come, Death, take us on such an afternoon, languid on the divan, lulled by her guitar, whose dreamy motifs and whose muffled tune keep time to our ennui..."

"It's beautiful, Constance Chlorus. So beautiful. Say again, *we shall not be old, but weary of life's faults*."

"We shall not be old, but weary of life's faults."

On occasion, she'll also read me a poem of her own. Around my neck, tied next to Christian's Zulu sun, I wear a genethliac speech she says she wrote thinking of our friendship. Here are the first four lines:

She was born. Oh, well! Oh, well! She is no more a lifeless stiff.

She was born, the little minx. And since that day, oh well!
She has been digging a hole—a grave, a great big well.

Yesterday she learned to walk! Today she's running off a cliff!

43

I think a lot, more and more each day. I think much better than those stale philosophers. Greek philosophers are philosophers from Greece. Italian philosophers are philosophers from Italy. Venetian philosophers are philosophers from Venice. Yet all of them are stale, sterile. They could all be from a country called the United Stales. Mixing imagination and will with a semblance of life can be delirious, become delirium, euphoria. And that idea is fruitful, very fruitful indeed, quite flexible, quite rich: it offers a thousand alternatives to loneliness and fear. When I admit that one plus one makes two, no delirium ensues. When a theorem is proven to me, some delirium may ensue. I've discovered that the more difficult it is to understand a theorem, the more delirium ensues from understanding it, the more a theorem challenges my will and my imagination, the more delirium it arouses in me. And based on that realization and the experiments that followed, I've concluded that there was delirium in me and that, for it to expand fully, for it to thrive, I had to give outrageous free rein to my will and imagination. It's not too clear.

I look at a city: it's black and grey as far as the eye can see, it's mighty, mighty far from my hands and my words. I could hack at it, yell at it in vain. I look at it and feel anxious, then weary, then bored. If I only look at the city, I can't have it any other way. Because a look, alone, opens a breach in the looker, an unconditional surrender, a loosening of the fabric allowing the city to penetrate the body like wind through open windows, and seize it. If, on the contrary, I look at the city and claim that it's half green, half blue, holding it like a gem in the palm of my hand, I experience a delirium akin to that of salvation or conquest.

I don't know what Mousermoth is thinking or doing right now. I don't know who owns the universe or which master I should serve. I don't know the source or purpose of my life. I don't know against what or whom I should shoulder arms. Should I stare blissfully at my own ignorance and let it drown me? No! Should I, like that famous poet, stare still at the shady saxifrage, waiting still until it tells me why it makes me feel something? No! I take stands, with all my soul. I establish certainties, with all my strength. That's what I do! I randomly change the shape of anything that's too insubstantial, too immense, impossible to grasp... and then, thanks to that new shape, I can grasp that thing, seize it with my hands, my arms, but especially my mind. To make up for my inability to act on life's intangible things or events, I define them, writing them in black on white, and subscribe with all my soul to the whimsical or sinister images I conjured up of those things and events. For instance, I claim that Earth (that the best astronomers still don't understand) is an elephant head floating adrift in a river of skyblue ink... and then, in my mind, that's all it is. I claim that the moon is a skull stuck in a spider web hanging from the black ceiling of a room that is my own big bedroom. Stars stridulate when, in August, the night is in full swing: I claim that stars are grasshoppers and crickets. Darkness is a conurbation of black uhlans, a magma of black uhlans fleeing toward Quebec, Waterloo, Verdun. I claim that whatever touches my skin is a caterpillar. When Constance Chlorus kisses my forehead, I firmly believe that a caterpillar, an orange and black caterpillar, is crawling across my forehead. As for Mousermoth, I know exactly where she is, what she's doing, and what she makes me feel. Mousermoth is standing in the middle of a street somewhere in Denmark, waiting for me, motionless, and I hate her. I know I hate her now. I know what to do about her now: hate. The universe, for its part, is ruled by a Titan who tries to scare me, who wants me to submit to him. Now, I know the universe is someone else's home.

"And death?" asks Constance Chlorus softly. "What's death?"

"In lay terms, it's a defeat. In delirious terms, it's called a triumph. But it remains to be proven that death is a triumph, you may say. Proofs are meant to establish facts, as everyone knows. But what good are the proofs when you have all the facts? I know for a fact that death is a triumph. You want proof? It's right there, waiting for me to die to prove me right. Now *you* call death a triumph with all the strength you've got. That's all. Call death a triumph with all the faith you've got. Why should anyone call it a defeat?"

"Triumph!" says Constance Chlorus triumphantly. "What a pretty name! I had a dream: standing on its hind legs, a frog as tall as me hugged me. And the very pale green skin of that frog was tattooed with big red roses. The frog, like an old chair, looked like it was covered in tapestry."

"That wasn't a dream. That did happen to you. A frog met you, stood up on its hind legs and hugged you. Why should you only want to experience mundane things?"

"It was a real frog, then?" asks Constance Chlorus dreamily.

"The sky is full of flying forks and spoons. Anyone who can't see that must be as blind as a bat."

"Look, Berenice: There's a dirty racoon sitting on the *bonheur du jour*. Shhhhh!"

It's snowing for the first time this winter. On the edge of a snowy park generously sprinkled with fluffy light, a mother and her child are waiting for the bus. The child, drawn to the snow, unable to resist its pull, tears himself away from his mother and throws himself into it, laughing, swimming in it like in water, kicking, sinking, splashing, spattering about. When they saw Canada for the first time, they called it the New World. The park, newly strewn with snow, is the New Sea. Constance Chlorus and I run all over it, and the more ground we cover, the more we discover. We roll, we fight in the snow. We talk in the snow, look at each other in the snow... Everything we do in this first snow becomes fresh like snow, novel, new like snow. It's as though I'd never spoken to Constance Chlorus, as though I'd never set eyes on her. We're caught, trapped, swallowed by the snow. With a lump in our throats, heavy hearts and burning brows, wearing our souls on the skin of our hands and legs, we are smothered by snow. Crappy cow crap! Shitty snow! With our hands full of snow, our feet full of snow, our clothes full of snow, we still run around in snow, and snow remains a mystery. I open my satchel and, one by one, throw my schoolbooks and notebooks in the snow. Constance Chlorus, impressed, imitates me. Knackered, at the end of our wits trying to solve the mystery of snow, we pick up our schoolbooks and notebooks and walk back to the columbarium. It's quite insulting when you don't understand the first frenzy that comes with the first snow. Shitty snow! Crappy cow crap!

There's no one in the cage's dining room. The dresser is lying face down on the floor in the ruins of its stained-glass doors and Dresden china. A velour hat and a pair of thick-soled shoes garnish the mess. The den's double door is closed. Judging from the clamour and screams coming from the den, we'll soon be catching a few haters red-handed. I suddenly get up on my hind legs. There, among all the shouts, I recognize the voice of daddy dearest. We step in without knocking. We've just walked into a true tornado. Einberg is there all right, very much there. With split suspenders, loose shoelaces, and their guns upside down, the two officers fighting to restrain him aren't fit for the task. Einberg is shaking like the devil, like a barman shakes a shaker. He's roaring, growling, foaming, drooling. He's struggling like a cock who's just suffered Holofernes' fate. He's fighting them off with his arms, his legs, his stomach, his head. At the end of their strength and sweat, the officers pull out their clubs and start banging him loudly on the head. The stronger they hit him, the more he rebels. He's now biting off big chunks of air. My muscles are tense, vibrating like violin strings. I can feel my brain popping out of my skull. Suddenly, Einberg's glare, blazing with screams, lands on me. He grows still. What will he do? His face, twisted like a dying cat's, finally relaxes, and he bursts out laughing. Hanging on by a thread, my brain falls out and I start screaming, and I see myself go mad. With his hair standing on end, his glassy bloodshot eyes, his face covered in bruises, his clothes muddy and torn, he walks toward me, arms outstretched, laughing even more.

"Come here, dear, dear child! I'm your father, my dear, dear, dearest daughter."

Barefoot, he walks with difficulty, as though he were wearing skis. He's drunk. He smells pungent, foul. He falls on his knees. His trousers are split. The gaping slit reveals his drawers. He gets back up. Jumps forward. He's right in front of me, arms wide open, laughing his heart out. He's about to fall over me. I step back. He falls with a bang and, with a daunting belch, purges his bowels all over my feet.

I couldn't sleep at all last night. Neither could Constance Chlorus. I feel at once violent and unable to move. It's like I'm possessed: I'm filled with a volcanic strength, a painful strength that nothing in the world could unleash or appease. I roll over and bite myself, desperate to know what to do. I feel this strength burning in my stomach, this useless, endless, pointless strength, like some kind of nausea that never leads to vomit! Constance Chlorus is crying, hugging me, kissing me, at the end of her wits. She would do anything to afford me some relief, but there's nothing she can do; she's utterly powerless. She gives me pots to smash. She tells me to beat her up. She kneels down in the middle of the bed, hands me a pair of scissors and begs me to kill her. Kill me, Berenice. Take the scissors and kill me! Leave me alone, Constance Chlorus. Go hang yourself, Constance Chlorus.

44

"These were the sons of Hur, father of Etam: Jezreel, Ishma, Idbash; the name of their sister was Hazzelelponi." That's all the Chronicles say about Hazzelelponi. In vain, I read the three preceding and the three following pages. There's nothing more on Hazzelelponi. Hazzelelponi never slept or ate, or drank anything. She was neither pretty nor ugly. She never carried a sword or a jug over her head. As I see her, Hazzelelponi was the sister of Jezreel, Ishma and Idbash, period; that's all she was, nothing else. Twenty-four seven, she was just the sister of Jezreel and of the other two. How marvellous! I would love to be like her, to be a sister like a statue is a statue. I would love for everyone to know at first glance, when I walk by, that I'm Christian's sister and nothing else. When the heteromyarian see a flock of yponomeuta rain down on a pear tree in bloom, they can tell right away what they are. Heteromyarian don't say,

"Friends, come quick! A pack of wolves are attacking a fruit-bearing apple tree." No sir! They say, "Come quick! A flock of yponomeuta is raining down on a pear tree in bloom." I would like human beings to be able to tell that I'm Christian's sister just by looking at my face. You should be able to tell that I'm Christian's sister as easily as you can tell that the wind is blowing. What should I do for the simple fact that I'm Christian's sister to be written on my face? Should I wear a uniform, like sailors or rabbis? You can easily tell that a fairy is a fairy from her wand and her bare feet. Fish swim. Coligny chewed on toothpicks. Napoleon wore his bicorn sideways. What does a sister do? Must I, to make it clear once and for all that I'm a sister, let my hair grow in long sewing needles, like a hedgehog? Yes! If a pear tree started to bear apples, lemons, and pumpkins, nobody could tell it was a pear tree anymore. To be a pear tree and go on being one, you must bear pears and go on bearing only pears. To be Christian's sister, all the things I do must look like pears. When I'm a real grown up, I'll make sure to do just that. Now I know what to do with my life. How great that makes me feel! How relieved! If I had a sister, I would call her Hazzelelponi and she would be exactly like Hazzelelponi. She would be my sister, and nothing else. I'll claim to be a sister, Christian's sister!

"Prove your claim!"

"I'm not bearing a single plum. You can see with your own eyes that pears are my only fruit."

During Physics, I think of Hazzelelponi. It's crazy. I think of her and can't shake that thought. Pears are a silly answer, dead silly. I know that. But that's the only one I could find. Staring at the ceiling, I'm so angry with myself that I can't hear anything the Physics teacher is saying. So the teacher, in the stentorian voice of an infundibular infusorium, cries out my name:

"Berenice! Berenice! Berenice! What's wrong?"

"I have a problem."

And, fancying himself dead witty, he hands me a piece of chalk and invites me to write my problem down on the blackboard. Thirty head are better than one, etc. and so on... A smart aleck myself, I take his joke hieroglyphically (or literally, if you will), and stand up. "The world sticks to my skin like lice stick to your scalp. I've had enough. And sufficiently." Permeated with this grim hypothesis, I climb on the podium, take the piece of chalk, and draw something like an elephant head.

"This is Earth," I say. "Got it?"

Then, I draw a small triangle inside the elephant head.

"And this triangle is me, Berenice Einberg. As you can see, Earth surrounds me on each of my three sides, Earth squeezes me on all sides. I'm just a spot on Earth. I'm just a pimple Earth will absorb and be cured of. And that can be easily explained by its circular orbit, a movement which is not unlike that of a churner. Therefore, I'm not a free or independent being, but a filthy lump, a kind of wart with arms and legs, a filthy wart that grew from Earth, feeding directly from the filthy beast that is Earth. What must I do to be myself, in and of myself, and cease to be a mere parasite of the beast that is Earth? What should I do to stop depending on it all, all the time, for all things?

Every time the Earth shakes, you shake. Haven't you had enough? Wouldn't *you* rather be shaking the Earth? What can you do to be free? Miss Constance Chlorus, what's your answer?"

"To break free from Earth, you have to elevate yourself above Earth."

"That's one possible answer, but it's neither one of the two I'm thinking of. And only I can be right. Therefore, I give you a big fat zero. Sit down! I'm waiting! Anyone else has a stupid answer for me? No one? Excellent! Truly excellent! Truly excellent indeed! So, Constance Chlorus gets zero, and everyone else gets one hundred percent."

I turn back to the blackboard and, armed with my piece of chalk, ferociously cross out the elephant head, being very careful, however, not to touch the small triangle.

"Here's what I need to do to be free: destroy it all. I didn't say deny, I said destroy. I'm the artwork and the artist. Everything around me, everything I see or hear, is the marble from which I must escape—hacking, carving, sanding my way out. A marble block contains a bust, but on one condition: provided you sculpt it. Do you get it?"

"If you destroy it all, what will you feed on?"

"Nothing, you idiot! And I'll starve to death! But, for two whole days, I'll have been free!"

"That's not much fun. I'd rather stuff myself full."

"Well, my dear, I'd rather eat nothing than be eaten by Earth. But there's another way. I'm afraid it may not please the faint of heart."

At my request, Constance Chlorus comes and wipes the blackboard, then draws another elephant head. Inside the head, instead of drawing a small triangle, she draws a queen moth. I tell her she's very talented and send her back to her seat. She hands me back my piece of chalk. Our fingers touch, recognizing each other. I go back to her drawing and circle it several times until the outline of the moth contains the whole elephant head.

"Here's what I must do to be free: swallow everything, spread over everything, enclosing it all, ruling over everything, subjugating it all, from the pit of the peach to the pit of Earth itself. You can swallow militarily, administratively, judicially. People usually go for the second option. In fact, to some extent, we're all victims. Who isn't being militarily, administratively, judicially, economically or religiously swallowed? Who isn't being swallowed by a bishop, a general, a judge, a king, or some rich man? Hence the need to incorporate it all. But I'd rather destroy it all. I don't know why. It's faster, prettier, more selfless. It makes me want to laugh, if you will. After all, doesn't my first answer presuppose that ultimate victory is a perfect synonym for death?"

I'm much applauded. I'm banished from class for the rest of the day.

I chase after every single Berenice in literature and history. I learn that Berenice of Egypt married her brother, Ptolemy Euergetes, and was then murdered by her son, Ptolemy Philopator. I like the idea of becoming Christian's wife. Just the kind of idea, if you will, that makes me want to laugh when my soul aches like today. As for Berenice, daughter of Agrippa I, I don't like her as much, even if she witnessed, without flinching, the conviction of one of Christ's apostles. As I read and reread Edgar Allan Poe's

Berenice, I get into the habit of acting like her, of being like her. All my namesakes have considerable influence over me. I need so badly to have faith in something, yet I'm so unable to have faith in anything others have faith in. I need so badly to find a path I would gladly follow, if I were given the chance, any Berenice's path. The powers of imagination must be great for the chance combination of a few syllables alone to provoke such an agreement of my whole being, and such a great desire.

I read that Ganymede was the most handsome mortal and that, after he turned into an eagle, Zeus or that other guy (Jupiter) kidnapped him to make him cupbearer of the gods. Triumph or defeat? Defeat! Defeat!

Constance Chlorus says that I'll be begging at the gates of Seville one day. I wonder where she gets such predictions. She must have seen an opera somewhere. She must love me very much to come up with such predictions just to please me.

Mousermoth came to visit, changed, with shorter hair, with short, comma-like locks. She was very sad and very beautiful. She looked like Joan of Arc with her short bob. It had been a good two years since I'd last seen her. Her shoes were so small, so sweet, that I wanted to hack her feet off. Two small feet, two small blows. Splat! Splat! She found me changed.

"You're all grown-up!" she said, all teary-eyed.

45

After completing an English horn course, I take a bugle course. I want to know everything. What's the worst that could happen?

It was written: I had to meet Ms. Menstruation. I'm full of ovaries now. Ovaries are eggs. Don't run too fast, Berenice, or you'll break your eggs. I'm starting to have teats. Don't run too fast, you cow, or your milk will turn sour. Last night, like every Monday and Friday, I walk over to my old music teacher's. Everything unfolds as usual. He holds my neck, and I blow overenthusiastically in my instrument's mouthpiece. I have cramps, and they're growing worse. I think it must be because the old bastard disgusts me, but unfortunately, that's not it. I thought I'd become an adult without suffering the throes girls whisper about in the locker room. I had to change my tune. I walk back to the columbarium doubled over in pain, unwittingly repeating to myself a sentence that stuck in my mind for some reason: *Her impurity will last seven days, and anyone who touches her will be unclean till evening.* I walk back to the columbarium, lonelier than ever. On the road, my eyes meet the familiar neon sign that says "Shoemaker." I read "Shitmaker." Nobody can know what happened. I walk back to the columbarium, lonelier than ever, telling myself that I'll put money aside and secretly go to a surgeon so that he can cut that disgusting sexual apparatus out of me once and for all. I vomit on a street lamp. I almost pass out on the sidewalk. God, I really feel like shit. Crappy cow crap! I've never had any luck! Nobody can notice. I climb up the fire escape to the ninth cage of the columbarium and get in through the small breathing-hole of the *buen retiro*. Streaks of blood and lymph and chyle are coagulating on my thighs, giving off a stercorarian smell. I get undressed as fast as I can, put my filthy clothes in a pile, set it on fire, and flush the ashes down the toilet. I fill the bathtub with ice-cold water. I jump in as though it were my saving grace, and spend most of the night in there, soaping up, shaving, cursing, swearing revenge.

White and pure, Constance Chlorus is asleep, curled up, snug, her neck and wrists drowning in lace, her curves completely lost in the ample folds of her long poppy-print nightdress. I hug her, crying. She's sound asleep; the columbarium could blow up and she still wouldn't wake up. She's sleeping, and her brow is moist.

"I would've given so much to be spared! I whisper to her beautiful face, deaf and blind. Poor Constance Chlorus! If you only knew what you risk when you sleep like this, unarmed, unguarded. Poor darling! Poor thing! Hang in there!"

I can see the pores of Constance Chlorus' pearly face open like the mesh of a sieve. I smell an oil stench seep into her breath, a breath so sweet, a breath that tastes like rosewater. I see nerves jutting out on her smooth hands and her smooth neck. I see her rock-hard flesh slacken, soften, and swell, weighed down with pitch. I see her diamond head shrivel up like a sickly apple. I see her put on a bra and nylons, with a cigarette dangling from her mouth. I see her skin turn yellow like rotten cheesecloth and bloated like whatever you will. I see her breasts, two empty sacks, fall on her globe-shaped belly. I see her change and change until she fades away. I need to save her, help her elude the sadism of the Titan. I must quickly come up with some harness, some hiatus, some poison, some place. She must remain as she is now and never change. I must pry her away from the roots devouring her, free her, cut off the wires of the waves sweeping her far away. She must remain to watch over the night like I'm watching over her tonight, guarding our childhood. Why must this night end? Why won't the night stop sinking? Why can't this night stay still and forever become a night we could stop by when we're old, a night we could visit like you visit an attic? Why isn't there, just outside of time, a sunny day we could go back to, where we could frolic in a river of daisies like we did yesterday or the day before? How can I consider stopping? The Khazars pose a serious threat to our rear guard. I must quickly go to sleep so I can regain my strength and resume fleeing tomorrow, bright-eyed and bushy-tailed.

46

Today, Constance Chlorus isn't speaking, running, or doing anything. She just sits there, emitting waves of sadness and angst. Not seeing Constance Chlorus be lively and gay worries me to the point of remorse, disorients me to the point of confusion. What's wrong with her? She doesn't know. She's got a bad feeling or something. She feels sort of depressed but doesn't really know why. Does she have a headache or a stomach ache? No. Like her, with her, I'm sort of depressed but don't really know why.

"What's wrong with you? Tell me!"

"Nothing. I've got a bad feeling or something."

"What kind of bad feeling? Tell me! You have no idea how it makes me feel to see you sad."

"I'm empty. I feel empty like when I heard that my three brothers had been killed. I'm sure Abel got killed too. I'm empty. I'm a house that people left, taking off with the furniture and curtains."

"I feel empty too. But I just don't care if anybody dies."

"Don't say that. What are we going to do, Berenice?"

"Let's run away, Constance Chlorus. Let's leave. I've had it up to here. Let's run away."

"If that's what you want. Everything matters so little to me today."

"Let's hop into the first caravel."

"Let's jump aboard the next three-master vessel."

We're on our way back from school. We turn around, half-hearted, and go wait for a trolleybus. We spend the whole night riding in circles, walking and jumping from one trolleybus to the next, without ever making it out of the city. Whenever the trolleybus stops, we end up somewhere downtown. It's as though we were the victims of a conspiracy.

It's dark out, as though we were underground. We walk fast. We must get out of this city. We walk as though we weren't the ones moving. We pretend that we're standing still and that the city's running, flowing like a river along either side of us. We watch building angles sail toward us like stems. Looking up in the air, we see huge neon signs fly over our heads like pterodactyls, spinning around, showing us the fantastic racks of their black carcasses. A procession of parked cars is silently inching our way. Built on a vacant lot, an isolated rental house is spinning like a live mannequin, showing us in turn three of its four faces. A ramp of reflectors fixed atop a department store window catches our eye. The colours of the flags they light up are twisting bright against the sky's perfect blackness. The trolleybus leaves us under a causeway. Under the causeway, our steps echo like in an empty cathedral. Excited by that echo, we start running between the huge concrete pillars. The faster we run, the more our resounding steps sound like storms of applause. Of course, we run as fast as we can.

"Look, over there!"

She's pointing far down below, where several causeways cross, like a large flight of bright birds frozen still between heaven and earth. She doesn't seem to realize what they are. Her eyes are open wide.

"Those are just lights. What did you expect?"

"But they're so white! Look: They're V-shaped, as though they had wings. I'm scared, Berenice. What if the world's ending? I've got a bad feeling about this."

I lead her to take a closer look at the tall V-shaped, infinite white lights that, perched on top of high gallows, illuminate the section of the causeway we've been running on. She doesn't look too relieved. A moment ago, she thought the wind was too soft to be natural. She just can't shake that bad feeling.

The sun is coming up. The city is bathed in an aquarium glow, an empty glow, a still, silent glow, a glow like I've never seen before and that doesn't look any more natural to me than it does to Constance Chlorus. The trolleybus we're on is running, almost empty, on a deserted avenue where no one, no car is to be seen. Constance Chlorus is nodding off, her head lolling from a quarter to twelve to a quarter past twelve. I shake her by the nose so she won't fall asleep. I'm so tired that I think I could forget her on the trolleybus if she fell asleep. Before us, a middle-aged woman with a cheek consumed by a scar is kissing, on the neck, a tall young black man with his fly open. The old drunk who just got on the bus is dancing a jig in the middle of the aisle; fancying himself funny, he looks at us, laughing. Constance Chlorus, convinced she's in hell, starts to cry softly. Dragging our feet down an alley, we're surrounded with small dirty old houses huddled against each other. Over that hedge of houses, in a white, ethereal haze, a skyscraper is standing, gigantic and spectral, merely made out, it seems, of translucent lit-up windows, that appear to stay put, always in the same spot, even though we keep walking closer and closer. I'm thinking, gravely, of a star vessel in distress, sinking in the morning marsh.

We end up, unexpectedly, in front of the columbarium. We go in. We delightfully fall onto our bed and delightfully fall asleep. For two days straight, in the cage, all our holey saints can talk about is our stupid, obscure, senseless, silly, foolish, crazy, dumb, dim-witted whim. But any talk eventually rots and dies, even when it's caused by a dim-witted whim.

I'm coming home from my bugle lesson. It's mild out. I'm in a good mood. I tell myself that learning to play the bugle or the accordion is better than learning to play the harquebus. The street is shrouded in splendid silence, the kind found only in the mountains. Twilight has raised its curtain beyond the fuliginous mass of skyscrapers. The four-leaf ash before Dick Dong's, the only tree in sight, turns red in the twilight. Someone is calling me. I stand on the tips of my ears. There it is again. It's the voice of Constance Chlorus who, despite the late hour and the avuncular ban, has come to meet me. At arm's length, she passionately waves what looks like a letter. She's running over like mad, slamming the sidewalk with her bare feet. Her locks are bouncing, dancing like tiny elves. All of a sudden, a car backs out of a basement, coming straight at Constance Chlorus—that filthy pile of scrap runs her over. I barely have the time to scream. She's already crashed, crushed. Blood already blackens the sidewalk. The ground gives in under my feet, like the trap under the hangman's feet.

I feverishly reach over with both hands, searching in vain for the familiar beating of her heart. Her broken chest is limp, sinking like snow under my touch. Moved by one last spasm, her fingers seize my arms and squeeze. Her livid eyes focus their very last spark into mine. Will she speak? Speak! Speak! Speak! Say something! Tears are crowding her eyelashes. Speak! Some kind of smile emanates from her face, still unscathed, some kind of true happiness. She speaks. Speaks my name.

"It's okay," she keeps repeating. "It's okay. Your letter."

Faces—awful, hostile, evil, silly faces—are swarming around me, suffocating me. I throw myself at them, wild. I brace myself and, with both my arms and all my weight, blindly force them back, push them off, away. One of the faces just leaned over the corpse, about to lay hands on her. I go right for its eyes, digging my nails into its skin, biting it. In one effortless sweeping motion, I lift her beloved body and run, carrying her far from the faces. She's so light, so light that *she* carries *me*, making me as light as the plovers we used to see trotting on the beach, lifting me like a balloon lifts a gondola until I go up in the air and fly off.

Constance Chlorus is gone. Funny thing. At the time, I lost it. Now, I feel nothing. So that was the death of Constance Chlorus. So that's what a late Constance Chlorus looks like. If the poor girl heard me... she had so much respect for the dead. But, sweet friend, am I to blame if I can't shed a tear? Is the well to blame if it runs dry?

I won't go to her funeral or to her burial. I won't bear any coffin or grief. They can think and say whatever they want about my behaviour. Good for them if my behaviour makes them boil. The next morning, in the aftermath of that first brush with death, I can't wait for the sun to come up, for the city to rise, for life to go on. Death, if you knew how anxious I am to see your face in the sun, for the sun to shine just enough for you to see me laugh in your face. Constance Chlorus is dead and I'm doing quite well. Dead, Constance Chlorus means nothing to me... Besides, the dead don't talk much, they don't say much to anyone. No mourning for me, thank you very much.

47

After she was cremated, Constance Chlorus was buried in the magnificent La Hêtraie ossuary in Montreal. I want to drop dead in the middle of a desert. And I want whatever remains of me to rot, right where I die, after the vultures, jackals, and ants have had their share. They made me vicious: I'm out for blood. Should it be seen as pure coincidence that I wished for Constance Chlorus to die? The answer is no. I wielded tremendous power over her, exerted a hypnotic fascination. I killed her: I state it coldly and firmly believe it. She couldn't go on living; it would've been an insult to her beauty, to her spontaneity. She felt that I wanted her to disappear. Why else should life have suddenly seemed so absurd to her? She erased herself to please me, like she would scamper behind me to please me. She got herself killed to conform to a mysterious imperative born out of my will. You can murder telepathically, and I did. I sometimes laugh over Constance Chlorus' death—sardonically, enthralled by my own power, as though I were intoxicated, like when you play a good trick on someone hateful. Is that madness? No: that's strength. And even if, holding all evidence to the contrary, I still wanted to be fully convinced that *I* had killed Constance Chlorus, no one could stop me. Now that's strength.

The doors of the neighbourhood cathedral remained open late into the night, as though they were expecting to welcome some Émile Nelligan. We often went there, Constance Chlorus and I. I remain standing for long minutes, still, under the vaults. With my head thrown back, head-strong, I listen to the words of Constance Chlorus coming back to me.

"Why do children hold hands? Is it because their parents told them to? Whey aren't we holding hands? Aren't you afraid to lose me?"

I'm standing in the middle of the nave, allowing myself to be stunned by the peace, the grandeur, the richness, the excessiveness of the place. Organs are thrumming, and I stand at their very heart, worried at first, then terrified, frozen stiff, as though I were caught in a winter storm.

"Hewn out of solid gold, a tall ship sailed…" I shut my eyes, and it feels like waves higher than mountains are rolling below my feet. Leaving. Again. Always.

I read *I the Jury*, *Kiss Me Deadly*, *Sylvia*, *The Hot Mistress*. No doctoral thesis was ever written on any of those books. My small ten-dollar monthly allowance would never be enough to pay for all the pornographic literature I go through. I generously resort to larceny. My furious taste for bad books comes from my furious taste for solitude and bad dreams. In a book, you're alone. In a bad book, there's murder and filth, everything I could possibly want. I don't despise them enough just yet. It would help if I could see them up to their necks in violence and filth. Also, I feel such a voluptuous pleasure exposing the scandalous covers of "my" books to the stupid looks of my uncles and aunts, cousins, teachers and classmates. This way, I've come to experience the strongest feelings scanning an Orrie Hitt novel at shul, stuck between Zio and his eldest son. I would also read some Christian, if only that villain dared to write. I haven't received one letter from him. Occasionally, Mousermoth sends me some news. He's well. He's on the other side of the Atlantic, in Europe, in Poland, in Silesia, in Walbrzych in fact. There, he lives off the Brückners. They say he started studying biology. They say he spends his time throwing the javelin. They say he prefers the javelin to his biology books. Mousermoth and Einberg come to visit me, too often for my taste. They come to see me but they never get to. I lock myself into my room and refuse to see them. I heard through the grapevine that Einberg and Mousermoth are trying to make peace. This, I think, means that Mousermoth is ready to sleep with Einberg again so she can get her hands on her holy family again. I would've never understood that if I hadn't read pornographic novels. Poor Joan of Arc. I'm weary. I've got a big mouth, bigger than the palm of my hand. Some sort of fuzz is growing, fine and white, barely visible, on my upper lip, like the fuzz on the back of a gromwell leaf. When I'm thirty, I'll have a moustache, a mole, maybe even sideburns. I'll be dead ugly. But unfortunately, I won't be able to enjoy it, because I'll never turn thirty. It's too good to last, as they say.

I learn, from a famous psychiatrist who gave a conference at school, that a virgin is someone like me. I also learn that I have some kind of tiny penis called a clitoris, that if I methodically manipulate it, I'll be masturbating, and that if the operation is successful, I'll experience some kind of tenesmus called an orgasm. Earth holds no more secrets for anyone: it's been fully uncovered, undressed. The atom has been fully undressed, uncovered. All that humans had left to do was to take off the girls' underpants; they didn't hesitate. There are no secrets anywhere anymore. What am I doing here? What surprises am I still waiting for?

"What about you? Do you masturbate?" asks an emancipated classmate.

"No, I'm grieving."

"Famous scientists or not, all those guys are pigs!" a square head cries out. "If I ever bump into one on the street, I'll beat him to a pulp."

You're so square, baby, you're so square! (Popular song.)

48

After withstanding a useless one-hour siege at my door, Einberg turns on his heels. I listen to him walking down the stairs. I part the curtains to watch him leave. What do I see? Mousermoth! She's walking up the alley to the columbarium. I'm seized with an eager curiosity, which makes me part the curtains wider. I need to have a good view of their encounter, of their hate making. I mustn't miss a single twitch of their face muscles. I sharpen my eyes like a cat sharpens its claws. I refused to see Einberg. I retired to my room and blocked the door with the bed, the *bonheur du jour* and two chairs. He spent an hour soliloquizing behind the door. For a whole hour, without ever losing patience or raising his voice, without uttering a single curse or threat, he begged me to let him in.

"I'm bringing you stillborn sheep gloves from Estrées-Saint-Denis. I ordered them myself, directly from the artist.

A girl your age of your standing should wear stillborn sheep gloves from Estrées-Saint-Denis. Tell me you want them."

Einberg comes out. They're walking, face to face, toward each other, between two wild rose thickets. Both of them are ostentatiously looking the other way. Both of them are deviating as much as they can from each other's path. Has either one of them said anything? They've just stopped. What are they saying with their heads down? I see them suddenly spread their arms open and take off, flying toward each other. Technicolor prostitution on a giant screen! How sweet it is to my little pornographic bookworm heart! They hug and grapple each other, twisting around each other like strands. They look quite ridiculous. It's quite a delightful sight. It's like watching a wrestling match. Einberg's starving snout is laboriously squeezing and squishing Mousermoth's sad and sweet mouth. In the heat of the moment, Einberg's velour hat flies off his head and falls on the wild roses, then lands on the grass. She could tower over him with her magnificent head, but she's not looking to exploit her advantage. She's bending down to his level. As she bends down to the task, her bright Moroccan crepe skirt swells up like a bell, pornographically exposing her shanks. They happily leave together, arm in arm, brushing hips.

An hour later, Mousermoth comes back, now in charge of the stillborn sheep gloves from Estrées-Saint-Denis. Unshakable, I remain silent and maintain my embargo.

Trembling anxiously, my forehead remembers the muzzle, warm and moist, of a wet rose—the mouth of someone marvellous. I will take revenge for the death of

Constance Chlorus. I will never forget her, Titan! I don't feel forced to take revenge or to remember. But I won't leave such a beautiful corpse lying there useless. Anyway, isn't the Titan playing a dirty trick on me if, instead of feeling forced to take revenge or remember, I feel forced to forgive and forget? And this bed is so empty, so big.

49

I've walled myself in so well, held my valves shut so tight during my last years of exile, that tonight, like many nights before, I'm dying, hitting my head against the floor like you'd hit a broken watch against the edge of a table. Everything is so tight, so violent in my body and my soul, everything hurts so much that I can't sleep. I'm stagnating. Especially since Constance Chlorus died, I can just hear the cage, the school, life rumbling from afar. I'm burning, half alive, half dead, in a brazen bull which I've locked my own self in. Will I push this stupid whining to the point of admitting that I'm unhappy? No!

I'm not happy because I never tried to be. I'm having enough trouble trying to hang on to the shred of dignity I have left! I haven't sought happiness in the first place because it means nothing to me, because it's ugly and implies that you're aligned with miasma. I refuse to do business with the foul world they've forced upon me, the world they threw me in without due process like a slave in the galleys. I was thrown into a mob, a bunch of guts and gobs that don't even know they have souls, a mob ready for anyone to chain them up and commit any crime against their souls or pride, as long as they have access to the trough their masters let them lick clean three times a day. O, Masters! I'd rather eat my own shit! O, Masters! I'll have you swallow all your cages—anchored or on wheels, in the air or at sea! I'll remain a bad inmate, a rebellious, disrespectful slave. I'll try to escape all the time. I'll support your strappados in silence as my curses' due rewards and will go on cursing. Whoever you may be, O Masters, and no matter how many, mortal or divine, I rebel against you, I carelessly spit in your face. I call you pathetic, pleasure-seeking sadists, I call you paranoid schizophrenics! My heart is hollow because I refuse to get on all fours and bark and fight four billion people to get your leftovers. I don't like wolves much, but I like them better than dogs, because wolves would rather eat each other than be walked to the curb on a leash to relieve themselves. Let me take this opportunity to mention that I like airplanes because at night, they wear coloured lights at the tips of their wings. I'm unhappy and my heart is hollow: I want to keep what's left of my dignity. I choose to be faithful, loyal, and defend a lost cause, the flag of a losing army, until I croak. My master is held hostage. My master is somewhere else. My master has lost. If my master hadn't lost, would I be locked up, at the hands of those icebox sellers? I'm suffocating here, alone, tonight, because, despite the heavy stone tied to my neck, I stiffen, stand straight, refuse to buckle or bow. I'm the handmaid to no President on earth, to no Yahweh in heaven. I will sacrifice no lamb for any of those poorly dressed generals. I will not pray or kneel for pardon, redemption, salvation, fictions, cars, or cash. I remember being beaten up, having another master. Here I stand, calling him back. I remember being in an enemy camp. I can really talk nonsense when I want to. I'm quite talented. Real gifted.

Since I have teats and no more zits, Murder-Quail, the eldest of my cousins, loves me in silence. Poor sweet donkey! He sets love traps in the staircase, at the dinner table, on doorsteps, in the den when I deign to go watch television. He breeds double entendres. His piggy eyes, his little Einberg-like eyes, let out guilty looks. I don't know what to do anymore to cool off the pestilent passion of that scrofulous fool. I offered to perform a little striptease for him. He claimed he was just looking for my friendship. If you're looking for my friendship, stop looking between my knees! I didn't mince my words! He didn't seem to mind. Quietly, with eyes full of tears and clammy hands, wearing his heart on his sleeve, he regularly gives it a try. He absolutely wants my friendship. He wants me to smile at him. What a sucker! He thinks I'm pretty! He must be frogging friendship-deprived! I grow up, excessively. I grow up so fast that, from one day to the next, I only see some kind of swollen, blown up version of myself in the mirror. Whatever! I'd rather grow as tall as Mousermoth than stay as short as Einberg. I'm through with having his eyes and his mouth! It seems like Dick Dong, who lives three or four blocks east from here, has a boyish crush on me. When we bump into each other on the sidewalk, he always says something weird to me. "Whenever you wish, milady!"

"Boy, do I love you!" "Let's leave together for Wyoming! They say there are so many cows out there they had to build pasture parkades." I must say, he makes me laugh, and I don't think he looks ugly. But I will never hang on a boy's arm, if only not to act like the rest of those two billion specimens of the female sex. I won't be any boy's girlfriend, and no boy will be my boyfriend. Count me out, you love factory forcing boys and girls to walk arm in arm! Count me out, you lusty love movie directors! If I ever get married, it will be to Christian or to a crocodile.

If Constance Chlorus were still alive, I would change her name to Constance Extinct. How could I, for five years, let her keep such a stupid name? Some things are real and some are fake. Real things make me want to laugh and fake ones make me want to puke. Love is fake. Hate is real. Animals are real. Men are fake.

50

The abbey has re-opened its doors. Yup! Einberg and Mousermoth are back together. Yup! Yup! Christian told me the news in the first letter he wrote in three years, visibly with a guided hand. He also tells me that he now speaks with a Polish accent. Here's my answer to my dear brother:

"My love, my honey, my sweet, my lover, my brother, I am very pleased to learn that you now speak with a Polish accent. For my part, I now speak with an American accent.

Your love, your honey, your sweet, your lover, your sister, Berenice."

I hope that'll chafe them and teach them to send me fake letters. When she was here, Constance Chlorus was the star of my show. Now that she's gone, Zio's the star. But only in contrast with the others—my aunts and cousins—who are so humble and mousy that they're not even worth casting as extras. I delight in saying the opposite of what he says and doing the opposite of what he wants me to do. It's easy. Zio has very strong views on everyone and everything. He bugs me. I'm realizing, since Constance Chlorus died, that he's convinced himself that I did everything I did over the past three years because he wanted me to. It's time to set him straight. If he's been leading me by the nose for three years, it's quite simply because I wasn't aware of it, because I found him so stupid that I didn't even notice he was there. If he thinks he has any authority over me, he'll be bitterly disappointed. I'm done with Saturday silence, fasting, stillness, and gloom! Enough with Zio! From now on, I'll spend my Saturdays eating myself full three times a day right under his nose and his long beard. Why should *I* obey *him*? After all, I'm as much a human being as he is! You better watch out, Zio, it's going to get ugly! And I'm done praying morning and night from now on, dear Uncle, I'm even done pretending. If Yahweh wants my prayers so badly, he can just come and rip them out of my oesophagus! What kind of behaviour is that? Why should *I* obey a filthy human being? It's going to get ugly! For verily I say unto you, things are going to get ugly!

51

The most ridiculous thing about Zio is his steely assurance, the steadfastness of his every action, the infallible machine-like logic guiding his every move. Now that I'm riddled with doubt, weak, limp, boneless from doubt, I'm not up to scaring him. I'm sure, however, that my doubt is better than his assurance. I'm convinced, however, that Zio is just a deaf and blind fool, just another one of those utter idiots who've made my world the way it is. To me, however, the fact that he believes me to fear and respect him like everyone else he knows couldn't be more ridiculous. Because all natural slaves see Zio as their master. Because all the cods see Zio as the great cod master.

On Yom Kippur, Zio always rises before the sun and walks all the way across Manhattan to take a pious, traditional dip in the Hudson River. It was very cold out this morning. I can picture him in his long mangabey beard, naked, stoic, confident, breaking the ice with his bludgeon. The Einbergs from Armenia would have never dared to start the day, any day, without cleansing themselves in the Aras or the Kura River. Cha cha cha. First thing on Yom Kippur, any human being must, Zio is sure of it, take a dip in the Hudson River. Unless said human is convinced to be something other than a human being. Maybe said human is convinced to be a Zio…

But people take Zio for a decent, respectable man. He's a powerful, trusted man. He has tremendous influence on everyone and everything they've done. He who left

Armenia in schmatte now manages a very large mortgage loan company in a British tweed suit and Italian shoes. Son of a cadet branch of the Einberg family, he slowly became, no one knows how, the undisputed head of all Einbergs. And there are a lot of Einbergs on Earth. They say there's at least one in each country. He's the pasha of Einbergs. He built them all a fortune. He found them all decent wives. He controls their sons' education. He makes them emigrate and immigrate back and forth.

On the surface, my relationship with Zio is almost non-existent. When he has something to tell me, he sends Zia to tell me. Because he holds all females in contempt. He allows women to talk among themselves, but forbids them to intervene when men talk among themselves. When a male guest dares to maintain a conversation with a female guest, Zio sees red; and the guests in question can be sure never to be invited again. He therefore contemptuously ignores women. Considering that I'm not a real woman just yet and that I'm a half-Barbarian on my mother's side, you can guess the depth of his contemptuous indifference toward me. As a general rule, he only addresses me once a year, on Pesach. He then tries to make me drink and laugh and see what I'm made of. There's nothing nicer than a tough man who's being nice. I'm moved. I laugh as much as he wants, drink as much as he wants, open up as much as he wants. Before, he often called me up to the Torah. Now, since my one-night escape with Constance Extinct, he never calls me up. When he's in a good mood, he calls me, cynically, "Fraülein." Mousermoth, who isn't too impressed with him, calls him "Santa Claus."

52

My bags are packed. My coat is buttoned up. The door is open. Mousermoth and Einberg have come to take me back and, any minute now, I'll be leaving this teeth-grating valley. To carry out my kidnapping, the husband-and-wife team counted on Zio being absent, but he suddenly shows up out of the blue, hitting all the brakes. The patriarch, great avenger of first-time widows, strongly objects. In an irrevocable tone, he tells me that I'm not leaving.

"That child is not going anywhere. Berenice! Take off that coat and those galoshes! Berenice! Go to your room and unpack your bags!"

Zio was the only one who still hadn't joined the ranks of those who look after my wellbeing as though it were their own. Now that he's joined the ranks of all those politicians, urbanists, philosophers, the SPCA, and sellers of extra-soft soaps, nobody's missing.

"I take full responsibility for Berenice!" claims the saviour of fatherless orphans.

Then, on the basis of that stunning hypothesis, the successor in title explains to the assignees that he doesn't deem me old or strong enough to take part in the little games they play on the island.

"Come back later, much later, when you have exhausted your disputes, in a year or two or ten."

Those last words cut Mousermoth and Einberg to the quick. So far stunned into silence, they now team up to launch a passionate salvo of blazing protestations. They could be a thousand and speak with Cicero's eloquence! Zio has built an impregnable tower around me: nobody can hit or hurt me!

My loneliness is too heavy. I'm slumping, crumbling, collapsing. Against my better logic and vows, I give in to Dick Dong's advances. He's late for our date. I'm waiting for him, and as I wait, in a desperate effort to save what's left of my honour, I keep telling myself that I'm a vestal and that I'll never let a man lay his dirty hands on me. Dick Dong finally shows up. He takes a long look at me without apologizing, then, still silent, mysteriously starts to count on his fingers.

"We won't be able to marry for six years," he finally says. "I have so many studies to complete! One more year in high school, five years in college... Will you be patient enough to wait?"

"Me? Marry you? Phooey, Dick Dong!"

Pulling the lace of my corset, I show him my precious pendulous things.

"I already have a fiancé. He's pursuing brilliant studies at a German university. We were only three when we were promised to each other."

"Does he study in Heidelberg?"

"I suppose."

Dick Dong, who has a lot of experience with girls, isn't shaken by my so-called revelations. We have ice cream and fries, like in French songs. It's not unpleasant. I must go home because it's nine o'clock and the trombone lesson I'm supposed to be attending ends at nine o'clock.

"We'll see each other again right here on Friday night," says Dick Dong.

"Is that so?"

"*Que sera, sera…*"

"How insolent! How arrogant!"

Like Zio, Dick Dong is cocky. But Dick Dong is not as dangerously cocky as Zio. Dick Dong is only cocky because he regularly uses "Hair Grease" deodorant. If he didn't feel forced to act like Marlon Brando, my life, at this very moment, might be quite different.

53

I'm watching the wind. The wind is sharp and cold. I see sparrows on the lawn, their down ruffled by the wind. Some are standing as still as they can, clinging against the wind. The wind is throwing others against the walls. Which leads me to talk about my business with Dick Dong. The sexual aspect of the human problem is completely ruining the unreasonable aspect of our rapport. Both of us are eager to be touched. Neither of us is starving for cash. Not succumbing to touch is unfortunately not a solution, because not succumbing is more time-consuming than succumbing. Human sexual dimorphism should be limited to the size of our feet.

If I were named Queen of Earth tomorrow, it would take me an hour at most to pull the world out of the ditch. First, I would quickly declare war, a state of perpetual siege between the two halves of the globe separated by zero degrees of latitude. My traitors, those of my subjects who would be caught talking about settling or submitting, wouldn't have their heads cut off; for them, I would have a more sophisticated torture in store: scheduled boredom. Their lives would be divided in hours, and they would be condemned to compile statistics until their very last gasp, sitting on a chair in some cage made of a few doors and windows. I would then build, in my kingdom's worst substructure, a forbidden enclave called the Republic of Love where, waiting for another alternative, thousands of women and dozens of men who all turned blind and deaf, would be exclusively devoted to perpetuating the species. I would accuse of treason any soldier of any sex found admiring the beauty or sadness of any soldier of the other sex, and that traitor would then be sentenced to scheduled boredom. The nature of humans or primates is not to drink, eat, or run after an orgasm, but to surpass themselves. If that's indeed the case, why have humans and primates come to stand on their hind legs and to insist on walking upright, swinging their two remaining legs, like show dogs? I forget, true enough, the ones who get around on wheels fastened to a jump seat… But those are old-fashioned and on the brink of extinction. Therefore, I've been queen of the elephant head for thirty-four years. It only took nine years for cities to fall and for humus to cover their leveled ruins. Cities only owed the soundness of their structures to the automotive industry. One by one, cars were launched into the Pacific from the mouth of an enormous cannon. Thus filled in, the Pacific became arable. The Gobi and Sahara deserts, having drunk the Pacific dry, became arable as well. Used to wearing armours and handling the blunderbuss and battle-

223

axe, human specimens of the female sex slowly lost their bumps and bounce. During the battles where my warriors kill each other, regardless of colour, for the sole cruelty of it, nobody cares about the gender of the fallen. Since each of the fallen is as nameless as the next, you'd have to slit their stomachs open to determine their gender with certainty, which would require the use of a blowtorch, since with time, the warriors' flesh and blood have merged with the steel of their armour. Besides, no one cares anymore about the gender of a warrior, dead or alive. In the Republic of Love, things are going great. The gynecologists ruling over my realm are swelling with pride in the reports they daily draw up for me using fountain pens. The Republic of Love will collapse soon enough, actually: its useless borders and filthy citizens are about to be razed and cleared. Tomorrow, just by chewing a horehound flower, an excessively bitter flower, my murmillones and retiarii, now true phoenixes, will be able to self-reproduce and, as though by fission, give themselves new lives, new bodies, new armours. Immortality has been achieved, and what's not to be sneezed at, it's there for the taking. The enormous cannon that launched cars into the Pacific was pushed into the Aral from the top of a mountain in Elburz (which had to be geographically adapted to that end), at the same time as all massive, massively destructive weapons. Also, there's just one blowtorch left on the elephant head.

Dick Dong and I are walking toward the docks, not holding hands. We sit down back to back on a capstan, just above the black surface reflecting the reflectors. With him, like with Constance Chlorus, I can't stop talking.

"I know why breaking, destroying stuff is so much fun. Let me explain. It proceeds from the nostalgia of having, possessing, possessing for real. Earlier, as we were walking, looking at our surroundings, a very sweet thought came to me: 'All of this belongs to me.' I compared the street to a doll I once had. I told myself that the street was mine as much as the doll had been mine, thinking, 'Everything I could do to my doll, I can do to the street—I can look at it, smell it, hug it.' Then I realized I was wrong, thinking, 'No! This street doesn't belong to me. Because I can't destroy it like I destroyed my doll.' Do you get it, Dick Dong? Do you understand my reification?"

Dick Dong thinks my explanation is queer, crazy, unnatural. Unnatural!... His opinion tells me that he's narrow-minded, that he has no faith, that he's fit to be thrown to the hogs. We climb on the top of a heap and sit down, swinging our legs between water and sky. We spit into the black water, aiming for the yellow-purple, green-orange oil stains. A liner sails by, close by, and the night seems to be soaking, watering down its whiteness. Suddenly, it bellows. Its roar is so deep, so powerful, that it shakes me like the wind shakes tree leaves, so powerful that it gives me goosebumps and makes me want to shout even louder. In reply, an invisible tugboat blows a hail of sharp whistles. The tugboat's shrieks are so shrill that I have to clench my teeth to contain the agony they've awoken in me. Dick Dong says that, unlike me, the tugboat's shrieks didn't make him think of tortured animals. It's getting late. We head back home. From all the alleys around, we choose the darkest, the narrowest, the most deserted and sinuous ones.

I'm running, pounding the pavement like a drum. I think of Christian, who spends his time throwing the javelin. This alley goes uphill. When I get to the top, I let myself fall down. Lying on my back, smack in the middle of the alley, I'm breathing, feeling great. I spread my arms and cross my ankles, just so I can look like Christ on the cross. I stare at the sky, on the spot where, right above the tip of a roof, the crescent moon is bathing in a hazy cloud. I turn over. Lying flat on my stomach, I am Antaeus: I can feel, through the cold macadam, the heat of the earth penetrating me, stirring my blood, making me grow roots and twigs.

Dick Dong has finally stomped over, catching up to me. He doesn't like to run or to walk sideways, or to stop and go. He likes to walk straight, like a pack horse.

"The poet said," I tell him, "*My dear child, you dance badly. Dance is a statelier pace, a paraphrase of the vision.*"

He holds out his arms to help me up. I tell him that I don't need anyone to help me back to my feet. He tries to kiss me on the mouth. I violently push him back, reminding him of our pact. Our pact stipulates that I alone can take initiatives with respect to touch, and that I'll only take such initiatives when I can be sure he's forgotten that we are a boy and a girl. When he forgets that we are a boy and a girl, he'll be the son of Fire and Wind, and, when I kiss him, his soul will shiver, as pure as a stream shivering under the blowing wind and the bright sun. He tells me that his heart is swollen with love, stretched to the limit, that it'll burst like a balloon blown too hard if I don't start showing him more affection. I find him vulgar, godless. I shower him with insults. He grows violent, pinning me to the pole of a streetlamp. Squeezing me, trying to trap me, to bind me, to make me submit, forcing his passion onto me as though he were tying a bull to a plow, his arms are making me sick. I call him a monster. He tells me that I'm the monster. Was I wrong to assume I had power over Dick Dong? Should I give up all hope to pull an ounce of soul out of his pluck? His last ultimatum is clear and concise:

"We've been going out for a month. Normal girls let you kiss them on the second date. If you don't let me kiss you on our next date, I'm leaving you."

"Where have you been?" Zio asks me, standing at the far back of the dark dining room.

"Go shave yourself!" I should reply.

But since I despise making scenes, since I despise drama, since I despise making a fool of myself, I quickly slip through his fingers with my head down, without saying a word.

54

Berenice Einberg, do you have any guts? I've got plenty of skin, but no guts, my Lord. And why is that, my child? I don't know, my Lord. It came to me just like that, little by little, bit by bit, day after day, slowly, without my realizing it.

Zio's authority over me hangs by a thread, I must say. Yet it's holding. The authority of generals over men hangs by a thread. Yet it's holding well. I pity Zio. He can do so little to me, for me, against the germs consuming me. I really pity him. He thinks that, thanks to his mortgage loan company, his Masoretic knowledge, his long moth-eaten beard, and whatever else he's helping to increase the overall wellbeing of all human beings. He would burst into tears if he saw how little I care about what he says, how much of a ridiculous fool I think he is, how little he matters, how alone he is, how alone he makes everyone feel, how unmoved and unchanged he leaves everyone. I have sort of a soft spot for him, the kind of soft spot any woman has for any man who tries to be manly. I would have a soft spot for any ant that dared to threaten me with a sword. Playing his game distracts me, keeps my heart busy.

Sitting alone before my mirror, I decide, without much enthusiasm, to launch a small strike against Zio. My hair is long enough to braid. I struggle to make myself two long thick braids and, in a Moorish twist, I tie them over my forehead with a big pink ribbon. I then take Constance Extinct's gouache set out of its hiding place, and carefully paint my nails, my eyebrows, my eyelids, and my mouth black. Later on, I show up at the dinner table with my braided hair and my painted face, heavily perfumed. I have an unspeakable impact on my female cousins. My aunts and cousins let out unspeakable ahs and ohs. With a tinge of apprehension, I throw a look at Zio. He'd been waiting for that look: he seizes it, staring back as only he can. He's laughing in his sleeve. He knows everything about my nightly outings. He'll take advantage of this opportunity to have a ball.

"Fräulein," he begins (in his mind, Mousermoth is German), "Mr. Klaust asked about you. He worries about your health. He can barely wait to see you back in class…

Trombone lessons, right? Your ballet teacher tells me she has never seen you before in her life. She looks forward to making your acquaintance."

What a face Zio is making! So stern, so harsh, so angry, so handsome! What a poor face! I feel disgusted to see how easily I can stare back into the vulture glare he's casting me to make me feel ashamed. I almost feel ashamed when I see how offended he is by my coldness.

"Lower your eyes, you insolent child! Only cats refuse to lower their eyes when they have been bad."

I comply. I can tell how vulnerable he is under his long beard. If I hadn't lowered my eyes, he would have started to cry or to beat me.

"You choose: if you don't start showing signs of kindness and maturity soon enough, I'll treat you like the bitch in heat you have been acting like for the past three months. But but but… are you not able, alone, to tell the difference between preserving and violating your own dignity as a young woman? Do you have no sense of duty, of obedience, of gratitude?"

No, Zio. I've got none of that. I'm a vile, void, vain, vicious, vapid, vanquished, thieving vixen. Since you can't cure me of insipidity, inconsequence, or any other cancer, I have to take care of it myself. My soul aches so much, Zio, and it's so important to have an aching soul when your soul aches this much, that I can't help caring for my soul, and for my soul only. Duty, obedience, gratitude, those are words that others, like you, are in a much better position to care for than a cancerous soul like me. Just go to them and leave me alone! My soul aches so much, Zio, and it matters so little to you! You should understand that all the woes those words give you don't matter much to me, that your beard doesn't matter to me as much as it does to you.

"You painted your face! You went to the hairdresser! You wretch! Go wash your face at once! Go brush your hair at once! How could you come to Yahweh's table in such a state? Do you take Yahweh for a libertine, for a philanderer?"

I stand up and go wash my face and brush my hair. All my soul said no, but my mouth said yes. What would have happened if I hadn't complied? He would have started to cry. He would have beaten me. He would have sent me back to Canada, far away from Dick Dong. Like Jupiter, he would have launched thunderbolts at me. Sometimes, it's best to do what an idiot tells you. Drastic measures have been taken so that I would attend my trombone and ballet lessons. A taxi will drive me there and back. The parents of "young Mr. Dong" were informed of his "bad behaviour."

I'm free. My will is inside my skull. Nobody can see it or hear it, or touch it. I alone can act upon my will.

55

I think it would feel good to be with Christian again, to find myself surrounded by the island's poplars and marsh. I receive one of Christian's rare letters. He conveys that he's glad to hear I'm starting to be interested in boys. "That's healthy." He conveys that he participated in the Hungarian athletics games, but that he came back highly downcast, having only succeeded in being eliminated in the first of four qualifying competitions. "The crowd petrified me, made me lose my grip. I'm irreparably shy." He speaks a lot about the grateful love that kind parental hearts should stir in their children's hearts. He barely even mentions our friendship, which is, for me, an inexhaustible topic. He drowns our friendship in the noxious grandeur of the homogenized and pasteurized family he longs for. I'd asked him to tell me if he too had gotten on the bandwagon, bewitching members of the female sex. He never complied with that request. I'd asked him to send me a photo of himself. He never complied with that request. To make him understand how thirsty I was for tender loving care, I'd asked him to start his letters with "My love" or "My sweet mistress" instead of "My dear Berenice" or "Sister dearest." He never did. "I am not your sister, I am your love, your honey, your sugar, your pumpkin, your princess, your sweet pea, your chickadee." There are no more chickadees in his letter than hippos in the St. Lawrence River! "Women like to feel small and stupid. I am not just your sister. I am also a woman. So call me your little lambkin, your little bunny. Remember that I am not your dearest sister, but your sweet mistress. Remember that the most beautiful thing in a man besides his tie is his tender loving care." But it seems that all those nuances are way beyond Christian. I'm not playing on words, even if I'm making it look like I am. I need tender loving care. I would really like for Christian to treat me like his mistress, in his heart and in his letters. My heart is shivering with cold.

My evenings are getting busier than ever. I now have more than twenty hours of ballet, trombone, karate,

Indology, Spanish, mechanics, electronics, and mythology lessons, spread out over the five school nights of the week. It would probably double the night count if I had to add the hours I spend bumming around downtown with Dick Dong, reading pornographic novels, maintaining my passionate one-way correspondence with my despicable brother, or thinking about Constance Extinct.

As for notions and knowledge, I'll swallow anything, anytime, any old how. My voracity delights my teachers. Zio seems to wonder about the overexertion such voracity must impose upon me. But he's not throwing wrenches in my gears. Without saying a word, he pays for whatever course I fancy taking. Once, as I was retiring to my room, I heard him whisper to Zia, "Yahweh has gifted this child with great energy. He probably has a great destiny in store for her. I wonder what worries her so much, what she's seeking so desperately." I'm on the go twenty-four seven. I study every single thing I see in its every detail. I follow my every thought to its utmost end, with actions. I decipher, register, and compare every single thing that comes to me in my sleep. Yet every night, at the very second when sleep finally hits me, the day I just had, even if it was brimming with activity, never fails to seem suspicious, devoid of any value, making me shake with fear. I always anticipate with fear the return of night, when I must fully face myself, when I must add one more zero to the sum of my past, when I come one full step closer to the border beyond which nothing lies, not even the future. You must not lose hope, dear Berenice, my little bunny, little bat, little lambkin, little lemur. There are still so many things left to consider before

232

the time comes for me to make my decision. The helicon and accordion must still tell me all their secrets. I've never smoked. I've never gotten drunk. I've never masturbated. The Sanskrit texts may be hiding some cosmic message that still hasn't been cracked by the billions of eggheads who've read them. I don't know how to pilot a plane. I've never ridden a motorbike. I've never seen the Barren Lands. I've never turned nineteen. We'll see what happens then. It dawns on me, suddenly, that I wasn't this clueless when I still had Constance Extinct. Phooey! Phoo-ey! Ph-o-o-e-y!

56

From the simple truth, the blinding blatancy that Zio is and always has been a mere figment of my physiological apparatus (a shadow in my eyes, a noise in my ears, a smell in my nostrils, and a shiver when he skims past me), I've come to stunning conclusions. I'm free! Free to open and shut my eyes! Free to punch here and there! Free to kneel before this woman or spit in that man's face! Tormented by the void's blazing lustre when I clumsily tried to distort its appearance, I refused to believe that Zio didn't exist, had never existed, had no existence whatsoever, that he only existed through me, that he only started existing when I focused on him and stopped existing when he stopped filling my thoughts. Enough is enough! Time to snap out of this confusion of senses and walk steadfastly into the light. Enough sleep! Time to stay awake at all costs! No one can exert influence over me unless I consent to it, driven by some devious ill will. You could argue that anyone can inflict physical injuries upon me without my consent. I agree, provided I may add that physical injuries don't occur between souls, but between things, so if the roof collapses, it too can inflict physical injuries upon me without my consent, and a snake bite can poison me without my consent. No one but me has power over me. Lightning, arsenic, alcohol, arrows and bullets have some power over me, but those are things, and things are likable. How many times must I remind myself of it? If I want to, I'm free to go to Chandernagor, Mahé, Joué-lès-Tours, or the docks! Enough shadows and ghosts! Time for tangible things! Time for courage too! But if I break all bonds, I'll jump head first into ether, and it seems to me (and whatever seems always seems important) that I'm more alone in this ether than on a wooded mountain... So be it!... It will be hard to live in ether, extremely difficult, painfully frivolous. So be it! Would you rather tame illusions and cuddle ghosts? Why wouldn't you? And if, following the light, you reached a place no one has ever reached? Light is a river calling me; there's something at its mouth. Someone strong enough to follow the truth to the very end is someone who'll climb on a sunbeam and wind up falling into the sun.

Zio and all the others only exist because I consent to their existence. I need three days and three nights to absorb the spirit of that solid logic. For slowly, over the centuries, my human soul came to lose control of my flesh, bit by bit. God! The thought of it! Willingly confined to the slow narrowing of their living space by setback lines (the front of your house must be perfectly aligned with the front of your neighbour's house) and other like stupidities, humans have degenerated so much that they have now totally forgotten what the lowest of rats still remember when, caught in a trap, they'll sacrifice any limb denying them the power to run as far as their eyes can see. A swallow would rather let itself die than give up any of the four winds. Therefore, I have completely adopted the stubborn logic of rats and swallows. Therefore, bit by bit, Zio's stupid authority over me slowly wanes, weakens, dwindles, dissolves.

Dick Dong and I have a date. We are to meet at nine thirty on the corner of Fourth Street and Fifth Avenue. I can't go to this date because I'm learning to play the trombone with Mr. Klaust, and by nine fifteen my faithful unbreakable hellhound watchdog of a taxi will be waiting for me at the door. This means I can only go to that date if I ditch Mr. Klaust, the taxi, and Zio. For one thing, such an option seems totally impossible to me. But as I keep thinking logical thoughts, it soon proves to be quite easy. I just have to want to go on the date, open the door (who can't open a door when it just needs a push?), and move forward, putting one foot in front of the other (who can't walk?). I want, I stand up, I walk away. I don't even need to run. Because Mr. Klaust, who is legless, couldn't possibly run after me.

"Where do you think you're going, young lady? Where are you off to now?"

I should give some kind of answer to Mr. Klaust's desperate questions, but I'm in the process of becoming a free human being, and a human being in the process of becoming a free human being should be tight-lipped.

Dick Dong is taking his sweet time, the rotten egg. That renegade always makes me wait. I have a headache. There's my rub: on my forehead. Constance Extinct, come rub your moist muzzle against my rub. My first pair of high heels hurt my ankles. Constance Extinct, come put your cold feet where my shoes pinch. My new bra hurts my clavicles. Constance Extinct, come back! You were always there, beside me, within soul's reach, yet I often didn't even notice you. How could you stand there, so gentle, so kind, so vulnerable, without me hugging you tight, squeezing you until you pass out? Dick Dong shows up, without fanfare or flourish, embracing the pole on which I'd been leaning comfortably while I waited for him. I want to shoot daggers at him. But I don't. I'm too lonely, too afraid. I smile at him sweetly. He's barely been here five seconds when I start exposing the infamous freedom scheme I've been devising over the past three days and three nights. He lets me talk, patiently and wearily. He lets me say, without interrupting me, everything that's been weighing on me. He figures the longer he lets me speak, the more rights he'll have over me. I'm done talking. Without missing a beat, he challenges me to prove everything I told him over the last two hours.

"If you're truly free, you can spend the whole night with me. And if you can spend the whole night with me, nothing can stop you from spending the whole night with me. If you spend the whole night with me, I'll believe that you're truly free."

He spoke American. That's the only language he speaks. I actually hold that against him.

"So be it! I'll spend the night with you. But where will

we spend the night together? I'd like for us to spend the night out on the street."

"Let's do it."

We've made up our minds. We morally get ready to spend the night out on the street, together. Throughout the night, Dick Dong tries to convince me to go back to the columbarium.

"Your uncle will murder you when you get home. If you stay here one more minute, he'll kill you. If you don't go to him now, he'll grind you to a pulp. I know him, you know!"

I roll up my sleeves so he can see my arms, and I start waving them right and left like mad.

"Look at my arms! See how they obey me! See how they answer to me! Who could ever stop such arms? If I wanted to saw them off, all I'd need is a saw. If I wanted to hammer three nails into my arm, all I'd need is a hammer and three nails. My arms only belong and answer to me. My arms are a piece of my soul. My arms are a sample of my soul. Nothing can stop my soul. I can ask my soul anything I want: it's obedient and faithful to me. It obeys me. I obey myself. I'm staying here. If Zio asks my arms to rise, even if he threatens to grind me to a pulp, will my arms rise? But this is all too deep for you. Zio can't stop me from wanting to stay here all night and stay for the whole night. Because, right now, he can't see me or hear me. Because he doesn't exist. From the second he leaves the scope of my eyes, of my ears, of my nostrils, he stops existing, stops living; he's dead, he can't touch me anymore. He may kill me, sure, but only if I want him to, if I bring him back to life, if I let him back into the scope of my eyes, of my ears, of my nostrils. Because Zio, like you, would never exist if I didn't have eyes or ears, or nostrils."

"You blow me away. You do. Really. You really do."

The sun is rising… again. I'm sitting on the edge of the sidewalk with my feet on the street, and it's as though I were sitting on a rock with my feet in the river. Dick Dong has deserted his post; he's chickened out. I put my trombone in my mouth and blow off-key. This daybreak reminds me of another, the one Constance Extinct and I had one early morning. The first rays of sun stir up the sounds of the city. It's as though the sounds of the city were mirrors meant to reflect sunlight. I play my trombone off-key, the notes harmoniously blending in with the cacophony of pitchy bugles, drums, and xylophones rising all around me.

57

The toothing must endure, the roof must hold. The wheel mustn't stop turning. I'm aching—ding-a-ling. But the zinc rains well. My hands are bloody; the shroud's hemp ropes peeled them like a grater shreds carrots. I'm dangling into space from a shroud hanging from the ceiling of the universe. To avoid falling into the void, I must, using the strength of my bare hands, support all the weight of my body, all the weight of my soul. My soul, any second now, will leave me with a piercing scream: I'm going mad. I must hold on to my senses with both hands, wringing their necks so that they won't disperse, or leave, or vanish into thin air, or escape from me like air from a burst balloon. I want to be a drama queen.

There's a soft spot in my heart for the chemistry teacher. Two pigeons once loved each other tenderly…

"What is phenol, Berenice? Speak! What is phenol?"

He wants me to answer that phenol is an oxygenated benzene derivative extracted from tar and coal oils, but I won't answer that phenol is an oxygenated benzene derivative extracted from tar and coal oils. I've had enough of giving him the answers he wants, that chemistry wants, that the whole world wants. He won't stop asking me about phenol, phosphate, phosgene, phosphines, phosphite, or phosphoric anhydride, and I've had enough. When I sleep peacefully at my desk, he wakes me up to ask me about phenol, phosphate, phosgene, phosphines, phosphite, or phosphoric anhydride. I've had enough answering the right answers. If Constance Extinct heard me answer, she would laugh, laugh like three hundred and forty-two groundhogs doused with laughing gas.

"I didn't avoid the reefs, Sir! I sailed straight into entire archipelagos and saw them burst into pieces like a flock of migrating egrets resting on the very spot where a bomb lands! Unfurling onto the mainland plains with the Mississippi's impetuosity, I destroyed everything, uprooted all trees, blew up all dikes, washed away all docks like nutshells! And I will soon spread into an enormous, clear gulf to merge with one of those currents that carry oceans beyond coastal borders and beyond the stars! And that, Sir, is why we must destroy Carthage!"

"And what is phosgene, Berenice?"

"It's a *con* pound, Sir, not a compound! Because, you see, from the depths of my Anapurna, I carved, in solid rock, a shaft leading to the light, to the tip of all things! Because, you see, sitting below my high mountain as you are sitting below this roof, I can finally breathe light and air! Do you even know what a gnu is, Sir? No? I'll tell you what it is! It's a bloodhound, a filthy beast, a despicable yak! And do you know what a yak is, Sir? No? I'll tell you what it is! A yak is a human being like you and me, a filthy teacher like you and me, a despicable chemistry teacher like you and me! And stop calling me Berenice! Only my brother is allowed to, the brother I'll marry right under your nose!"

"We shall see about that."

They saw about it. And I was kicked out of the Einstein school for good.

Zio starts holding me captive, keeping me locked up for days with no more bread and water than wind or sunlight. They barricaded my bedroom door against a whole army. There's only one way out: the window. But if you jump from the ninth cage of a columbarium, you could break your toes or even die. And I don't want to die before I take my revenge. I jump on my bed with both feet just to annoy our holey saints, just to make enough noise to keep them up all night. But as I keep jumping on my bed like mad, I feel that I'm losing my grip. I hear myself laughing like crazy. I feel the exhilaration of insanity hitting me in the stomach, in the heart, in the head. Suddenly, with a frightful crash, the base of the bed breaks, the four iron legs cracking all at once on the spot. I can't see straight. Armed with two iron legs, I run all over the room, hitting the walls as hard as I can. Suddenly, after a few frantic iron blows, the window is smashed to pieces, frame and panes included. Then the winter air blows in, freezing cold, palpable like water, flowing in, taking me like a river. Whatever! I'm jumping! I dive headlong into the winter breach, and, instead of dying after a stunning hundred-foot fall, I collapse into a snow-bank. I can't believe my own body as I get back up. I've sprained both my ankles, but I can walk. So I walk for four days and four nights wearing only my nightgown. Thinking I must be some kind of character shooting a movie scene, people let me walk in peace. I get to the Canadian border. Then, for lack of a better country than my own, for lack of a better destination than the abbey, I decide to double back. Shaking from head to toe with every layer of my skin, I head back to the columbarium.

All agriculture talk is over between Dick Dong and me. Totally over. He keeps talking about one thing and one thing only: love. He wants to turn me into his essential handsy-Peeping-Tom kit. He wants me to become his own little Jezebel, his shut-up-so-I-can-explore-your-anatomy partner, his own real-life pornographic novel. He's got no fucking clue. I need tender loving care, but I don't need it that badly. Hands on my knees, then on my thighs! Hands on my shoulders, then on my breasts! Crappy cow crap. You want breasts? I'll buy you a sweet pair. Enjoying my female parts, sweetie? Let's go to the store and get you fat juicy ones.

"Get your hands off me! Stop groping me or I'll lose it and gouge your eyes out! If I wanted to be groped, I'd still be up in the columbarium, doing it myself. My arms are as long as yours."

"You don't know what you want, Berenice Einberg. You're completely lost."

"Yes, I'm lost. And we've been going out long enough for me to know I could never count on you to find me. I bid you farewell, Sir Dick Dong. Adios amigo! Off vee there Zen!"

"Off vee there Zen? Again?" he says laughing, sure his filthy hands made a big impression.

"Off for the very last off vee there Zen!"

I'm so angry that I almost killed Murder-Quail, the sweet fool. We're at the dinner table. It's time for dessert. And since his first sip of soup, Murder-Quail hasn't been able to take his eyes off my haunting self. He's looking at me, teary eyed: he longs for my friendship. If I were humble and sappy like him, I'd also long for my friendship. That milquetoast makes me sick! I kick him under the table, so hard that, after a while, I'm afraid I'll break his shins. I've made faces at him, sticking out my tongue. I've tried everything. Nothing seems to divert him from his atrocious contemplation. Over the past few days, the irritating feelings he arouses in me have increased geometrically, as my ex-chemistry teacher would say. It feels like he's clinging to my skin and my soul with all his pustular clamminess. This has to stop! I've had enough! I stand up so abruptly, so violently, that I knock over my chair. With tears in my eyes and my hair standing on end, I scream, I shriek.

"Enough, Murder-Quail! Do you hear me? Enough! Enough! Enough! Gosh! Be a man already! React, for frog's sake! Straighten up and hide your soul! Cover that filthy soul! Punch me! Don't you want to rise above your mediocrity, zit-face? Haven't you had enough, yucky yack? Punch me! Do something! Stop looking at me like that! Haven't I done enough to you? Haven't I rejected you often enough? Haven't you had enough being nagged by me, a girl? Don't you long for a breath of fresh air, you disgusting anaerobic microbe? Don't you want to be worthy and strong?"

Zio is out. Poor Zia is doing the best she can: she's making a fuss. The other cousins are disappearing under the table one after another, letting themselves slide off the backs of their chairs. Murder-Quail is crying softly, with his head down and his eyes buried in his hands. Seizing the fruit salad bowl, I walk around the table and tip it over his head.

"That child has always been kind to you," begs Zia. "What's wrong with you? You lunatic!"

"Fight back, you big chicken!"

Then I slap Murder-Quail. Then, riled up by my own violence, I slap him again and again. No reaction. I grab him by the hair and pull with all my strength so he'll stand up straight. No fighting back. The chair topples over, and Murder-Quail bangs his skull and loses consciousness, it seems. I tell myself that I want to kill him and that I will kill him. I'm overwhelmed. I take off my shoes, hitting Murder-Quail with them in an effort to revive him.

"Look at me! Come on! Look at me! Do something! Move!"

I hit him again and again. As soon as I feel a twinge of pity, I hit him harder to shut him up. My heart beats so loud that I can hear it. It's so hot in my head that I feel like the walls are melting. Moving at last, Murder-Quail makes a run for the stairs. Terror has given him wings. He's running so fast that I only manage to catch up to him on the second flight. I grab him, hold him back for a second. But he's shaking so much that I suddenly feel like this is hopeless, that nothing matters anymore, and I let him go, brutally pushing him off.

"Run! Bolt! Beat it! Scram!"

I pushed him so powerfully that he falls over, tumbles down the stairs like a ball, and rolls onto the sidewalk. Someone calls the police. Someone calls the fire department. Someone tells the electricians. An ambulance arrives, buzzing like a swarm of bees. I don't give a damn.

58

They locked me up in the bathroom closet. My lower spine is burning, hurting, killing me. I've been trapped in here for two weeks. Sitting at the back of the bathroom closet, I can't see a thing. When Zio opens the hatch to hand me another ration of black broth, I see Zio's hand, the nails on Zio's hand, the small black hairs on Zio's hand. I always hear the same noises: soaping up, tooth brushing, gargling, urinating, defecating, flushing. It's black, jet black, pitch black. I'll only be set free when I feel some kind of genuine remorse for my behaviour. There's nothing I regret less than what I've been accused of. I refuse to apologize for trying to stop hurting. I won't say a word. I keep busy as best I can, driven by the vague hope I might escape, pleased that I didn't beg, swearing that I'll never beg. I've undertaken to remove all thirteen tiles from the floor of my small rectangular realm. I'm not exaggerating when I say this task is as hard and absorbing as putting a boat in a bottle. My only tool is a safety pin, and the tiles are so firmly cemented that I'm having a hard time telling, just by touch, where the joints are. I haven't yet managed to remove my first tile. But the first tile is always the hardest. Once I've done it, the other twelve will come off readily. Then, I'll get on with the floorboards, the beams, the chimney. Who's never dreamed of dismantling a ten-cage columbarium with a single safety pin? Wherever you are, there's always some great task to tackle, some impossible feat. Drawing on my desire never to beg for mercy, I'll do whatever it takes, with my safety pin, to pull the whole world to pieces. And then it dawns on me: when the columbarium is fully dismantled, I won't be trapped in my closet anymore. Anyway, in a year from now, I certainly won't be trapped in my closet anymore, my beautiful closet fortified with wall plates. I should add that I'm fully naked—they stripped me bare for fear I might kill myself with whatever I was wearing. Being buck-naked, I can't do a striptease, so I suffer from an awful lack of hobbies (all work and no play makes Jack a dull boy). When Zio puts his hand in the hatch to give me my ration of black broth, I really let him have it!

"You're a laughing stock, Zio! I scoff at everything you do to trick me! In fact, I Cheshirely laugh at your foolishness! You'll never defeat me! You'd have to kill me to subjugate me, and you don't have the heart or the mind to do it!"

I've been thinking a lot about Constance Extinct. When I suffer my worst bouts of despair, I take her ghost in my arms, squeeze her real tight, and feel her bones bend. Gone are the days when I beat my head against the walls! To calm down, cool off, and comfort me, I've got a ghost. No living creature could give me more human warmth than that ghost or cause me to relax and sleep like that ghost. Even talking to her helps.

"I haven't betrayed you, fair ghost. I won't betray you, fair ghost. Because you're the object of betrayal they want to pry away from me, right? Because they want me to beg and grovel at their feet so that I'll lose you, right? Because it's you, your innocence, your kindness, and your beauty that I'm fighting for in this very closet, right?"

I also think of Christian. I think of him out of habit, because I trained myself to do it. He's got no guts. I think of Constance Extinct. I remember everything clearly, her every movement, her every word. And what a revenge that is! What a wonderful revenge! Thanks to you, Constance Extinct, and our handful of memories, I'm avenged in advance, victorious in advance, radiant in advance. Thank you! Thank you! Thank you! I remember every mango we stole, every starfruit we stole, every candle stub we lit. If only I could remember more! If only I could remember more fiercely! We drew matchstick men and women on the pavement with graphite scraps. And snow! How many first snowfalls have we welcomed together? Two? Four? What a beautiful egg you left in me before you left! I think of you and it's wonderful, so wonderful, so incredibly wonderful! One night, it was cold outside and you hugged me, laughing and shivering, clinging to my back with all your strength. You said you felt good. "This feels so good! It feels so good to be together when it's that cold outside. It feels so good to be in our bed. I feel so good. It feels like I'm sleeping with my eyes open." You told me that when you were little, you owned a big Saint Bernard, and that you slept side by side. You told me that the dog refused to lie under the covers with you, preferring to lie on top, and never got mad. I said something that I didn't think was funny. But you found it funny and started laughing. You hugged me so tight that I could feel you laugh through me. You fell asleep. In your sleep, you slowly drifted away from me to your side of the bed. Shortly before I fell asleep, you threw your leg over my legs. When I woke up in the middle of the night, your leg was still lying on my legs, still cold.

59

Things happen in a certain way, often in a disturbing way. If you let them go by for fear of being poisoned, it's over: you've missed your chance. Things won't happen again. You must take things, altogether, no matter which way they happen. You must grab the embers, seizing the fire in the thick of the flame. You can't just sit there, watching things go by and remain stupidly intact, comforting yourself with the thought that if you'd taken the things that just went by, you would've been burned to death. When something or someone comes my way, they're mine. The plane that flies over the city knocks on my door. I won't kill myself because I don't want to leave. When you want something, you're safe. I won't leave because once I'm gone, I won't want anything anymore, and then I'll have to eradicate myself. My own logic scares me.

Constance Extinct's moist muzzle and cold feet are screaming louder and louder, calling out ever more fiercely. Wandering in the street, I run into a little blond girl. I grow morbidly interested in her, as I would in any little blond girl. I watch her getting closer, as though I were a tiger. She has Constance Extinct's skinny arms and skinny legs. When she walks past me, she looks at me with Constance Extinct's big black eyes, as though she shared the same thoughts as Constance Extinct. My muscles stiffen. My breathing becomes heavy. I turn around and see her vanish around the corner. I let her walk away! Gears start shifting inside my soul, loud and fierce. With no way out, their energy gathers, dilating, distorting me from within. It's a death wish, the wish to be saved. Where would all that spinning take me if I let it? I distinguish murder patterns. I should've never let that little girl walk away. I should've grabbed her. I should've told her to turn around and come with me.

"Come and be my friend," I should've said. "Come and live with me. We'll find a hiding place. I won't let any adult cast a shadow on your childhood joy. I'll shelter your childhood joy for you. As long as I live, nothing or no one will tarnish it. I'll arm myself to the teeth to save your childhood joy. I'll fight to my last drop of blood to keep you safe from adulterity."

Why did I ever let that little girl walk away, she who spoke so much to my soul, she to whom my soul had so much to tell? I'm such an idiot! When will I be free to do what I want? Soul-sick to death, I decide to play truant. In Mousermoth's memory, I go to a Polish cinema. The small movie theatre is almost empty and smells mouldy and cold. To be alone with the screen, I sit down in the first row. Let's relax, let's breathe in. Beautiful and umbrella-free, a woman and a man are strolling on a shore in the pouring rain. They're walking slowly, almost staggering, holding each other, as though they were walking on intoxicating riches, on the jewels of a huge pirate trunk. Swoony-eyed, they're kicking pebbles with the tips of their feet as if the stones were rubies and emeralds. We can hear sad guitar music. We're carried over to a street. We can see tin roofs glisten white in the rain's grey shadow. We can see a rivulet coiling around a manhole. These images move me. What do you do when you're moved? Do you write poems, paint, sculpt? Why were that beautiful woman and that beautiful man strolling in the rain without umbrellas, kicking pebbles with the tips of their feet as if the stones were rubies and emeralds? I'm quite intrigued. What will happen next? We're in a bedroom. I should have seen it coming. We can see a bed, love in all its glory. The little sweethearts are naked! We can see a mouth mounting a breast that fills the whole screen. The pretty rain and pebbles have found their purpose. It all becomes logical. Here I am, educated and disgusted. I storm out of the theatre. What we breathlessly call beautiful, oohing and aahing with our eyes split open, has shown me its true face. Beauty is a seductive shimmy worse than a belly dance. What are art and poetry? Phenol! What is phenol, Berenice? Who will turn all those museums into barracks, those bagpipes into blunderbusses, those bucolics into hoplites? Sir, at what time is the train of the Messiah, the God of Armies' son, scheduled to arrive? And until sundown, I wander adrift on this earth, tirelessly singing, "Beauty is a seductive shimmy worse than a belly dance" to the tune of *Old MacDonald Had a Farm*. Let's get drunk on disgust. *Let us, my pet, grow our rancours tenderly* (Nelligan).

Once a week at my new school, on Wednesdays, I'm a gymnastics instructor. I'm in charge of the fifth-graders. I never miss school on Wednesdays. When I'm with these young girls, I feel sort of ecstatic. They love. It seems that they just can't help but love, and love with all their hearts. They even love me, a person in no way loveable, and loved me right off the bat. They flock around me as soon as I show up, hugging me with their laughs, their bright eyes, their wide-open faces, their eager souls. They're wooing me. Each of them tries to win me over. I feel shy, humbled, clumsy, overwhelmed, overjoyed. One of them makes me howl at the moon, and I think of her when I run to avoid being late. Her name alone is enough to make my heart race: Constance Klorüss. I step onto the basketball court in a sweat. I feel like I've entered a sanctuary. All my little courtesans are there. It feels so warm inside my soul! I can feel it overflow with riches. They've just seen me. They all buzz over to greet me, with Constance Klorüss at the head of the hive. I dive into her eyes as deep as wells. I take as many of those clammy little hands, wiggling like fish, as I want. I tousle their locks, softer and smoother than grass. My arms are loaded with arm clusters. I love how I love to love, and am loved just as I love to be loved. I'm so happy. They're taking me to such a beautiful world, with no arts, no literature, no politics, no business, no cars, no hanky panky. I extend recess. They have so much to share, and everything they say is so sweet, so harmless, so easy to understand. I don't speak. I listen to them with all my strength. I strictly use my mouth to hear them better, as though I had a third ear. Once the gym class itself is over, I take Constance Klorüss aside and tell her she was so nice to me that I almost feel compelled to give her the rest of the day off.

"And I'm taking you with me!"

"Wow! Wow! For real? I'm so happy! You're the nicest gym teacher ever!"

"But come here so I can help you comb your hair and freshen up a bit. You wouldn't want to walk on Fifth Avenue with your hair in your face and your face all sweaty, would you now?"

I help her freshen up and carefully smooth her hair. They can think whatever they want! This afternoon, Constance Klorüss is mine and mine only, fully mine, as though she were my own child.

We go through Central Park, walking from one tree to the next, but on the grass, not on the paths. I suggest we play who finds the biggest pebble. This game captivates us. A big pebble spotted in the distance is cause for a ruthless race and endless arguments.

"I saw it first. It belongs to me."

"Taking it first is what matters, not spotting it."

We go into a drugstore and sit down at the counter. She wants chocolate ice cream and I want vanilla. She puts away her big pebble in her satchel, fearing I might steal it from her, takes her chocolate ice cream with both hands and savours it mouthfully, as though it cost a million dollars. On one of the drugstore's rotating displays, there's a dagger that I've been eyeing for quite a while. Using Constance Klorüss as a cover, I steal it. Constance Klorüss finds herself utterly shocked, utterly sad, utterly sullen. I hate my pretty dagger so badly I could eat it. We visit every shop and store on Fifth Avenue. She wants to buy it all. I wish I were a millionaire. Mesmerized by the darkness of the Lincoln Tunnel, she wants us to walk through it. Although I know from experience that the Lincoln Tunnel is closed to pedestrians, I want to fulfill her desire. Barely twenty steps inside the dark, curb-free tunnel, we're apprehended by the police. Late that night, I walk Constance Klorüss back to her life, a life from which I had to borrow her, but where she belongs. Her sobbing mother and her shouting father promise they'll report me to the school authorities. Turning vulgar, I insult them, calling them lousy people makers, threatening them with the stolen dagger. Through my anger and my hate, I see Constance Klorüss' heart breaking. I know by heart every face of the night. I know that tonight, I won't be able to sleep or read, or withstand the tartness of my thoughts. I light a cigarette. The night is so quiet that, as I blow on the flame, I hear it flap like a wet flag, roar like a motorcycle. I'm really thirsty. But I don't get up, for fear I might disturb the numbness that seized me for keeping still too long. Merciless, my thirst grows more intense, unbearable. I get up, but I'm determined to take revenge and drink something other than water. The decanter full of manzanilla that Zio secretly keeps for Pesach behind the volumes of an encyclopedia is made out of thick crystal encrusted with opal vermiculations. I head back to bed hugging the decanter, which, four centuries ago, a Bragança gave to some gypsy girl who became the great-grandmother of Zio's first wife. I've been leaving the window open since Constance Extinct died so her ghost can come and go as she pleases. Suddenly, a bat storms in. With my hair standing on end, I watch it and hear it beat its wings as it flies three times across the ceiling and grazes the bedsheets on its way out the window. When Constance Extinct and I woke up, I always had a bunch of her locks in my mouth. When I had a pebble in my shoe, I liked to lean on her to raise my foot. At night, she was afraid to go to the toilet alone: I had to go with her, sit on the edge of the bathtub and wait until she was done. I awaken our memories one by one. Now that my arms are loaded with manzanilla, there's no harm in getting all worked up about getting drunk. I get back up. Let's drink standing! I stare at the almost full decanter. To drink is to act like Mousermoth. I'm the one drinking, but it's Mousermoth's lips on the bottle. I've taken all the candles we had left and lined them up on the floor like tiny tin soldiers before lighting them. Standing in the middle of the candles, my legs spread wide as for a duel, I swallow the dark fluid. I gulp it down as fast as it can flow into my stomach. I only stop when I must stop to catch my breath. Drunkenness will soon ensue. I hiccup, wobbling, laughing without realizing it. Overly elated, I recite a snippet from the *Song of Wine*: "*So glad am I that I fear I shall break down and sob outright!*" To hasten my intoxication, I stagger more than I usually would. I soon lose control, walking on candles without realizing it, retching like a cesspool. Each spasm makes me scared I might spit my heart out. I'm afraid to die. I'm crying. I throw the empty decanter against the radiator. It bursts into pieces. I'm laughing. I'm not afraid to die anymore: I *want* to die. I look for the dagger, my pretty dagger. I'm disgusted with myself and I intend to restore order fast and sweet. I see a big flame go up the curtains. I find the dagger and, slowly, systematically furrow my skin every which way.

"I'm festering! Do you hear me? Festering! I'm full of filth!"

Now Zio and all his holey saints are standing there, staring at me, speechless. Have they been there long? The firemen show up and put out the fire.

60

So, I'm tired of being all alone. Whom could I visit that I still haven't met, whose dreadful tedium I haven't chanced upon yet? A crazy idea comes to mind: I could go meet my favourite pornographer. I strongly approve of said idea. Let's go meet him at once. If he lives in Oklahoma City, I'll walk to Oklahoma City. If he lives in Yakutia, I'll travel to Yakutia. Who knows? He may be some kind of wonder-worker. Maybe he breeds unknown species. He might give me a hippo squirrel to thank me for my lovely visit. I find his publisher's number in the phone book and call him. My name is Berenice Einberg. I'm a reporter with the *Saturday News*. Do you know where I could reach Blasey Blasey? One moment! they say.

"Blasey Blasey here. I'm listening."

"Listen, Mr. Blasey. I'm not a reporter. I'm all alone in the world and I want to meet you. I need to meet you. I need to meet someone I don't know, like you. Don't hang up! It's not a joke. I'm desperate. I've read almost all your books, and would love for us to meet and discuss them."

"Okay. Come over to my place tonight around six. We'll have dinner."

He makes me write down his address, says goodbye, and hangs up. I'm overexcited. A pornographer! If Zio only knew! If Mousermoth only knew! This date makes me happy anyway. At least, today, I did what I needed to do with my life. What should I do? Where should I go? These questions have been dealt with.

The basement of the columbarium where Blasey Blasey's cage is located is just as parallel and perpendicular as Zio's cage. Being a pornographer isn't worth it, I think to myself, disappointed. However, when I take a closer look at the columbarium, I feel it's more stylish, more refined. For instance, the lobby is full of fake flowerbeds filled with fake rushes. Also, abstract paintings are hanging on the walls in the hallways. Because it's been raining non-stop for days, I carefully wipe my feet before ringing the doorbell of Cage 3456. Blasey Blasey welcomes me in a bathrobe, smelling of perfume.

"Judging by the sound of your voice, I thought you were older, more mature. But valour does not depend upon age. It's from Rabelais, I think. In any case, you have nothing to fear. I'm not an ogre. I'm a most bourgeois bachelor. Come in! Come in! Make yourself at home. You have nothing to fear. I don't eat little girls. I have a wife and four children, and I adore my wife. And take off those shoes. Hand them to me so I can put them by the radiator to dry off. Because of the somewhat unusual genre of my novels, everybody thinks I'm a pervert. But again, you have nothing to fear. I write books like others work in a factory. I must provide for my family."

He can't stop talking. He won't even stop to let me say yes. I can live with that. On the small table lit by a fake chandelier, there's a bottle of champagne waiting in a bucket, a fully feathered pheasant, bread, and a whole lot of fruit and pastries. It's quite a spread! Without waiting for his invitation, I sit down at the table and start eating. Seeing that I've sat down at the table and started eating, he also sits down at the table and starts eating, still speaking non-stop. I feel good. I am… somewhere else, delightfully disoriented. I'm having dinner at a pornographer's! Tomorrow, I must have dinner at a taxidermist's.

"Goodnight, Mr. Pornographer. And thank you. The pheasant was very much excellent."

"Goodnight, Miss Einberg. I'm now convinced you don't believe one word of those gossips tarnishing my reputation. You've seen it yourself: I'm an over-devoted father and inveterate bachelor, as honest-to-God as they go. Don't be scared to come back. It was my pleasure to meet you. I really like you. Blah blah blah…"

In my mind, over time, the gardener has become as beautiful as his suicide. He never said "No frigging way!" No! He said "No frogging way!" He never called his dog "Fido." No! He called it "Zero." He didn't like talking about the wars he'd fought in Africa and Belgium. "'You travelled quite a lot. Tell me about your travels!' 'No frogging way! I don't like to. It makes me blue.'" He constantly wore his brown fishing hat with the edges bent up. He rolled his own cigarettes. He drank like a fish. There were always a hundred empty beer bottles or so lined up against the shed's footings. He often talked to me about his son Renaud, who died at the same age I was then, run over by a truck. He told me about Renaud's tremendous agility. "Renaud could catch a running weasel and jump as high as the quarry winch." That gardener never laid hands on a spade. In fact, Mousermoth has always despised cultivated plants. I wonder what he was doing on the island. Are there gardeners who are meant to watch dandelions grow?

Jerry de Vignac is as cute as a button. We all agree. But he has a lisp. He has a lisp, and since he enrolled at the Krostyns', that speech defect has caused a schism between us ballet pupils. I like his lisp. It seems to me that, without his lisp, he wouldn't be so shy, so gentle, so sweet. In his defence, all those who've taken his side, including myself, maintain that he has the same lisp as Alcibiades. The others, those who are against him, maintain that he has the lisp of a pervert. He and our Classics teacher are cousins. I almost didn't get to meet him at all. There was a vote to decide whether *Swan Lake* would be performed with or without male involvement. And I won. The Krostyns are planning to put on our *Swan Lake* in a big theatre and make it a smash hit so they can fill the school they just built. We sometimes rehearse into the early hours. During breaks, Jerry de Vignac teaches me South-American dances. And wherever his hands hold me, they blow me away. In his hands, I feel myself come to life, like a crocus in the first light of day. I'll sleep with him, if only to despise myself even more. I *will* sleep with him. I'll pay him if I have to.

61

Human languages are evil tongues. They have too much vocabulary. Their most abridged dictionaries are a thousand pages too long. Such superfluity creates confusion. Feelings are perceived to the touch. Everything my stomach, my heart, or my eyes recognize as one and the same phenomenon should bear only one name. All the states of visceral oppression designated by words such as sorrow, suffering, hatred, disgust, angst, remorse, fear, desire, sadness, despair, or spleen, actually refer to one and the same reality. I've always mixed them up, shamelessly. So should linguists and gabbers. Every human being is alone, and the hostility of our species comes from that loneliness. When I was a child, I would call "fear" the painful defeat I met each time I rebelled against my loneliness. Pasteur was able to cure rabies because he detected the same pathogen in every case of rabies. If humans insist on confusing lice with lions, stingrays, wolves, eels, hyenas, and triceratops, they'll never be able to find a cure for any of their diseases. And you heard it straight from Berenice Einberg.

Here's the story of a handsaw. One crisp September morning, in two different spots, one foot apart, the earth's crust shook, swelled, split, and two heads sprang up. Thus were born two fifteen-year-old humans, whose coincident release from subterranean swamps prompted a mutual friendship. They lived together. People saw them travelling hand in hand from one country to another. Although they both felt a burning desire to communicate, Grebelda and Adleberg never understood each other. There was a lack of transparency between them. This deficit was most obvious when they engaged in dialogue. Grebelda would say, "I'm famished, let's eat pepper." Adleberg would answer, "Tea corals." Grebelda would say, "This hill is so small that it does not even rise above the plain." Adleberg would answer, "Enamels in May." Grebelda would say, "That worm is sour, yuck, nasty, yuck." Adleberg would answer, "Stones in noses." Grebelda would say, "The prince who ran was no prince charming; he was a panting prince." Adleberg would answer, "Stained glass widows." Grebelda would then get mad and say, "I don't understand a word you say!" To which Adleberg would stoically answer, "Bull dice." Grebelda faced the facts: she had to act. There was a wall between her and her birthmate, and that wall should be breached. Scratching the wall with her nails, she extracted a few molecules, and entrusted them to a man of the highest expertise so he could study it. "'It is a malleable, resistant metal.' 'What do you suggest I use?' 'A handsaw.'" Grebelda went to a bookstore, bought a handsaw and went looking for her friend. She made him say a few things to make sure that the barrier was still there, drew a circle in the air, seized the handsaw and, following the contours of the chalk circle, she started sawing. After she was done sawing, she removed the small moon cut-out from the wall and inserted her elbow into the hole. Adleberg started laughing like a horse and finally said something that made sense: "You are tickling me!" Horrified, Grebelda burst into tears, slit her throat with the handsaw, and died. Jerry de Vignac told me that story. When a human being's anxiety reaches a certain level, verbal diarrhea ensues. A perfect example would be the pornographer, aka writer, author, novelist, and poet. Since anxiety is so hard to distinguish from a head cold, I'm surprised so little has been written under the inspiration of a head cold. The confusion comes from the fact that the level of human anxiety, not the level of a head cold, is used as a basis to assess beauty and describe the blows we're dealt. Indeed, things are only said to be "beautiful" when they cause anxiety, and "more beautiful" when they cause more anxiety. What's a sky or a dreamy sunset? It's a sky or a sunset so painful that you have to pause and ponder your pain. What do you do when you have a splitting headache? You pause and ponder. What's anxiety, pain, an aching soul? Heal them! By order of Berenice Einberg!

The theatre is full, so full that the walls are bulging like a pregnant woman's belly, like barrel staves. It's the intermission. We danced quite badly, received much applause, and our teachers are now congratulating us backstage, bouncing like kangaroos with cestode-ridden encephala.

One of them, a sexy Slavic teacher, comes over to Jerry de Vignac and me.

"You two are quite a hit. Bravo, children."

"But I tripped twice."

"Never mind! Never mind! As the old Chinese saying goes: *When you fall on your face, you are moving forward!* Keep going!"

"And when you fall on your behind?"

"Bravo! Bravo! Keep going! Now give me your pretty faces so I can kiss your sweet lips! Mmmmm! Mmmmm! What a treat! I'm so proud of you!"

I drag Jerry de Vignac outside. It's raining, like in that medieval tapestry depicting the flood. It's pouring white, straight, parallel, tight drops as thick as chains. The patella-like fixture holding the electric bulb over the door projects a cone of yellow light where huge raindrops are haloed with gold. I circle around an invisible tower with my eyes closed and my arms up in the air like a flamenco dancer, pounding the mud with my poor satin slippers. As I feel my insides flare like Danaë's, my hairdo and my tutu's big tulle crown are dissolving.

"What's gotten into you?" Jerry de Vignac keeps asking, shivering on the front step, covering his head with his raincoat. "What's wrong?"

I stop swirling, go over to him ,and give him my answer.

"You must store everything in your memory through your right eye: the decadent grey backside of those houses, the black mesh of that tin fence, the red shade of the bricks covering the theatre's backside, the queer oval contour of that brown rain puddle—everything. Close your left eye and commit everything to your memory."

Suddenly, the sky slowly starts to shake. Look! Look! Just above us, the green and red lights of a four-engine airplane are flashing.

"You're insane! Insane! When will you say anything that makes sense?"

I kneel down, hugging one of his legs and kissing it from knee to toe.

"Yes, my love, right away. Let's go away! Let's go away from here without wasting one more second! I can't dance anymore. It's absurd, too absurd! What's the use of all those digressions, twists and turns, periphrases, and entrechats? Why should we submit to such nonsense? Let's rush right to the point! Why wait, day after day, for sixty years? Here's what I have in mind. I have a bit of money. We'll rent a hotel room and then, we won't make love; we'll make warmth; and then, we'll make warmth until we're drained, dried out, delivered, dead. I've had enough beating around the bush. Just a little warmth and death… That's all. There's nothing else to expect. Let's go and get it over with—tonight!"

Hauling myself up against his body, I throw my head back and I open his mouth, leaving my own lips up in the air, half-open, so he can take them. That quickly triggers the expected response. He doesn't want to kiss me! He doesn't like me! He pushes me away. Livid, Jerry de Vignac mumbles a few excuses, steps back, and scampers off. Hee-haw! Hee-haw! Hee-haw! Hee-haw! Hee-haw! Hee-haw! I find myself backstage. Mrs. Krostyn herself greets me. She can't believe her eyes. She refuses to believe my muddy slippers or my melted tutu. She's shouting at me. You can shout all you want.

"You idiot! Unbelievable! Good God! Good God! What were you thinking! But...! You're almost next! *Next*! You must hurry and change! Come with me! Quick!"

"I'm going home."

"You... What? Where do you think you're going?"

"I'm going home."

I'm walking toward the stage, with my interlocutor at my heels.

"Berenice Einberg! Berenice Einberg! Come back! Where are you going?"

"Home. You can shout all you want, sweetheart. I'm going home. I'm walking across the theatre because it's the shortest way. I've had enough walking around the shadows!"

At the foot of the curtain, Mrs. Krostyn catches me, clings on to me.

"You're rebelling, just like that, without a word? At least take the time to explain. What happened to you? Did someone hurt you?"

"I've got nothing to say. I'm rebelling, just like that, for no reason. Why should there always be a reason to rebel? Do motives change anything about actions?"

I slide under the curtain. I walk across the stage, bowing beyond expectations. I make my way through the orchestra drumming my fingers on the head of every bald musician. I proceed through the audience, moving forward on my ankles, then on my knees, then on my hands. I try to be funny. Some people sort of laugh. I call a taxi. I give the driver the columbarium's address, as though it were the most natural thing in the world. I tell myself, looking at the back of the driver's swollen neck, that taxi drivers are full of pipes.

263

"Tell me, Mr. Driver, do you know someone who, for twenty dollars, would make warmth to a trained bitch wearing a wet tutu until death do them part?"

62

Zio throws in the towel. Zio abandons me to the acids corroding me. Zio flings me over the nettings, over the railings, over the copings.

"You win! I cannot stand you anymore! I cannot suffer you! I cannot stomach you! Pack up your things at once! Leave this virtuous home at once!"

I don't know which of my latest schemes sparked the blaze. Just yesterday, he said, "I will break you in, even if I shall lose my soul in the process! I will crush the vermin flowing in your veins instead of blood!"

It's been almost five years since I left the island. I haven't seen it in five years. I haven't seen Christian in five years. The island hasn't seen me in five years. Tomorrow, I will roll in the thick soft wheatgrass again. Am I too old now for wheatgrass? I haven't seen wheatgrass in five years. Do I still have a knack for wheatgrass? Will the wheatgrass recognize me? Does Mousermoth still have Three, the Abyssinian cat?

It was five o'clock when he told me to pack up my things. It's now six twenty, and I'm all set, all packed up. My plane leaves at eight twenty-two. I just can't believe what's happening to me. I still live at the same pace as five hours ago. Despite the cousins' suffocating silence, despite that burning feeling I exude, time still crawls by as slow as a crab, as always.

Christian… Christian, from the other end of my exile, I call you softly, flatly, half-heartedly. I'm too crazy and too greedy to dig my own salt out of the ground; I'll become part of you like broomrape grafts onto alfalfa. I'll eat from your hand like a trained crow. I'll eat only what you give me to eat. I desperately give you whatever will I have left. Take good care of it. I give you my mouth. Protect it from all bitterness. Christian, will you find me pretty?

I suddenly realize that I'm not a child anymore. In Constance Extinct's old notebooks, I find most of our "surreptitious dialogues," beautifully handwritten and carefully compiled. They move me to tears.

BERENICE

My boots are full of smoke. (I sniffle). Goodness gracious, my hands stink! Where was I? Dreamland? (I shake my head like a barman shakes cocktails.) Goodness gracious! And my head is also full of water. My, oh my! Am I alone?

ME

Why yes, Bubblehead. You are completely alone. You are always alone, wherever you are.

BERENICE

Oh… really? Really… oh! The walls are so black! The ceiling and the floor are so black! My, oh my! But I cannot see anyone! Actually, I cannot see a thing! Am I truly alone, completely alone?

ME

Yes, Bubblehead. You are always alone, wherever you are. Now leave me alone!

BERENICE

The air too is so black! What have we here... I finally see something. A short red line, up in the air, drawing circles, squares, triangles, rectangles, trapezes, parallelograms... What is it?

ME

It is the geometry, the trigonometry of yesterday, of the day before, and of all other days before that.

BERENICE

I thought I was done with filthy geometry and stinky trigonometry.

ME

They came back to you. They are truly, madly, deeply faithful.

BERENICE

Are they faithful for that long?

ME

For several years.

In a dictionary that suddenly spreads open before my eyes, I read this: "Caligula lived to be ninety-nine years old. He ruled for three years, ten months, and eight days." Is this what you mean?

ME
Yes, Bubblehead, that is exactly what I mean.

63

To leave is not to heal, because you're still there. To come back is just the same. It's time to get started. It's time for me to start killing white men, white women, and white children with a poker. Tomorrow, it will be too late. The time has come to crush hands and feet slowly and collect the fresh blood in a mug. To drink blood. Blood is so warm, like milk coming out of a cow. I want a drop of aqua fortis on my pasty tongue. I want to burn down to its roots the rotten banana taste infused into my mucous membranes. I want the hill to have more sides, a dozen more, a thousand more. Daisies don't grow fast enough, and it makes me steep in my own juices; the time has come for their buds to burst out like thunderbolts, for their petals to soar up to the sky like flying shrapnel. Please no more of that tiny tremor in my bellybutton; any other tremor, a dozen others, a thousand others. When you're alone, you're no dozen, no thousand, no different from your unchanging face. Is there anything beside brine in the work of a slug? Is there anything beside that progressive, very slow softening taking hold of my body and soul, leading me to paralysis? Meanwhile, the first hair of the kind that fall for good and never grow back, falls from my head. *Meanwhile, back at the ranch…*

In the room that used to be my bedroom, I feel cramped, oversized. My bedroom has shrunk. Compared to what it used to be, it looks like a doll's bedroom. My bedroom doesn't fit me anymore, like the old dresses and shoes I found in the attic. I'm fifteen. In a moment, I'll be thirty; if my speed doesn't increase soon, I won't have made a single step outside myself. At my age, Romeo and Juliet had already exhausted their supply of arrows and bombs, giving in to the Titan, Earth, and the Mineral King.

My arrival at the Dorval Airport is a sad one. When I show up at the top of the ramp, I find no regiment of imperial Grenadier guards playing a cavalry march. It's windy, and a flurry of newspaper pages are screeching across the tarmac. I set foot on Montreal soil like an astronaut stepping into a lunar quarry. No one has come to greet me at the foot of the ramp, not even Christian, not even Mousermoth, not even Einberg. I end up on a never-ending bench in a great hall of lost steps. Here, in this hall with a ceiling as high as a cathedral's, no one moves a muscle. The slightest whisper unleashes an avalanche of deafening noises. In the middle of the hall, a white car shines on a revolving stage, wrapped in ribbons like a gift. The young soldier seated in front of me is looking at my knees with sickening sadness. His khaki uniform is a mirror reflecting my own image as sharply as a scalpel. I hate sadness so much! Suddenly, a set of speakers starts speaking to me: "Miss Berenice Einberg, please report to the luggage department." Mrs. Glengarry is standing before the luggage department, waiting for me. She doesn't recognize me. Noticing that I'm staring at her, she shrouds me from head to toe with that horse-dealer look any well-educated human will bestow upon any stranger who dares to stare. Mrs. Glengarry doesn't have one female bone in her body, not even in her teenage breasts or her fine features: she's pure support and devotion. I've barely revealed my identity than she's all over me, breaking out in amazement, compliments, public displays of affection. I remain silent and stiff before her throes, as cruelly indifferent as I can despite feeling painfully sad.

"So you're the welcome committee? The immigration department?"

I'm wearing eyeshadow. I was so sure that Christian would be there to welcome me that I went all out. I soaped myself up to the bone, putting on powder and perfume down to the back of my nostrils. I put my hair up like Madame Bovary. I'm sporting a beautiful canepin southwester and a beautiful black raincoat with golden bows on the shoulders, at the cuffs and on the pockets. I want to yell, *that's enough, chubby cheeks, enough!* at slender Mrs. Glengarry, but I remain silent. I let her hug me to the point of exhaustion, then I say, "Drive me to a flower shop." *And where we found her bones, a columbine has grown* (Nelligan). Very few flower shops sell columbines. I must have come out empty-handed of at least twenty of them before I could find some.

"Drive me to the La Hêtraie Cemetery."

"Nonsense! Why? What for?"

"To pick a beech tree. And since you're only my chauffeur, don't ask questions. The chauffeurs' motto is *Stop talking and start driving.*"

Before the grave of Constance Extinct Cassman, using a trowel, I dump three dozen columbines into the ground. I throw them in upside down, petals down in the earth and roots up in the air, so she can really smell them.

No one told me of Christian's whereabouts. I should say that I didn't ask. Mousermoth is ill. She's been bedridden for a week. Despite all of Einberg's pleas, promises and injunctions, I refuse to go see her. If she could live without me, she can die without me. What more do you want? A glass of water from Spain.

65[*]

I know a woman called Kimberley Ann Jones. Yesterday, I didn't know her. Today, I feel happy, hopeful again. Like pain, hope comes and goes. Like pain, hope is also a plunge. Pain is when you break your teeth falling down from an elm. Hope is when you break your heart falling up into the clouds. As though they were acting in collusion, all of today's events match my good mood. For instance, I get the chance to spite Einberg. I make him writhe in anger, triggering his every tic.

_____

[*] There is no chapter 64 in the original French text.

Mousermoth suffers from foot and mouth disease, a disease cows catch from other cows. Largely because I keep refusing to see her, her rash eventually caused a twenty-four-hour bout of apnea during which we all believed her to be dead. She's now well enough to receive compassionate visitors, so Einberg makes another break for it. He can't understand that the minute he wants me to do something, I lose at once any desire I may have had to do that thing.

"I command you to go upstairs and see your mother!"

"No!"

"Go see her right this minute! And apologize to her for not going before!"

"No! No frogging way!"

He comes closer. He wants to collar me and compel me by force. Making a classic obsidional move, I jump across the table.

"Come on! Catch me if you can! Come on! Jump across the table if you can!"

I beat the table frantically, as though it were a war drum. I also make tiger faces and let out tiger roars like the soldiers under Hamilcar Barca. Einberg scolds me. Einberg scorns me. To make me go over to Mousermoth, he'll resort to all modern handling means if he has to!

"I ordered you to go upstairs to see your mother. My order will be obeyed, even if I must resort to an escalator or an airborne monorail system!"

What *I* want is to make him run. I want him to chase me. Climbing on top of the table, bouncing like a boxer, I bring the fight to him. He looks like he's about to move. He takes a step forward. Swinging his arms as though they were lassos, he threatens me with a chair like a lion tamer performing a show. He's in full furious mode. His thorax is twisting and untwisting. His skin is spotting. His eyes are bulging over his cheeks. Strange, transitory tumours are growing at the back his neck. But he won't run or jump over the table. Pushing my boldness to the max, I jump off the table, right at his feet, landing toe to toe with him.

"Run! Come on, you invalid! Run after me! Come on, you crippled fool! Run, you limping loser!"

He doesn't want to run. No! He's resisting. No! He won't run! Standing so close to me, he thinks he just needs to let himself fall face-first like a wall to weigh me down and detain me. He thrusts himself forward and fails. The hateful convulsions caused by his failure are so strong that he loses all restraint. He starts running, bravely, activating his atrophied leg with both hands. You can run all you want. I'm gloating.

"*I, the jury!*"

I get a head start and squat to laugh at him.

"Look at yourself! You could turn to dust with a single push. Look at me! I'm too swift to be caught by a jackrabbit! Long live the young! From now on, only I, the young, will rule! Only I can save the world from sinking!

I catch my breath and proceed to shout quotes from the dictionary off the top of my head: "The planks of this ship are coming apart! Hate makes you free! Goodwill and humility are just other forms of collusion! They only protect the old, the sick, and the crippled kings. They allow the old, the sick, and the crippled to impose the old, the sick, and the crippled upon the world, in all impunity."

Pillars of mosquitoes akin to smoke pillars are hovering over the marsh. I feel sleepy. I wrap myself in sand. I close my eyes, trying in vain to picture the birds I can hear singing, just by the sounds of their voices. Just by paying close attention to their smells, Constance Extinct could tell me the names of the creatures strolling arm in arm under our feet, between the blades of grass. She would sniff really carefully and say, "I smell a tiger beetle near that daisy." She tried to teach me, but I had neither her gift nor her soul. She only ever succeeded in teaching me to identify that ugly plant with yellow flowers called the common rue. I like plantains because I've known them for a long time, as long as I've known Christian. When I see a plantain leaf, I can confidently say to myself, "This leaf is a plantain leaf." The plants whose names I don't know are like human beings whose names I don't know. I'm asleep on the shore. In my dream, I see the magnificent Tharandt Castle standing on a tall hill, decked with a thousand towers, pepper mills, salt mills, and vinegar bottles. I walk toward the hill and see no other trees around but plantains. A common rue opens the castle gate for me. In the voice of Constance Extinct, she tells me her life story: "I am a common rue. I am hemagogic, anthelminthic, soporific, and sudorific. I haunt dispensaries. I met my first husband in a dispensary while sipping a glass of sulfuric acid. With Barnaby, life slowly became unbearable. Being a rose, he kept insisting that *he* smelled the nicest…" I'm asleep on the shore in the evening sun. A swimmer suddenly wakes me. She's squeezing her nostrils, blowing her nose. She twists her hair like a rag to wring out excess water. She tells me she's hungry.

"I'm hungry. Don't you have anything to eat?"

I run to the abbey and come back with a basket full of bread, meat and fruit.

"I'm thirsty. Don't you have anything to drink?"

I run back to the abbey and find, in the cellar, nothing less than a hundred-year-old bottle of Châteauneuf du Pape. I ask the swimmer where she's from.

"Port Hope, on Lake Ontario."

"Did you swim all the way here?"

"Yes."

"Where are you headed?"

"Finland."

"Will you swim all the way there?"

"Yes."

"What will you do over there?"

"I'll never make it. It's too far away."

"What's your name?"

"Kimberley Ann Jones."

I must never forget that name.

66

One day, the gardener's dog, Zero, came back from the mainland with its head down, its snout bloody, and its ears torn off. The gardener, who was drunk, threw Zero a scornful look, and said, "You got beat, you frogging old fox, eh?" I remember it like it was yesterday. I enter the bedroom of our seriously sick patient, squeezing my eyes shut.

I don't want to see her ugly. It's rather common to refuse to see your mother in an ugly state.

"Cover your face. I don't want to see you ugly."

"I just did, little lemur. Come here. Come take care of me."

I keep my eyes shut. I don't want to see her bent over, sobbing.

"Are you going to cry like a fool? Are there tears in your eyes? You sound like you have a heavy heart."

"No, little lemur. Don't worry. My heart is light, light as air. So is yours, I hope."

I open my eyes. She hasn't covered her face. She smiles at me with her ugly, horribly swollen yellow face, as though nothing had changed.

"I tricked you."

"Yes, you did. You're hideous! Where's Christian?"

Christian is in Vancouver, competing in track and field events. Then, aware of my determination to remain mute, our seriously sick patient proceeds to ease our silent discomfort by telling me, in a cheery, raspy voice, a story long enough to make my ears boil over.

"Christian only stayed for one night. He didn't seem to feel at home here anymore. He was up all night, walking and smoking, and walking and smoking. He left at the crack of dawn. He didn't even take the time to eat. He almost didn't kiss me goodbye. But I'd been planning his return for a very long time, sure to please him. I don't know if you've been to the cellars... Sit down, Berenice. Come sit next to me. I won't give you any trouble. I'll lead the whole conversation. You won't have to say a single word. And

I won't say anything personal. I won't say how pretty I find your face and your figure. Come and sit next to me, okay? If you've been to the cellars, you must have noticed the change. That was all thanks to me. I, alone, did everything myself. I installed the shark tank by myself. And I even managed to put the shark in there by myself. There are forty aquariums; I designed every single one. Did you see the amoebas' aquarium? It was my idea and mine alone to put twin lenses to make them look two thousand times bigger. Now that's smart thinking, and you can't deny it. And you can't deny that what I've done with the place is a real masterpiece in its own way. You can't say that you, who are as big a fan of aquatic creatures as he is, haven't at least enjoyed the look of it. Did you notice the lighting?... You could swear it's coming from the water, right? Those ideas, again, were all born in my head... And the salt water, huh? Who do you think drew it straight from the Atlantic Ocean? I did! And, again, I did it alone. And Christian didn't stay two seconds in the cellars. I worked like a dog for a whole year so I could throw him that surprise. Well he came right back up, telling me he was pleased that I'd gotten into fish. I felt my heart break like an egg in his grip. He only ever thinks of that darned javelin. I think he's just putting on an act with his biology studies. He surely doesn't like biology as much as he claims. Anyhow!... At the start, I didn't even know what an amoeba was. I'd heard from one of his professors that Christian was interested in amoebas; that's all. I read thousands and thousands of pages from the most inaccessible books, I consulted all kinds of biologists, to the point that I managed to raise a flourishing colony of amoebas. Some have trouble raising a cat. Imagine: three million amoebas!"

Our seriously sick patient bursts out laughing. I don't dare to laugh, for fear I might start crying if I open my mouth. Why should being in the presence of that witch always, more or less, make me want to cry? I should shut my eyes. Because when I see her, I'm toast. I should shut my ears. Because if I yield to the temptation of listening to her, she'll get to me, and I'll be done for, dead, defeated.

"White octopuses—wholly white, truly immaculate—only live in the waters around the Amami Islands, in the South of Japan. And the pearl fishers, the only ones who can catch those white octopuses, are some barbaric Ainu who've turned those creatures into gods and would never accept, for any price, to catch any other specimens then the ones they worship. You can tell how knowledgeable I've become thanks to my endeavour!... Now, I wanted to have a white octopus couple. Nothing, including barbarians, could stop me. I chartered an old beat-up junk owned by two young pirates from the suburbs of Kagoshima, boarded the ship, and we set sail for the Amami Islands. My two little Asian friends spoke only Japanese, and I don't speak a word of Japanese. I often thought they were heading toward another Amami archipelago, but I was doing this for Christian: my intentions were pure and I felt no fear. But then the sea went wild. And I, who could never stand the slightest roll, had to face the Sea Giant himself: Adamastor. A mile or so off the shores of the archipelago, my two pirates wimped out. They dropped anchor and gestured at me, making it clear that I was to do my best and deal with this alone. If you want those white octopuses that badly, go fish them yourself! I waited until nightfall. I hadn't swum in ages. I jumped in the water and effortlessly swam that mile. I had faith: I was swimming to make my son happy. My two little pirates had guided me well. I ended up on the right island. At the top of a cliff was a great blazing pyre. I followed the smoke. The Ainu were dancing wild around the pyre. Just before the pyre, on a stone altar, stood a great cauldron. I knew (thanks to my infinite wisdom…) that my white octopus couple, the father and the mother, were calmly waiting for me in that very cauldron. I comfortably sat down in a thicket, waiting for the Ainu to go to bed. Once they did, the rest was easy. I fished the octopuses out, put them in my bag, threw the bag over my shoulder, dove back into the sea and swam that mile back. How did I lay my hands on a medusa with a black swimming belt? I forget. How did I acquire strawberry anemones, eyed cribellas, catworms, and all those rare species no one would let me have? I forget. I often wonder how I even managed to remember their names. For a year, I read illegible books, took impossible seminars, travelled throughout the world, sweating blood, water, and grey matter. And all my efforts came to nothing."

Mad mountain wanting to birth a mouse! Mad mouse wanting no mountain for a mother.

"I wanted to show my son that a mother is not a doll that you must hug willy-nilly. I wanted to tell Christian that I was kind, keen, brave, bold, strong, industrious, ingenious, worthy of interest, and maybe even of wonder. I wanted to tell him that a mother is her children's delighted slave. And to prove him that I was no clumsy slave, I tried to dazzle him. I tried to dazzle you both like a showman auditioning for a job. And it all came to nothing. That's what being a woman, a mother, is all about, and it's marvellous. It gives you faith, Berenice. And I know you know what I mean. What faith can make you accomplish is marvellous."

"Enough! Enough!"

It's time to shut her up. How can I let her know?

"I don't want you to love me! Christian doesn't want you to love him! We want nothing from you. We need nothing. We don't want anything from you. We don't want to owe you anything. We don't want to owe anything to anyone. We don't need you."

"If I'm no good to either of you, little lemur, what am I good for?"

"Yourself. Which means you're good for nothing, like me, like everyone else. What good am *I* to anyone? Am I complaining? It's not so bad. You'll get used to it, you'll see. Stop talking. Stop trying. Leave me alone."

My anxiety gland is now oozing. I'm trapped, once again, as always. I lift the bed of our seriously sick patient with one foot and let it fall back down. I mechanically go through the same motion, again and again. A weightlifter mechanically lifts his dumbbell and lets it fall down with a bang. Her arms, pale and still, look like dead fish. I stare at the spot where the quilt covers her stomach. If I let my head drop on that spot, I would feel lighter than air. If I let my head drop on that spot, those dead fish would stroke my hair. I feel my hair stiffen as a deep slumber swallows me. I can't stand it anymore. I storm off and slam the door. I flee.

"You got beat, you frogging old fox, eh?" I say to myself.

279

67

Mousermoth is cured. The doctor has just told her she can go back to eating *sub utraque specie*. Mother. Mommy. Mamushka. Mamaminha. Stop! Stop! Stop! I know that, for a few minutes, you could carry my burden on your belly. I don't want you to. Thanks anyway. Since you'll have to give it back to me anyhow, I'd rather stay true to my own burden, carrying it alone all the time. I feel like kissing Mousermoth. I won't do it; I'd be kissing her for nothing. When you reach a dead end, you have to retrace your steps. No matter onto whom you pass your anxiety, it will bounce back at you. No matter where you hide your anxiety, it will come and find you. Even if you can run as fast as a weasel, your burden will catch up to you. You must live restlessly, fearlessly, constantly confronting your anxiety. You'll only hurt yourself trying to fool, forget or defeat your anxiety. There's barely enough time to make your burden bearable and bolster your bones so they can withstand the weight. People who unload claiming they just want to rest can be crushed when their burdens fall freely back on their shoulders. When two profligates reach cloud nine, they have to retrace their steps. And you can only retrace your steps by falling down. Since the return fall cancels the flight over, the way up to cloud nine is, at least, always sterile. Societies that condemn opium should also, if they were consistent, condemn orgasms, religions, or anything else that'll fly you high above the sky. I think that if humans got used to living without dreams, delusions, or excuses, choosing to tackle their burdens head on, they could eventually produce individuals fit to cure them. Stop!

Stop! Stop! Shut down all the trains, all the factories, all the engines! I see it as though I were there myself. Everything stands still. And the real Adonai rises. He speaks. He speaks to us.

"We do not have a backache, but a soulache. Does someone have a cure to offer, someone whose voice may have been drowned by all those hissing jet engines and those thundering steam hammers? No one? What a shame. True enough, we could only expect ready fools to tolerate the uproar, to survive the uproar. But there is a cure. There *is* a cure. There is a *cure*. There is a way—yet to be discovered—to feel beautiful and good, forever and ever. It is a *certitudo sine qua non*. There is a cure. We just need to *find* it. We *just* need to find it. Let us get to it and clear away those ruins. Let us get down on all fours and look for it at once. Off we go! Off we go! Get to work! We all know what we must do now."

The animals that best adapted to life on Earth are those that renounced, once and for all, life at sea. Amphibians are as bad at walking as they are at swimming. Crocodiles and the like are weak. They sleep all the time. They do nothing but eat, sleep, and breed. Only human beings who have renounced, once and for all, life in the soft darkness behind closed eyes will be able to adapt when Earth becomes overpopulated, and we all have to live in the light. We must seal off all dead ends, burn all umbrellas, parasols, and sunglasses, fill all burrows and clefts, take an axe to all nests, cathouses, and conjugal beds. When houses have no more roofs and mountains no more caves, humans won't have any other option but to live in the sun, in the light, in the universe; their only insurance, their only respite, will be oblivion. You heard it straight from Berenice Einberg. And there you have it: Berenice Einberg is back at square one.

68

He's arriving tonight, no one knows when. I have the devil's own time trying to fall asleep. I finally do, with tremendous difficulty. On Earth, getting to sleep is a challenge. A few hours later, I'm startled awake: I know he's here. His presence, like rain, has soaked the stones of the abbey. I went to bed naked to play with my clitoris, waiting to fall asleep. On Earth, you play with whatever you've got. He's here! He's finally here! I run to him, putting on my nightgown. I sprint body and soul through the hallway, flinging myself body and soul against his bedroom door. My heart is banging so hard against my ribs and my temples that I can't hear my fist banging on the door.

"Open up! Open up! Open up!"

The vermin flowing through my veins instead of blood turn to boiling pitch: if he doesn't open up soon, I'll blow it all up. I'm eager as the devil.

"Open up, scoundrel, or I'll knock the door down!"

I'm eager as the devil, wrestling with myself like a trout in a dip net. The latch clicks. The hinges creak. A bright crack slowly swells, until it frames the outline of a human similar to thousands of others walking everyday in the streets of New York. It's a young man in red pyjamas. He looks knackered, his face shaded by a two-day beard. One of his feet is in a huge filthy cast. Two crutches are jammed in his armpits: they seem too big for him, seem to cause him pain. It's Christian all right. That hostile string bean figure is Christian. Any small dog will grow up if God grants it life. That tall disappointing dog, that dog with long legs and a long muzzle: that's Christian. I recognize him somewhat instinctively. Everything in him, except maybe his eyes, seems suspicious, fake, half-baked, packed, polished, stretched, stuffed, clipped. For an hour, we stare still into each others' eyes, petrified by each other, overcoming a five-year chasm.

"Will you at least let me in, you killjoy!"

In a kind gesture, he throws his crutches in a corner, leaning on me to walk back from the door to his bed. We sit down on his bed. A bunch of names have been scribbled on his cast. I lean closer to read the names. As I lift up my head so we can both laugh at a funny signature, I notice that he's teary-eyed, and we fall into each other's arms. I hug him as hard as I can. My chest fills with sparks. I won't stop hugging him until the last spark wears off.

"I was run over by a bike. I have to schlep that cast for another month."

Now that his accident holds no more secrets for me, what do I need to ask him? Now that I know he'll be wearing that cast for another four weeks, what do I need to tell him? Will we start talking about the weather now? Nobody cares about the weather. Will I tell him that I'm fifteen and counting, though I've lost some teeth and hair? What news could I possibly give him? None. So I start babbling.

"The vinegar in vinegar bottles is meant to make salads in salad bowls taste a bit vinegary. Empedocles plunged into the Etna's mouth, and no one ever saw him again strolling arm in arm with his wife on the sidewalk at night when it was nice out."

I want us to shut up, so he can go back to bed, back to sleep. I want to watch him sleep. I want us to shut up so I can watch him sleep.

"I'll turn the light off... Okay? Go to sleep!... Okay? Stop talking. I'll watch you sleep. Watching you sleep will mean something to me. You look dead tired. Go to sleep..."

He's asleep, snoring. You must be old or exhausted to snore. Between his eyes, like a frontlet, hangs a black lock of hair, really black, black like a black pistol. Just like that, for nothing at all, I take this lock of hair and push it back with the rest of his hair. I lie down next to him. Lying as straight as a straight coffin with my hands crossed over my belly like Henrietta of England, my feet perpendicular to the ground, my heels cheek to cheek like that carriage called vis-à-vis, and my eyes wide open as wide as can be, like an ambitious soldier, I'm a recumbent effigy of the female sex. I am, therefore I think, watching, as calmly as I can, yesterday's dawn stealing back in, then the day before yesterday's dawn, then the dawn of everyday past. A dazzled tit crashes into the window. "That means someone in this house will die!" Constance Extinct would have said. I dozed off. I tiptoe back to my room. The sun, all fired up, rises on the horizon. It's gleaming, but its light seems so pale that I mistake it for the moon.

69

Erratum: It's not the taste of a rotten banana that's forever taken root in the mucous membrane of my mouth. No! Not at all! Not one bit! It's the taste of a catfish that died two hundred and thirty-nine days ago!

Early this afternoon, Mousermoth locked herself in her bedroom with a coloured clockmaker. It's now past midnight and neither of them has come out yet. What kind of things could my mother be doing so late at night in her bedroom with a black clockmaker who's not her husband? I obsessively wonder what the mother of my brother and of my brother's sister could be doing so late at night with a black clockmaker who's not our father who art in heaven hallowed be your name your kingdom be gone. I press my right ear against the door. I can barely hear anything. I can't make anything out. I can hear laughs, but I can't hear words. The black clockmaker laughs like a child. I manage to silence my breath. The acoustics still bite. By truly extraordinary means, I manage to silence my past. Now that my past is quiet, I take a deep breath of darkness (at night, you never know if you're breathing air or gloom), and proceed to press my right ear once more against the door. The same static scrambles the sound of their voices. I run to the attic, break into every century-old suitcase, and find two stethoscopes. I wake up Christian and hand him one of them.

"That ugly clockmaker is still in our mother's bedroom. And it's well past midnight."

I help Christian sit down in his wheelchair, wooing him a little as I push him through the hallway.

"I love you, you know. I feel good when I'm with you. Do you want me to spend my whole life with you? What I feel for you is hard to describe. With you, if I want to, I can feel kind, easy-going, calm. Take care of me. If only you wanted to make up for three quarters of our friendship! Then I'd gladly make up for the remaining one hundred. What the heck! I would do anything, as long as it's not halfway done. Imagine: one hundred and three quarters of friendship! I sound like a silly fool with all my quarters, right? Shoot!"

We hold the suction cups of our stethoscopes near the keyhole. The conversation is still in full swing on the other side of the door. Unfortunately, even with our stethoscopes, we can't make anything out. If the keyhole weren't blocked, we could hear and see everything. Unfortunately, it's blocked. That's just the way it is. What should we do about it? What could be blocking that keyhole?

"It might be the key," Christian suggests quite cleverly.

I have an idea. The wheels of Christian's wheelchair are like the wheels of the bicycle that ran him over on the way to the Vancouver stadium, like the wheels of any bicycle. I unscrew one of the spokes off Christian's wheelchair, put it into the keyhole, and push it further in. Whatever object was blocking the keyhole falls off, just like that. The coast is clear! The bedroom light flows freely through the keyhole. Christian refuses to look. I don't need to be asked twice. Marvellous! I wonder where the clockmaker got all those clocks from. He came in empty-handed, I'm sure of it. I can't believe my eyes. If we were to string together every clock of every colour lined up like little tin soldiers all over the floor, the ceiling and the walls of Mousermoth's room, we could easily circle the Earth. With my own eyes, I see the black clockmaker take out of his pant pocket a clock taller than the door, then another, no bigger than my pinky finger. Mousermoth asks him if he has more. No, he doesn't; but he's got something else. He bursts out laughing and takes out of his jacket's inside pocket a mast taller than the CBC Tower, with that Swiss flag floating on top. Sitting on the floor, Mousermoth holds a small transparent clock with four dials. It's the one she likes best.

"I think that's the most beautiful one, Mr. Clockmaker. However, I'm afraid it's not working. The pendulums are swinging all right, but the hands aren't moving. I must have been looking at it for an hour, and the four dials are still showing midnight. But if you can fix it, that's the one I'll buy."

"If it keeps showing midnight since you've started looking, Mrs. Einberg, it's simply because you haven't been looking for a whole hour just yet, despite what you're claiming, if I may say so. On the stroke of one, it will show one o'clock. This clock works quite well, despite what you're claiming, if I may say so. The hands move once every hour. It really is that simple, Mrs. Einberg."

"Oh! Ah! Ah!" Mousermoth cries out. "They're moving! Look!"

The hands are moving so fast that they're turning into a wind machine. They're such a powerful wind machine that Mousermoth's hair gets all ruffled and dishevelled. With her hair still all over her face, she starts counting the few pennies he asked for his queer clock. The black clockmaker slips his other clocks back in his pockets.

"Quick! Christian! Let's go! Let's run! They're about to come out."

Alone, straddling the quarry wheel, I recreate the wild feats Christian and I used to perform before we turned into filthy adults. I went to the mainland to gather maple branches, and Christian, with a small axe and a large knife, transforms them into multicoloured javelins that he throws in the river as soon as they're done. With great love, I feel it, he straightens the branches, trimming, polishing, beveling, and fledging them. He's making javelins, whistling in his wheelchair, like a non-union house painter. I've learned to talk with him again. With Christian, everything is wonderfully easy: he never fights it. If you want, you can do anything with him. He's like clay in the artist's hand; you can shape him any way you like. You could do anything with him, even a miracle. He's kind, softly passive. He just sits there, waiting to be used. He's the human being I need. I'm the hands, he's the material. There must be hands and material, and I'm no material. When there are two sets of hands, they come to blows, they wrestle, and that leads to nothing, that doesn't work, the hands can't stop fighting. Besides, he's my brother, and the word *brother* is the most beautiful word in the world.

"It suits you well…"

"What does?"

"To be making javelins with my branches. Do you know what I want when I watch you work?"

"What do you want so badly?"

"I want you to stay… in this wheelchair making javelins with my branches for the rest of my life. I feel so calm…"

The sidewalks are packed. I see a sandwich man and think of a ham sandwich. A set of traffic lights turns from yellow to red. Instead of asking me if I was happy, Constance Extinct would ask if I felt like laughing. The air I'm breathing is so thick, so thirst-quenching, that I can never get enough. Christian turns to me, his face stuffed with two eyes as small and as black as crowberries.

"Have you run out of fuel, Berenice? Did you forget to fill your tank?"

I stopped without realizing it, leaning on the back of the wheelchair, gawking around, waiting, maybe, for the light to turn green. I need nothing more. I'm fulfilled. I don't see why I should resume walking, move further down the sidewalk, or go on pushing that wheelchair. Tight rows of humans filled with hate and malice hastily march by us right and left, terribly annoyed to have to walk around us. Imperatively, they motion me to move. Move, Berenice Einberg, you bloody Aussie Kiwi!

"Move yourself, you bloody paranoid nutcase!"

I'm proud of Christian, confident in us both. I'm suddenly struck with a crushing, dizzying feeling of fullness and freedom. It's the truth; I swear. I see another sandwich man. It might be the same one as before. He reminds me of the thousands of sandwich men you can see in New York and Newark. If I had their guts, I'd become a sandwich man at once. My two silver spangled boards would say, "That's my brother in the wheelchair."

We head home. Einberg stops me on the way in and brings me to his office, a murderous look in his eyes. He shuts the door. He pulls out a portfolio protruding from one of the dark green drawers of his four-drawer filing cabinets with silver handles. In a hateful motion, he tosses the portfolio on the chrome-plated table, right under my nose.

"Inside, you'll find some of the odd six hundred letters you wrote to your brother during your stay in New York. In all good conscience, and I'm sure you must understand why, I couldn't let them reach their recipient. I want you to reread them at once and reflect upon them. Off you go! You're free to go."

"Free to go? Free? What's freedom got to do with it? Tell me what's weighing on your conscience! Speak! Make yourself clear! What's the matter with those letters, huh? Tell me! You find them anticlerical? You find them unpatriotic? You find them filthy? Go on! Speak!"

70

Einberg leads me once more into his office. And, suddenly, yesterday's metalepsis magically means something. A shunning! Again! Yet another shunning!

"Your so-called friendship with Christian crossed a line. Beyond that line, there are no limits. You're leaving for Israel tomorrow at the crack of dawn. What you'll find over there should knock some sense into your head. *SheElohim yevarach otha!*"

"I'll be the one knocking some sense into your head, Mauritius Einberg; and I won't even need a weapon! You're the lord of the flies! You're so much worse than anything poor William Golding ever came up with! You're just a filthy piece of fly shit! You're hurting the tip of my thyroid gland!"

I call Christian to my rescue. Meanwhile, I grab a Montreal newspaper (*L'Opress*), skimming the room-for-rent section of the classifieds.

"Christian, my love, if our friendship is more than a word, help me rid my life of that raving maniac that is our dear father."

"No!" he answers, faintly yet firmly.

"If you're truly my brother, come and share the misery in which I want to plunge to escape the merciless anxiety of that raving maniac!"

"No!" he answers, faintly yet firmly.

"We can rent a filthy, fully furnished apartment swarming with cockroaches, in some basement of Montreal's most squalid slums!"

"No!" he answers, faintly yet firmly.

"I'll support you, like those Parisian prostitutes support their pimps in French movies. You'll see how quickly I'll find a job. I've got the gift of the gab, and I'm street smart and fearless. I can dance. I can play the English horn, the bugle, and the trombone. I can give karate lessons. To make more money, I'll learn touch typing and shorthand. Pornographers will snatch any typist who knows shorthand! I speak all kinds of languages. I'm a qualified mechanic; from five to seven, I'll patch flat tires, oil U joints, replace spark plugs, change contact brushes, fill gas tanks. I'll work night and day; I'll be making enough dough for you to buy a European sports car. We can put money aside and play tourist every year in Cunaxa. Over in Cunaxa, we'll run among the ruins of Cyrus' defeat, barefoot and barelegged, like when we were kids. I can see us in Cunaxa as though I were already there. I can see us bend down to pick up the shoe that Tissaphernes' horse lost running after the Ten Thousand…"

"No!" he answers, faintly yet firmly.

"Xenophon's own feather! The goose feather he dipped in his blood to write history!..."

"No!" he answers, faintly yet inflexibly.

"When you're fully recovered, you can go back to being a javelin thrower or a biology student, as you wish. I'll pay for whatever you choose to do. Say you decide to study meteorology and come home knackered from campus. What do I do? I carefully copy your notes, with all my heart. If you love women, I'll make the most beautiful women of Egypt kneel down before you."

"No!" he answers, faintly yet inflexibly.

"*Amid gold streams on Egyptian vases…*" sang Nelligan.

"No!" he answers, faintly yet firmly.

"Sometimes, we'll get drunk. And just so my being female doesn't stop me from hanging out in taverns with you, I'll wear pants and get a crew cut. And just so my undue femininity doesn't cause us trouble, I'll wear a bowler hat and a dotted tie, and the fakest fake beard in the world."

"No Berenice! Stop fooling around! Stop with all that nonsense!"

"We'll sleep in the same bed, like when we were kids."

"No!" he answers, faintly yet firmly.

"We'll die tragically, like Pyramus and Thisbe, for

instance, or like Castor and Pollux if you will, or like Queen Elizabeth and Prince Phillip if you prefer."

"No!" he answers, faintly yet firmly.

"Let's live together. Together! Let's go live together."

"No!" he answers, faintly yet firmly, well aware that I'm in no mood to laugh.

No? Again! Still no? Okay, then! Israel it is!…

The engines are on, but the plane seems to be standing still. It feels like we're stuck in this cloud, white and thick like bread. From where I sit, the wing of the aircraft reminds me of a rapier plunged in cream of mushroom. And cream of mushroom makes my stomach turn.

His unbecoming air force major uniform only exacerbates his skinny scarecrow build. He has no cheeks anymore, no flesh on his chin. A nasty pink scar almost splits his left hand in half. There's nothing left of Rabbi Schneider but the big cow eyes of Rabbi Schneider. We're skirting Lake Tiberias in a haze of red and gold dust that seems to be part of the twilight hubbub… not of the jeep roaring in front of ours. Around the corner, young women sporting khaki shirts, khaki skirts, and black berets, with rifles on their shoulders, are goose-stepping in line. Rabbi Schneider drives the jeep into the ditch, waiting for them to march past us.

"Saluuuute!"

All at once, they turn their heads to face Rabbi Schneider, and, all at once, stiffly swing their right hands to their right temples. Rabbi Schneider salutes them back, limply. They seem to have a heck of a lot of what Mousermoth calls faith.

"They'll guard a border marked by barbed wires. They'll spend the night in the desert, scattered, in groups of three or four, face to face with a sly, devious, evil enemy."

"Aren't all enemies evil?"

"I'm not evil. Some of these girls aren't older than yourself. Last night, fifteen were ambushed, raped, violently tortured, and killed."

"Violently tortured and killed…" Something tells me I'll like it here. Major Schneider leads a reconnaissance squad and a flight school.

"I train fighter pilots. I only train soldiers who were born in Israel; that's a must to make sure we have the best National Guard. You've just landed in a country infested with swashbucklers."

"I want to learn to fly a plane. Will you teach me to fly, Major Schneider?"

He chuckles softly.

"Nonsense! Time to get off your high horse, little Apache. Everyone who lands in Israel these days is viewed as another swashbuckler; and air force majors have been ordered not to teach swashbucklers how to fly."

71

Here, the war has allowed human beings to find themselves again. Here, human souls strike back. Here, once freed, triggered by faith and violence, humans blow up, spurt out like lava from a volcano; they blow up and unfurl like a million startled egrets. Here, people die doing something funny; people die fighting. Here, humans recovered sight thanks to bursts of fire and steel; they can finally see enemies, finally know where to shoot. Here, you can blow the horn at full blast. Here, you can finally resound with every single pipe of your organ. I'm out of control, like a mustang next to a running train. I'm a Jew, a Jew, a Jew! This country is mine; its golden dust flows through my veins. Quick! Give me a gun! Or at least hand me a knife, like Judith! I thought I was floating above Earth, as wild as fumes. I thought that I was part of nothing, that I had nothing to answer for. Here, I feel roots thrusting me into the centre of the Earth, into its very core. At the headquarters of the Student Militia, which I've contacted several times, they misunderstand my enthusiasm, merely pouting at my impetuosity. I've told them over and over that I heard the call of Moshe, of Joshua, of the Shoftim, and so on. I've told them over and over that I heard the bowels of the Earth cry out, and that those cries unleashed a great wrath within me. They just won't believe me, not even close. How wonderful it feels to be a Jew after having been nothing! Why didn't I have them throw me back into the past sooner?

72

Miss Bovary was in love with bombs and grenades. A grenade belt would soon be tied around Miss Bovary's waist. She had a few seconds to make up her mind: she became a Mystic. That Miss Bovary is me.

Today, in this world, a weapon must pierce through your skin for there to be a crime; blood must flow before you have the right to retaliate. Today, humans are so obsessed with charters that they don't even dare to enjoy the privilege of defending themselves (passive verb) called the "power of life and death." When humans hurt your soul or try to kill your soul, you have the right to beat them to a pulp as though they tried to make you bleed or blow away your legs. Tomorrow morning, tomorrow at dawn, Equality, Fraternity and the other one will have made humans so weak, so craven, that they won't even dare to own (nobody builds castles anymore) one single acre of the land they could once take whole. I thought I was a Jew; that ship has sailed, obviously. I believed in Yahweh for two days, and got a bellyful. With me, illusions die fast. If a Syrian had given me the rifle that Israelite gave me, I would still relish the lush, pungent smell that oozes out of the barrel when a bullet is shot. Razing a mosque to erect a synagogue is just some gyral way of revolving and spinning back and forth. All gods are of the same race, a race that grew in human soulaches like bacteria in cankers. When you fight for your country, you fight for a cradle and a coffin; it's stupid and fake, and it reeks of rotten excuses. The only logical fight is the fight against everyone. That's my fight. It's also, unconsciously, the fight of all those who wage war. I, for one, am crazy for fresh jejunums, still warm with blood, throbbing with life. That's why I stand against all human beings... Because what kind of humans would let me slash their stomach and steal their jejunum? You can only reach your full potential as an individual by subjugating all human beings. Say a woman cheated on her husband, and he wants to cut her throat. Now if he wants to cut his wife's throat without getting caught by the law, he must take control of all executioners on Earth, which means all humans. Right? Who wouldn't want a city instead of a hut, a jungle instead of a cat, a harem instead of a wife? Which humans aren't spending their whole lives waiting for things other humans refuse to give them? Who wouldn't rather rule than be crushed? Who doesn't feel fated to rule? How many have the guts to stand?

Now that I've gotten a taste of it, I find the Student Militia disappointing, pathetic even. I pictured them holding their own guts in their hands. I find them thick and bored. In a nutshell, my one-week watch on the front has left a depressing mark. A yawning chasm separates us from the enemy. A peace treaty was signed. The slightest act of aggression will cause the culprit to be court-martialed, and the State to come before the World Court. Anyway, I don't understand much about it.

"Your weapons are symbolic. A treaty was signed, and the State, very much bound up with its allies, can't afford to break it. If you stay on this side of the barbed wires, you're protected by the UN, you're untouchable. There is, theoretically, no danger: you can bring books and read, you can bring wool and knit."

The Arabs, less fearful, it would seem, want hostilities to resume at all cost. But they refuse to shoot first. They don't want to alienate the UN. To make us shoot first, they're calling us cowards.

"They're sly, full of tricks. They'll throw shards and stones at you. They'll insult you. 'Cowards!' they'll shout. Just let them. They'll set all kinds of traps. They'll try to make you believe all sorts of things. Do *not* open fire. Do *not* open fire. Do *not* open fire. The terms of the truce state that a single corpse can be considered an act of aggression. However, not just any corpse can be considered an act of aggression. If a corpse comes up, do *not* pull the trigger. Contact your commanding officer and wait."

Enough to drive anyone up the wall! But I haven't lost hope. The war lies dormant: the war is here. Some smoker will eventually wake it up, asking for a light. If it takes too long, I'll do it myself. I need to know. What do you see when you're in the war, in its very core?

I know my basic herd instincts. I like to be heard, so I speak and laugh loud and clear. I like to lead. I go to the leader and defy him. I mostly hang with the Canadian crowd, thirty-odd youths gathered around Major Schneider who meet in the basement of his pavilion on Monday and Wednesday nights. Their circle is very tight and very high-strung. Contacts are frequent, fertile, and risky. Graham Rosenkreutz is the star of our group. I watch him closely, furiously spying on him, searching for his weakness. Guided by my anxiety, I deny myself the right to admire him or to let myself be won over. Gloria (aka "Lesbian") finds that Graham Rosenkreutz has panache, not like a peacock or a bird of paradise, but like a reindeer, that is, he doesn't need to display it, and it doesn't keep him from running. Graham Rosenkreutz isn't even twenty yet, but you can tell he's found himself and his way, imposing on himself as easily as he could on anyone else. No one knows much about him. He came from nowhere in the thick of the war, skinny, undocumented, was arrested and imprisoned for swashbuckling by the Colonel, whom he then asked for a uniform and a rifle. He escaped and ran to the front, where he stole the identity and the clothes of a soldier who died at his feet, and proceeded to fight with distinction. He was then arrested again. He refused to disclose his identity or his origins. Once again, he slipped past his jailors. This time, the very same night, in the heat of an exceptionally violent battle, he managed to destroy two tanks and four machine-gun nests, armed with a pistol and a bayonet. Schneider, then Lieutenant, noticed Graham Rosenkreutz when he represented him in court-martial and offered to vouch for him. We've stopped trying to solve Graham Rosenkreutz's mystery, the most troubled and troubling thing about him—we've just taken it for granted.

I have to stay true to Constance Extinct and to Christian; I owe it to myself. I know it's crucial, vital, essential to me; but I don't quite understand why. The second I consent to betraying them, to breaching that duty, I'll fall apart. I must stay true to those two faces from my past: I keep repeating it to myself like you repeat something that you want to remember, but that keeps slipping your memory, a quote in a foreign language, for instance. I must stay true to them; that's my salvation. That's my key, and since the clock started ticking, its hands getting ever faster and slimier, I struggle like the devil to hold on to it. Eternity is like an hour that never ends. I refuse to die. If I cling to the fragment of time when I still believed in Constance Extinct and in Christian, I'll only ever be one hour old and I'll never die. You must cling to the moment in time when you wished for everything to stop, cling to that moment, in the past, when you thought you were beautiful. You must cling to something. But I don't understand much about it. Stay unrelenting in your fight against the Titan, stay fierce and tenacious... Remember that, Berenice Einberg; remember, you fat noodle; never forget, you dingleberry. Resist. Deny the facts. Stay put and screw the pot's lid tight so that no steam comes out—stay cooped up until you're done cooking. Hold on to the beauty in yourself and in your life like Tarcisius held on to his ciborium, like a castaway holds on to a beam. I think about all that after reading what Lesbian wrote on the flyleaf of the book she lent me. "If you create a void around a memory, there's nothing left but that memory in the surrounding infinity, and that memory becomes infinite." Am I not letting it all escape? "*Can we escape them?*" asked our beloved Rimbaud.

Major Schneider has one obsession: Sabras. Everything must originate from Israel: soldiers as much as violins, violins as much as vegetables. If I understood correctly, real Sabras are human beings born in their own graves: they don't move much, no more than a root; they twist left, then right, then stop twisting altogether. I'm aggressively stateless, wildly heimatlos. I long for one place only. And the only way to get to that place is through the crack I sprang up from. What does that mean...

I'm just back from the basement of the Major's pavilion. Everyone was incredibly articulate. The UN took a heck of a beating! I unleashed my own tirade. It wasn't ultra-Zionist enough for them, so it was booed.

"I'll go to that Congress of Troppau and play nice, at first. I'll stand up, request to speak, take the floor, and, like all those kind, helpless old folks, I'll plead for armistice and amnesty, for the status quo and the sea's dead calm, for disarmament and deflation! Then, when all the lead has been melted into spoons and violin strings, I'll stand up, pull out my machine gun and aim at them. I'll say, 'Hey! You!' and add, 'Hands up!' I'll shoot the armless ones, to enlighten those who don't intend to put up their hands, giving them all a fair idea of what obedience means to me. Slowly, I'll say, 'Hey! You!' and add, 'Now I'm the one who calls the shots.' Breaking and entering like that, I'll achieve universal royalty. I'll have them call me Caligula, like the emperor who deployed his men before the sea and ordered them to charge. Aiming at humanity with the only firearm I have left, I'll finally be able to indulge at will my passion for fresh jejunums. I'll sit on or under a throne. An endless line of children, women, and men will spread out before me. Two grand viziers with perfect dexterity will feel their abdomens. They will set aside for me the one human being in a thousand with the most promising stomach. With a diamond-wire blade, I'll carve a window in the most promising stomachs. As I wait patiently for my mouth to water, I'll marvel at the exposed viscera before extracting the precious jejunum."

73

Adults are soft. Children are tough. Adults must be avoided, like quicksand. Planted on an adult, a kiss will take root, sprout, and grow tentacles that grab you and never let you go. Nothing can penetrate a child; a needle would break, a francisca would break, an axe would break. Children are not soft, slimy, or fertile; they are tough, dry, and sterile, like a granite block. The thighs of an adult are flaccid. The skin of an adult dangles from the bones like blobs of egg white. Constance Extinct's forehead would reflect my mouth. Her cheeks would reflect my lips, unsoiled, like the flat gold cheeks of a freshly felled tree. What's slimy and soft stains. What's ugly uglifies. You should never touch anything ugly.

I take a handful of soil as though it were a ten of clubs. What does the soil do? How does it react? If I shake it close to my ear, will I hear bells like you can hear beans when you shake a rain stick? If I throw it against the wall, will it bounce back like a ball, like my mouth would have bounced back against Constance Extinct's, or will it break like a crystal ball or a cathedral's rose window? If only I could grab a mosque as though it were a jack of clubs...

I hate adults so much, reject them with such rage, that I had to lay the ground for a new language. I shouted, "Ugly duckling!" I shouted, "Lame duck!" and felt confounded by the weakness of such insults. Struck by a flash of genius, I morphed into ectoplasm and shouted, stressing each syllable, "Floodoglobe Spetermaganax!" A new language was born: Berenician. I borrowed from ready-made, rare languages. When two friends drift apart in the woods and can't see each other anymore, and try to find each other, they echo each other's call. "Nahanni" is a call-calling call. When Constance Extinct calls me, I answer "Nahanni," lengthening each syllable, isolating each syllable. Berenician has many synonyms. "Bexeroceeding Moononster" and "Floodoglobe

Spetermaganax" are synonyms. In Berenician, you always need the verb "to have" to conjugate "to be."

I swim with Lesbian in the university pool. The reeds of our music instruments vibrate to air strokes. Memnon's Colossi, of mysterious design, sang to light strokes. Fish live in water and die of water. Human beings live in air, and die, of air. There is water, air, and light. Water and air are toxic. Only light remains. Berenician has filled a void, calling "daynians" humans who live in light, and calling "grandreedlets" the reeds of tomorrow. Remove the air present in light. Remove the air that stands between humans and their lodgings of tomorrow: all the light, all the air that keeps humans from reaching a daynian state. Rub-a-dub! Rub-a-dub!

I have a gift for war. A weapon, whatever weapon, never weighs down my arm or feels heavy at the tip. It's an extension of my arm, like my hand. I only need to feel it touch my skin to gain full knowledge of a weapon. It's as though it were pre-integrated in my proprioceptive system. It's intrinsically jointed, like my fingers' phalanxes, as though my blood were flowing through it like it flows through my hand. The sergeant who trains our company, a fat, phlegmatic cow, cried when she saw me, after one demonstration only, unassemble and reassemble a Lebel rifle in the blink of an eye. There was a tank in the middle of the armoury, an archaic dismantled machine nicknamed "Top" because it would only move in strenuous spins. One night, between two thirty and three thirty, I got up and took a seat in Top's belly. Sitting before levers and dials, with all that steel between me and the world, I felt great, safe, as cozy as ever. During the day, when I could, I'd steal a cup of fuel and empty it in Top's gas tank. Once fueled up, she looked more alive to me, more vulnerable, more fiery. One night, the temptation became unbearable and I turned on Top's combustion engine (that's an understatement!), and made her spin two hundred and thirty-nine times as I recited a Nelligan poem. When I lifted a window to get out, I saw the soldiers whose sleep I had disrupted circling me, hostile. I barely had time to save my melinite-stuffed skin before Top exploded. The army had mistaken me for one of those Arab dogs.

At the armoury this afternoon, a rifle blew up in the hands of a girl, ripping off both her arms. Our old rifles have a mighty kickback. At target practice, the faint of heart stuff the hollows of their shoulders with sponge pieces. In the basement of Major Schneider's pavilion, the rage triggered by the division of Jerusalem is in full swing. "Death to the Mosque of Omar!" To shout louder and clearer than every-one else, I'm standing on the table. "Death to the Mosque of Omar!" There are brothels. Why aren't there other sporting houses called, say, "crusades," where a human being could kill other human beings for a couple of bucks? In the basement, Lesbian and I slowly fall for each other. If you don't want to tarnish your reputation, you better not smile at Lesbian too much. I like being seen with her, being considered her friend. I like to hear them talk in hushed voices behind our backs. Nothing feels more delightful than seeing them think that I'm like her, that I'm her mistress, if I may say so.

A letter addressed to Christian, sent to the abbey, was returned to me, marked "Unknown here."

74

Here's a cup no one ever drank from. It's filled with violet wine, as clear as a mirror. If an angel comes near, he'll drink the wine and throw away the cup. If a pauper comes near, he'll wipe the cup with his sleeve after drinking the wine, and drink from that cup until it's covered with such a thick crust of filth that using it becomes an issue. Masters never wash their hands. Pashas never wash diamond-studded chalices—they drink up and crush them with the heels of their shoes. An angel won't cauterize his wound—he'll let it consume him. Once a drunk, always a drunk. Once a believer, always a believer. If you've washed your hands once, you'll wash them again.

It was raining. The pavement reflected, matching them with our steps, queer pictures whose unpredictable movements, incredibly supple and graceful, were setting us up in a sort of sad waltz. On the pavement, our Technicolor shadows twisted as we walked, as though they'd fallen under someone else's control, through some trick of the light, as though they'd morphed into flags of ourselves, wielded by underground winds. Pointing at the pavement with her middle finger, Constance Extinct said, "How nice it would feel to be down there, always floating upside down, quietly, in the winds blowing within the earth, like two muslin drapes."

Angels won't eat twice in the same house or at the same table. For them, a house where they once ate, a table at which they once ate, is over. Satraps open their mouths once, then they stay silent. If no one listened to what they said, they don't repeat it—they get mad and they strike. It's raining, and Gloria and I are walking side by side. My very first step by her side in the rain has put me in a state of betrayal, a state of iteration. I'll do much worse. I'll push the betrayal to blasphemy, push the fall's infamy to faithful parodic accuracy. With Constance Extinct's middle finger, I point at the illusions projected at our feet like adventures on a movie screen. Words from the past surge up my throat, tormenting me, irrepressible, like an urge to vomit. I can't stand it anymore. I speak. I desecrate her grave.

"How nice it would feel to be down there, always floating upside down, quietly, in the winds blowing within the earth, like two muslin drapes."

"The winds blowing within the earth," chuckles Gloria.

I surrender to iteration. I get used to iteration. I let myself die a natural death. I waver. Fall flat. Crawl. The apex calls the abyss. The higher you ascend, the scarcer the air, the steeper the climb, the harder the effort, the greater the pull of the chasm below. I've slowly developed, for everything I ever denied and despised, a bulimic craving. I would like, for instance, for a man such as Graham Rosenkreutz to tell me I'm beautiful, and to do so in a descriptive fashion, in a flurry of details, flattering my vanity in every aspect of my body.

"Your teeth are small, very white, really even and square. Your nostrils are extremely cute; they remind me of old mountainsides. You have legs the likes of Praxiteles' women. Your breath is warm and fragrant like an August evening breeze in Canada. There's something charming about the contours of your arms, but I can't find the words to explain it. Wiggle your toes. Wiggle your nose, move your eyebrows up and down. Move your eyes. You wiggle your nose in a wonderful way."

I need to be comforted, cradled, coddled. I was never meant to die a virgin or a martyr. I'm an entranced maenad. I have an epic, a monstrous need for tender loving care. However, the laugh I laughed at the tender loving care I want was even more epic, even more monstrous. I could never afford to bestow or receive the slightest touch anymore without drowning it in cynicism. Give me a drop of honey, and I'll give you a sea of bile.

Earlier, with Gloria, I allowed myself to forget my duties to Constance Extinct. Earlier, in the rain, I enjoyed Gloria's company. Opening up to her, I sought and found comfort and calm. I betrayed. Now I must pay. Now I'm sitting on the edge of my bed as on the edge of a cliff, disgusted, hating myself, beating myself up like a couple of cats fighting each other, with my toes curled under my stiff feet, and I can taste the desire to split open, from the bottom up, a belly riddled with red ants, trampled by white hippos. I'm making the same painful mistake I made with Dick Dong and Jerry de Vignac: trying to re-enact, like a play, the happiness I think I may have felt with Constance Extinct. Here's a cursed soul trying to break out of hell. There's a criminal trying to pry himself away from his crime. Here's an armless man struggling not to sink in the middle of the ocean. The worst way humans can insult their souls is by repeating themselves, making themselves hear the same thing all over again, forcing themselves to watch the same show twice. My poor soul!

75

Constance Extinct, the little queen, set up a mausoleum in one of those churches where her poet, mad about words, would spend his nights. Split in two, I stood guard on each side of the church's great portico, standing as tall as I could, dressed in a silk jerkin and striped breeches, holding a gun at point blank in two of my hands, using the remaining two to hold two rabid lions captive, one against each of my two stomachs. Once ripe, pumpkins fall off the tree. I suddenly collapsed, fell asleep, and ever since, the little queen's mausoleum, like a coop, is occupied by cocks and hens. Why, despite that wall of bones, can't the memory of her hovering over my chest cast a stronger shadow over my soul? Like a saint, I renounce all earthly possessions. I'll enjoy oval glory when I die. I become a well-obedeviant servantress of the Titan. I now only rebel out of habit. A few minutes ago, I polished and varnished my chains; all buffed and shined, they look dazzling in the sun. For batter or for whirs…

Gloria dreams of a Ph.D. in digits. I first liked her because she's in the habit of saying "It's decimal" to mean that nothing's worthy of attention. The principal of Tel Aviv University is a decimal. The professors of Tel Aviv University are decimals. All lieutenants, sergeants, and corporals of the Militia are decimals. Major Schneider is a decimal. Graham Rosenkreutz is a decimal. As a philosophical system, it's easy to learn by heart and to apply.

"Major, I came to see you to remind you, once again, that I'm dying to learn to fly, and that your role as a father requires that you teach me how."

"You're not old enough. You're not a man. You're not a Sabra."

"Graham Rosenkreutz is not a Sabra."

"You're not a hero."

"One heroic deed is all I need to become a hero."

"Here's a piece of advice from fake father to fake daughter: don't trust Gloria."

"Come again?"

"You're a starry-eyed little Apache. You'll be an easy prey for her. Have you cut your pretty hair?"

"I love Gloria like a sister. I forbid you to make such innuendoes. You're insulting me. You're disappointing me!"

"If you value my friendship, I advise you to stop flaunting yourself with that piece of trash."

"Advice for advice, I advise you to get this into your head, once and for all: I'm more than just my sex, I have my own two arms and my own two legs, just like Bellerophon and like Achilles of Oileus, called Achilles the Lesser."

"Get out, Berenice. Come back when you've knocked some sense into that head of yours."

"Exeunt," as Shakespeare often writes in his plays.

Music History and Theory in Antiquity. That's the title of the book Gloria wants me to read. If I don't read that colloidal tome by Gevaert, Gloria will feel offended. Reading a borrowed book creates a bond. Let's browse and bond. I dutifully, three times over, run through the pages at the top of which I notice a set of imperative exclamation marks. Dear Anna! In my mind, Anna is the feminine for anus. Drawing an eight-storey high ink spiral, she laboriously circled "The young ladies danced together." What a dear girl! So devoted!

So thoughtful! Between page one hundred thirty-nine and page one hundred forty, I find a poem by Verlaine, the one where two girls play husband and wife. Between page two hundred thirty-nine and page two hundred forty, I find the poem where two Greek goddesses of gossip play husband and wife. With how many girls before me, dear fickle Gloria, have you shared these poignant poems? Pastures and crops make up the mother milk of France… Gloria prides herself in being the most lecherous woman ever born on this earth. She says that when she reads the conjunction "but," she systematically reads "butt." In her mind, a woman has six vulvas: the one between her thighs, the two that are her armpits, the one that is her mouth, and the two that are her eyes. She says that when she reads the adjective "ole," she sees a naked señorita taking a bath. She says that she only smokes niñas because, for her, smoking niñas feels like kissing a Swiss lady called Niña.

Like the guitar player's thumb rolls down every single string, Major Schneider's coccyx rolls down every single step as he free-falls from the high, steep, rail-free staircase to the basement. Stunned into silence, everyone turns around. Major Schneider gets up, as dignified as ever, his yellow tie hanging backwards over his shoulder. Then, after a few hiccups, he turns toward the trap and orders someone to come down. Thrown vigorously, two eggshell shoes hiss above our heads before crashing on the basement window. A pair of bare feet stick out from the opening, followed by a pair of overly plump calves. The woman's yellow dress sticks to her skin like the skin of a snake. The size of her knees and bulk of her bum are greeted with boos. Then the scandal erupts.

"Children," says Major Schneider between hiccups, "allow me to present my mistress. I'd like you to meet, in rather full flesh, the mistress of a rabbi."

She doesn't look like a Sabra. She shares a family resemblance with "our" French pilots. Staggering like the devil, he takes her by the arm, about to go around the room and introduce her to each and everyone of us.

"Let's leave this place! Let's get the hell out of here! The Major's gone mad!"

Word gets around. Keeping their heads down, everyone stands up and walks, as a group, toward the stairs. Suddenly, Gloria, Graham Rosenkreutz and I are the only ones left sitting at the table. As a show of gratitude for our support, the two lovers gracefully bow before us like actors on a stage. At first, the whole scene leaves me cold, feeling quite foreign to me. Suddenly everything changes, the whole scene turns into an unexpected opportunity to move out of the Militia's camp. I curtly call out Major Schneider.

"Now that you've got nothing left to hide, maybe I could pack up and come live here."

He responds sententiously.

"Have I ever refused you a favor, little Thyestes with twice one ear?"

"No, Major Schneider."

"Well! Ask Céline dearest if she agrees."

I ask Céline dearest if she agrees. Céline dearest spews a confirmation of sorts.

"Good!" says Major Schneider. "Now ask Graham if he agrees."

Because being a tenant makes Graham Rosenkreutz subject to democracy.

"Agreed, Graham Rosenkreutz?"

"Yes, pumpkin."

I have a three-hundred-word essay to hand in first thing tomorrow. The topic is discretional. I choose to demonstrate the superiority of the bullet point over the boiling point. Read backwards, the Spanish article "el" becomes the French article "le," meaning "the." Hence Abou-Djafar El Mançour, aka The Invincible. Whence, I think, the señorita and her ablutions. If I keep being good at forgetting how Constance Extinct taught me to drive, I'll surely be decorated by the Dutch Academy. The Academy of Luxembourg might even give me the Dannebrog Cross. And when I die, the Titan's priests will place a mandorla around my picture—a sign of oval glory, of almond-shaped glory.

I remain with Gloria, alone with Gloria and her fat oily face, alone with stinking smelly Gloria. She brags about never bathing. If anyone denigrates her stench, she starts to cry. She's got some sense of humour.

"When I have to pee, I take off my panties, pee right on them and put them back on. That keeps away decimals like you."

I still don't get why, in her story, she can't just pee with her panties still on.

76

In the fall, at night, the mainland gravel road was littered with small sulphur yellow butterfly corpses, reaped along with the wheat. They all lay there with their wings closed, clasped. When I tried to spread their wings, they turned to dust.

My blood was evaporating like milk in a casserole. Where I was, it was too hot for my blood to keep. I chartered a floe, beautifully blue, bluebottle blue, and dashed off. Berthing occurred one hemisphere north of the launch. I'm at the most southernmost polar point of Adélie Coast. I'm now thirty-nine years old. With one cigarette on each corner of my lips, I'm as right as rain. Everything here shines white, including insects, and even trees. But my hair shines red, beetroot red. I'm now a male. Each of my many wives gives birth to one whale a year. In Antarctica, people's teeth fall out, rotten. My own teeth don't fall out, rotten. They grow, sharpen, and multiply. I'm now thirty-nine and have thirty-nine teeth.

"Voorrrf! Voorrrf! Voorrrf! Voorrrf! Voorrrf! Voorrrf! Voorrrf! Voorrrf!" barks the white Scottish terrier at anyone who'll listen. The Greeks called cynical those who lived like dogs (*kuôn, kunos*). Felicity (Felix the Cat) comes from caressing cats.

I wake up purring in my new bedroom. I get out of my new bed, meowing. Yesterday's dogs are all but forgotten. I feel kind of delicious. My body releases a waft of baking bread. Here's how I come down the stairs: on my bum, sliding down the rail. I've reached the utmost depth of my solitude. I'm in a place where the slightest mistake, the slightest doubt, the slightest pain can't exist anymore. I'm in a place where, stripped of all bonds, all footings, all air, my life, by sheer miraculous blossoming, intoxicates me with power. I'm in the place where the eaglet lands and, after almost succumbing to the shock of the void we call sky, stunned by its immensity, suddenly sees that void as its true domain, finding quite dull the former space where it was confined. No one dares to venture into the void. When you do, you can see that all fears are gone for good, leaving you invulnerable. The void is what you fear most. What could you possibly fear when you're within the void, once you've broken through the cloak that concealed it? Once you've severed all roots, there's no more cause for painful cuts— just amazement, ever-renewed. There's no death since, by committing the very act she's presumed to commit, Death takes away all means to verify her existence. A smile strains my lips, like life strains my unbridled, triumphant heart. I enter the room where Major Schneider, Céline, and Graham Rosenkreutz are eating at a round green table. I'm struck by the incongruity of those characters. Unable to foster or hamper my state of grace, they're absurd—a flaw of reason. The sight of them spoils my appetite. I immediately leave the room. I hum a Strauss waltz to mock my other self, who always despised Strauss waltzes. I run non-stop across the street, zigzagging from one row of bomb-blasted houses to the other. Suddenly, I see myself reflected in a filthy store window. I'm as deeply overwhelmed today by the serene beauty of my face as I was yesterday by the din of its disharmony. Everything is so peaceful, so harmonious!

I'm floating inside the void!... I have no memory, no one with me!... I see Gloria at the other end of the street. I swiftly vanish from her line of sight. I take to my heels. If we talk, I'll be back at square one. I'm in the void. I have no Constance Extinct, no Christian, no Mousermoth. There's so much space to fill! What a relief! There's nothing and no one. How could I ever stop believing in that truism? I've been such a fool! Nothing and no one! It's as though, at this very moment, the one half of the globe lying at my feet were falling into an invisible abyss, kind of like an apple half falls off with the stroke of a knife. How can you fear or doubt anything when there's nothing there yet, when everything remains to be done? To do...

I won't stop harassing Major Schneider. With him, I'm a mean praying machine. You must teach me to fly! You must take me into training!

Nothing existed before me. I can prove it. For instance, the longest letter ever written didn't exist before me. I wrote Christian, with Gloria's help, a letter that was one page longer than the letter that, before me, had the highest page count in History. That letter is made up of only one sentence, repeated countless times: "I am not sure why, noble brother, but I have faith in you." A beehive will only hold bees.

77

With my gawky cheeks as stiff as saucers, I show up late to class. Dame Ruby, ignoring me insolently, goes on teaching without interrupting her History lesson.

"Entrusted with this important parchment for Lord Selkirk, the intrepid Métis trapper left the room, put his snowshoes back on and, without wasting any time, dashed to his destination. It was November 1893. The snow, rock hard, as thick as sand, was swept with such force by the wind that it seemed to crash like true ocean waves against the houses. Lagimonière pulled down the flaps of his fur hat, and just like that, he walked right into a polar storm that could make stones shiver, knock down mountains, or disorient the sun. Merely guided by his flair, merely armed with courage, merely moved by his own legs, that hulk of a man had to break through a jungle of silver whirlwinds and torrents of hailstones every second of every day, when any other man would have needed an axe to carve out a path. It was so cold out that he didn't dare to loosen his lips throughout the entire journey, worried that his saliva might freeze on his very tongue, worried that his teeth would burst like bottles in a fire. Lagimonière set foot in Montreal in early January, less than two months after leaving Winnipeg, his mouth black and his eyelids welded shut, pleased to have carried out his mission."

I could swear I've just heard Dame Ruby's very voice, her very own words. But I must have imagined it. Because Dame Ruby didn't neatly stitch away at her subject; she slashed away at it. Memories sprout, growing trees inside your head. Only stones have a faithful memory. The mind will kill off anything that it can't feed or boost through laborious toil. There's no winter here. I find myself longing everyday more fervently for the bitter, almost sour fragrance of the cold season. I ache ever more feverishly for those nights when I woke up in the quiet of the abbey and felt the cold crushing my eyes.

Since early this morning, rumour has it that an Agonalia might take place. But not because today is St. Honoratus'. Why isn't it St. Honoratus'? This question is perfectly useless. Why is it a perfectly useless question? That's also a perfectly useless question. St. Honoratus had a nanny who once drove her bread peel into the ground and, lo and behold, branches loaded with leaves and fruit sprang up from the ground, like some kind of sun suddenly shedding its beams. Christian would go to bed like a good boy, and Mousermoth faithfully went to kiss him goodnight and tell him a story. In winter, those displays of affection would stretch, getting longer and longer, embellished by clever games. I spied on them, studying their every word, dissecting their every gesture, taking full advantage of the plentiful pasture feeding my gluttonous anger, feasting on crimes to avenge. Born violent, convinced that hate had to be justified, I coolly inflamed my envy, stirring it until the pain became unbearable, invidiously atrocious. I was so small that I needed to let myself hang from the doorknob to keep my eye in front of the keyhole. Followed by her cat, with her vellum missal inlaid with amethysts under her arm, Mousermoth would enter Christian's bedroom, gently closing the door behind her. She would hold Christian in a vice-like grip against her breasts. She would rub his chest and his legs to warm him up. She would go to the closet and get ten wool blankets of various colours that she then softly piled on him. She would laugh, her mouth hovering over his face. They would fight. Then things would calm down. As he would go back to bed, she would bring a chair and sit by his bed. She would open her huge missal with cinnabar edges on her lap and start reading with her beautiful, raspy voice, the story of that day's saint. Christian would stop her to ask perfectly stupid questions.

"What was Honoratus' last name?"

Like St. Honoratus, I just had a fat ugly nanny to sleep with. But we should close at once that infelicitous digression and get back to this morning's events.

Since early this morning, rumour has it that an Agonalia might take place. I don't know why. It's not St. Honoratus'. Because Israel isn't Catholic. Because in Israel, on St. Honoratus', no flock of white communicants comes tumbling down the hill in pairs, holding hands. Suddenly, a corporal, covered in mud, comes down into the basement, shouldering two beer kegs wrapped in flags, two kegs reminding me of two coffins. We all drink immoderately. All of us are soon drunk. I, for one, chugged so much beer that my belly's brimming with billiard balls, and my head, frothing with soapsuds. There's about thirty of us, each one of us belching and shouting more loudly than the next. We want to be heard, but won't hear any of it. We can't hear ourselves anymore. I, for one, am screaming like mad, dangling from a beam.

"Re! Rex! Roi! King! Monosyllables! Just monosyllables! Those were mankind's first cries! Who'll answer them? Huh? Who?"

On all fours under a stepladder, Gloria gives a disconnected speech, straining her silver tongue as she overstresses vowels and consonants.

"We're oout of daiingerr! Since urrgly Urrlyseez, that decimal, killed that Cyclap, we're oout of daiingerr! There's no Jo-Ann of Arrk left, as there's no Aiinglish left, not one, not a seengle one! Go on and take foorty weenks! Since urrgly Hurrcules, that decimal, killed that Erymanthian Boer, we're oout of daiingerr!"

Major Schneider is preaching, having grabbed a curtain that he wrapped around his waist like a tallith.

"I've had enough!" cries Céline around the room. "I've had enough, enough, enough!"

"Mommy!" yells a stranger. "Mommy! Mommy!"

Gifted with a thunderous voice, that guy manages to gather a dozen fanatics, including myself, then leads us to the foot of the stairs. If only we could climb up the damn staircase, the Mosque of Omar would be doomed. We'd take it and burn it down! Graham Rosenkreutz stays still, quiet and cold. After a few days living together, the spell he'd cast on me finally broke, just like that, without fanfare or flourish. I walk to Graham Rosenkreutz with the firm purpose of finishing him off.

"Here's how you oust an impostor! Here's how you knock down a bronze!"

Turning my words into action, I grab the back of the chair where our new Joshua sits and topple it over. We both end up on the floor, flat on our backs, and the bold audacity of my attack, along with my victim's embarrassment, cause a silent cataclysm. Graham Rosenkreutz tries to hide behind his usual puffiness, unsuccessfully: it doesn't fit him anymore.

"Go powder your nose, pumpkin; it's looking shiny."

"Don't let that decimal insult you, Rebenice! Take up the gauntlet! Since the Nomitaur died, we're oout of daiingerr!"

Gloria's support is greeted with unanimous boos.

"I spit in your face, Graham Rosenkreutz! Rosenkreutz! Rosenkreutz!"

Once again, I turn my words into action. But this time, the victim's soul revolts like the French revolted against Louis XXXIX in 1789. Graham Rosenkreutz gets up, suddenly facing me, and he grabs my throat in one stroke, with one hand, squeezing it as though he meant to strangle me, his bones crackling with ire. He lets go of me, out of pity it seems, and throws me forcefully to the foot of the stairs. He then grabs hold of my throat again and lifts me up before speaking through clenched teeth.

"Go back to bed, pumpkin! Go on! Back to bed! Go rub your vulva a bit before you go to sleep; it'll soothe you, calm your nerves."

I feel like throwing up all over him. By some miracle, I'm suddenly sober. I can now gain advantage over my opponent, who's so drunk that he can only stand by leaning over me. I feel a surge of violence hit me at full speed and I pin it on Graham Rosenkreutz, who crashes his skull against the concrete floor. He bucks up, visibly furious. He stands back on his feet with the flexibility of a cat, raises his fists, brutally showering me with uppercuts. He's lost all pity, all control.

"That's what you wanted, right? You want to be treated

as an equal, treated like a man... I'll be a good sport. Take that, you lion! Take that, you goon!"

His every blow sends me flying, leaping from table to table, jumping from chair to chair with my severed tongue, my broken jaw, and my cracked ribs. The pounding suddenly stops. Spread-eagled on the floor, sore from head to toe, I can barely move. Gloria helps me back on my feet. My eyes are open, but I can't see a thing. They're covered in blood. If I had a gun and could see Graham Rosenkreutz, I would kill him. I'm crying like crazy, blood and tears trickling down my face.

78

Gloria's in my room with a pair of scissors. To get in, she had to climb up the wall, like Romeo. Gloria takes off her shoes and sits down on my bed. Her feet are smeared to the ankle with a gritty coat of filth. Her toes are long and crooked, like monkey toes. She wants me to crop her hair, as close to the skull as I can. As I cut her hair, full of dandruff, as close to the skull as I can, she wets the tip of her finger with her tongue, drawing small pristine-pink circles on the top of her feet.

"You could at least swab you ears; they're making me sick."

Gloria shrugs, letting out snippets of laugh. But who am I to tell her what to do? You're fine just the way you are, Gloria. You sure dazzle my crowd. You'll never chafe them enough. She asks me if I want her to cut my hair. I ask her not to shave it as short as I shaved hers. I don't want to look like a boy. She tells me not to worry. And, while she's clipping away, I tell her about my void.

"I'm alone. So there's no one here but me. And if there's no one else, what are the people I remember, see, and foresee? They're illusions, mirages, figments of fiction. They're abstract, docile bearing points for the host of forces haunting me. Like you, Gloria, for instance. You're just an image projected by a force of my soul. Am I making myself clear?"

"I guess," answers Gloria. "Go on."

"I was launched to the face of the universe in a leaky felucca. Five billion shadows are stirring within my view. What do I do with those shadows? I impose upon them the only image I know: my own. How could I picture them otherwise? I coloured one of those shadows with the most beautiful colour, yellow, and coincidently called it Constance Extinct, just like I was called Berenice Einberg. Then I took your shadow and coloured you blue, the opposite of yellow. I still had a bit of white at the bottom of a jar that I'd left open. A shadow fell into the jar; I called it Mousermoth. Christian is my green shadow. I've got a pit filled with red; I don't know what to do with it… I have a plan: I'll empty it in the lake where, in summer, the rest of the odd five billion shadows or so come to swim. I've got all of my shadows wrapped around my little finger. They're only what I tell them to be. A shadow that I coloured blue remains blue until I colour it over. If I felt like seeing you in pink, I would just need to colour you pink. Is that clear enough, as a vital way to see other beings? I'm alone; I'm willing to swear on it. Is that clear enough for you?"

"It's clear, crystal clear."

"Remember! We met an old woman on the street. She reminded *me* of Melpomene. She reminded *you* of Thalia. What exactly *did* we meet? Was it *really* and old woman? Or wasn't it rather a shadow, a reflecting surface, a mirror throwing back an image of our own souls?"

"Let it go, Berenice. Let me be. Let yourself be with me."

"Miasma! Chyle! Chyme! Only I can taste the flavour of thirst in my throat! Only I can feel the cold stickiness of a frog in my hand! I'm the only one who knows what my own voice sounds like to me!"

"Like you, I'm hungry, hot, and thirsty. Stop talking nonsense."

"I can only imagine that you're like me; nothing proves it. Your pains are altogether different from mine. Mine are primal, pressing. Yours are virtual, mute, and have no coercive impact on my nervous system, on my digestive system, or on my solar system. Your pains remind me of those of the Duchesse de Langeais, heroine of Balzac, of Zola, of Cyrano de Bergerac, and of the Barber of Seville. I'm alone in the space I fill, wherever that space may be. No one can enter the space I'm in, wherever I may be. I'm alone! Is it clear enough for you now? Have I given you enough proof? Besides, what justifies the belief that you should only believe in what's proved by facts or tests?

"I only believe in what's disapproved," answers Gloria, laughing. "How do you like your new 'do?"

I pat my hair a bit. It'll do. Now get out of here, Gloria;

I'm sick of your hands in my hair, of your stench in my room. I undress, slip under the covers and turn my back to her. If Gloria slipped under the covers with me and tried to feel me up like her misty eyes suggested, what would I do? I'd let her, saying, "Go to town, Gloria... Repulse me real good." I used her so much, it would only be fair for her to use me a little. Besides, I'd like to see her in action. I'm almost sure that her wild theories on perversion are just a bluff; in fact, I'm so convinced that I'd like to try and seduce her just so I can see her chicken out. I open my eyes and turn around to see if she's still there. She's gone. Constance Extinct, can you read my mind? If so, aren't you ashamed that you ditched me like that?

79

My seals are asleep. When the seals sewed into my fingers thaw and realize they've been trapped, tricked, they tussle. And sutural scars bleed. When I press my hand against my ear, I can hear the beating hearts of my seals, and I'm scared. When the massive eagle stuck inside my chest seethes and shakes its chains set in stone, its wingspan wide and white, the inexorable cyclone that ensues makes me swell, shake, suffer, and sweat like a birthing broad. I'm swampy, furrowed, arboreal: my place isn't here, among those mammals. I'm a deathly mining bee; I selected every flower, every field. I don't belong in this nest. Human concerns are sexual. My only concerns are creepomoral. Sexual is English. Creepomoral is Berenician, and its meaning is and always will be obscure.

Gloria, I can't say it enough, is wonderfully vulgar, divinely sinful. She never washes herself or her clothes. Her person releases a rich stench of sour milk. We're sitting under an olive tree, philosophizing. A pair of freshly minted corporals march four times around our tree and plant their feet right beside us, left and right.

"Which of you two stinks, soldiers?"

"I do, Captain!" squeals Gloria, visibly pleased.

All smiles, she stretches out her armpit to the corporal, offering it to him to take a sniff. Gloria doesn't passively reek. She wittingly, carefully, consciously reeks. Here's how she explains the features of her aesthetics to the corporal.

"To be repulsive in order to repulse. To repulse so that people will stay away, won't come near or mislead me, or disturb me while I peacefully sleep my sorrows off."

"Send the injured to the Apothetae! Send all corpses to the graveyard! And send the poor, the old, and all the unemployed fathers of five to the gallows!"

Thus speaks Gloria after unfolding a communist pamphlet on her lap.

"The bearer of burdens won't go far with such burdens on his back. How far can humankind go with a leper on each shoulder? It'll collapse at the first hurdle, out of breath."

Must we lend a serious ear to the words of that so-called lesbian whose father, mother, brothers, and sisters were burned alive by the Gestapo?

"Send the rest to the Mosque of Omar! To the tallest minaret! Let's behead every dwarf, every striker, every eunuch, every drunk! Dwarves needlessly weigh on the earth's stomach! Strikers will thank us for crucifying them; they'll be grateful that we're giving future strikers an excuse to strike some more! Eunuchs, thinking they're God's little darlings, will sing as we set them on fire; like countless others, they'll laugh and dance in agony! Don't deprive drunks of their only possible glory; make them burn; turn them into martyrs!"

That feeling of being your true self, of having lived and living on, that soul you're talking about, couldn't we just call it memory? And conscience, the science of good and evil, isn't it just a form of dead memory, a steering instinct based on recollections degenerating into inextricable conditioned reflexes? When humans are born, they have no soul; they'll only get one after childhood. If human beings were born at fifteen, they'd be just like me without my past, without seals in their arteries, without condors in their chests. Cha cha cha!

I read from my dictionary. I just read the words. I skip their definitions.

"Chenopodiaceae. Chenopodium. Cheops. Cheongjin. Cholula. Chungli."

Six pyramids! Six, including four of my own invention! That's too much! What a thrill! I throw my dictionary over my head. The dictionary hits the ceiling light, turning it off as it breaks. I'm lying across my bed, with my head at the foot and my feet on the bolster, staring at that spot in the corner of my room where the walls meet the ceiling. The pharaohs' roads, I imagine, ran between two rows of standing sphinxes leaning on each other's paws to create an arch. I see red metallic sphinxes as tall as sequoias. In the middle of the floor lies the telegram Einberg sent. "You're wasting your time writing to that woman's son! All your letters are intercepted and destroyed." When I rest my forehead on a mirror, my eyes merge into one big blurred eye, and I remind myself of a Cyclops. I keep staring at the spot where the walls and the ceiling converge. I got a postcard from Mousermoth. "*Vergiss mich nicht*, string bean. Don't forget me, string bean. Mom." That spot in the corner, I focus on it with all my strength! In my bedroom, there are four such corners above my head, and four more on the floor. I'm thinking that if I cut off the corner where I'm sinking my eyes and put it on the *bonheur du jour*, I would get a pyramid. It would be empty, but no one would notice since the pyramid would be sitting on the *bonheur du jour*. Oh the horror! Suddenly, on the very spot I've been staring at, a pyramid sprouts, grows, and swells, descending upon me. I see the base become bigger, and bigger, and bigger. I feel the pyramid coming right at me, crushing me, swallowing me, expanding at record speed, growing beyond the floor, beyond Earth, beyond the universe. I scream, biting my fists. Graham Rosenkreutz, whom I've woken up, now viciously pounds on the wall. I scream louder; my blood is gushing out. Graham Rosenkreutz appears above my face, paved with good intentions. I violently push him off, knocking him down. I don't eat anymore. I'm never hungry. Eating makes me sick. To hang on, you need to eat. The spiders that used to crawl on the marshes' surface are called diving bell spiders. The few copepods we caught each spring, awe-struck by their mythological look, are called cyclops. Diving bell spiders and cyclops! Ten whole years went by between my first encounter with those little creatures and the day I learned their names. I still don't know the name of the small brown mollusks that stick to soaked rush stems and make eggshell noises when you crush them between your thumb and your index finger.

80

At the table, Céline and Graham Rosenkreutz are fighting, each barricaded behind their glass of orange juice.

"And, my pudgy petal, when an idea pops into my head, it doesn't pop into thin air."

"Good for you, my precious pet! Too bad only sad ideas pop into that head of yours! If you had a fun idea in your head once in a while, it'd be helpful. If you had a fun idea for tonight, for instance…"

Clearly stung, Graham Rosenkreutz takes on the challenge, throwing her a mean look.

"Does stripteasing sound like fun to you?"

"That sounds like fun, yeah…"

"Well, my pudgy petal, I bet that I can make every woman here tonight striptease before you, except for Berenice, of course, poor girl…"

"You've already lost your bet, my precious pet! Any pig-headed fool who wants *me* to do a striptease for him must be even more stubborn than you are!"

"Let's make a deal, my pudgy petal. I vow to make every female guest do a striptease on this very table tonight. Under one condition: that you vow to do one yourself if I fulfill my part of the bargain."

"And how do you propose to convince them, my precious pet? With a machine gun…?"

"I won't threaten anyone. I'll just use, like it or not, my own personal charm."

"It's a deal, my precious pet! If you succeed in making the chaplain's wife undress on this very table, in front of everyone, without threatening her, you can make *me* do whatever you want!"

We spend the day on campus. We spend the night banging our heads against the walls. We slip under the covers wondering how long we'll be lying there with our eyes wide open, listening to our souls writhe in tedium and fear. Suddenly, Graham Rosenkreutz bursts into my room, followed by a trail of laughs and songs. He's staggering and, exceptionally, he seems to be a happy drunk tonight.

"Did I wake you, pumpkin?" he asks me affectionately in a gravelly voice.

"No! But I don't like to be woken up *ever*, even when I'm not sleeping!"

"What you're saying is not super clear, you know… Not very super clear at all, you know… What you're saying is confusing as hell, you know… Let's go! Come on! Surprise! Surprise! Graham's got a great surprise for you! You know, I don't hate you. You know, I have sort of a soft spot for you. You're a bit like my little sister, and I'm a bit like your big brother. Let's go! Come along! I can't have you die of boredom in that big black hole of yours anymore. Come on! Turn that frown upside down, old chum. Surprise! Surprise! Get up! Get up!"

In one stroke, with one hand, he grabs all my blankets, flinging them over his head. He crouches to touch the floor. He finds it cold.

"It's too cold! Way too cold! I won't let you set your bare feet on the floor. Where are your slippers, your socks, your shoes, your boots?"

"I have no slippers, no socks, no shoes, no boots!"

"Don't play tough. It's no use. I know you. I *know* you. I bet I could make you cry, just by being nice to you, just by being a good boy. I know you. You're like me: you have a soft heart, a good heart. So you have no slippers, no socks, no shoes, no boots? No problem. When you have a friend, that's no problem."

He takes off his shoes, puts them on my feet, lacing them up. Disarmed, touched, I let him. Now that he's made sure I have shoes on, he picks me up, lifts me out of my bed, and takes me away.

"But now that I think of it… Come to think of it, what will *I* look like stripteasing without my shoes on…? But shhhhhhhh! It's a surprise! Surprise! Surprise!"

In the living room, there's the Protestant chaplain of the French headquarters and his wife, Colonel Schlyt and his wife, Colonel Schlyt's aide-de-camp and his wife, and two strangers and their wives. Graham Rosenkreutz shows me to the most comfortable seat, and whispers in my ear that I should keep my eyes peeled.

"Watch this, pumpkin. You'll have such a laugh! See those fat old cows? Well, they're gonna climb on that table and take their clothes off! Watch this, buddy. You'll laugh so hard! All those fat old fat cows are gonna get up on that table and take their panties off!"

Céline fills me in. She's drunk, like everyone else.

"The bastard won his bet, you know! He asked them,

'If I do a striptease for you, ladies, will you do one for me?' And all the old bitches said yes!"

Then, in a sea of laughter, like in a nightmare, climbing on the table one after the next, Graham Rosenkreutz, the five old cows, and Céline get naked.

All cats look alike at night. Everybody knows it. At night, when Major Schneider's done with Céline, he sends her to Graham Rosenkreutz. When Graham Rosenkreutz's done with Céline, he sends her to hell. Céline always sleeps alone. Sometimes, Céline tiptoes into my room, and flicks her lighter above my eyes. When she sees I'm not asleep, she gives me a cigarette and sits down beside my head. We don't talk much.

"Shoot! I forgot to bring an ashtray again!"

"Don't beat yourself up, Céline. There's an empty glass on the *bonheur du jour*...

When she feels desperate, she tries to make me feel sorry for her. She turns on the light and makes me count along with her the deep furrows under her eyes. She lifts her nightgown and shows me her shanks, her fat gelatinous shanks, her yellowish skin streaked with red and milky blue branches of bulging veins. Why does the skin turn yellow like that? Why do the veins bulge like that?

"I wish I knew, love. I just tell myself it's because life's unfair."

"Poor Céline. That's awful. That's dreadful!"

When I feel like playing, she plays along. Stepping into my room, she finds me awake, dancing, wearing a poncho I made by cutting a hole in the middle of one of my blankets. She likes what she sees. Without saying a word, she returns to her room and comes back with a quilt and a pair of scissors.

"How did you achieve such a great look?" she asks me.

"It's easy. Let me show you."

I take her quilt and, with her scissors, I cut out a diamond-shaped hole in the middle. I try to put it on her. It won't fit. Why won't it fit? It's hard to say. Either the good Lord made her head too big, or I made the hole too small. After I make the hole bigger, I try to put it on her again. It fits like a glove. I straighten her poncho and proclaim my new identity.

"I'm Aricia! Who are you?"

"Who's Aricia?"

"I'm Aricia, the Athenean princess nobody cares about. Who are you?"

"I'm Jupiter himself."

"You're Jupiter?" I ask Céline, handing her back the scissors. "Good for you! Here! Take your thunderbolts! And don't spare me!"

I retreat within myself to get into character, to become a soft princess.

"I'm Aricia. I'm sweet and shy, dreamy and naïve. They keep me locked up. I don't belong with the sharks; I don't have a place in the sun; I wait for the sharks to make a little room so I can have my place in the sun. Behind the door, they're fighting over my beloved husband. I lost him because I lack hatred and violence. I was deposed for my delicate soul. My voice is too soft; no one can hear me. My eyes are too soft; they think I'm impaired. I wait, in silence and in prayer. Soon, when the sharks are gone, I can squeeze his broken corpse against my breasts, and surrender one last time to Hippolytus."

Heavy tears are pouring down my cheeks. I'm crying more than I ever cried. I'm crying like a sieve, with my every nerve, every muscle set loose, with my viscera gushing out. I'm so limp that I collapse, like a coat falls off a coat rack.

"Pity me, Jupiter! Please pity me!"

Jupiter kneels, takes me into his arms, cradles my head against his neck, strokes my back.

"I pity you with all my heart, Aricia. Go on, cry; it's such a gentle slope…"

"Leave me alone! Don't touch me!"

"Don't fight it, Aricia. Compassion will help you cry, and crying will help."

"Don't insist, Jupiter."

I feel my tears grow bitter, toxic. What do we look like, hugging each other like that? We look like a couple of lesbians! Enough! I get up, wipe my eyes, and spot my ink bottle. I love ink. Céline fills my cupped hands with the silent, swift, volatile, ethereal liquid, as light as a flock of butterflies. I dunk my face in the soft blackness that fills my hands. Once my own face is well blackened and my poncho well stained, I apply the rest of the soft blackness over Céline's decaying face.

"Now we're a couple of blackface freaks. Let's have some fun!"

Gloria is a great diver. She bolts off the springboard, arches her back, glides down with her arms outstretched before she curls into a ball, performs three backflips, straightens her core, and enters the green water, as square as a nail, leaving a mere wrigglet of froth in her trail. As for me, between heaven and earth, I lose all touch with my bodily form. And I make more of a splash than an atomic bomb. All is quiet on the Western Front. The Arabs are singing. We're asleep, hugging our rifles, while Gloria burns, page by page, her Calculus textbook.

81

"We shall not be old, but weary of life's faults!"

At the courthouse, where voices echo like in a tunnel, Constance Extinct presides, bitter, wearing a robe and a hood. Constance Extinct is chanting, as though she were rattling chains, lines from Nelligan: "*We shall not be old, but weary of life's faults! Let us, my pet, grow our rancours tenderly!*" Each syllable is irrevocably sharp, resonant. What are you doing there, Berenice, so far away? Kill yourself, quick! What are you doing so far away from my corpse? Each syllable hits me, stuns me. Quick. Berenice, secure in our coffin what distension hasn't managed to distend in your face as I knew it, as I held it, under whose shadow I walked and slept! We were meant to be bled by the same rapier, like bark and trunk! We were meant to be buried, still warm from each other, in the same crypt, like one single tree! You should have passed onto me the death that plagued you, by touch, when we last hugged, while it was still plaguing you! Graham Rosenkreutz eats his meat raw, between two slices of bread. That bread gets soaked with blood. To look like I'm not alive, like I'm being faithful to Constance Extinct, I only consume water, a sterile nutrient.

We're wilting, rotting, decaying. And we do nothing about it. In order to seem like you're not too compliantly betraying what was once beautiful in itself, you pretend you're not hungry.

Constance Extinct snaps at me.

"Look, Berenice Einberg, you filthy pig! You're putrefying! Soon, there'll be nothing left for you to save! Soon, you'll be reduced to binge drinking and debauchery! Remember, you deceitful bat! You gave me your word! You promised me you'd never let them fool you!"

As though I'd misheard, I answer, "Nahanni! Nahanni! Nahanni!" I have fits of madness. I have eras of truth. Madness is no folly; it's a devastating bout of lucidity. During such moments of thunderous clarity, the idea seizes the object, the mind seizes matter, twisting it, the forces of the soul are engaged to the fullest in my every action. When I played Aricia with Céline, I was mad, I was Aricia. When I get one of my fits of madness, my sight sharpens, and I can only see what I want to see, and I can only see in me whom I want to see. I hate. Where should I pin down my hate? What should I affix it to? When I'm mad, I'm violently aware that nothing can be held accountable for my torture, that a given thing doesn't deserve my revenge more than any other given thing. Choosing is no option, becomes impossible. But hate must land somewhere. Mine will alight on a branch, like a bird. I hate right away, indiscriminately, anything that captivates my senses or my imagination. Anything that violently takes shape is hated. I hate acute angles as fiercely as the Greeks hate the Turks. Far from me to decry Greek haters! Instead, I decry that genuine feeling of entitlement to hate the Greeks. That's a flaw of reason. Expert hate technicians, true magicians of this craft, aren't looking for excuses. They've learned that no passion is defendable. Let's not base our hate on data extracted from a memo or a page of history; that's pure deception. My friends, let's hate right off the bat! I let the water flow out of the faucet until the floor is fully drenched. Fascinated, I kneel down and watch the thin flat puddle spread, its edge slightly rounded. I watch the water slowly gain ground, and see a continent sink in an ocean. I'm thirsty. I fill a glass with water. I try to drink it through my ears, then through my nose. I take a little water in the palm of my hand and try to grind it. I pour a bit of the clear liquid on my red sleeve, and watch my red sleeve turn black. I go to the market place, and, once there, I speak Berenician at the top of my lungs. Nothing I've said to date has been fruitful. Hence none of those human beings can hear me. As I shout my hate out, I'm only doing what any plant does when it grows.

"Istasquorum hemativieren menumore soh, tantalying apostrofoons! Boo! Boo! Borogenous Demonotremes! Moo! Moo! Moo! Quod templum terra shan't make mi treble! Id shall make mi dance!"

A twenty-five-mile jeep ride brings Gloria and me to Outpost 70. The jeep bids us farewell, and we walk around a bit to stretch our legs. The sand has almost swallowed the famous bunker. In the shape of a rotunda, its wide loophole makes a kind of human mouth. We go in. The radio is on. The bunker is full of great big logs. We won't need to go get wood. Just as well. All we need to do is maintain, all night, a fire big enough for the backup troops posted on the hill to see what goes down with their filthy telescopes, with their filthy microscopes. And something *will* go down. There's always something going down at Outpost 70. Almost every time the Militia lost, it lost here. Fifteen militiawomen were massacred here just before I arrived to this country. Not that something goes down every night at Outpost 70. But when, like tonight, they only risk sending out two volunteers, you *know* something's about to go down. Two Syrian scouts show up behind the barbed wire. They make obscene gestures at us, then leave. When night falls, fifty, or maybe a hundred more will come.

A sequentially brief purple yellow crescent moon pierces through a thin cloud. At least fifty Syrians have gathered behind the barbed wires. We can hear the dogs bark. Each time we go outside to put another log in the fire, we get bombarded. We get bombarded with rotten eggs, shards, cans, rocks, insults, and laughs. We've told our backup troops. They keep telling us to lie low so they can see it all with their filthy telescopes and their filthy microscopes. They tell us to lie real low. They call us five times every five minutes to remind us not to open fire under any circumstance. I'm at my wit's end. If I lose patience, not a single member of those filthy backup troops will stop me from shooting. We need two volunteers for Outpost 70. If only I had known! I'm perfectly able to throw rotten eggs at myself when I feel like it.

"Ninety for seventy! Ninety for seventy! Seventy, do you copy? Do you copy? Feed the fire, for God's sake! We can't see shit anymore with our filthy telescopes, our filthy microscopes!"

Feed the fire! Feed the fire! If you were right in front of me, you filthy peeper, I'd feed you like no one's ever fed you before. I'd stuff you full of eggs, you rotten egg! We go outside: Gloria carries the log, I carry the machine gun. The desert is dead quiet now. There's no round of rotten eggs greeting us, no flying laughs or insults, no barking dogs. We hurry. What do they have in store for us this time? Will a fanfare suddenly come blowing out of nowhere? Still nothing but silence. Will they suddenly blast machine-gun music on a record player? We go back inside the bunker—nothing was launched, nothing broke the silence. Gloria reports back to Ninety. Wait five minutes and go feed the fire some more. What does that filthy peeper think? That he's playing chess? Is he taking us for pawns? That rotten egg! I never ever felt this angry! That rotten egg!

"I think this is it!" says Gloria suddenly. "Yes, this is it. When you're on death row, you get one last favour. I'll grant yours, and you'll grant mine… Okay?"

"Stop talking nonsense. You're making my hair stand on end. Come on! Take your log and let's go! Take two if you can."

Under Gloria's horrified gaze, I release the safety of my machine gun and put my finger on the trigger. For fun, to cheer her on, I hold the barrel to her back.

"Let's go, you nasty lesbian! Come on! Let's go!"

Outside, the silence and stillness seem to harden as I prick up my ears. We hobble forward in the sun and the wind. Suddenly, Gloria's head jerks up. Like me, she heard those screeches behind us, the rustle of running feet. We turn around.

"Don't shoot! It's the dogs! The dogs! We're dead!"

Too late! I fired. The ejected sockets graze my arms, burning hot. Dog entrails are scattered all around, glistening in the firelight. The Syrians are quick to react. Already, thunder breaks out, bullets whistling past my ears. We're impossible to miss. Only Gloria can save me. I drop my machine gun, grab Gloria from behind, squeezing her against me as hard as I can to shield myself from the bullets. She struggles, screaming like a banshee. I manage to hold her still; terror and madness are making me all-powerful. I keep her pinned to me, facing the fire. I can feel the impact of each bullet penetrating her, shaking her, stinging her. She grows limp, falls apart. Her weight is harder to bear than her rage. The bunker isn't very far. I let my shield collapse and, on all fours, dragging it before me, I crawl backwards into the trenches skirting the bunker. Suddenly, I see hundreds of soldiers running right and left. It's those filthy backup troops. Those filthy microscopes, those filthy telescopes. Then I black out.

Gloria will be buried on Tuesday. I got off with both arms in a sling. I lied. I told them Gloria appointed herself to act as my human shield. If you don't believe me, anyone will tell you what good friends we were. They believed me. They happened to need female heroes.

Translator's Note

Somehow, life keeps setting me up with Ducharme. In July 2011, while I am in Berlin, Till Bardoux comes to me for insider help with his German translation of *L'Avalée des avalés*. We start poring over difficult passages, and I end up writing a preface for the book.* Fast forward to December 2017: Dimitri Nasrallah comes to me for a new English translation of *L'Avalée*. I end up writing this translator's note.

Barbara Brey penned the first English version of *L'Avalée* in the UK, back in 1968. I have not read or seen her translation—it is hard to find, and to be honest, I do not really want to. Not now. Maybe not ever. My translation is not a *re*translation. I hate that word—it implies that a translated book comes in second, that it must "revisit," "refresh," or "repair" some *original* translation. There is no "re" in translation—just different readings, interpretations, incarnations. Translations do not have expiration dates—just different readerships. Some will love a given version of a masterpiece; others will hate it. One version is never enough.

---

*Ducharme, Réjean. *Von Verschlungenen verschlungen*. Till Bardoux (tr.). Deitingen: Traversion, 2012. (Apparently a new edition is forthcoming.)

As I translated *L'Avalée*, J.D. Salinger's *The Catcher in the Rye* and Carson McCullers' *The Member of the Wedding* were companions of choice. Ducharme's Berenice Einberg has a lot in common with Holden Caulfield and Frankie Addams. Uncomfortable in her own skin, she constantly rebels, swearing, kicking, and screaming. She loves, hates, and hurts—all at once, and with the same passion. She is unlike any girl her age, unlike anyone you know. Her language is also unique—it's neither Québécois nor so-called "standard" French. In the original novel, Berenice exhausts all registers of the French language, including rare and technical words, borrowing at times from English, Yiddish, German, or Spanish, and creating new words when existing languages fail her. Even native speakers of French may not understand everything right away. An unreliable narrator, Berenice does not care much for the truth: several quotes, idioms, or historical references are a little or completely off. Do not try to set her right. Berenice is no fan of smooth transitions either: new characters pop up unexpectedly; known characters change names without notice. Never seek explanations. Keep reading.

The only way I can tackle this daunting Ducharme, I thought to myself from day one, is if I channel Berenice. I made friends with her, followed her around, allowed *her* to follow *me*. I let her haunt me. I let her swallow me so that I could share her feelings and thoughts, and learn to use and abuse language exactly like her, but in English. Berenice took the lead, and I played by her rules, however mad, mean, or mind-blowing they felt. *Swallowed* did not only become my working title, but an ongoing condition affecting my state of mind, my way of life. Then it became a book.

It took Berenice and me over a year to finish our game. We both survived. So will you.

Madeleine Stratford, April 2020

Translator's References[1]

Corneille, Pierre.[2] *The Cid*. Roscoe Mongan (tr.). New York: Hinds & Noble, 1896. 16.

Nelligan, Émile. "Walled-In Dreams." *The Complete Poems of Émile Nelligan*. Fred Cogswell (tr. and ed.). Montréal: Harvest House, 1983. 20.

———. "Sentimental Winter." *The Complete Poems of Émile Nelligan*. Fred Cogswell (tr. and ed.). Montréal: Harvest House, 1983. 26.

———. "Creole Fantasy." *The Complete Poems of Émile Nelligan*. Fred Cogswell (tr. and ed.). Montréal: Harvest House, 1983. 56.

———. "Fan." *The Complete Poems of Émile Nelligan*. Fred Cogswell (tr. and ed.). Montréal: Harvest House, 1983. 58.

———. "Glooms." *The Complete Poems of Émile Nelligan*. Fred Cogswell (tr. and ed.). Montréal: Harvest House, 1983. 77.

———. "Song of Wine." *The Complete Poems of Émile Nelligan*. Fred Cogswell (tr. and ed.). Montréal: Harvest House, 1983. 77-78.

Polo, Marco. *The Travels of Marco Polo, the Venetian: The Translation of Marsden Revised, with a Selection of His Notes*. Thomas Wright (ed.). London: Henry G. Bohn, 1854. 20.

Rimbaud, Arthur. "Lightning Flash." *Arthur Rimbaud: The Works: A Season in Hell, Poems & Prose, Illuminations*. Dennis J. Carlile (tr.). Philadelphia: Xlibris, 2000. 42.

St-Denys-Garneau & Anne Hébert. F.R. Scott (tr.). Vancouver: Klanak Press, 1962. 19.

Soulary, Joséphin.[3] "L'ancolie." *Oeuvres poétiques de Joséphin Soulary*, Vol. 1. Paris: A. Lemerre, 1872. 47.

---

[1]There are frequent quotes from the Bible throughout the book. Depending on the context, different official English versions were used (see https://www.biblegateway.com/).

[2]In chapter 60, Blasey Blasey erroneously credits Rabelais for a quote taken from Corneille's *Le Cid*.

[3]In chapter 63, a line attributed to Nelligan is actually from a poem by Joséphin Soulary. I could not find a published translation into English, so I provided my own.

ESPLANADE
Books

THE FICTION IMPRINT AT VÉHICULE PRESS

A House by the Sea : A novel by Sikeena Karmali
A Short Journey by Car : Stories by Liam Durcan
Seventeen Tomatoes : Tales from Kashmir : Stories by Jaspreet Singh
Garbage Head : A novel by Christopher Willard
The Rent Collector : A novel by B. Glen Rotchin
Dead Man's Float : A novel by Nicholas Maes
Optique : Stories by Clayton Bailey
Out of Cleveland : Stories by Lolette Kuby
Pardon Our Monsters : Stories by Andrew Hood
Chef : A novel by Jaspreet Singh
Orfeo : A novel by Hans-Jürgen Greif
[Translated from the French by Fred A. Reed]
Anna's Shadow : A novel by David Manicom
Sundre : A novel by Christopher Willard
Animals : A novel by Don LePan
Writing Personals : A novel by Lolette Kuby
Niko : A novel by Dimitri Nasrallah
Stopping for Strangers : Stories by Daniel Griffin
The Love Monster : A novel by Missy Marston
A Message for the Emperor : A novel by Mark Frutkin
New Tab : A novel by Guillaume Morissette
Swing in the House : Stories by Anita Anand
Breathing Lessons : A novel by Andy Sinclair
Ex-Yu : Stories by Josip Novakovich

The Goddess of Fireflies : A novel by Geneviève Pettersen
[Translated from the French by Neil Smith]
All That Sang : A novella by Lydia Perović
Hungary-Hollywood Express : A novel by Éric Plamondon
[Translated from the French by Dimitri Nasrallah]
English is Not a Magic Language : A novel by Jacques Poulin
[Translated from the French by Sheila Fischman]
Tumbleweed : Stories by Josip Novakovich
A Three-Tiered Pastel Dream : Stories by Lesley Trites
Sun of a Distant Land : A novel by David Bouchet
[Translated from the French by Claire Holden Rothman]
The Original Face : A novel by Guillaume Morissette
The Bleeds : A novel by Dimitri Nasrallah
Nirliit : A novel by Juliana Léveillé-Trudel
[Translated from the French by Anita Anand]
The Deserters : A novel by Pamela Mulloy
Mayonnaise : A novel by Éric Plamondon
[Translated from the French by Dimitri Nasrallah]
The Teardown : A novel by David Homel
Aphelia : A novel by Mikella Nicol
[Translated from the French by Lesley Trites]
Dominoes at the Crossroads : Stories by Kaie Kellough
Swallowed : A novel by Réjean Ducharme
[Translated from the French by Madeleine Stratford]